Praise for
The River Gum Cottage

'Leonie Kelsall has a way of writing that makes you feel as if you are a part of the town, and that the characters are people you know and care about . . . a delight to read.' **Beauty and Lace**

'Leonie Kelsall has done it again . . . a beautiful and emotional story that dug deep, not to be missed.' **Family Saga Reviews**

'Intriguing and beautifully written . . . an emotional story filled with alarming secrets, betrayal, courage, heartbreak, misunderstandings and romance.' **Ms G's Bookshelf**

Praise for
The Wattle Seed Inn

'Written with warmth, humour and sincerity, offering appealing characters and an engaging story, *The Wattle Seed Inn* is a lovely read, sure to satisfy fans of the genre.' **Book'd Out**

'Léonie Kelsall makes a welcome return that offers plenty of happiness, fun and heartbreak . . . With a wonderful message about letting go, seizing the day and embracing all experiences on offer, *The Wattle Seed Inn* is an encouraging read I highly recommend.' **Mrs B's Book Reviews**

‘Heart-warming.’ ***Family Circle***

‘Endearing and full of possibilities.’ ***Country Style***

‘[*The Wattle Seed Inn*] is a meditation on the city/country divide, as well as a salutary tale about the importance of finding community. It’s also a rollicking good read.’ ***Australian Country***

Praise for *The Farm at Peppertree Crossing*

‘Kelsall is a bold and fearless writer who is unafraid of presenting her readership with a plethora of darker style themes . . . authentic, insightful and sensitive in the right places.’ **Mrs B’s Book Reviews**

‘Léonie Kelsall’s skilful portrayal of life on the land and the people who live it comes alive. An absolute gem of a book!’ **Blue Wolf Reviews**

‘. . . moves from foreboding, funny, breath-holding, sad and sweet. I loved the way Kelsall unwrapped the secrets slowly throughout the story—little teasers that kept me glued to the pages.’ **The Burgeoning Bookshelf Blogspot**

‘It’s a mark of Kelsall’s unique storytelling ability that she is able to combine both the dark and light elements of this story to create something so appealing.’ **Jackie Smith Writes**

'A fantastic tale with relatable and loveable characters.' **Happy Valley BooksRead**

'. . . told with plenty of heart and humour . . . a charming book full of strong, unforgettable characters you'll fall in love with.' ***Glam Adelaide Magazine***

'A thoroughly delightful read that had me thinking of the characters long after I'd finished the book.' **Claudine Tinellis, *Talking Aussie Books***

Raised initially in a tiny, no-horse town on South Australia's Fleurieu coast, then in the slightly more populated wheat and sheep farming land at Pallamana, Léonie Kelsall is a country girl through and through. Growing up without a television, she developed a love of reading before she reached primary school, swiftly followed by a desire to write. Pity the poor teachers who received chapters of creative writing instead of a single page!

Léonie entertained a brief fantasy of moving to the big city (well, Adelaide), but within months the lure of the open spaces and big sky country summoned her home. Now she splits her time between the stark, arid beauty of the family farm at Pallamana and her home and counselling practice in the lush Adelaide Hills.

Catch up with her on Facebook, Instagram or at www.leoniekelsall.com.

Also by Léonie Kelsall

A Farm at Peppertree Crossing

The Wattle Seed Inn

The River Gum Cottage

LÉONIE KELSALL

The Willow Tree Wharf

This is a work of fiction. Names, characters, places and incidents are products of the author's imagination or are used fictitiously. Any resemblance to actual events, locales or persons, living or dead, is entirely coincidental.

First published in 2023

Allen & Unwin
Cammeraygal Country
83 Alexander Street
Crows Nest NSW 2065
Australia
Phone: (61 2) 8425 0100
Email: info@allenandunwin.com
Web: www.allenandunwin.com

Allen & Unwin acknowledges the Traditional Owners of the Country on which we live and work. We pay our respects to all Aboriginal and Torres Strait Islander Elders, past and present.

A catalogue record for this book is available from the National Library of Australia

ISBN 978 1 76106 609 2

Set in 12.4/18.2 pt Sabon LT Pro by Bookhouse, Sydney
Printed and bound in Australia by the Opus Group

10 9 8 7 6 5 4 3 2

The paper in this book is FSC® certified. FSC® promotes environmentally responsible, socially beneficial and economically viable management of the world's forests.

For Taylor,
who shares the journey
and maintains her (and my!)
enthusiasm for the adventure . . .

. . . but also for all of my fractured,
messy, argumentative, tempestuous,
improbable family who,
divided and together,
make my life . . . well, interesting.

I wouldn't be who I am without
each and every one of you.

Prologue

Samantha knew everyone's story. But, even after spending the entirety of her thirty-seven years in the town, she'd make certain no one would ever know hers.

That was the beauty of owning Ploughs and Pies, the only cafe in Settlers Bridge. Locals might be a little cautious about what they discussed in front of their hairdresser, or perhaps monitor what they shared at the CWA meeting, but somehow a perfect cappuccino, a golden pastry and a slice of cake had a magical way of opening mouths and easing inhibitions. Best of all, Sam's role taking orders and serving the beautifully plated food seemed to absolve her from reciprocal sharing.

Thursdays at the end of winter were possibly Sam's favourite days. The windows of the cafe were comfortably steamed beneath the short, lacy curtains, and the smell of hot pastry and simmering soup—pumpkin, today—drove away the chill of the damp wind sneaking inside each time the bell above the door cheerfully announced another customer. And the promise of spring was only around the corner. Many of the older farmers came into town on pension day to do their banking as, despite the impressive facade of the stone building at the high end of the street, the Commonwealth Bank was only open Thursdays and Tuesdays. They'd pick up their groceries from the IGA and then head to either the Settlers Pub or the Overland Hotel—directly opposite one another, and both overlooking the bridge spanning the Murray River—or catch up with friends at Plough and Pies.

Not only the older farmers, though, Sam corrected herself as Lachlan MacKenzie quickly closed the door to keep out the scurrying breeze.

'Morning, love,' she called, although, in his early thirties, Lachlan was only a few years younger than her.

For a second, the cafe fell quiet: Lachlan's mum was dying, and rumour was that his wife was playing the field. She was also a local, but the town's sympathy—always a tangible, fluid thing—was firmly on the popular farmer's side. Not that he was aware of it. As usual, although hungry for gossip, the town had doubled down to protect him. Not least because rumour was that Emily's fling was with an out-of-towner, which basically meant she risked excommunication from the community.

'How's your mum, love?'

The lull in chatter stretched for a few seconds as customers held their breaths, waiting to see whether there'd be fresh information to be gleaned from Lachlan's sombre expression.

He gave a slight shake of his head, lifting an eyebrow in wryly amused acknowledgement of the interest, but kept his gaze strictly on her. 'Same, Sam. Any pie floaters?'

'No pea soup, love. It's pumpkin today, thanks to Jack.' Her brother had nine hectares of organic market gardens and orchards, down near the river, and kept his family, their grandparents, and the cafe well supplied.

'You reckon that'd work?' Lachlan said, his shoulders set to block the interest of the other patrons.

'Give me five minutes, and I'll make it work,' she said as an idea came to her. Pie floaters—meat pies centred in a bowl of thick pea soup and generously topped with tomato sauce—were a South Australian specialty, but that didn't mean she couldn't create something new.

'Sure.' Lachlan cast a glance around, then moved toward one of the few empty seats. The other locals greeted him with a nod, or sympathetic smile, but let him be.

'Tara, can you get the drinks on for the mothers' group?' Sam called, aware of how her waitress had frozen, an adoring gaze glued to the farmer.

'Sure, sure,' Tara trilled back.

That was another reason Sam loved Thursdays: the extra crowd meant she had an excuse to throw a few more hours the teenager's way. It was hard for kids in a town the size of

Settlers to find enough work, and far too easy for them to be seduced into moving to the city. Tara's brother, Hayden, had recently found his way back from a dark place and, after a rough couple of years, the family could do without worrying that Tara might move away.

Sam snipped some garlic chives from the tray she kept on the prep counter. Ladling the rich orange pumpkin soup into a bowl, she sprinkled it with deep green chives and finely diced red chilli. Then she selected a butter chicken pie from the pie-warmer, one of the range she brought in from McCues Bakery in neighbouring Murray Bridge. She carefully placed the pie in the middle of the soup, then topped it with a dollop of sour cream, swirling that with sweet chilli sauce. A grind of black pepper over the whole lot, and she gave a satisfied nod. 'No charge,' she said, delivering the dish to Lachlan. 'Just let me know what you think of it; I might add it to the menu.'

She always felt something of a fraud, delivering well-plated food with almost as much pride as if she'd baked the pastry. But there was no point setting herself up for failure, far better to stick to what she was good at.

Making a loop of the room, she slid dirty dishes onto a tray. Sam paused, resting one hand on the child-safe fencing that sectioned off a corner of the cafe. For a few years, the area had seemed a waste of space, but slowly the number of kids in Settlers Bridge was increasing. Plus, she now had the buses from the Monarto Safari Park stopping by twice a week.

Toy cars and farm animals were strewn across the cheap rugs, and the low, brightly coloured table was filled with creations from the playdough she'd whipped up that morning. It was school holidays, so Roni Krueger had brought Marian and Simon in. As usual, the five-year-old twins were in deep negotiations with Keeley, Sam's unofficial step-niece: Jack, and his partner, Lucie, were far too alternative to make their relationship official, but Sam was claiming Keeley, no matter what.

'Auntie Sassa!' Keeley hadn't been able to manage 'Samantha' when she was younger, and the mispronunciation had stuck. At four she was still baby-chubby, but she had the slightly older twins wrapped around her finger. 'Me and Simon and Marian are going to see Pa-pa's puppies today.'

Simon nodded importantly. 'We're going to have one each.'

'Said who?' His mum, Roni, made horrified eyes at Sam, as though adding more animals to her rescue farm was unthinkable.

'We saving them,' Keeley said gravely.

Sam suppressed a grin. Keeley was quick—she already had the measure of Roni, who could never turn down an animal in need. It was funny how people changed: a few years back, when Roni had moved to Settlers Bridge from Sydney, she'd been insular and standoffish. Now, married to the town vet, she was on the school parents and friends committee, a member of the CWA, and had taken Lucie under her wing when the young mother moved into town almost a year ago.

'Saving them from what, exactly?' Lucie asked her daughter.

'From being sad without us,' Keeley answered with a slight air of scorn.

'You already have Dash.' Lucie's lifted chin indicated that the dachshund must be in their car, parked on the street. 'I'm not at all sure we need to add to our family.'

Sam's ears pricked. She couldn't read anything into Lucie's choice of beverage: the natural therapist favoured a range of odd blends of tea over coffee. But Sam hoped it wouldn't be long before an announcement was forthcoming. Though he could annoy the crap out of her on occasion, her brother deserved some happiness. And their grandparents, who had pretty much raised Jack and Sam, would be thrilled to have an addition to the family.

'Are you coming to the farm on Monday, Sam?' Lucie asked. 'We never see you out there anymore.'

Sam wrinkled her nose. 'Everything's so crazy busy lately, isn't it?' Ploughs and Pies was closed on Monday, and for years she'd had dinner that night with her brother and grandparents, while her husband, Grant, was at bowls. But a few months back, Grant had headed home early. He'd worked himself into a panic when he discovered that she wasn't home, apparently imagining all kinds of back-roads accidents. Sam rubbed her wrists, as though the memory marked them: he'd only grabbed them to shake her, but after more than twenty years together, he should know her low iron count meant she bruised easily.

Lucie deftly retrieved a piece of playdough that Keeley had fashioned into a pancake and was persuading Simon to eat. 'Your grandmother's trying to get the CWA enthused about making macrame potholders for a new fundraising push but Mum's worried that, without her overseeing the project—' Lucie rolled her eyes, Monica's overbearing personality was a source of both fear and amusement around town '—there will be too much variation in the product. She's wondering whether you'd let the CWA meet here.' The vivid blue and pink dye beneath Lucie's choppy auburn cut caught the light as she shook her head in mock despair. 'I don't know how many people Mum thinks will show. She already murdered the book club back home, but there's Ma, obviously. Tracey, Christine—'

Sam hiked an eyebrow. 'Christine Albright's going to come to a crafternoon where she's being told what to do?'

Roni chuckled. She and Christine had a long-running feud, though Christine held the grudge far more tightly than Roni did. 'I think Christine is probably working on the "keep your friends close, your enemies even closer" campaign.'

'Sounds like one of *my* mother's sayings,' Lucie groaned. 'Anyway, I just wanted to give you a heads-up, Sam. Though it won't be until the weather gets warmer, anyway.'

'No worries,' Sam said. 'You know it's the more the merrier around here.' She grinned at Lucie. 'See, your mum's contagious, got me doing it now.'

She loved the idea of people holding meetings in the cafe. Surrounded by familiar faces, noise, light and warmth, busy behind the register or in the kitchen or at the counter, Sam was never lonely.

And she never had time to think.

1
Samantha

Samantha tensed, her eyes stinging as she strained to peer through the gloom. She knew there was no reason to panic: the noise that had woken her came from the small alley that ran alongside the cafe, linking First Street to Main. During the day, the knocking of the vines against the rusted gutters wouldn't bother her—Sam wouldn't even notice it over the dinging of the bell above the front door of her cafe, the hum and chatter of customers, or the babble of the local radio station. But at night, everything took on a more sinister slant.

And yet, still she felt safer at Ploughs and Pies than at home. Which was ridiculous, she told herself, thumping the cushion she'd retrieved from the back window ledge of her old hatchback. She shoved it more comfortably under her head. The tiles beneath the bright, crocheted knee rugs she'd bought from the CWA fundraiser for her customers to use were cold and unforgiving against her back, and she shifted restlessly.

The problem was, Grant's stress levels were through the roof. Things weren't going well at the meatworks, and even worse—according to him—the bowls team wasn't ranking. So when he stomped into the house last night already half-cut and made directly for the TV cabinet where he kept the Jim Beam, she'd stayed out of his way. An hour later, with him snoring on the faux-suede cinema suite in front of something-or-other streaming on the TV, Sam had decided it would be best to make herself scarce. With a hangover, Grant could be a bit of a loose cannon.

Previously, she had crashed at Hayley and Angela's, texting Grant that she'd had a couple of wines after netball practice and couldn't risk driving home. Despite the text, Grant had turned up at Hayley's place, hammering on the door and yelling that Sam needed to get her arse home. Hayley laughed it off, saying it wasn't a drama, the odd hubby on a bender wouldn't raise an eyebrow in a place the size of Murray Bridge. The rural city held the strange distinction of being only a few kilometres and yet a world away from Settlers Bridge. And that was exactly why staying with Ma and Pops wasn't an option: everyone in Sam's small home town had their nose in everyone else's business. If Sam lobbed up on her grandparents' doorstep, the entire town would know something was going on.

Though it wasn't, not really, she told herself, staring up into the darkness. Grant was just going through a bit of a rough patch. They'd been here before, and come out the other side. It would all be fine.

A particularly loud bang in the alley jerked her halfway to her feet. She groped for the row of shelves that stretched the length of the closest wall, as though the familiarity of the tea, coffee, sugar and basic baking goods would soothe her. A tangle of macrame rope and beads from the successful crafternoons Monica had started hosting early last summer snagged her fingers. Her other hand closed around the phone in her pocket. The light switch was only metres away, but the darkness surrounding her was inky and impenetrable. It would be safer to flick on her torch than to push through the oppressive cloak of blackness. But she couldn't risk anyone seeing the light in the cafe. Then there would be questions.

Questions that could not be answered.

Because she loved her husband, she truly did. She wasn't hiding from him. Not really. She was just . . . taking a break. They had been together since she was sixteen, and after twenty-two years it wasn't surprising they occasionally got on one another's nerves.

Besides, her phone was turned off. Grant had installed a free tracker app in case she broke down, so he'd be able to find her. If she deactivated the tracker he'd get a notification, whereas if she simply turned her phone off, he would probably drunkenly sleep through the night.

The wind was getting up. She should make a run for her car, before the weather truly woke. Though it was only mid-autumn it was already cold and there was rain forecast.

The weather, plus the fact that it was pension day, meant the cafe would be busy. She needed to get to the car, drive home, shower, change, then get back to work and clean up any hint of her overnight stay, even though she didn't have any help rostered on until mid-morning. But she had to time it right, arriving home after Grant had left for work. His hangovers always seemed more manageable on the slaughterhouse floor than in the privacy of their house.

Groping in the dark, Sam found her rain jacket and stiffly pulled it on. She could have done with the extra layer for warmth last night, when the cold from the tiles seeped into her bones, but the nylon had been sodden from her tramp to the cafe. She had parked a couple of kilometres out of town, on a dirt track, because the sight of her car overnight in the main street—or even on one of the few side streets—would spark talk.

Outside, the road was dark and rain-washed, and she pulled the door to the cafe closed quietly. There were no residences in the main street, just a handful of businesses: Ant's pub and opposite that the posher hotel, the Overland; Lynn's IGA; a newsagent and post office; the butcher shop. Sam's cafe, Ploughs and Pies, sat directly opposite Tractors and Tarts, which had been vacant for a decade.

Beneath the insipid, antique yellow glow of the streetlight, a possum skittered across the empty road and into one of the giant pots of bougainvillea in the windswept centre strip. There was no sign of life other than the faintest thread of dawn to the east, over the river.

Sam shivered. Next time, she would make sure she grabbed extra blankets from home.

No! She shoved the keys into her pocket, tucked her long ponytail into her collar and pulled up her hood. There wouldn't be a *next time.* This was a one-off, while Grant got himself sorted, that was all.

It took only minutes to reach the outskirts of town, switching from the bitumen road to the rambling dirt tracks she knew from childhood. As she left the houses behind, paddocks ranged either side of her. Cleared of the low-growing mallee scrub, the rocky ground was cultivated for crops, or planted with feed for stock. Wildlife corridors and windbreaks of remnant bush and she-oak created puddles of darkness at the edges of the track.

The occasional noise in the hedgerow was disconcerting so she kept to the middle of the narrow track. Flicking on her torch would only make the periphery darker: if she kept her eyes on the path, each time she glanced up it would be a touch lighter, and she would feel safer.

Yet she could turn on every light in her beautiful home, and it wouldn't have the same effect.

She breathed in deeply, the fresh air centring her. How could people survive in Adelaide? Even Murray Bridge was too big, too populated for her; she only felt truly free when she was out here. The tiny town of Settlers Bridge had been a comforting, almost maternal presence her entire life. Sam knew every shop, every street. She knew which side of the road to walk on to catch a river breeze in summer, which of the shop verandahs leaked in winter. Which street the local mad magpie, Mike, chose as his swooping territory, coming in silent and deadly, a black-and-white missile exploding in a fusillade of beak clacking. She knew which of the willows along the riverfront twisted its roots in the perfect position to sit upon while bludging off school, and where to drop in a yabby net, or a baked-bean can punched with holes and baited with a stocking full of soap, to catch tiny shrimp. And she knew everyone here. Heck, she even knew their dogs. Maybe familiarity should breed contempt, but for her it bred content.

Sam sucked an achingly cold breath of air through her nose, hoping the chill would sear the fog from her mind. Though being *home* temporarily lifted a weight from her shoulders, she knew she couldn't continue to exist like this. It was no kind of life—she was marking time, aware of a creeping sense of dissatisfaction as the years passed.

She let out a soft sound of surprise. Despite the growing light, she had almost missed the unmarked turn onto another dirt track. Even in his absence, Grant threw her off balance. And maybe that was because of the guilt she felt, knowing that the fault lay with her. Grant couldn't imagine a life for them apart . . . and yet perhaps she could.

She took a shortcut across a floodplain covered in saltbush, eager to outpace her thoughts, to reach the banks of the river, where she always felt at peace beneath the majestic river red gums that had stood for centuries.

Threading beneath the sparsely clothed, dripping branches of the deciduous willows, she clambered across the twisted, gnarled roots that formed a platform above the broad river.

The peaty smell of moss and rotting leaves filled her lungs with a velvet smoothness. The water flowed beneath her—the muddy, soothing, almost invisible movement calming her mind. It didn't matter what was happening in her life: the sun still rose, the seasons turned, the river ran, the plants grew and the birds sang.

Sam closed her eyes to absorb the timeless serenity. Arms lifted from her sides, she wobbled. Yet would it be so bad if she fell? She could swim, but even if she couldn't . . . the water would embrace her. A final soft blanket. She was tired of pretending, tired of the restless nights, tired of the emotional exhaustion from years of wariness.

One of her sneaker-clad feet slipped from the moss-covered root and she gasped, instinctively snatching at a nearby branch. The flare of adrenaline cleared her head, and she grinned with bleak humour at the realisation that the water looked horribly chilly and far more of a wake-up than she needed.

She held her breath as a darter, his snakelike glossy black neck and narrow-beaked head above the water, glided by before disappearing beneath the surface in search of breakfast.

Which reminded her, the breakfast rush at the cafe wasn't far off.

She climbed back through the cave of twisted branches and roots, and dropped onto the narrow, muddy path, breaking into a jog.

Fortunately, it wasn't far to the dirt road she'd parked the car another kilometre or so along. She checked the time on her phone, then popped her earphones in to catch the start of the breakfast show on 5MU. *Up and Adam* was unfailingly cheerful, and the music helped block her thoughts.

Sam didn't hear the car sneak up behind her. It wasn't until the sinister black bonnet slid into her peripheral vision that icy prickles of fear warned her that she was no longer alone.

She jerked around to face the danger. Stepped back as far as possible, the border of tangled mallee and she-oak making escape impossible.

The car window buzzed down. The driver, dark hair cut in a tapered fade, the length on top elegantly dishevelled in a manner that had to be deliberate, was a stranger, and she breathed a little easier.

She would unpack the reason for her relief later.

His mouth moved, and then he grinned and tapped his ear. Sam realised she had her earphones still in. She yanked one out, raising a brow at him.

'I wasn't too sure if you were an actual person,' he said. 'Or some kind of river nymph wandering along here in the dawn.'

Obviously, her relief had been too hasty. She eyed him warily, her hand moving to the phone in her pocket. Though who would she call? Jack, she supposed. Her brother's riverside block wasn't far away, and she could rely on him.

The driver lifted a hand as though either surrendering or calming her. 'Sorry, I didn't mean to startle you. Or sound like a creep.'

'Said every creep ever.' Yet her wariness lessened, she peered more closely at him. He was probably a few years older than her, judging by the silver that flecked the short sides of his hair, and the deep furrows that carved his cheeks. From what she could make out, he was well put-together, too, at least for a town that rated clean jeans as Sunday best.

'Fair. Guess I screwed up on both.' He flicked a finger toward the road. 'I think I'm kind of lost, and you look like you must know your way around here. I'm trying to get to . . . Wirildi?' He pointed to a dash-mounted GPS screen. 'The signal dropped out right after I left the town. Guess we're all too reliant on technology. Until the robots rise up, at least.'

Creep and geek. 'Do you mean Wurruldi? The Wattle Seed Inn?'

'That's it.' His relief made it apparent he had genuinely thought himself lost. Which meant he was definitely a townie: it was hard to get lost here, with the sun rising in the east and the river providing an uncrossable border. And the inn, recently restored by Tara's stonemason brother, Hayden, and his partner, Gabrielle, was on the river, so all the guy had to do was head upstream, and he was bound to arrive in Wurruldi . . . eventually. Few roads around here led directly to their destination. Like everything in the country, they tended to meander but as long as you maintained a sense of direction, you were fine.

He tapped the useless GPS screen, as though it would wake up. 'I promised Gabrielle I'd be there last night, but

I got held up at work. So now I'm trying to make amends by coming ridiculously early, bearing gifts.' He picked up a white cardboard box from the passenger seat. 'Do you like Italian cakes?'

'I don't—' she hedged warily.

He groaned and leaned his head against the steering wheel, then glanced sideways at her with an appealing grin. 'Sorry. I'm coffee-deprived and not making much sense. I'm discussing catering an event at Gabrielle's in a few months, and wanted to check out the venue . . . if I can ever find it,' he added, with a questioning lift of one eyebrow.

'Oh, yeah, sorry. You're clearly not the only one who needs caffeine. Just head—' she stopped as she realised that the unmarked lanes she'd grown up with probably weren't all that easy to find. 'Tell you what, my car is just around the corner. I'll show you how to get to Gabby's.'

The guy looked startled. 'I don't want you to go to any trouble.'

'No trouble,' she said cheerfully. 'I'm flipping frozen, so I'll take any excuse to sit in the car a little longer and warm up. It's not far.'

'Look, if you honestly don't mind, that'd be fantastic. I only lost signal about fifteen minutes ago, but I swear I've driven past this same tree ten times already. And,' he held out the white box again, 'you must take this as thanks for rescuing me. I insist.'

'Will you have enough left for your job?' she said as she took the shoebox-sized container.

He shot her that disarming grin again. 'I'm Italian. As my mama says, "*Il cibo è vita*".'

She lifted one shoulder to indicate she didn't have a clue what he was on about.

'Food is life,' he translated. 'We've always got enough.'

'Sounds like a good slogan for a caterer.'

'Pierce di Angelis,' he said, sticking a hand out of the window.

She juggled the box to her other arm, taking his warm, dry palm. 'Sam. Samantha.'

'Samantha, you are absolutely freezing.' He closed his hand around hers as though he'd warm it. 'I'll give you a lift to your car?'

She shook her head, retrieving her hand to gesture at her rain jacket. 'I'm soaked. And, in any case, my car really is just around the corner. Drive on ahead, you can't miss it.'

Pierce looked dubious. 'Seems a bit ordinary, driving off and leaving you in the dark. By the way, you shouldn't walk with earphones in. Or you should at least take one out.'

His brief charm hadn't lasted long. Sam felt her face harden as familiar resentment solidified inside her. 'And maybe you shouldn't tell me what to do.' She had a husband for that.

2
Pierce

Pierce tossed the potato gnocchi in flour, indenting each with a practised flick of his thumb. Dad said Nonno always claimed the hollow was so the handmade pasta would hold just the right amount of the basil-infused tomato passata Nonna bottled each year.

Nonna's brown beer bottles no longer cluttered the shelves of the commercial kitchen: Pierce wasn't sure what had become of them when she and Nonno passed away within two years of one another. But the huge gas boiler they had always used on tomato day still lived in Dad's garage, and at the end of the season the family would spend a day chopping and salting bright red egg-shaped Romano tomatoes—Nonna would be back to haunt them if they used any other variety—then sieving the cooked puree into the clear Fowlers preserving bottles, which now filled an entire shelf.

He tipped a plateful of the soft pillows into a pot of boiling salted water and then, as they floated up almost immediately, scooped them out to drain. About twenty years back, he'd persuaded Dad to start bottling sugo as well as passata. The rich tomato, olive oil, onion and garlic sauce made a far better base for the classic Italian penne arrabiata and all'amatriciana dishes. But for potato gnocchi he didn't like either of the tomato-based sauces, preferring a decadent butter and sage finish.

The frypan hissed and spat, and he quickly sautéed the pasta to golden, dripping with rich butter. It was ridiculous how much people were willing to pay for plates laden with what was basically peasant fare: mashed potato mixed with egg and flour. And the larger and emptier the plate, the more customers would pay. But Mum would chase him around the kitchen with her wooden spoon if she caught him trying to send a customer out who wasn't practically groaning from being overfilled with good food. They might be in the restaurant business, but Mum treated customers like family, and wasn't above chiding salad-eating millennials to '*Mangia!* Eat up and enjoy, you'll be dead soon enough.' It drove her nuts that he fasted at least two days a week, but once he'd turned forty a while back, he'd discovered that spending eighteen hours a day on his feet wasn't enough to counter a lifetime of finding pleasure in food. He didn't believe in denial, but moderation worked. Though, as he plated up the gnocchi and placed the order on the servery, slamming a palm on the bell to let Amanda know the meal was ready, he smacked his other hand against his flat belly, trying to quieten the rumble.

Dad slid a charcuterie plank—always one of their most popular meals, the rustic board piled high with quality sourdough, piquant and creamy cheeses, and the finest smallgoods, separated by mountains of glossy black olives, cherry tomatoes and oily anchovies—onto the ledge. 'We'll cash out the till tonight, hey, Pierce?' he said.

Cash out meant Dad wanted all but a minimal float transferred to the safe. Though it was old-school, they always kept extra cash on hand because most of their original suppliers had been home growers. That had changed over the last decade, though. They still bought from market gardens, but Mum complained their produce didn't taste like it used to. Still, she liked to make sure there was money in the drawer, beneath the register tray, on the unlikely off-chance someone would wander into suburban Adelaide selling eggs or zucchini or tomatoes she couldn't resist.

Pierce's jaw tensed as he clenched his teeth, but he kept his focus on tossing hot ravioli in a cream and sundried-tomato sauce. There was only one reason they cashed out. 'So Dante's making an appearance,' he said flatly.

'Sometime tomorrow,' Dad said. But they both knew Pierce's brother wouldn't show up until after closing, when any risk of being called on to help out had passed.

Pierce snorted. 'If he can stay out of lock-up long enough.'

His father grumbled deep in his throat, a noise Pierce had learned in childhood was a warning. Not that Dante had ever heeded it. 'Don't upset your mother,' Dad said, though Mum wasn't working tonight. He gave a cautionary glance around the kitchen, indicating the dishy and the front-of-house staff who darted in and out. 'Dante was in *Bali*.'

'Yeah. Three months of Bali with no tan to show for it,' Pierce muttered, knowing that his reaction was immature. He added a smidge of blue vein to the *quattro formaggi* sauce on the range. Which would technically make it a five-cheese sauce, not four, but he found the sharpness of blue vein enhanced the creaminess of the others.

At thirty-two, his little brother was still 'finding himself', according to their mum. Defending Dante was the only time Mum departed from her fierce practicality, and she seemed oblivious to the fact that Pierce hadn't been given time to 'find himself' but had instead been expected to step up in the family business from before it was legal to pay him a wage.

Dante had been an unexpected baby, fifteen years after Pierce, and Mum chose to consider that a miracle rather than an imposition. By the time Dante was born, Pierce was already helping in the family restaurant after school each day, so he didn't have much to do with his brother. But he'd been aware of Dante's string of minor infractions throughout school, despite his parents discussing the issues in hushed voices. The offences escalated when Dante turned thirteen, and started hanging with a pretty wild crowd who fancied themselves a street gang. By seventeen, Dante had done two stints in juvie.

Of course, that wasn't Dante's fault, Mum would say. He was led by the other boys. And she'd give Pierce a hard look, as though to reinforce that he should be watching out for his brother.

He'd tried. Even had Dante live with him for a while. But his brother was slipperier than olive oil: he'd have everyone convinced of his best intentions—then he'd go do whatever the hell he wanted. And that *whatever f*requently involved money going missing from his family's wallets. Or the restaurant till.

Occasionally Dante would put in a couple of months' work here or there, but every time he lost a job, he would come crying poor to Mum, saying how misunderstood he was, how he was destined for better things, how he had all these plans and dreams that just required a start-up fund. The guy was a smooth talker.

He was also a drug dealer.

Not that he'd been in lock-up for either of those things: he'd done time for domestic violence. And, while Pierce didn't know the details, any lingering brotherly bond had been destroyed by the realisation that Dante was the kind of guy who thought it okay to hit women.

'It's slow.' He lifted his chin at the restaurant. 'I might take off early, if you're okay to lock up?'

'Sure thing,' Dad agreed quietly.

Sometimes Pierce thought Dad got it. That he realised how deeply it wounded him that his parents accepted Dante's behaviour, while Pierce was expected to shoulder the burden of making sure the family business ran smoothly. But even

Dad didn't seem to recognise the personal cost, what Pierce had sacrificed to keep the restaurant operating. Instead, his parents made occasional mention of his reliability, level-headedness and trustworthiness. Vague praise that was couched in expectation, keeping him tied to the family business, trapped in his parents' dream rather than pursuing his own.

Dad rarely closed up because Pierce was always the last out of the restaurant, locking the door, then taking the fifteen steps to the adjoining building he'd bought more than twenty years back. Originally, he planned simply to snap up the real estate—Dad was always big on encouraging them to invest in bricks and mortar. Not that Dante had—he was waiting for an inheritance.

Within months, Pierce had moved into the tiny upstairs apartment, and opened a brunch cafe downstairs. Serving a tight, niche menu from seven on weekdays, he closed mid-afternoon to get a couple of hours in the gym before heading into the family restaurant six nights a week.

Pierce moved along the counter to pull down the next order clipped to the overhead rail. He was relieved to see the dessert orders were flooding in. As usual, they averaged only one per couple, with the patrons too full to really want dessert but too tempted to completely resist the lure of the award-winning sfogliatella, flaky pastries filled with luscious custard cream and black cherries. He slid one on to a plate: it had been twelve weeks since he'd last baked the crescent-shaped cakes: he remembered, because that was when he'd headed out to the riverside inn his friend, Gabrielle, had renovated at Wurruldi.

He'd offered a boxful of the cakes to the woman tramping through the scrub in the middle of nowhere. And she'd refused them. In fact, she had barely said a word to him after she shoved them back through his car window, stalked off to her own vehicle and led him to Wurruldi.

Initially, he had been struck by the fear that froze her face when he pulled up near her—though the reaction was understandable, given that it was barely light and they seemed to be the only two people in that part of the world. When she had thrown back her sodden hood, he'd found it hard to look away from her unusual blue eyes, one splashed through with a bold stripe of hazel. It had been one of those awkward moments where to look away seemed to make it more obvious that he'd noticed the aberration, but to stare also made it apparent. His brain had kind of frozen on the conundrum and he'd ballsed up his side of the conversation. Yet she had seemed friendly enough.

Until she hadn't.

Pierce shook his head. He didn't need to worry about whether he'd offended some *pazza*. Probably lucky she'd refused a lift in his car; she could be the local axe-murderer. He reached for another plate and sliced an extra-generous wedge of the layered, coffee-flavoured tiramisu: the order was from a young couple with a newborn cocooned in a sling tied across the mother's chest. From the way they inspected the menu, he suspected they were intent on celebrating, but within a budget. There was no harm in giving them enough dessert that, even allowing for sharing, they'd need a container for the leftovers. On a whim, he picked up a white cardboard box and slid in the last two cannoli, then wrote *Table 7, N/C* on the lid of the box. Whoever was on the register would hand it over when the couple paid their account.

With the cannoli cleared out, he'd have to decide on the next menu. Each week he put up a choice of only four desserts, then changed three of them the following week. The quirk guaranteed repeat customers who wanted to claim to have sampled each of the creations.

He spooned mixed berry coulis over a gently wobbling panna cotta. Like the pasta, the dessert was a minimalist's dream. Four ingredients: cream, sugar, gelatine and vanilla. Allow to set, garnish to taste, and there was an eighteen-dollar dish on the counter. The profit margin on something like that made Trattoria di Angelis a rewarding business venture, though it was the superb food and outstanding service that made it an award-winner. Not bad for a migrant Italian family who had absolutely no culinary training between them, just a passionate love of great produce.

Dad could handle plating the rest of the desserts now the dinner service was finished—after all, he had four decades of experience. But since Pierce had taken over the rostering more than ten years ago, he rarely put Dad on mains. His father was old-school, seeing it as a compliment when patrons lingered over their dinner. Which was fine, but he also expected to be able to take his time preparing the food, and didn't realise that, while customers were happy to flash the cash, time had become a commodity that people were increasingly careful about spending.

Pierce cleared the till of all but a basic float, putting the money in the safe beneath the counter. He caught Dad watching him and gave a slight shake of his head: he'd said his piece, he wouldn't make any comment on the necessity to empty the register. Dad knew what Dante was like, yet still he chose to keep the fiction alive.

'Last coffees,' Pierce called to what remained of the restaurant staff an hour later. As usual, he would be the only taker at that time of night: a large espresso before he cleaned the machine and closed it down. Over the years, he'd become immune to the caffeine hit, yet still fully dependent on it. Though it was already eleven thirty, once he'd finished up here he had to go next door to set up for the morning service, plus bake a couple of desserts for Thursday night at the restaurant. So he needed something more than the plate of salt-and-pepper calamari he'd inhaled during a lull to carry him through the next couple of hours.

'I'll get the coffee for you,' Dad said.

His father hated fighting the large silver machine, so Pierce knew the offer was an apology—or at least acknowledgement—of the drama the re-emergence of Dante would bring to their lives.

And that was the way it always played out: Dante breezed in, put everyone on edge, then buggered off again.

3

Samantha

'Morning, love,' Sam chirruped with a false brightness she was nowhere near feeling as the door opened, introducing a gust of fresh air into the cafe. For years she had hidden behind being matronly, the frumpiness of excess weight and exaggerated heartiness accompanying her from high school to premature middle age. It was safe: if you were chubby and adopted an upbeat, cheery facade, people assumed you were happy. They didn't suspect that you were stuffing yourself with the cafe's leftovers to muffle the voice that whispered perhaps being content wasn't the same as being happy.

More than a decade ago, in desperation to shake Grant from his complacent acceptance that bowls on Monday, darts on Thursday, and the Riverview Speedway on Saturday night was all they needed in their lives, she had floated the idea of separating. It backfired. Grant decided she was interested in someone else and demanded a baby as the cure. Which was nice, she supposed. Having babies was what everyone aimed for, wasn't it? And Grant's jealousy proved he loved her. Not that she needed proof. He said it often enough, though sometimes the words seemed almost a defence, 'You *know* I love you', uttered after he'd become frustrated with her over some misdemeanour.

She'd been surprised to discover that her weight was one of the few things she could control. The initial loss hadn't been deliberate, but a result of a constant feeling of vague nausea. She'd hoped—for Grant's sake—that it was morning sickness. But the third time the familiar cramps started, she simply stopped eating.

As her early-morning customer made her way into the fragrant cafe, Sam lifted a bakery tray onto the counter and started loading the cake cabinet. Christine Albright folded her lips in on one another and cocked a steel grey eyebrow, as though she hadn't heard Sam's greeting hundreds of times. 'Samantha.' Her helmet of grey hair didn't dare move as she inclined her head toward the cake cabinet. 'Are those Veronica's lamingtons, or Tracey's?'

The question, the same every Friday, made Sam chuckle, though she was careful to keep it silent. Everyone—Christine included—knew that Roni used Tracey's recipe. In fact, Tracey had taught Roni to bake, several years ago. 'Tracey's today, love. Roni is too busy with the twins and the rescue centre to bake much for me.'

'I'll take a vanilla slice then. They're from McCues?'

'They are.' Fleetingly, Sam again wished she had the courage to try selling her own baked goods, but way back when she was a child her father's constant criticism had killed her confidence on that front. 'I'll bring it out with your cappuccino.'

The early spring sun slanting beneath the verandah made the interior of the small cafe bright and cheerful. Entirely unlike her mood, Sam thought as she plated up the vanilla slice, adding a chocolate curl to the top. Though that was largely due to lack of sleep. At least the kitchen floor wasn't as cold as it had been through the winter months—not that she had slept there regularly. And she had made the area a little more comfortable, hiding a cheap Kmart sleeping bag behind the canned goods, and keeping a wash bag and toiletries handy so she didn't need to rush home to Murray Bridge to prepare for the day's work on the odd occasion she was forced to seek overnight refuge in the cafe.

As Christine took a seat in a patch of sunshine in front of the large window, the doorbell tingled again.

Sam's smile froze as her husband strode into the shop. She blinked rapidly, then tried to force a lightness into her tone. 'No work today, love?'

Grant's eyes were bloodshot, he hadn't shaved, and he reeked of the Beam he'd downed last night. 'Couldn't bloody go in because I was too worried about you. You didn't answer any of my texts. I was up all bloody night.'

She darted a glance toward Christine, whose ears would be pricking, and lowered her voice, hoping Grant would do the same. 'You know I had to start early because I've got the coach coming through this morning.' And she knew that Grant had not been up all night texting her. In fact, when she'd dressed in her cramped cubicle at some ridiculous hour this morning, so that she could yet again go and fetch her car from the back roads, there had been precisely zero messages on her phone.

She winced at the blast of alcohol as Grant leaned across the counter.

'I bloody got pulled over by the cops on the way here.'

'Did you blow over?' There was no way he couldn't. His words were slurred.

'Check your damn messages. I told the cops you were coming out to pick me up.' He dangled a set of keys from his index finger. 'Lucky I hid the spares in the wheel arch.'

'They took your keys? So . . . your licence?'

Grant waved off the question. 'Get me a coffee. If I hadn't had to come searching for you, I wouldn't have been on the road.'

He would. He frequently drove to work under the influence of alcohol, but she consoled herself that the meatworks were only a short distance from their house, and he was unlikely to encounter much traffic at that hour.

Sam quickly made a coffee, then slid a pie into a brown paper bag and passed it to him.

Grant took a bite, then slammed the bag on the counter so hard that it split open, gravy and sauce oozing across her clean benchtop. 'It's bloody cold! No wonder you're not bringing any money in if you can't even serve your food hot.'

She wiped the counter, keeping her temper and voice low. And trying not to tremble at his evident anger. He'd lost his licence, it wasn't surprising he was mad. 'It's too early for the pie-warmer to have kicked in properly. No one comes in for pies at this time of day. Wait five minutes and I'll do you a croissant. Or I can microwave the pie?'

'I don't want your microwaved crap. I want you at home, making my breakfast,' Grant grumbled, his voice still pitched well above the radio.

Christine wasn't even making a pretence of not listening; instead her hard gaze pinned Sam to the spot. With a start, Sam recalled Christine's order. She purged the steam wand for longer than necessary, clinging to the noise puncturing the oppressive silence.

Pressing his knuckles into the counter, shoulders hunched, Grant stared balefully at her. As the coffee machine quietened, his bloodshot eyes filled with tears. 'What are we going to do now, Sam? I need my licence.'

She heaved a tremulous sigh, relieved that this time he'd settled down so quickly. 'We've still got the mountain bikes in the back shed. You can ride one of them to work.' Grant's shoulders tensed, and she hurried on. 'Or I can run you there. I'll close the cafe early to pick you up. Or get one of Wheaty's sisters to cover it.'

'I don't want to be waiting on you all the time,' he muttered. 'Jesus, Sam, why did you have to pull this stunt?' He sounded tired.

'I didn't make you come here,' she ventured carefully, encouraged by his unusual calm. 'You know the cafe hours, you knew where I was.'

'I didn't know where you were all bloody night,' he yelled, pounding his fist on the counter. 'I even called your grandparents, trying to find you.'

She cringed. She'd have to go and see Ma and Pops, come up with some story to cover why her drunken husband was calling them early in the morning. Careful not to make eye contact, she took Christine's cup to her table, startling as the older woman's hand briefly covered the back of hers and gave it a little pat.

'Men, right?' Sam murmured, trying to make Grant's behaviour into a joke. Still not meeting Christine's gaze, she hurried back to the counter.

Grant had straightened up, tucking his shirt into his pants. She noticed that he had bare feet. 'Give me a couple of custard tarts then, Sammie,' he said. 'Don't worry about doing a croissant just for me, you'll need them all for the coach.'

Grant was always like this, his flare-ups short-lived. After so many years, she should know better than to provoke him. 'Here you are, love. Do you want me to call in Tara to watch the shop and I'll run you home? It won't take her fifteen minutes to get here. If she's up, that is. You know teenagers.'

'I don't *know* teenagers.' Grant snatched the paper bags. 'And I'm not being run around because you made me lose my licence.' Without another word, he stalked from the cafe.

'Make yourself a coffee, Samantha,' Christine called imperiously from her table. 'There's no one else in, you can take five minutes to chat.'

Hidden by the machine, Sam closed her eyes and blew out a long breath. The last thing she needed was to have any part of Settlers Bridge involved in her marriage. As she headed toward Christine's table she realised she should have made her coffee lukewarm, so she could escape quickly.

'You could report him to the police, you know,' Christine said without preamble, as Sam pulled up one of the wooden chairs, catching the floral cushion as it skidded off the seat.

'For driving unlicensed?' Sam's voice rose in surprise. 'I'm sure it's a one-off. I'll run him around.'

'How about for that "fall" you had a couple of months ago?' Christine's dark eyes locked on Sam.

Sam knew it was unusual for women her age to take a tumble. Even more unusual for them to do it on a semi-regular basis. The bruises were always minor, though, and generally easy enough to hide. It wasn't as though Grant was hauling back and giving her a deliberate shiner, or anything like that.

But it didn't matter: she couldn't afford the town's busiest busybody to go shopping rumours around.

Sam evidently took too long coming up with her reply, and Christine gave a sharp 'humph', though it seemed to signal her decision to share. 'There are places you can go, you know. People you can talk to, Samantha.'

'About Grant's drinking?' she said, deliberately misunderstanding and frantically chugging her coffee, ignoring the burn. She had to escape.

'You know what I'm talking about.' Christine glanced around the cafe, as though making sure it was empty. 'You're not alone, Samantha. This happens to many women. And men, supposedly,' she added, though she sounded disbelieving. 'But you do have to speak up, take action.'

She'd take action, all right: Sam stood abruptly, collecting Christine's half-empty cup. 'All done? I've been meaning to ask, have you thought about getting Netflix to change things up from those daytime soaps you love? I'll see you next Friday.' She deliberately didn't mention the weekly macrame crafternoon, inferring the invitation was revoked.

Safe in the galley kitchen, on the pretext of needing to immediately wash the cups, Sam hid until she heard Christine leave. Then she slumped against the sink, nerves and exhaustion trembling through her.

Why couldn't people just leave her and Grant alone? Every relationship had its problems, theirs was no different.

~

Although she had called earlier and left a brief message so her grandparents wouldn't be concerned about her, Sam headed out to the farm after she closed up in the late afternoon.

She couldn't remember when she last visited Ma and Pops, but the moment she walked into the kitchen it felt like coming home.

'Well, hello there, stranger,' Pops said, looking up from his seat at the kitchen table.

'Not so much of the *stranger* stuff, Pops,' she replied, hefting a box full of baked goods onto the counter and then dropping a kiss onto his head. She had considered moving in to care for her grandparents as they became increasingly fragile, but Grant resented any time she spent at the farm, so it worked out perfectly when Jack's partner, Lucie, was able to arrange home help for them.

Except Grant had been quick to point out that Sam no longer had a reason to go there regularly. 'I seem to remember you cleaning me out of Kitchener buns in the cafe only a few days back,' she teased.

Pops had a killer sweet tooth, and often nagged her to start baking again, even though it had been well over two decades since she'd felt comfortable working on her own creations.

'You had Jack deliver them,' he said gruffly. 'And it's not the same as having you come home. And you know it.'

'Enough, Paul,' her grandmother interrupted. 'I see Sam every week at the macrame crafternoon: I keep telling you, you can come along. The old ducks will get a giggle out of you tying them up. Tea, love?'

Ma already had the kettle under the tap, and Sam knew it would be pointless refusing, even though she was nine-tenths liquid, having survived on coffee alone all day. She was never sure whether the coffee made her jittery, or if it soothed her permanently frayed nerves. But after a bad night's sleep, coupled with Grant's tantrum this morning, she'd needed something to fuel her and, like most days, she couldn't stomach the thought of food. 'Do you have any of Lucie's herbal teas?' she asked.

'Any?' Ma chuckled, pulling open a drawer. The kitchen was old and the drawer moved jerkily, wood rubbing on wood. It was overflowing with boxes of carefully labelled herb blends. Lucie made sure her partner's grandparents—and everyone else in Settlers Bridge—were well provided for when it came to natural therapies.

Sam widened her eyes comically. 'Do you have any idea which do what?'

'Other than chamomile, not a clue,' Ma said.

'Then I'll try—' Sam's words dried up as a car crunched in a wide circle in the farmyard before coming to a halt. Years of living at the farm had her attuned to every noise: without being able to see it, she could tell the precise location of the car, near the side gate—where Grant parked on the rare occasions he visited.

Ma frowned at her. 'Are you all right, Samantha?'

Sam nodded jerkily, moving toward the window above the sink. Why the hell had he come out here? Hadn't he done enough damage, making her grandparents worry that she hadn't been home all night? She still had to answer for that: she knew Ma's cup of tea was merely lubrication for the inquisition.

The last thing she needed was Grant firing up in front of her family. She had managed to keep him and her relatives fairly well separated for years—made easy by the fact that

Grant didn't like socialising with them. Or with anyone he hadn't chosen to be in their small circle of friends. At first she had resented that he controlled who she spent time with, his sulking if she didn't conform being far harder to tolerate than her friends' and family's disappointment at her cancellations. But she came to realise that it was because Grant wanted her home, waiting for him. That was how his parents were; his mousy little mum hadn't worked since she got married but stayed home looking after his dad and her two boys. Grant often remarked that his parents' relationship was perfect and, to be fair, she had encouraged his desire. When they married she had thought it fun to role-play the ideal 1950s housewife, always making sure she looked nice when he walked through the door, having his food ready, acting as though she hadn't had a hard day at work, because he was the breadwinner and only his day was important. She had grown out of that phase, and now it wasn't so much a case of her wanting to be that wife, as realising that it was better for her to become the wife that *he* wanted.

Ma's hand landed on her arm. 'It's just Mark from the fodder shop, Samantha. Dropping off some chook feed.'

Sam hadn't realised how tense she was at the prospect of Grant's presence until relief washed through her. She lurched toward the chair, trying to disguise the reason for her weak knees. 'I'm going to have to get Tara Paech to come in for more hours. I'm knackered. The coachloads coming through are full on.'

Ma remained standing across the table from her, her forehead even more lined than usual. 'Samantha, I'm worried about you—'

'I told you there was no need. Pops passed on the message, didn't he? Grant just got confused, forgot I had an early start today.' The words tumbled out on top of each other.

'That's not what I mean,' Ma said. 'And you know it isn't, young lady.'

Sam closed her eyes, dropping her chin to her chest so her grandparents couldn't see her expression. She didn't have the mental or physical reserves to take on an argument today. 'Ma, you know you'd be the first person to tell me to do whatever it takes to make your husband happy.'

'No, she wouldn't,' Pops interjected. 'I would be. And I'd be damn well wrong. I don't like seeing you unhappy, Samantha, and that's what you are, isn't it?' His voice was rough with emotion, and if she still had the ability to cry, she wouldn't have been able to hold the tears back. 'I don't know what's going on, but it isn't right. Grant's always been a standoffish bastard, but we've not seen him for months. And now we barely see you, either. What have we done wrong?'

'You!' Sam exclaimed. She was so invested in covering up what was going on in her life, her marriage, it hadn't occurred to her that her grandparents could consider her absence their fault. 'Nothing. I'm just . . . busy,' she finished lamely.

Ma snorted. 'You've always been busy, Samantha, right from when you were little. But never too busy for us.

Or for your brother. I have to go along to those ridiculous crafternoons so Monica can tell me my knots aren't tight enough, even though I was tying them before she was born, just so I can see you. And Jack said that when he calls, you won't make time to talk to him. The only way he can see you is to go into the cafe, but even when it's empty you barely speak.'

Sam rolled her eyes. For a guy made quiet by his speech impediment, Jack had sure been dishing the dirt on her.

'Have we said something to upset you, Samantha? Hurt you in some way?' Pops' dry, cracked palm covered her hand on the table. And his hand was trembling. Bloody hell, her grandfather was crying over her!

'It's not that, Pops. It's not you guys,' she said, frantic to take away their evident pain. 'Just Grant and I are . . . I don't know, we're at each other's throats all the time at the moment. So I'm trying to go with the flow, not make him upset.'

'You don't "make" him,' Pops said, his hand clutching hers so tightly her fingers ached. 'He's a grown man, you don't *make* him do a damn thing.'

'I knew it was him!' Ma sat down in a flurry of floral apron and whiff of Cashmere Bouquet talc. Sam wasn't sure whether it was relief or accusation in her grandmother's tone.

'It's not him, Ma.' She couldn't allow them to blame Grant, even though it was so tempting to let them think that, to let them take her back in, to regress twenty years, to be cared for and cosseted. But Jack already did more than his share of keeping the family fed with his sustainable farm. Without Grant, Sam had nothing; and she refused to be a burden on either her grandparents or her brother. 'It's not Grant, it's *us*. We're just . . . going through a rough patch. It'll shake itself out. It always does. Now, I thought we could do a high tea kind of thing? I brought along both savoury and sweet.' As always, she turned the conversation before her grandparents got fixated on her life.

Besides, she needed them to eat early, so she could get home to Grant.

4

Pierce

Pierce had managed to avoid Dante the previous day, but obviously his luck wasn't going to hold. Standing behind the counter in his cafe, he had a clear view of Mum crossing the busy street on the fringe of Adelaide's CBD. Dante hulked alongside her, putting up one hand to signal a car to slow down. *Tosser*, Pierce thought, the car was still fifty metres down the tree-lined road. Dante was no doubt disappointed as, navigating between the parked cars, Mum failed to notice his dramatic chivalry.

Pierce tilted his head to one shoulder, then the other, trying to loosen his neck. He'd have to slam it hard in the gym this afternoon, work off some of the tension that the sight of his brother triggered.

Though, looking at Dante, perhaps he'd lay off the gym. His brother had evidently used his time in prison to work out and help himself to steroids. Pierce knocked back his espresso without taking his gaze from the approaching trouble—Dante looked like he belonged on the door of a seedy strip club. He kept his arms braced in a version of the weightlifters' crab: hands fisted at his navel, elbows jutting out to enhance his biceps. Out of proportion with his relatively short stature, his over-enhanced deltoids and traps swallowed his neck. He strutted across the road with an odd gait, his torso rigid and his legs so thickly muscled he had to throw them out slightly to the side with each step.

For a brief moment, Pierce hoped Mum would head to the restaurant next door, but he knew better. She was always determined to force him and Dante together, like she could forge a bond that had never existed.

'Bro!' Dante roared as he stepped sideways through the doorway, as though his shoulders were too wide to fit.

'Dan. Good to see you . . . back.' He wanted to say 'out' but wouldn't let his sarcasm hurt Mum. No one would benefit from him outing the Bali fairy tale his mum was choosing to believe. In any case, he was adult enough to realise that half of his dislike of Dante was caused by jealousy, a juvenile sense of having been ousted from his place in the family by his little brother.

Of course, the other half stemmed more reasonably from the fact that his brother was a waste of oxygen, someone who would spend his life taking—money, time, affection—without ever giving more than lip service. The perfect conman, loudly proclaiming his evolved conscience, empathy, outstanding morals—while working out how he could fleece everyone he knew.

Dante thrust one meaty fist across the counter. 'Good to see you, man,' he said, as though there was no bad blood between them. He was always over-the-top friendly in front of their parents, a deliberate act to make it seem that any bitterness came solely from Pierce.

'Oh, you're very quiet,' Mum said, sounding disappointed as she looked around. A couple of customers sat in a back corner of the sleek chrome-and-timber-fitted cafe. A woman hunched over her laptop in a window seat. She often sat there, consuming only a couple of lattes during the entire day. Pierce didn't mind. He figured she was either writing a book or lonely: whichever, a customer in the window was always a drawcard.

'Yeah, you've caught us in between rushes,' he said warily. Mum rarely came into the cafe, this was his domain; she had final say in the restaurant next door.

'You'll be busy again once it gets to lunchtime, though?' she said too eagerly.

'Before then. Mid-morning. This is just the after-breakfast lull.'

'But you'll have time to do the *torta di ricotta*?' Mum pushed, as though he hadn't been running the cafe and pretty much managing the restaurant for over a decade. She knew he preferred making pasta or putting together the mains, but creating desserts was a task they had shared for years.

He crossed his arms over his chest. 'Of course.'

'Perhaps Dante could help you?'

His gut twisted and he gave a sharp shake of his head. He hated saying anything that would disappoint Mum, but no way was he having that thieving piece of crap behind his counter. 'All under control, Mum. Besides, cooking's not really your thing, is it, Dan?' His jaw ached with the pressure of his clenched teeth, as he fought to stop himself from qualifying the statement with a list of just what his brother excelled at. All the 'skills' his parents chose to ignore.

'Rustling up some sangas isn't exactly rocket science, bro.' Dante laughed. 'I'll pick it up in no time, yeah?'

Pierce bristled. Sure, he had no formal qualifications, but both his cooking ability and the management of the two restaurants had come at a high price. 'You'd be in like Flynn if it was science. Chemistry, at least,' he muttered. Meth was probably about the only thing his brother cooked. 'But I don't own enough teaspoons to share kitchen space with you.'

Mum frowned, her gaze switching between her sons, but he knew the drug references would go over her head.

Dante chuckled. 'Not my scene anymore, bro. I like my brownies baked, and that's about it.'

Pierce jerked a thumb at his brother's overdeveloped muscles. 'I can see you've gone for the organic approach.'

'True 'nuff, bro. Nothing but protein and testosterone. Guess we haven't caught up for a while, yeah?'

That was true. Pierce had put Dante's bulked-up frame down to his time in jail, but he'd not seen his brother in almost a year. There could be some truth in his claim of being clean. Didn't excuse the rest of his failings, though. 'Hadn't noticed.'

'Enough,' Mum said, a flash of annoyance lighting her dark eyes. 'I don't know what you two are on about, but you're like a pair of street dogs, as usual. Pierce, Dante needs a job.'

'I don't have anything,' he said, folding his arms across his chest. 'Any extra shifts, I've already promised to Stefan.' The guy was studying for a double degree at the nearby Adelaide Uni, and doing it tough. Pierce made sure he took a free meal every time he worked.

'That's fine,' Mum said. 'But Dad said we're short a dishy next door from Saturday.'

'Dan doesn't want to do dishy.' And he didn't want Dante anywhere near the trattoria.

'Dan can speak for himself, big bro. And Dan says he'll take whatever he can get, yeah?'

Dante's words had a menacing undertone, but Pierce met his brother's gaze. 'We're talking about working, not *taking*,' he ground out. 'Might be an unfamiliar concept.'

'*Basta!*' Mum's hand sliced the air. Both of them knew that when she swapped to Italian, her temper was well up. 'I said enough. Dante will work as dishy in Trattoria di Angelis,' she made a point of saying the full name, as though reinforcing that it was a family business. 'Until something that suits him better comes up.'

Pierce's guts hurt as though he'd just spent twenty minutes with the medicine ball. He turned away to ring up the bill for the couple who had hesitantly come forward from their back corner seats, uncertain whether to intrude on the family drama. Holy shit, this was his worst nightmare. Even as a kid, Dante had just breezed through the tratt, always too busy with some great scheme or plan to bother mucking in. He lived a charmed life of irresponsibility and endless second chances. It was typical that now he would be handed a job on a platter. Sure, Pierce derived a great deal of satisfaction from growing the small-scale family trattoria into an award-winning restaurant, but the truth was, although he had done the bulk of the work for years, it was still Dad's business and would be run the way Dad wanted.

Dante, though? Dante got to do whatever the hell he liked.

Which was really the only blessing: Dante wouldn't stick around for long.

5
Samantha

Sam had planned to bring home one of the large beef steak pies she sold at the cafe but, remembering Grant's reaction to his cold food that morning, she ducked into Woolies on her way back from Ma and Pops' place, picking up a lasagne and bagged salad. She couldn't stand the stodgy, slippery, tasteless mass, but Grant loved premade pasta dishes. He'd whack a ton of salt on top and devour it along with half a loaf of white bread, completely ignoring the salad.

It meant another night she would skip dinner, but as her stomach seemed perpetually queasy, alternating between being tied in knots of tension and being acidly liquid, that was just as well.

When she pulled up in the driveway of the neat brick-veneer home, she could hear Black Sabbath blasting on the sound system Grant had installed. Her hands tightened on the wheel: the music was never a good sign. Grant was incapable of listening to heavy metal without accompanying it with heavy drinking. She paused a heartbeat, her right hand on the car door handle: she could drive away right now, go back to Settlers Bridge. Heading toward her home town always soothed her.

She couldn't face another night on the floor of the cafe, though. Maybe she should take a room at the Overland Hotel? Lynn would be sure to have something. But that would open her private life to scrutiny.

Besides, even the idea of taking a room was ridiculous: she had a perfectly good bed and house here. She couldn't run away simply because her husband was in a mood. God knows, it wasn't like she didn't have a temper herself, but she'd learned to stay small and silent at home.

Sam hefted the bags out of the car, refusing to give in to the sudden wash of nerves.

The glass panes alongside the front door vibrated with the beat of Grant's music, but she actually felt a little relieved. If her husband was fully into his music and Beam, she could slip into the kitchen without speaking to him, get his dinner warmed up while hoping he hit the 'happy spot', where he'd had just enough booze to turn him from angry to maudlin. Either way, she would be blamed for whatever was wrong in his life: but his tears were less terrifying than his anger.

She grimaced as she popped the lasagne into the oven and turned it on: this time, she actually was to blame. If she hadn't slept at the cafe, Grant wouldn't have come looking for her, and he wouldn't have lost his licence. Heaviness centred in her chest. Regardless of whether Grant was happy drunk or melancholy drunk, they'd have to discuss how he was going to get to and from work each day. They couldn't afford the mortgage payments on the house on her income alone, not after the expenses for the cafe had been deducted.

Forty minutes later, she had sorted out the cutlery drawer, the plastics cupboard and the pantry, clinging to the kitchen as though it was a safe zone, and working quietly in case Grant heard her over his music. She desperately needed to go to the loo, but that meant passing the lounge room where Grant would be in his recliner. Stoically ignoring the demands of her bladder, she donned the quilted gloves Ma had given her for Christmas, and pulled the lasagne from the oven. She was officially out of excuses to avoid Grant.

As she turned to place the hot tray on the draining board, she almost dropped it: Grant was slumped in the doorway, one shoulder against the doorframe, his ankles crossed, left hand wrapped around a Jim Beam can. She knew instantly that he was melancholy drunk, and the deep breath she was finally able to draw felt life-giving.

Though his lips moved, she couldn't hear what he said, and pointed to the Bluetooth speaker on the kitchen counter.

Grant fumbled for the remote control in the pocket of his jeans, and turned down the music . . . a little. 'Babe, we're gonna have to sell up.'

She froze, ignoring the hot foil tray burning through the oven mitts. 'What do you mean?'

'I mean, we can't afford to keep this place.'

She put down the tray carefully. Though Grant looked after their finances, they'd never had an issue making the payments. But when he was drunk, Grant easily slipped into 'half-empty' mode, and she had to ease him out of it, assure him that life was good. 'We've been paying the mortgage for eighteen years now, hon. Surely we're actually ahead?'

'You don't understand!' Grant yelled, slamming the doorframe with his palm.

Sam flinched. She didn't usually misread his mood, yet this time Grant had switched in a flash from melancholy to angry.

'And why the hell would you? I have to look after every damn thing around here, not you. I have to pay for the house, the cars, the furniture, the . . . the . . .' He cast around the room, as though looking for something else to claim, then crushed the can in his fist. Dark liquid fountained from it, and he threw it to the floor. 'Every bloody thing, even the piss. And what do you do? Fuck off to Settlers Bridge every five minutes. You're not even here to make my bloody dinner.'

'I've made your dinner,' she almost whispered, gesturing at the lasagne.

'And what fucking time is it?' he roared.

Just after seven, the same time they had dinner every night. But Sam knew better than to point that out. 'I'm sorry, hon. I'll dish up right now.' She bent to pull plates out of the cupboard below the island bench, and the entire tray of lasagne flew past her head, slamming to the floor.

'You call this a dinner?'

Lava-hot pasta sauce splattered the walls, the cupboards. Her bare legs. She gasped and instinctively wiped at her skin to stop the burn.

'Leave it!' Grant yelled, his ugg-booted foot slamming down into the mess on the floor, right beside her. 'You're not listening to me.'

'I am,' she pleaded, trying to back away from him but brought up short by the kitchen counter. 'But I don't know what's wrong. We can afford the mortgage, we always do. And the cafe's doing really well now, so we could even put a little extra in . . . if you wanted to,' she added. Grant didn't like it when she tried to help organise their finances.

'The cafe.' He seized on her words, his bloodshot eyes struggling to focus on her. 'That damn place takes up all your time, all my money. That's why you're not here doing what you bloody well should be. That's what we'll sell.'

'But there's nothing there to sell, hon. You know if anyone wanted to open a cafe they'd take Tractors and Tarts over the road. That's been on the market for next-to-nothing for years. No one's going to want to pay decent money for my place.'

'*Your* place?' he said, his sudden quiet more menacing than his anger. 'Don't I fund that shithole? Aren't I paying for your hobby?'

There was no point trying to persuade him that the cafe turned a nice profit; money he saw in his account every month. In any case, fear dried up her words, her throat so constricted that she was fighting to get air down it. Grant rarely got this angry. God, she wished she hadn't slept at the cafe last night; she should have just stuck it out here.

Grant stooped, grabbing a handful of the mashed pasta, seemingly oblivious to the heat. He smeared it against her chest, using her shirt to clean his hand. The cold shock of her fear stole the heat from the food. 'And what do I bloody get? My dinner on the floor, like some damned dog!'

She hadn't actually seen him throw the tray on the floor: maybe it had slipped from the bench. She had to cling to that thought. What else could she give him for dinner? Frantically she rifled through the contents of the freezer in her head. Because cataloguing that was preferable to being in this moment.

The fight suddenly left Grant's posture, and he slumped against the counter, his hands covering his face. She knew that stance: the sorrow and self-hate would kick in now. Normally, she felt sorry for Grant when the depression got to him, but tonight she was just relieved.

Cautiously, she gripped the hem of her shirt, pulling the cotton from her chest to ease the burn.

'The fuckers canned me, Sam,' Grant mumbled from behind his hands.

'What?' She surreptitiously blew down onto her chest, trying to cool it.

'Meatworks. They fucking sacked me.'

She froze. Grant had been there all his life, starting on the process line at sixteen and working up to slaughter. He'd even done a Certificate III in meat processing. The meatworks had cutbacks sometimes, like any industry, but they wouldn't fire a qualified slaughterer. 'Why?'

He slid his hands up to press against his forehead, so he could gaze at her blearily. 'It's your fault. I went into work after you pissed me off this morning, and they had bloody rando testing. Made me piss in a cup.'

Sam closed her eyes, despair washing through her. Grant had been off his face when he stormed into the cafe, driven home unlicensed, and then gone into work still drunk. 'Shit,' she whispered. 'Why did you go in? You could have called in sick, you were late any—' She hadn't even finished the sentence before she saw her mistake. No one ever questioned Grant.

'Because I bloody had to, Sam! Someone has to keep this *family* afloat.' He sneered the word. 'Though I don't know why the hell I bother. What am I fucking getting out of this?' He cast an arm wide, encompassing their neat, Caesarstone-topped kitchen. 'All I ever fucking asked you for was a couple of kids—a couple of boys to kick the footy around with. But you can't even get that right.'

She knew their repeated miscarriages had gutted him. Yet, even though the dream had been his, not hers, he'd never had to deal with the anguish of flushing the remains of a life down the toilet, wondering if it was his fault because he hadn't been able to find it in himself to want the baby desperately enough. She'd tried to do right by him, tried to get pregnant, month after month, even though it tore her apart. Tried until he had rejected her more than a year ago, saying there was no point to having sex with her anymore. As though it had never been anything more than a means to an end.

'You know that isn't my fault,' she whimpered.

'Of course it is.' He groaned. 'There's bloody nothing wrong with me, Sam. We're not a family, we're not shit, thanks to you. Everything is your fault. I'm working my guts out ten hours a day trying to keep everything together, but you're just off who-bloody-knows-where all the time. Are you seeing someone else? Because I'll kill the bastard if you are, you know I will.'

'I'm not,' she said, trying to appease him. 'There's never been anyone else, hon.' That was the god-honest truth. He'd been her first and he'd be her last. She had spent more years with Grant than without him, so they had to fix this. She loved him too much to be without him.

Didn't she?

Doubt blossomed too quickly, as though the thought had always been there, niggling, waiting to flourish. She'd always known Grant loved her, needed her, more than she needed him. But never before had she allowed the traitorous thought that perhaps she didn't love him at all. Perhaps what they had was convenience and habit and familiarity. And nothing at all like love.

'Then where the fuck were you this morning?' Grant raged. 'Why weren't you at home? Where you're supposed to be.'

'I went in to Settlers early because you were snoring so loud I couldn't sleep. You know how you get when you've been on the Beam.'

'Snoring? What if I'd fucking stopped breathing again, Sam? Did you think of that?'

Yes. Yes, she had thought of that. She'd wondered what it would be like if his sporadic sleep apnoea kicked in again, if his loud snores cut to silence. Would she shake him awake so he'd take a breath? It had been better that she left, rather than give herself a chance to find out.

'I'm sorry,' she whispered, evading his gaze. 'I just needed to clear my head.'

Grant lurched across the room, his fingers fastening around her neck. His index finger pressed hard against her throat, his thumb and middle finger digging into the arteries.

She pulled frantically at his hand as she struggled for breath, trying to choke out a plea.

He lifted her with one hand. Dark patches bloomed on the periphery of her vision as his fingers closed tighter. 'I could just slap some sense into you, Sam. But you know why I'm not going to?'

She couldn't answer, and he shook her like a rag doll. 'Because I don't want to hurt you.'

His fingers cinched tighter, and reality exploded and then disappeared in waves in her head, as though her brain rejected the truth of what was happening.

'It has to be slower, like this, so you understand. So you have the chance to learn, Sammie. I could punish you, but instead I'm teaching you.'

Her legs jerked spasmodically. With an immense effort, she dragged her gaze up to the air-conditioning vent in the ceiling. She wanted that, not her husband's deranged countenance, to be the last thing she ever saw.

'I've been too soft with you, and you've forgotten that I'm in charge. I love you, Sam, and that's why you have to learn to listen to me.' Grant lowered her so that just the tips of her toes touched the floor. He loosened his grip a fraction, but he still had her throat, her life, in his hands. 'We're going to lose everything because I love you too much, because I let you have your stupid cafe, let you hang around your grandparents all the damn time, let you pretend that you're actually contributing to this bloody family.' He groaned, pressing his cheek against hers. 'I give you every damn thing, Sam, so why the hell did you have to make me chase you?'

She hadn't wanted him to chase her. Never wanted him to.

The realisation was sudden and absolute.

She wanted Grant gone.

6
Pierce

'Bro, you want to try some of this?' Dante shook a plastic container at him. His brother seemed to spend half his day mixing up smoothies and shakes from the vast array of supplements he'd moved onto a shelf in the trattoria kitchen. 'You look like you're a bit stiff. Work out too hard last night?'

It didn't help Pierce's mood that his brother was right: since Dante started at the trattoria, Pierce had been hitting the gym harder. He wanted to pretend it was only to release some of his anger, his frustration that their parents had, yet again, let Dante back into their lives, but he knew it was also due to the longstanding, undeclared rivalry between him and Dante. Anything Dante could do, Pierce was determined to do better—mostly so he didn't have to hear his parents go on about Dante's 'achievements'. It was lucky his brother didn't aspire to much. 'No, thanks. I'll have a couple of eggs later,' Pierce replied.

'The stuff is here, bro. You help yourself. It's all kosher, check the labels.' Dante seemed almost as determined as Mum that they have a relationship. He constantly tried to engage Pierce in discussion about his workouts, or commented on the female customers he ogled through the service hatch, as though he and Pierce had some kind of macho buddy thing going.

Like hell.

To be fair, Dante also seemed intent on proving he'd turned over a new leaf, doing at least three shifts a week as the dishy over the previous month. Not even close to a full-time job for a grown man, but it was so unlike Dante to stick with anything, Pierce was grudgingly impressed. At least, he was prepared to be while the end-of-day takings balanced and Dante stayed out of his face.

'Dan is working out okay, huh?' Dad said a week later as they worked together on that night's special, dotting teaspoons of ricotta and spinach filling evenly across sheets of pasta covering the width of the trattoria's stainless-steel bench.

As each sheet filled, Pierce draped another piece of dough over the entire creation, pressed gently around each mound of filling, then sliced the pasta into squares with a pastry cutter. 'Guess so,' he replied. 'If by "working out" you mean he rinses the dishes before they go in the dishwasher. Not too much that could go wrong, though, is there?' He hated that he let the petty childhood jealousy creep into his tone.

'Been meaning to talk to you about that.' Dad dusted each of the ravioli with flour and set them aside to dry out. 'It's time Dante took on a bit more responsibility.'

Pierce stiffened, his heart racing. And not in a good way. 'How so?'

Dad hefted a tub of beef and spinach mix from the commercial fridge and thumped it onto the counter as Pierce rolled out fresh sheets of dough. 'Mum and I were thinking that maybe it's time he did some work out the front.'

The tension that had been creeping up the back of Pierce's head expanded in a blinding flash. Somehow he had convinced himself that, given Dante's unreliability, his parents would be content to keep his brother in the kitchen until he decided to move on. 'We don't need an extra at front of house.'

'It's not so much about need, Pierce. At least not in that sense. It'd be good for Dante to be more involved, take a sense of ownership in the business. It would give him something to focus on.'

Pierce turned away, flipping the tap over the sink to full pressure as he fought to contain his anger. What the hell could he say? He was a grown man, so to complain about the obvious unfairness would sound self-indulgent. Yet he had devoted more than thirty years to supporting his parents, building both their business and his own. Dante had barely hit thirty days, yet he was already to be rewarded. 'Front of house means access to the till,' he said tightly. 'You're comfortable with that?'

Dad blew out a long breath, then started carefully spooning out the ravioli filler, as though the steady pace would help maintain his calm. 'Dan is trying. You don't know if you can trust a dog off leash until you let him run and see if he'll come back.'

Pierce snorted. As far as he was concerned, dogs shouldn't be allowed in a restaurant. 'Your business,' he said tightly. 'Just keep him out of my cafe.'

'It's not my business, Pierce. It's the family business.'

Pierce shrugged.

'It was built so you'd both have something.'

'I know that, Dad. And I appreciate the start you gave me. I just don't want to see it screwed up after everything you've put into it.'

'Everything we've put in, Pierce. It's been a family effort.'

Yeah, a family of three. 'Dan may not even be interested.'

'Mum spoke with him. He's keen as mustard.'

Of course she had. Mum was determined to force them into family togetherness. 'What exactly do you plan to have him do?'

'I want to discuss it with you. You know you're my right hand; this place doesn't run without you.'

Pierce glanced up at the unusual praise, but then recognised it for what it was: a softener.

'We're thinking if we put him on greeting and taking orders to start with, he'll get some experience in customer handling.' Dad's words proved Pierce's suspicion. 'We'll shift Amanda from the front to be your sous chef, she'll be keen on that.'

He didn't miss the fact that Dad had promoted him to chef: with no qualifications, they'd never bothered with titles. But Dad had obviously been primed by Mum to keep him sweet.

'Probably not the best idea to put Amanda in here,' he said. Amanda would be far too keen to work in the close confines of the kitchen with him. While he pretended to be oblivious to her interest, he wasn't stupid enough to put himself in a position where it would become an issue. His entire focus was work, the two businesses: he didn't need anything that would get messy.

'Well, there's no point keeping Dan in the kitchen, he doesn't have your ability.'

'It's not about ability. You, of all people, bloody well know that. It comes down to practice,' he said bitterly. Hours, days, weeks and months of repetition, practising the skills that didn't come naturally. Practice that had been at the expense of . . . dreams, opportunities. And relationships.

7
Samantha

Sam had steered clear of joining the CWA when she was younger because it seemed like something more suited to old ducks. Yet, she'd gradually come to recognise that, although she saw people in the cafe every day, it was possible to be both surrounded and lonely. Perhaps that was what happened when you chose to keep secrets?

With the CWA meetings now held on Thursday afternoons while Grant was still at work, she had a rare window where he didn't know what she was up to. Tara appreciated the chance to pick up an extra shift in the cafe, and Sam got to feel like an actual person for a couple of hours, although she didn't really participate in any of the activities. Craft and sewing weren't her thing, and she didn't dare attempt to bake something to add to the array of goods for the Friday stalls or the bigger fundraisers.

But it was nice to simply . . . relax. Lately, she felt like too much adrenaline was pumping through her body, leaving her constantly on edge, a nervousness she tried to hide behind over-enthusiastic friendliness.

Though Grant had lost his licence a few weeks back, he'd been wrong about losing his job: his foreman had merely marked him as sick, and the urine test had been bogus, obviously staged to straighten him out.

Grant decided that his foreman, Talbo, was the greatest mate that ever lived, yet the relief of keeping his job hadn't been enough to stop him from sulking for days, completely cutting her off. He'd turned the latch on the bedroom door, locking her out as some kind of imagined punishment for being the cause of his embarrassment.

So she'd slept in the spare room. And she'd worn a thick, knitted scarf around her neck, although the house had ducted heating throughout, and spring was kicking in.

Somehow, she never got around to moving back into their bedroom; instead she scurried in to grab her clothes when Grant was at work. But she often woke to find him standing in the doorway to her room. He never said anything, certainly never did anything. He simply stood there, ignoring her questions. Then he'd walk off, presumably back to the main bedroom.

Without lifting a finger, he managed to put her in a state of constant wariness. It was like water torture, leaving her permanently on edge, waiting for the next drip to fall, the next outburst that would drown her. She could no longer sleep through the night, repeatedly startling awake and rearing up to see if Grant was standing there.

Last night, he had been.

In the bright, safe light of day, she told herself that her behaviour made no sense. Grant didn't hurt her—well, hardly ever, and that had only been to make her listen. He rarely even yelled at her, now. She had shared a bed with the man for two decades, so how could she now be afraid of him simply looking at her?

Yet the truth was she slept better on the floor of the cafe than she did at home.

Sam dug the heels of both hands into her eyes, trying to force away the weariness. Then she picked up a cardboard tray and slid open the glass cake cabinet to choose some slices for the CWA afternoon tea. As always, she felt a pang of wistfulness as she selected the McCues red velvet, apple crumble, and Chester squares. Slices were simple, basic fare she'd made when she was a kid; there wasn't much room for her to get it wrong. Grant was more a pie and chips kind of guy, but her passion had always been for making desserts. At least, it had been until her father repeatedly heaped shit on her efforts, even though Mum never baked a darn thing. Perhaps that had been deliberate, though: Mum wasn't giving him a chance to put her down. He did that often enough with his fists. It had always perplexed Sam that their mother—intelligent, attractive, university-educated and now working at a small newspaper in Singapore—had stuck it out with that bastard for so long. Well, a few years, anyway. Long enough for Jack to cop some good thrashings from their dad.

Sometimes, she wondered whether it was Dad's fault that she'd married so young. It had made her feel safe, knowing someone—other than her elderly grandparents—cared about her. Though her father had been long gone, Grant had wanted to beat him up when she told him about the abuse.

She wrapped her arms around her waist, holding the memory close for a moment. Would Grant fight for her now?

Probably. He was fiercely protective of her.

Possessive, a little voice inside her corrected.

She snapped the cabinet closed and forced a smile into her voice. 'You're in charge of lock-up, Tars. Don't forget to turn the warmers off by three.'

~

'They look nice,' Christine Albright said with a lift of her angular chin toward the tray Sam carried into the Rovers' clubrooms where the CWA meeting was held. Sam had been goal defence for the Rovers, but when she moved to Murray Bridge, Grant insisted she join the local netball team, sister to his football team, even though it meant playing against her friends each time the towns faced off in a game.

Christine's words had Sam immediately on guard. The woman rarely complimented hard work and was even less likely to be nice about desserts brought in from a commercial bakery. 'They're from McCues,' she said cautiously.

'I know,' Christine replied, moving some of the plates already ranged on the long bench in the clubroom kitchen.

Sam cast a longing look at the table, mentally baking each dish, trying to find the courage to risk turning that dream into actuality. Lamingtons, vanilla slices, ginger snaps, scones, coffee kisses. If she allowed herself, which recipe would she tackle first? The cream horns, she decided. They were old-fashioned and rarely seen, the cone of sugar-crusted, flaky golden pastry filled with cream turned just a touch tart by whipping it with cream cheese, then garnished with whatever berries were in season.

She inhaled deeply, the aroma of chocolate, vanilla, berries and hot pastry tantalising, despite her working in a cafe filled with the smell of good food. It wasn't that she wanted to eat, but that she longed to *create*. If she allowed herself to try, she wouldn't need to tell Grant, she could simply give the baking away to the after-school crowd. But what if her father was right, what if she really was useless? To try meant risking failure, the loss of another dream. It was safer if she stuck to plating up food, helping someone else's creation look delicious.

'McCues are always reliable, aren't they?' Christine said. 'Unlike some of the things that turn up here.' She waved a hand to indicate the tea table. 'I mean, really, Tracey is still putting out her "secret ingredient" lamingtons, as though we don't all know it's orange essence.'

This was more the Christine that Sam recognised, and she relaxed. 'I love the zing of the orange essence. And I can't believe how well Roni's learned to cook, thanks to Tracey. She said she'd never done more than heat baked beans before she moved here.' Too late, she remembered

Christine's fury when Tracey and Roni had teamed together to win the lamington baking contest a few years earlier. Maybe Grant was right, she shouldn't speak.

'Yes, well, you can't believe everything anyone tells you, can you?' Christine moved down to the urn and filled two cups with hot water, giving the machine an admonishing glare as it dared to burp. 'I suppose you've learned that for yourself.'

Sam frowned, accepting the cup with the teabag label draped over the side. 'I think everyone around here is pretty much what they seem. I mean, most of us have known one another forever, haven't we?'

'It's not here I'm talking about, Samantha,' Christine reproved. She pursed her lips, glancing around the room as though she wanted to keep their conversation discreet . . . which was unusual enough to set off all the warning bells in Sam's head. 'I'm talking about your life.'

Oh god, Christine was going to do this here? Now? Sam had managed to avoid being alone with her the last few weeks in the cafe, delivering her meal or coffee and disappearing with barely a word. 'I've no idea what you're talking about,' she said stiffly, eyeing the doorway. She couldn't escape without physically pushing past Christine, and she was certain the older woman had deliberately manoeuvred it that way.

'Enough, Samantha. You know perfectly well what I'm talking about. I've tried to give you opportunity to discuss it in private at the cafe, but you've chosen to ignore me. Anyone can see that you're not well. For goodness' sake, you used to look older than your age because you let yourself go, but now you're . . . haggard.'

Sam took a step back, shaking her head in bewilderment. Where did Christine get off, chastising her as though she was some kid who'd told a lie? Acting as though she had a *right* to Sam's secrets?

'Look.' Christine glanced around again, and Sam realised that the older woman was actually nervous, as though she genuinely didn't want anyone to hear their conversation. 'I want you to know that some of us understand the situation you find yourself in.' Her tone wasn't exactly gentle, the words clipped by Christine's habit of snapping her mouth shut at the end of each sentence, yet it was . . . compassionate. 'It's not your fault, and there are ways out.'

'Ways out of what, Christine?' Sam blustered. Sure, she'd thought of escape; but without Grant, without their marriage, she was nothing, had nothing. And people like Christine Albright liked to encourage other women to fail so they could make sure everyone's misery matched their own. It was like being in high school again, with girls looking for drama, egging each other on to dump their boyfriends so they'd all be losers together.

'I realise you don't want me to spell it out here,' Christine lowered her voice. 'And, frankly, I don't want to get into it. But you don't have to stay with your husband.'

'Not stay with my husband?' Sam repeated, shocked. Not so much at the thought but at the fact that anyone would come out and openly say it. 'Why would I leave him? Because we argued that one time?'

Christine cocked her head, her expression oddly sympathetic. 'Only once, Samantha? It wasn't; it never is. They persuade you that they lost their temper that one time, and that it was all your fault. As though you're an imbecile who can't count.' As Sam started to disagree, Christine held up her hand. 'I heard him. He was drunk as a skunk, and trying to make it all your fault. And I'll bet it didn't stop there, did it? And nor was it the last time.'

Sam's fingers reflexively went to the scarf she'd taken to wearing. She had figured it would be less remarkable if she frequently wore a colourful piece of chiffon around her throat. Then it wouldn't look as though she was hiding something if she ever *needed* to wear it. 'You don't know what you're talking about, Christine. Of course Grant was angry; he'd just lost his licence. You're trying to make this into something it isn't.' She cast a frantic glance out into the hall, where women were grouped around the various craft tables, pursuing their hobbies. She couldn't go out there, couldn't risk Christine following her, continuing the conversation more publicly. But she also didn't want to stand here, didn't want to have this talk, didn't want to be forced to face any kind of . . . truth. She had spent hours persuading herself that she wasn't a victim, and to have Christine thrust the label on her was belittling. She wasn't the sort of woman who was abused. She was smart, ran her own business, had friends and a house and a marriage and . . . and . . . surely everything any woman could want?

Except peace of mind.

Security.

Independence.

But they were things you traded to be married.

'Grant isn't violent.' The thought of revealing her secret was too humiliating to even consider. 'He just loses his temper, like you saw. He doesn't mean anything by it. Maybe you should look after your own business, instead of listening in on mine.' She slammed her folded arms across her chest, to keep them from trembling.

'There is no *just* in this,' Christine hissed, tapping a bony finger against Sam's forearm. 'The man is a controller.' She glanced out toward the main hall, where a gust of laughter went up from the macrame table. Then she leaned in closer, her breath laced with peppermint. 'I've seen it before.' Her mouth tightened for a moment, as though she was holding words in, then she exclaimed, 'I've *lived* it! And you need to get out. Now. While you don't have children. There's nothing to stop you from walking away.'

Cold fury swept through Sam. She drew herself up straight. She was so sick of being judged for not having children, sick of the inference that her lack of maternal desire meant there was something wrong with her. Obviously, in Christine's eyes, if she had children she should be willing to stay and get beaten. Which meant that if she chose to walk away now, she was a coward. 'You women with children don't realise that those of us without can't see how it makes any difference,' she snapped.

But she did know how it made a difference. If they'd had children, Grant would be happier. That was the problem: he wanted to be a family, not a couple. And she couldn't give him that. 'The success of a marriage isn't based on whether you've got kids. It's worth fighting for either way.'

'And the failure of a marriage also has nothing to do with whether you have children. Sometimes that marriage isn't worth fighting for, no matter how much you want to believe it is,' Christine insisted. 'Sometimes your happiness is better found somewhere else. Even if that happiness is only the freedom to make your own choices, to do what you want when you want, to wear what you want, eat what you want, without being constantly scared of retribution.'

'I'm not scared,' Sam lied. 'You're deliberately twisting what you saw to make it sound like Grant's violent.'

'At the very least, he's controlling you. And he'll go there, eventually. You're a smart woman, Samantha: you know the truth, deep down inside, even if you're hiding it. That's why you're scared. I swear, you've turned into a shadow of the girl I've watched grow up over the last thirty-odd years.'

'You watch too many soapies, Christine. Grant's not doing anything wrong.'

'Oh, trust me,' Christine sneered. 'It's most definitely wrong. It's abuse. I don't care what anyone says, coercive control is domestic violence.'

Sam glanced frantically toward the sink. The words she'd forbidden herself to even think made her feel physically ill, as though Christine had punched her in the stomach with each syllable.

'I can see it in you, Samantha. I've seen it all before. You'll waste so many years on dreams of holding your marriage together, believing that anything that went wrong is your fault, that it is your job to fix everything. They are years you will never get back.'

She hated Christine for shining light on what should be a dirty, dark secret. Yet, at the same moment, she wanted to clutch onto the life raft that Christine was offering. The thought that someone understood so intimately, that there was someone who possibly wouldn't judge her failure, tempted her to share. She chewed her lips. 'But I don't know what to do,' she whispered harshly, her tone angry, even though what she truly felt was desperation. 'Everything is in Grant's name.'

When Sam married she'd happily spent the next five years neglecting friendships while cementing her position as a perfect housewife in Murray Bridge, doing a bit of part-time work at Coles while waiting to fall pregnant. She'd been a bit miffed when Ma suggested she take on the vacant cafe: she wasn't going to have time to run that, she would be busy with the babies Grant wanted. 'The cafe was a tax dodge,' she added to Christine, as though she could defend her own stupidity. 'My grandparents helped out with the deposit, and Grant said if it was all in his name he could write off the costs against his income.' He took care of the money, giving her cash to cover groceries. He promised he would handle the finances, and later they would rent their house out and buy somewhere bigger, nicer. For their family.

'We just never got around to changing the business to my name when the cafe started paying its way, because Grant said we'd lose more in stamp duty and capital gains tax than we'd saved in negative gearing.' It had made perfect sense, planning for their long-term future together, so the house, both cars and the business were in his name. And she was a prisoner. 'I can't afford to leave.'

'Can you afford not to?' Christine asked bluntly.

'He said that if I leave, he'll kill himself.'

'And if you stay, there's a chance he'll kill you.'

The words should shock her, but instead they just seemed exhaustingly inevitable. She shrugged. 'Isn't that the better option?' she said. 'I don't want to be responsible for his death.'

'You're not,' Christine hissed fiercely. 'He's a grown man. You're not responsible for him, any more than he is responsible for you. What you are responsible for is taking charge of your own happiness. But sometimes, seeing the way forward becomes impossible.' Her cold fingers closed around Sam's, her grip surprisingly strong. 'I want to help you, Samantha.'

'I can't go, Christine. You're not listening. *Everything* is in his name.' As Sam whispered the words, she was aware of how ridiculous she had become. When had she allowed a man to take control of all she had, all that she was? A man who, she now fully accepted for the first time, she had not loved for so very long.

'I'm sure a lawyer can help sort that. But in the first instance, you have to get out. I have some money. I'll help you all I'm able,' Christine said firmly. 'And you know Settlers Bridge will close ranks around you. You're one of our own, through and through. Not like Veronica,' she added as a gust of laughter came from where Roni and Tracey stood chatting with several other women. 'Though I suppose she is earning her place. But if you don't want to involve the town, I know a group that can help. They'll come and pick up your things while Grant is at work, move you wherever you want to go. A safe place. Can you stay with your grandparents?'

Sam shook her head. 'If Grant came there . . .' She knew her words were an admission that she suspected her husband could get violent toward someone who mattered, instead of only to her. But the escape she hadn't realised she so desperately wanted suddenly seemed excitingly attainable and terrifyingly real.

Christine nodded. 'I understand. Your brother?'

Again she shook her head. 'Jack's only just getting his life on track. And I'm his big sister, you know, I'm supposed to be the one who looks out for him.' She winced, realising that she had been strong enough to protect her little brother against their abusive father, yet somehow she had walked into the same trap as her mother.

'Somewhere else, then,' Christine mused. 'Give me a day or two, I'll find something. I promise.'

Gratitude and relief flooded Sam, and she felt as close to crying as she ever came. How was it possible that this woman, who had always been hard and demanding, interfering and imperious, was coming to her rescue?

'Have you heard?' Roni Krueger rested both hands on the serving counter, between the trays and plates of afternoon tea. She was almost bouncing up and down in apparent excitement.

'Heard?' Sam repeated, hoping Roni hadn't caught her own conversation.

'Sharna is engaged. And typical Sharna, it's all a big rush: the wedding will be at the end of spring. At the inn, of course.' Sharna had lived and worked at the Wattle Seed Inn for the past couple of years. The owner, Gabrielle, ran the century-old building as a B&B and served high teas, always making a point of sourcing her baked goods from Sam's cafe, to keep the money in the district.

'She's finally come to her senses then?' Christine said sourly. 'I'm surprised one of our boys is brave enough—or foolish enough—to take her on.'

Roni cocked an eyebrow at Christine. 'She and Taryn have announced their engagement,' Roni said reprovingly.

Christine snorted. 'Well, that's neither an engagement nor a marriage then, is it?'

'It absolutely is,' Roni said firmly.

Normally, Sam would jump in to back Roni up, but now she was torn. Somehow, Christine had become her unlikely ally.

'Of course it isn't.' Christine waved away the notion and set her mug down with a sharp crack. 'Marriage is for a man and a woman. The bible says so.'

'And the law says otherwise,' Roni retorted with a roll of her eyes. 'Anyway, Sam, I wanted to let you know. We're throwing an impromptu party at the Wattle Seed Inn next weekend. You'll be there?' She paused, as though she was done, then added in a slightly grudging tone, 'Open house, Christine, so of course you're welcome, too.'

'I'm quite certain I'm busy,' Christine replied.

'Shame,' Roni said dryly. 'Do make sure you come, Sam. It's on the Sunday, and it'll also be Sharna's farewell, as she's moving to Adelaide with Taryn.' She stuck out her bottom lip, pulling a sad face. 'It'll be weird not having her around.'

'Yeah, it will—' Sam started.

Christine interrupted. 'Moving out, you say? She's still living at the inn, isn't she?'

Roni nodded. 'Gabrielle repurposed a couple of the upstairs rooms into a bigger suite for Sharna.'

'Interesting.' Christine clamped her mouth shut, signifying the conversation had ended. But her eyes gleamed as she shot Sam a meaningful look.

Sam's breath caught, her heart pounding hard enough to make her chest shift. Could escape really be this easy?

8
Samantha

'You're late,' Christine said, as though Sam didn't own the business.

Sam's heart had sunk a little as she pulled up behind Christine's SUV parked outside Ploughs and Pies. For all that Christine was determined to defend her—and organise her—she was still low-key terrified by the woman.

She dragged her tote from the car as she clambered out. 'Only five minutes. It takes a bit longer coming in from Wurruldi than it did from Murray Bridge because of the dirt roads. Maybe I should give you a key, save you standing out in this sun,' she joked, fanning her face.

Christine moved into the deep shade of the hooded verandah. 'If you're going to make a habit of being tardy, maybe you should. I never run late.' She gave a tight smile, which Sam suspected was supposed to be gentle. 'Even though you've moved out, it's important to maintain routine as much as you can. You have to assess what was good about your old life, what worked, and make sure that's what you cling to. I know how easy it is to tell yourself everything about that life was wrong, to give in to the temptation to discard it all, to become someone else altogether. But that will just bring you a whole new set of problems. It's not how you move forward.' Christine impatiently rapped a knuckle against the cafe door. 'You can't recreate or ignore your past; you have to acknowledge it so you can build on the experience.'

'I don't know that you can call twenty wasted years an *experience*.' Sam scrabbled in the bottom of her tote for the shop keys, trying to ignore Christine's lecturing tone. 'Anyway, you've always been in Settlers, haven't you? So what did you discard? What changed in your life when you . . . left?' She wasn't sure of the correct term for running away from your husband and your life. Fled? Escaped?

Christine's face shuttered. 'The details don't matter. I'm giving you the benefit of my understanding. And my advice now is don't use the upheaval in your life as an excuse to run late.'

Sam held up her phone. 'I'd forgotten this was off. I had to pull over to fiddle with the darn thing.'

'Turned off so *he* can't bother you all night?'

'Off so *he* can't see where I am,' Sam muttered, shoving the key into the frame of the cafe's glass-paned door. Provided she could get Tara in to do lock-up each day, she was out of Settlers Bridge before Grant had a chance to get there after his shift at the meatworks. By the time Sam reached the steep cliff down into the tiny, five-building township of Wurruldi, she breathed easier, knowing he couldn't find her. But was this any way to live? It couldn't be a long-term solution.

'What do you mean?' Christine asked sharply. 'Is that a feature on the phone? There's not much we can do about him knowing your whereabouts while you're here, but the rest of the time it's imperative he cannot locate you.'

Sam waggled the phone. 'I don't know about phone features, but no matter how I fiddle I can't seem to disable this tracker app except by turning the phone off.' She realised her mistake before she finished speaking.

Christine snatched the phone, strode toward the road and dropped the device into the gutter. As Sam watched in stunned disbelief, the older woman climbed into her Pathfinder, slowly drove over the phone, then clambered out of the vehicle. She picked up the mangled phone from behind the front tyre and tossed it into the public rubbish bin.

She returned to Sam's side. 'There. You can have my old phone and *he* can enjoy tracking that one all the way to the dump. I'll pop into Murray Bridge later and get you one of the card things from the post office. I don't suppose Cynthia has them at the Australia Post outlet here.' She waggled an admonishing finger as Sam continued to stare at her. 'And now you are ten minutes late. Come on, hurry up. I thought we could spend some time in between customers discussing what we're going to do for Sharna's *celebration* cake.' Although Christine hadn't attended Sharna's rather lively engagement party, her disapproval evidently did not extend to keeping her nose out of the wedding plans that had the town buzzing.

Hours had gone by, the lunch rush finished, before Sam had a chance to carry two cappuccinos over to where Christine had entrenched herself—as she had done every day for the past two and a half weeks—in the window seat of the cafe. She swept aside the tiny hexagons of her latest patchworking project as Sam approached.

Sam sighed as she nudged the chair out with her foot and deflated into it. 'I love that the buses for the safari park have put Ploughs and Pies on their route, but, wow, it makes for an exhausting day.'

'Not helped by starting ten minutes behind,' Christine said. 'There's no playing catch-up if you wrong-foot yourself that early in the morning.'

Sam ignored her. 'And only half an hour till the kids come in from school for another rush.'

Christine parked her needle by threading it through the fabric, then settled her hands in her lap. 'Did you try something new for them?'

Sam puffed out her cheeks to release her nerves. 'I did. You know, Gabrielle's kitchen facilities are so awesome, it's a shame she buys in the baked goods for her high teas.'

Christine waved off the information as unimportant. 'So you made . . . ?'

Sam nibbled nervously at her lower lip for a moment. 'I tried a French vanilla slice. It's in the fridge. But I think perhaps there isn't enough cream in the custard, it's a bit too yellow and maybe a little heavy.'

'I'm sure it's not improving while you're sitting here talking.'

Sam dragged herself to her feet. Christine had yet to openly criticise any of the recipes she encouraged—demanded—Sam try each day. But she had also yet to be enthusiastically complimentary.

The cake carefully plated, Sam added a fanned strawberry on a crosshatch of chocolate sauce to the side, then thickly dusted the golden pastry top of the slice with sieved icing sugar. If she couldn't get the baking right, she was at least confident in her plating. She chose one of the tiny souvenir teaspoons Lucie's mum, Monica, had gifted from her extensive collection—the Eiffel Tower spoon, of course—and lined it up carefully with the flaky pastry base. Then she took a deep breath and delivered the dessert to Christine.

The pastry cracked sharply under the edge of the spoon, and Christine nodded approval as she sliced into the fluffy custard and down to the middle layer of pastry. Sam tensed. Would that fresh-baked pastry have gone rubbery or soggy beneath the weight of the custard? She should have tested it herself before giving it to Christine. But the constant nervous anticipation of Grant's messages—which alternated between brokenly begging and aggressively demanding she return—had stolen the last of her appetite weeks ago.

The second sheet of pastry shattered, and Christine actually smiled. 'I think you may have succ—'

The bell jangled frantically as the door smashed back on its hinges.

Sam's heart plummeted with a rush that left her hands cold. Grant was unshaven, his hair dishevelled. His favourite Black Sabbath tee was stretched out of shape, as though he'd been pulling at the neckline.

'Sam, enough.' He reeled against the counter and squinted across the room at her. 'It's time you came home. I've thought about it, I get it. You're not happy. And that's down to me. But I'll change, Sammie, you know I will. We've always been good together, right?'

Even if she hadn't seen his bloodshot eyes, she would know from his rapid-fire speech, the irrational change from angry to wheedling, that he was off his face. 'Why aren't you at work?' Sam countered as she stood.

'Don't go near him,' Christine murmured, and Sam was surprised at the fear in her tone. She shook off Christine's restraining hand. No matter what Christine thought, this was her husband. And he clearly wasn't well.

'I can't,' Grant slurred pitifully. 'I just can't get it together without you. It's always been you and me, Sammie. You and me against the world, since you were in school, remember?'

'I remember,' she said, trying to stop her chin from wobbling. God, she remembered. She had loved Grant back then. Loved him with the absolute devastating intensity a sixteen-year-old was capable of.

But he had loved her, too. He'd cared for her, protected her, cherished her.

At what point had that turned into controlling and possessing her?

'I remember,' she repeated. 'But that was when we were kids, Grant. We're different people now. We've changed. We don't fit together.'

He shook his head. 'Don't say that, Sam. I don't know where we went wrong, but if I've changed, I'm sorry. I'll do anything it takes to make you happy again. I want you back. I want the old Sammie back. I want *us* back, Sam.'

He sounded so pitiful. So betrayed. Maybe all she'd needed was a couple of weeks' break, a chance to get her head straight.

They had history. She couldn't throw that away. She took three swift steps toward him.

Christine's chair screeched as it skittered across the floor, and the older woman's surprisingly strong fingers closed around her wrist. 'No, Samantha!'

It was Christine's fault that she'd left Grant, Sam realised. She snatched her arm away, shooting Christine a scowl. Christine had always been a meddling old cow.

'I'll give up work, Sammie.' Grant's words were broken by harsh sobs, and her own throat ached. She could still see the eighteen-year-old boy she had fallen in love with, all those years ago. 'Then we can spend more time together. It's work that does my head in. It's the slaughterhouse, all the blood, the death, you know?' His hands formed a circle, as though he was choking the life from a sheep.

She was close enough to smell the whiskey on his breath, his clothes, and she froze. They had history together, but not one she wanted to recall. 'But it was me you choked, Grant. Me. Not an animal. Not a damned sheep.'

He shook his head and leaned slightly back, frowning. 'Choked you?' His gaze slid past her, to Christine. 'Come on, Sammie. You know that's not true. Well, not in a bad way, anyway.' He leered, though it looked strained. 'That was just messing around, remember? A bit of rough play to spice things up. I never hurt you.'

Her hands flew to her throat, aching with more now than just repressed tears. 'Don't lie to my face! You *choked me*! Get out. Get out now. I never want to see you again!' The words weren't premeditated, only seconds earlier she'd actually been considering giving in to his pleas, but now clarity flooded her mind. If Grant couldn't admit to what he'd done—hell, if he couldn't even see what he'd done—then Christine was right: her husband was dangerous. 'I told you, Grant, we're finished. Get the hell out of my cafe! Get out of my life!'

'No!' Grant roared, slamming his fist on the counter, his mood flipping from pleading to demanding. 'You're my wife. You're *mine*!'

The malice in his tone drove her back as Grant lurched forward, trying to grab her.

But somehow Christine was between them, her phone shoved into Grant's face. The woman's voice cracked with authority, although her hand trembled. 'Look at the screen, you piece of filth. You're on camera. Live to the Murray Bridge police station. So I suggest you do as Samantha has asked, and get off her premises.'

Grant's head swung bull-like between the phone and Sam, as though he expected her to demand Christine stand down.

Sam staggered back, though she hated herself for deserting Christine. But every inch that she put between herself and what remained of her husband was permanent. She understood that now. She deliberately took another step. And another. Never breaking her eye contact with Grant, willing him to understand that this was it; this separation was now irrevocable.

The door brought her up hard, and she reached behind herself, dragged it open. 'Get out.'

Grant gave a bellow of rage, then spat in Christine's face. 'Fuck you, you interfering old bitch!' He shoved past her and paused at the door, staring at Sam. 'I never hurt you. You know that. This is all in your fucking head.' He jabbed rigid fingers into her temple twice, the pressure snapping her neck sideways.

Sam braced herself for the final blow, barely able to breathe, her jaw locked.

Grant stared at her for a long moment. 'Thank Christ we never had kids, otherwise they would have inherited your fucked-up genes.'

Sam whimpered, doubling over. Her arms wrapped around her stomach as though Grant had punched her, his words bruising deeper than any blow. For the first time, she realised there was no limit to her husband's cruelty. Yet, in trying to wound her, he made her face her own truth. She'd never wanted a baby because she couldn't take the chance of her history—her parents' history—repeating. Her mother had failed to nurture or protect her children.

And Sam didn't want to find out whether the fault was hereditary.

9
Pierce

Arms folded across his chest, Dante leaned back against the kitchen bench. Pierce recognised the stance was supposed to be intimidating—his brother's 'no nonsense' look—but all he could think was that the disparity in their height was made more obvious by the fact the steel top on the commercial kitchen bench dug into his brother's backside, where it would hit his own thighs.

In contrast to Dante's belligerent posture, Dad was hunched, hands in the pockets of the white chef pants he liked to wear in the trattoria kitchen, his grey hair sticking out at odd angles as he stared down at his shoes. Mum kept both hands clasped in front of her mouth, her knuckles pressed to her lips as though she was holding in tears. Pierce knew better than to make eye contact with her. All his life, he'd kept his head down, done his job and turned a blind eye to his parents' *necessary* favouritism, designed to keep Dante on track. But this was too much. 'Manager?' he repeated his father's words incredulously. 'You said that you wanted to get Dan out front to learn, but *manager*?'

'Come on, bro,' Dante said. 'You know it's just a title. It doesn't mean a thing.'

'That's where you're wrong.' He pointed at his brother, but yanked his hand down as he realised his finger was trembling with rage. 'It means every damn thing. And they know it.' He jerked his head at his parents, who stood beside Dante, the three of them ranged against him. For so long he'd swallowed his anger. But not now. 'Doesn't it, Dad?' As hurt as he was, he couldn't attack Mum. But Dad? That was a different matter. Dad knew what Dante was, he didn't blind himself to the facts, merely chose to go along with Mum when she kept trying to pretend that her youngest son wasn't a steroid-pumped conman. So to find that Dad would now do this was . . .

Jesus, Pierce knew that he didn't have it in him to forgive this betrayal.

He took a deep, shuddering breath. 'You're making Dante the manager after all the years I've put in? Then what the hell am I?'

'What you've always been,' his dad said, keeping his tone reasonable, though Pierce could read desperation in the way his fingers kept flexing and curling. 'You know you're my right-hand man, you always have been.'

'But not the *manager* of the Trattoria di Angelis, right? I'm not management material?'

'Bro, the staff all know you, they know you run this joint,' Dante wheedled. 'I'm the new kid in town; I need a title, or they won't respect me.'

'Why should they respect you?' Pierce exploded. 'Every single one of them has more experience than you. You washed dishes here for all of five minutes before you got jack of that. So you got your *mummy*—' he ignored that Rosa was also his mother '—to put you on as front-of-house, so you can strut around like you're running the place. How does that earn respect? Where have you been all the nights Mum's here baking till three in the morning while Dad scrubs the floors?' Not to mention the nights, the *years*, he'd sacrificed. All for Dante to step in and take whatever he damn well wanted. Just like he always had.

'Cool it, bro,' Dante said, but the fake brotherliness had dropped from his tone. 'It's my family business just as much as it's yours. You don't fucking own it.'

'I don't own it, but I bloody worked for my place here, Dante. I didn't take a nice little holiday in jail—' he ignored Mum's muffled gasp '—then come sniffing around for handouts.'

'You've been living off Mum and Dad your whole life,' Dante shot back. 'You've never done a damn thing for yourself.'

'Not if doing a *thing* means selling drugs to kids. Or stealing from . . . everyone.' He backed off, trying to get a grip and take his accusations down a notch as Mum's sobs cut through his rage. She knew what her youngest son was, there was no point hammering it home.

Pierce tipped his head back, staring at the ceiling for a long moment before he closed his eyes and drew in a massive, slow breath, the air laden with the familiar fragrances of basil and oregano and garlic. 'You know what? I'm done. I quit.' He gave a short, mirthless laugh as he tugged free the chequered tea towel he always tucked into the top of his jeans, screwed it into a ball, and tossed it onto the counter. 'I quit *whatever* my bloody job is here. And you—' he eyed his father, his anger laced with sadness at Dad's betrayal '—can clear out your own damn till.'

Dad knew what he meant. Grief flashed across his dark face, but Pierce was done with being the scapegoat, with carrying the weight of his brother only to have his loyalty treated as though it was both expected and worthless.

Dad took a step forward but Pierce was already on the move, letting the kitchen door slam behind him.

Dante's words, deliberately loud, chased him. 'Don't worry, Mum. You know I'm here for you both.'

The warm spring air hit Pierce as he strode away from the trattoria, and he stopped to take a deep breath. His heart was racing, the pulse pounding in his temples with a beat strong enough to make him feel sick. What the hell had he just done? He'd never considered quitting the restaurant before. Not seriously, although there had been periods in his life when he should have. But this time something had snapped inside him; he couldn't continue bottling up his resentment of Dante, nor his pain at the unfairness of his treatment.

Yet, considering the magnitude of his impulsive decision, how was it that he felt . . . lighter? Relieved, as though the weight he had shouldered all his life had been lifted. He was no longer responsible for his parents, their restaurant, their employees, their menu, their desserts. For the first time in more than forty years, he was free. He owed no one anything: no loyalty, no time, no obligation.

The notion was terrifying in its breadth and exhilarating in its potential, as though a universe of forbidden possibilities was now spread like a feast before him. But to enjoy it, he'd have to push his parents' wounded expressions from his mind.

Pierce checked his steps as he drew level with his brunch cafe, his elation dropping as he eyed the darkened window: plus there was that, of course. No matter how he chose to distance himself from his family, they were always going to be, quite literally, right next door.

Maybe he just needed a couple of days' break. He hadn't had an actual weekend off since he couldn't remember when.

He closed his hand around his phone: Gabrielle had invited him to some open garden thing at her inn. Of course, he'd refused the invitation: not only because he had zero interest in plants but because, although his cafe was shut, Saturdays were the restaurant's busiest day.

But that wasn't his problem anymore.

He unlocked the cafe, simultaneously flicking Gabrielle and Hayden a message. He was pretty sure the invitation would still stand: Gabrielle had changed a lot in the couple of years she'd lived in the country. She was far more laidback than when she'd barely been able to find time to slot in marketing the trattoria alongside a full schedule of corporate engagements for her company, Small & Sassy. The tree change—even though, in typical Gabrielle style, that involved her owning an entire village—had clearly worked for her.

The glow from the humming drinks fridge was enough to guide him through the cafe to the stairs at the rear, which led to his austere apartment. He pressed a hand against his chest. He could do with a dose of whatever it was that had eased Gabrielle's stress levels: as the adrenaline from the confrontation and his resulting snap decision receded, reality seeped in. And right now, he hurt so bad he wasn't sure whether he was having a heart attack, or his heart was breaking.

~

Pierce pulled the car in against the high gutter edging the Settlers Bridge main street. He must have passed through this town months ago, on his way to Gabrielle's, but it had been dark so he'd barely noticed. Not that there was much to see even in the sunshine. He didn't understand how people could live their entire lives going in and out of the same handful of shops, seeing the same people, no doubt having the same conversations, with the choice of only a couple of cafes and pubs to dine at.

He'd never had time to do much dining out himself.

He pulled out his phone, swiped the latest message from Dad off the screen without reading it, and checked the mud map Gabrielle had texted. He wasn't going to rely on some friendly—or, per previous experience, temporarily friendly—local showing him the way to Gabrielle's secluded retreat on the banks of the Murray River.

Buggered if he knew how he'd so royally cocked it up: the map looked simple enough to follow. Nothing like the twisting, turning back tracks Sam had led him down last autumn. She had driven aggressively, swapping direction on the loose gravel and slippery dirt with barely a warning flash of her indicator, as though challenging him to catch her. Even now he wasn't sure what he'd said that had made her flip moods, and it wasn't until he'd driven out of Wurruldi in the full light of day that he realised sections of the road were little more than a goat track, switchbacks slicing up the edge of a cliff that dropped to the mighty Murray River hundreds of feet below. A cautionary warning from Sam would have been nice, Pierce thought, instinctively checking his rear-view mirror to make sure there was no half-crazy woman following him.

He didn't need to worry: there was no one around. Despite it being early afternoon, the broad, four-laned main street was completely devoid of life, although four utes were parked nose-to-tail in front of the double-storied building at the end of the street. Almost directly opposite, a burgundy and gold-lettered sign swung back and forth from a horizontal pole protruding from the stone wall of the Overland Hotel, the rhythmic, silent movement adding to the ghost-town feel of the place.

'Bizarre,' Pierce muttered, clambering from his sleek black sedan.

His glance ranged the short street, book-ended by the pair of pubs near the bridge and two equally impressive buildings with bank logos at the opposite end of the road. He needed to top up his caffeine: there had been an espresso before an early morning session at the gym, and another two while he packed the car.

The town centre appeared to be caught in some dusty, sleepy time warp that dated back to the fifties, the quaint little shops hiding timidly beneath hooded verandahs. It seemed Settlers Bridge had the necessities covered, though, with a butcher, newsagent, cafes, post office and a supermarket. But no bottleshop, even alongside the pubs, he noted with a grimace. He had packed a couple of bottles of his current favourite wine, God's Hill Aglianico, along with one of their black olive merlots, into the hamper, but had intended to pick up a few more mid-range bottles. Just in case he stayed longer than the weekend.

Not that he had any plan to. Yet somehow, once he'd made up his mind to escape Adelaide, the Murraylands had begun to beckon with all the promise of a proper holiday. A weekend would be enough, though. He needed a couple of days to get his head straight without the risk of running into his brother around every corner.

Both cafes were dark, clearly closed, and the sandwich board in front of the IGA was the only thing that hinted at a chance of getting customer service. In which case, he'd have to settle for iced coffee. He doubted he'd make it to Gabrielle's without a shot.

He found the fridges at the back of the small supermarket, then carried his drink to the long wooden checkout.

'Just that then, lovey?' the cashier greeted him.

'That's the lot, thanks,' Pierce said, sliding the bottle closer as he realised the counter wasn't automated.

'You're passing through?' the woman said, keying figures into the register.

'Headed out to Wurruldi for the weekend.'

'Oh, Gabby's place? Well, it has to be Gabby's, doesn't it, she owns the entire village. Seems half of Settlers Bridge has gone out there. Deader than a dodo in here today, least until the tennis is finished.' She took the twenty he handed over, raising an eyebrow. 'Don't often get folding from you young ones.'

'My folks are old-school.'

She nodded consideringly. 'Good way to be. What the government doesn't know won't hurt them, right? I'll see you out at the Wattle Seed myself, once I close up.'

Pierce grinned, her easy manner reminding him of his mum. Which promptly wiped the smile from his face. 'Maybe I should hold off and follow you. Got myself all kinds of lost last time I tried to find the place. Though it was pitch black and bucketing down.' Slight exaggerations, but he didn't want to sound totally incompetent.

The cashier closed her fingers around his change. 'Back in autumn? It was you that Sam rescued down near the river then, lovey?'

'One wrong turn and I'm straight into local legend?' he said with a rueful grin. He'd heard how small towns worked but wouldn't have thought his adventure gossipworthy. 'I lost the GPS signal but thought I had a fair idea where I was going.' He hiked a thumb towards the shop window. 'Reckon I took a couple of tracks instead of the dirt roads I was after.'

'Ah, well there're dirt roads and then there're dirt roads,' the woman responded, releasing his change. He dropped it into a collection tin hand-labelled with *Settlers Bridge CFS* on an orange Post-it. 'The ones with a rubble topping are official roads, maintained—if you can call it that—by council. Anything that's plain dirt are farm tracks or fishing access to the river. I imagine, if you're not familiar, you could get yourself in a bit of a pickle.'

'And it was dark,' he repeated, not entirely sure whether she was taking the mickey out of him. 'Anyway, last thing I expected was to almost run into some woman out walking in the middle of nowhere. Not sure which one of us got the bigger scare.'

'Walking?' the cashier looked momentarily puzzled. 'Oh, yes, that was before . . . guess she was out to clear her mind.' Her gaze moved beyond him, to the faded fly strips hung over the wide doorway. She straightened, her impressive bosom alarmingly thrust out.

He glanced over his shoulder.

'Afternoon, Lynn.' The newcomer paused in the cascade of orange vinyl to run a hand over his shining head. Pierce wondered whether it was a habit from when the guy had hair, or if he was checking for sweat. The sun was more than cheerful. 'We still on for this arvo?'

'Wouldn't miss it, Anthony,' Lynn said with a bright smile.

'I'll pick you up at three?'

'Better make it four, so I can get tizzied up. You'll be able to get away from the bar?'

'I've got Spence managing for the night. It should be a quiet one anyway. Last time I checked in, Bowhill are killing us, so there'll only be a few lads in, drowning their sorrows, I suppose.'

'Shame for the boys. Tara ducked in to tell me the girls won the doubles, but she needs the afternoon off because they're all getting tarted up to head out to Gabby's.'

'Most of the lads will be dragged out there anyway, then,' Anthony said as he circumnavigated a huge carousel full of postcards, and headed like a guided missile toward the counter. 'I mean, not dragged . . . but . . . y'know . . . ah, going along to keep the girls happy.' He looked stricken.

Lynn waved away any misunderstanding. 'Must say, I'm looking forward to an excuse to get done up myself. An afternoon out will be lovely.'

'You don't need to do any tarting up, Lynnie. You always look good.' Anthony leaned his thighs on the Peters ice-cream freezer that sat horizontally across the end of the checkout. His hands clenched where they rested on the chill-misted glass lid.

'Get away with you,' Lynn said, smoothing the maroon apron over her ample curves, managing to make it sound as though 'getting away' was the last thing she wanted Anthony to do.

'Thanks.' Pierce held up his carton of iced coffee and waggled it in farewell. Though he was well out of flirting practice, even he could see he clearly needed to give them some privacy.

Lynn startled, as though she'd forgotten he was standing there. 'Oh, yes. Well, we'll see you out there, then, lovey . . . if you don't get lost,' she added with a teasing grin.

~

He didn't get lost. Although he did almost miss the right-angled turn from the bitumen onto the dirt road that led to the cliff-edged switchback track.

After the white-knuckled descent, the road threaded between lagoons surrounded by gum trees. Their trunks suggested they'd been there for centuries. He wound down his window and let in a blast of fresh air, rich with a confusing mix of lush growth and sweet decay. A cloud of grey and pink galahs swooped in front of his car, playing chicken before soaring to cackle loudly at him from branches a hundred feet above. On his left, a backdrop of deep orange cliffs across the water framed stands of lime green willows. Diamonds sparkled as though cast by the handful onto the river's surface.

Wurruldi was only a couple of kilometres along the flats. The town consisted of three stone cottages perched on the banks of the river, a slightly larger building that looked like an old shop in the centre of a rocky paddock, and Gabrielle's impressive, double-storied sandstone inn, set further back from the water.

Last time he visited, he had followed Sam along the majestic swoop of a white gravel driveway from the river-front right up to the inn. Now there were a couple of dozen vehicles parked in the paddock alongside the old shop, so he followed suit.

A cobbled path meandered from the improvised car park. It skipped across the dirt road and picked up on the far side to lead through a small gate in a drystone wall, almost hidden by wattle trees. A thick, honeyed scent came from the yellow-covered bushes, noisy with bees, and he ducked beneath the arch of branches.

In contrast to the well-grazed paddock, the lawns of the inn were lush and green, bordered by crowded garden beds. Other visitors strolled the grounds, pausing to admire flowers. His mum would have a fit: despite the extensive gardens, there didn't appear to be any fruit trees or vegetables.

In the centre of the grounds, a lacy-leafed tree spread a deep purple canopy above clusters of white tables and chairs. Gabrielle sure knew how to present her property, he thought, pausing to take it all in. But she would, considering she was in marketing.

Each table was draped with a cloth in a soft pastel shade, many of the chairs occupied by visitors sipping from champagne flutes and, to his surprise, given the rural setting, beer in tall glasses rather than bottles. Clearly, the drinkers were about as interested in the gardens as he was. But he was sure looking forward to kicking back with a glass. It would be a change to allow himself to completely relax for once. And not think about any damn thing.

Because he couldn't afford to let himself dwell on what had been torn from him. Or on what he'd thrown away.

10

Samantha

Sam wiped the smear of flour from her cheek, and determinedly faced off with the pastry again. 'I'm not going to let these cream horns defeat me,' she said to Tracey, who was working on the opposite side of the wide bench in the inn's kitchen. 'Not this time.'

'Don't you worry, love. They'll come right.' The older woman's bangles jangled madly as she beat a bowl of cream with a wire whisk. She had to be the only person in Australia who still did it manually. 'I tell you, I've never known a girl love cream as much as that Sharna does. Lucky her dad runs the dairy.'

'Except in her coffee. She goes nuts if you get a speck of cream in there,' Roni added, dipping pale gem cakes in jelly, then expertly flipping them in coconut. A wire rack already held jelly cakes in a rainbow of pastel shades—pink, orange, yellow, light green and baby blue—waiting for Tracey to load them with fresh cream. 'She must've got a shock when she moved to the city and discovered what it's like to have to buy cream in a carton.'

'I'll have to teach her how to make it,' Lucie piped up from the far end of the kitchen.

'Make it? You mean beat it?' Tracey said, swapping whisking arms. She blew from the side of her mouth so that a spiral of her fluffy golden hair jetted up off her forehead, then resettled on top of the pastel-shaded scarves knotted around her head.

Lucie's nose stud glinted as she shook her head, carrying a mixing bowl over to the bench. 'No, I make it. Milk, organic sugar and gelatine. It's so easy. And unadulterated.'

Sam bumped her hip against Lucie's. 'You're so *alt*, Luce. But we love you anyway.'

'Not sure I'd love that cream,' Christine sniffed disparagingly.

'Is that mock cream?' Roni asked. 'It doesn't matter that I can get the "good" stuff now, I'm always going to have a love affair with mock cream.'

'Done.' Tracey set her bowl down with a sigh. 'And no, mock cream is made with whipped butter.' She brushed a couple of wild ringlets out of her face. 'It sounds like Lucie is on to something altogether different. You'll have to teach us that one, Lucie.'

'Or not,' Christine muttered. 'We already have fresh cream, and we *all* know how to make mock cream.' She shot a triumphant look at Roni. 'I'm sure we don't need to find *alternative* recipes.'

Roni's eyes danced with laughter. 'Well, I'm totally down for learning your method, Lucie. Even with two cows, I can't keep up with feeding the twins. If making cream is quicker than waiting for it to separate, count me in.' She wiped her hands on a tea towel stained with the food dye she had added to the jelly to enhance the colour. 'When I first moved here, I couldn't get my head around the fact that cream comes out of the cow, ready to use.' She lifted her chin toward the large, glass drink dispenser full of milk. As the cream separated and moved to the top, it was skimmed off each day and added to a jar in the fridge. 'Well, almost ready to use. But all up, it still seems a lot less effort to buy a carton from Lynn down at the shop.'

Sam chuckled. 'Whenever you say things like that, I picture you as a Kardashian. You know, living in some ritzy Sydney apartment with a fluffy white dog and a team of minions.' She winced as she recalled that Roni's estranged mother had a white lapdog.

Roni didn't seem to make the connection, though. 'You have no idea how far I was from living anything like a Kardashian life. Aunt Marian rescued me . . . in more ways than one.' Roni had moved from the east coast a few years earlier, when she inherited a huge wheat and cereal property. And a huge farmer, to boot.

Sam ignored the loaded snort from Christine—no fan of Marian Nelson—who was decorating a tower of palm-sized meringues. In keeping with the theme, each crisp, flat disk was tinted a delicate pastel shade, and Christine carefully sandwiched them with cream and complimentary fruit:

raspberries, strawberries, and fresh sliced apricots. Her fine work was in contrast to her clamped lips and dour appearance. Though Christine looked like she would be more inclined to hack off a wedge of heavy fruit cake and slap it onto a plate than produce anything beautiful, she carefully finished the top of the stack with delicate white chocolate curls between hand-piped pink cream-cheese rosettes.

Sam floured her marble rolling pin, eyeing the pastry critically to make certain it was an even thickness. 'I meant that city folk are so far removed from the whole cycle of life, the chain of production,' she clarified to Roni. 'You know, milk comes in cartons, salad comes prewashed and chopped in sealed bags, meat comes on disposable trays. Even Murray Bridge was more than enough suburbia for me. It was such a relief to come back to this.' She gestured at the high windows in the open attic of the barn-style kitchen. The thick branch of a flowering red gum, the white bark mottled grey and russet, was silhouetted against the bluest sky.

It wasn't only a relief to move back to where the air was fresh and the constant white noise of a large town didn't burrow into her head, it was escaping Grant that had changed everything.

She had intended to stay at the inn for a week or two, until the story of her marriage break-up made its way around town, then she would get a room at the Overland Hotel in Settlers Bridge. But Gabrielle had unquestioningly made her welcome at Wurruldi, even before Sharna had vacated her suite to move to the city.

Sam discovered that being able to meander the riverfront, spending hours watching the birds, the water, the sky, without making an excuse or giving an explanation, was freedom beyond imagination.

She shot a grateful glance at Christine, who responded with the customary frown that no longer intimidated her. Christine was right: the world had looked different from the moment she threw her belongings in the car and pulled the door on her house closed for the last time.

And even better once Grant left her cafe.

Without the insidious whispers that had filled her head, suggesting Grant's behaviour was her fault, the possibilities and choices had become endless—although slightly terrifying. She felt as though she was finally an adult; for the first time every decision was hers to make, from what she wore, to where she went, and what and when she ate.

Over the years she had become weighed down by a subconscious sense of oppression: if Grant wasn't one hundred per cent happy—and realistically, he rarely was—it had seemed disloyal for her to embrace any joy. After almost two decades together, she had forgotten what it was to allow herself to love life. Now, she rose early to watch the sun top the river cliffs each morning, the daily miracle a reminder that the world turned independent of the madness or sadness of her life.

Swiftly, two weeks at the inn had turned into two months.

'It's not just the groceries, though,' Tracey said as she landed mugs of tea along the bench. Sam was impressed she could remember how each of the five women took their cuppa. 'Imagine living where the only animals are cats and dogs, and a vegetable garden is a raised box in the courtyard.'

Sam sliced the pastry into even strips. 'A courtyard veg garden would be an upgrade for me. I haven't grown anything since high school biology, when we had to do that "grow one tray of radishes under a light, one in the shade" experiment.' She scrunched her nose. 'Don't tell old Mr Read, but I never even planted the seeds. I just logged what would have happened if I *had* grown the radishes. There's a reason I don't even have pot plants.' Other than no longer having a house to keep them in, that was. 'I rely on poor Jack to do the growing.' Her brother's paddock-to-plate sustainable acreage went a long way to keeping their grandparents fed.

'You know he loves it,' Lucie reassured. 'He always says he owes you for back when . . . well, you know.'

Yeah, she knew. Back when she'd protected her much younger brother from their abusive father.

'There's no harm in picking and choosing what you're best at,' Tracey said comfortably. 'Marian always said "play to your strengths".'

'Oh, for goodness' sake,' Christine muttered. 'Even now Marian's not here, we still have to hear her thoughts?'

Sam winced. Though Marian had been dead a few years, it was clear that Tracey still missed her best friend terribly. She took a fresh ball of puff pastry from the glass-fronted industrial fridge. Flouring the cold marble board, she rolled it out to a rectangle, folded the top third down to the middle, then the bottom third up. She rolled the dough back out to the original size, turned it ninety degrees, and did the thirds trick again. 'You know, no matter how many times I do the math, I don't see how doing this six times makes seven hundred and twenty-nine layers in the pastry.'

'I don't get the math, either, but your puff pastry is beautiful, Sam,' Tracey said. 'You wouldn't want it to be a degree warmer in here, though, or the butter will melt.'

'She knows that,' Christine snapped.

Sam hid a grin. Tracey had taken Roni under her wing years earlier, and now Christine had clearly decided Sam was to be her protégé, and no one else was permitted to interfere.

Under Christine's beady gaze, Sam hadn't been given a chance to doubt her ability—she was too afraid of getting a rap over the knuckles with Christine's wooden spoon. Christine had cut her some slack, though, not insisting she enter the annual Christmas lamington contest that year. But she had been resolute in her determination that Sam tackle a new recipe each day, distributing the results to the afternoon rush of school kids in the cafe for free. Obviously, the word had gone around, as Sam ended up having to push closing back by a half hour, and put Tara on to handle the orders for the super creamy milkshakes Christine suggested she offer as a paid extra, to offset the increase in non-paying customers.

Roni moved around the bench to watch her shaping the cream horn by spiralling centimetre-wide strips of raw pastry around the cone she had created from aluminium foil. She had already made enough cream horns to see them through the day, but with the ovens empty, she had decided to whip up some reserves for that evening. The pastries always tasted better after they had been filled and allowed to sit in the fridge for a couple of hours.

'Perfect!' Roni said. 'Tracey always says the secret ingredient is love.'

Sam avoided Christine's gaze, knowing she would be rolling her eyes. 'Guess I'd have been quicker at nailing this one if the ingredients included bitterness, despair and anger, then,' she joked.

'That bad?' Roni screwed up her face sympathetically.

That was the problem with always being deliberately upbeat and cheery: the moment you let the guise slip, someone noticed.

'Not really anyone's business, is it?' Christine said immediately.

Sam winced. Sometimes Christine's staunch defence actually made it harder to brush off the questions. 'No, I'm just sooking. I mean, Grant's being an arse, but it's so much better being away from him.' She pretended the strip of pastry needed all of her concentration. Though Settlers Bridge had closed ranks around her when the story of her separation made the rounds—as she had known it would—she still found it impossible to admit the reason for their split. Instead, she tried to downplay the whole thing, waving it off as an early midlife crisis, boredom in the relationship, or an accumulation of minor woes. She knew she had no right to sympathy: she wasn't a victim.

Not only had she willingly put herself in a position where her husband controlled her finances, her personal life, her happiness, but for years she had been perfectly happy to live like that. She couldn't go crying to her friends now.

She gave a huff of frustration. 'You'd think I would have been smart enough to walk out ten years back, wouldn't you?'

Roni sighed. 'It's nothing to do with being smart, Sam. We just hang in there, hoping we can fix them.'

'And if that's not being dumb, I don't know what is,' Sam tried to joke. 'Though Grant sure wants me to believe that he's fixed. I found a note under the door the other week, promising me everything will be different.'

'A note?' Tracey's blue eyes rounded in surprise. 'Didn't think you young ones were into exercising your penmanship.'

'He doesn't have my number,' Sam said shortly. The women didn't need the sordid details of her husband's attempts to keep tabs on her. 'He came into the shop a couple of times when I first moved out, but I told him if he didn't stay away I'd get some kind of order from the cops.' She didn't meet Christine's eyes as she minimised the situation.

Both the threat to call the police and Christine's supposed video link to them had been a bluff, as Sam wasn't about to admit to anyone that her husband had ever laid his hands on her. She had expected that the payoff for Christine's protection would be having the details of the encounter spread far and wide, but it seemed that so far only the basics of her separation—that she had walked out on Grant and was living at the Wattle Seed Inn—were common knowledge.

She gave a light laugh, trying to recapture the carefree persona everyone expected from her. It wouldn't do to have Lucie too concerned and running stories home to Jack. Her brother wouldn't hold his temper. 'Grant hasn't been around for a while, so I figured something must have finally penetrated that thick skull.'

Sam's encounter with Grant in the cafe had been like a boulder dropped into a pond: the splash drenched everything, but worse, the ripples spread out in unsettling circles. It had taken days before the waves stopped churning, and she was able to settle again. But each day he stayed away, her relief had grown, the gnawing pit of despair in her belly easing. Though she would neither forget nor forgive the cruelty of his parting words, his absence allowed normality to shove the cafe door open inch by inch, determined to creep back into her life. She had stopped jumping each time the bell jangled, stopped listening for the familiar tone of Grant's car pulling up outside, stopped checking up and down the street before she stepped off the verandah.

She pulled a wry face. 'But no such luck. The girls from Murray Bridge dropped by the other week, and they mentioned he got busted for drink driving. Again.' She rolled her eyes, trying to make a joke of it. 'Second time's the charm, so his car got impounded, and he can't get to Settlers unless he can cadge a lift.' She couldn't keep the elation from her tone. Although there was a slight chance Grant might get a ride to Settlers and harass her at the cafe, she no longer had to worry he would turn up at Ma and Pops' place, demanding to know where she was. His mates were all good guys; they'd have no part in that kind of business. Her grandparents were safe.

'Is someone keeping an eye on the time?' Christine cut in. 'This chit-chat is all very well, but we have a job to do, ladies. And I won't thank any of you if my meringues go soft because you're running behind on your little bits.'

Sam hid a grin at Christine's insinuation that her own tasks were of greater importance.

'I do think perhaps you shouldn't have put the cream on them yet,' Tracey ventured. Sam winced. Then she caught the wicked glint in Tracey's eye. Although the elderly woman seemed sweet and scatty, she had known Christine all her life, and clearly recognised just how to push her buttons.

'And I told you, I'm only doing two meringue towers right now as a test,' Christine bit back. 'I want to see how long it will take the cream to bleed in this heat. Absolutely ridiculous holding a wedding in November,' she huffed. 'And a garden wedding at that. Though, of course, it's not *really* a wedding, is it? Just some sort of make-believe commitment ceremony, so they can pretend they're normal.'

'No, it is *really* a wedding,' Roni said firmly. 'And they are *normal*.'

Sam gave a quick shake of her head, warning Roni off. There was nothing Christine liked more than an argument. 'We're fine on time,' she diverted the conversation. 'But you're right, Christine, we do have a job to do.'

Having taken Sharna under her wing a couple of years back, Gabrielle had made a sizeable donation to the CWA in return for them catering Sharna's wedding. Some of the other association members were bringing in pre-cooked finger foods—salmon and cream cheese puffs, miniature pasties and sausage rolls, tiny quiches and pinwheels—to warm in the kitchen's huge oven in time for the late afternoon celebration, but the core group had decided to bake the more delicate desserts on the premises.

Quick to pick up on the need to head off a major altercation, Lucie gestured toward the counter that ran the full length of a wall opposite the sink and oven. A mountain of fifty-cent-sized pale shortbread hearts sat beside cooling racks of cockle-shaped golden madeleines, both waiting to be iced to match the pastel theme. 'Who's on icing duty?' Lemon, rose and pistachio macarons, already filled with ganache, lay in neat ranks to the left of the biscuits.

Sam smiled as she eyed the desserts. Although she was nervous about what was to come later in the day, for the first time that she could recall, she felt . . . fulfilled. While she still had much to learn, over the last few weeks she had overcome her fear of failure thanks to Christine—and the non-judgemental, bottomless pits of the local kids. Now, working alongside a team of women she trusted and admired, creating something beautiful that would bring joy to the newlyweds, she felt unspeakably happy. Life suddenly seemed as sweet as buttercream.

11
Pierce

Pierce scowled as he toyed with the leather cord lacing the open neck of his white shirt. Maybe it was a country thing, but the other visitors seemed overdressed for a relaxed afternoon spent admiring gardens. Evidently, the locals agreed with Lynn about seizing the opportunity to get done up.

'Pierce!'

Shading his eyes, he followed the call. His gaze tracked the front of the imposing inn. A timber balcony ran the length of the upper storey, overlooking the gardens sprawling down to a rustic wooden dock jutting out over the river. Gabrielle's effortlessly graceful form was easy to distinguish, even without her welcoming wave.

Placing his empty glass on a vacant table, Pierce made his way into the building and up the main staircase. Last time he'd been here, Gabrielle had enthusiastically recounted the restoration of the timber treads and broad, glossy handrails. Rooms opened off a short passage that ran in both directions from the central stairs. He headed to the left, admiring the paintings that graced the deep burgundy walls of the corridor, the plush carpet swallowing his footfalls.

'Hey, Juliet.' He kissed Gabrielle on both cheeks in the European fashion as she stepped in from the balcony.

She held him at arm's length, raising one dark eyebrow. 'Juliet?'

He gestured toward the balcony, hidden by the soft billow of filmy white curtains. 'I thought we were having a *thing* for a moment there, with you calling down to me.'

Gabrielle gave a deep, throaty chuckle. 'I'll have to suggest that to Hayden. No, I'm up here checking the placement of the tables. You've got a great eye for that, come help me.'

'What's with all the fancy togs?' he said as they gazed from the balcony at the latest influx of guests, who wandered through the side gate to stroll the expansive gardens.

'Fancy?' Gabrielle said. 'Standard version of black tie around here: Rossis, moleskins, cocktail dresses and just a few suits.'

'And some wildly retro gear,' he added, spotting a houndstooth jacket, worn in apparent defiance of the late spring warmth. 'But is black tie the norm for an open garden?' Despite the absurdity, in his blue jeans and raw linen shirt, he was the one who was out of place.

'It's not an open garden.' Gabrielle's forehead creased in amused puzzlement. Her hair was longer than when he'd last seen her, still thick and impossibly blonde. She had put on a little weight and looked more . . . natural than he was accustomed to seeing her in the city. Either being in the country, or being all loved-up, sure suited her. 'Though it's most definitely a black-tie garden wedding.' She threw her arm wide, indicating the elegant white table settings dotted across the vast lawns like mushrooms. 'A terrifyingly open-invitation garden wedding, that is.'

It was so clearly a wedding. How the heck had he missed the white wooden arch above the side gate? He groaned, plucking at the lightweight shirt he'd pulled out of his wardrobe after realising the local forecast was several degrees warmer than Adelaide. 'I didn't only come casual, I came beach casual. I thought you'd have jet skis out on the river, maybe a barbecue.'

Gabrielle patted his arm, and he noticed she no longer sported immensely long, richly coloured nails. 'You're definitely the most handsome pirate here,' she teased.

'I was going for Zorro,' Pierce said with a rueful grin.

Gabrielle chuckled. 'Don't worry, you'll fit in fine: wait until you see what Sharna's wearing. And, by the way, Sharna is the bride.' He caught a whiff of a soft floral fragrance as she turned to gaze out over the vista.

'Open garden or garden wedding, this looks amazing,' he said. 'I can't even wrap my head around how you work with this much space.'

Gabrielle rolled her eyes. 'I need it! Like I said, open invitation. And everyone around here loves Sharna.'

'Open invitation, not open garden. Got it,' he muttered, surveying the grounds. He was accustomed to having just enough room for his restaurant staff to thread between the tables and for the customers not to knock knees—although elbows occasionally collided. In the cafe there was more room, but the hustle and bustle of phone conversations and work meetings created a discordant buzz that echoed from the polished cement floor—a feeling of intense, focused activity, rather than a pleasurable relaxation.

Gabrielle was feeding the masses on a grand scale—and yet nothing was crowded. Wooden tables clustered in twos or threes were dotted across the swathes of lawn. White Adirondack chairs lounged in casual groups near the riotous flowerbeds. A number of trestles stretched along the golden hedge of wattles, and intimate wrought-iron settings nestled beneath the purple shade of what he now recognised was a jacaranda. It looked impressive from the ground, but from up here the layout was nothing short of stunning, the white and pastel theme tying together the mismatched furniture spread across the acreage. 'You must have seating for over a hundred, but you've made it so . . .' He waved a hand around, searching for the words.

'*Élégamment éclectique*,' Gabrielle supplied in her soft French accent. 'Elegantly eclectic. And it's two hundred seats. But I can't claim credit for any of it. Hayden's sister Tara is keen on being an events planner. She doesn't get much chance around here, so she's gone all out for Sharna. And *because* it's Sharna. Only the flowers are down to me.'

'And the amazing venue.' He waved a hand across the park-like grounds, toward the river, where towering sandstone cliffs on the opposite side glowed in the afternoon sun like apricot gelato.

Gabrielle shook her head. 'I can't really take credit for that, either. This is more the result of—' She sighed, though the noise was of utter contentment. 'I guess it's more a case of the perfect storm of circumstances. The inn is a beautiful building, the river makes the most spectacular backdrop, but it's the people out here that tie it all together.' She nodded decisively. 'It's a different world, Pierce. The people are amazing. Everything I've created here comes down to the local community mucking in with working bees, plant cuttings, food, advice.' She gave a low laugh. '*Lots* of advice! That's why the wedding is open invitation: no one chooses friends around here. Sharna knows everyone, and I owe everyone.' She turned her back on the view and gestured at the glass door that led into the inn. 'Come on, I'll show you to your room. And Hayden's hanging to catch up with you again.'

~

The wedding might be open invitation, Pierce decided, but clearly everyone else here knew each other well. Groups formed, broke apart and reformed, like olive oil poured into water. And then there was him, the lone drop of balsamic.

Though he wasn't shy, he clearly didn't fit in. He rubbed his chin, wondering if he could get away with ditching the party and instead wander down to the dock over the river and chill there.

Gabrielle made her way across the lawn as he did yet another circuit of the gardens, admiring the flowers. 'You okay, Pierce? Looking a bit lonely over here.'

He gave a sheepish grin. 'I should have brushed up on footy or tennis.'

Gabrielle wrinkled her nose sympathetically. 'Sorry, I forget it can be a bit of a culture shock. I don't suppose there's a chance you know anything about crutching sheep? Or whether lupins are going to sell high next year?'

He frowned and squinted, as though sifting through his knowledge. 'Nope. Bit rusty there, too.' He waved a hand at his clothes. 'If you don't mind the attire, I could give the wait staff a hand?' At least then he'd feel useful. And rather than make conversation, he could fall back on the rote patter of inanities he'd perfected over six days a week for the last three decades.

Her fingers toying with the full bloom of a deep burgundy rose, Gabrielle glanced across the lawn to where hospitality staff in black jeans and white shirts wove between the guests. Shards of light refracted from the glassware on the silver trays they carried, creating shifting patterns over the tableau. 'You're almost in uniform, but I've put on half-a-dozen high school kids for the day. There isn't a lot in the way of work for them around here, so I like to give them a chance whenever possible. And they've got the energy to keep those trays circulating—plus, being busy will keep them out of the booze, at least for a while.' She glanced at her fine silver wristwatch. 'Actually, do you think you could help me start herding some of the outliers in the right direction?'

'Herding? I'll impress the locals with that, for sure.'

She flashed him a grin. 'I'm going to go check on Sharna, but I need everyone to gather closer to that water trough.' She pointed to a two-metre-long carved wooden manger beneath an arch of pink and lavender roses. 'So if you can maybe rock a bit of that Zorro vibe, crack a stockwhip or something and get everyone headed that way, we'll get this show on the road before the CWA ladies start complaining that the food is ruined.'

'CWA?'

'Country Women's Association,' she clarified as they strolled toward the largest group of guests.

'I know, I'm not *that* city!' he protested. 'I meant, you have the CWA catering a black-tie function?'

'Absolutely.' Gabrielle nodded emphatically. 'When one of Tracey's pastries melts in your mouth, or you go back for sneaky seconds on Roni's lemon meringue, you'll know why. Then you'll be trying to steal my girls for the trattoria.'

He flinched. For a few sunny moments, he'd forgotten what he was running from.

'Gabby!' a deep voice boomed.

'Justin!' Gabrielle gasped as a guy threw his arms around her and lifted her from her feet. She extricated herself from his grasp, flicking a finger against the silver collar tips on his white dress shirt. 'You came! And super fancy.'

'Of course I did.'

'I thought you might not because . . . you know, *Sharna*,' Gabrielle said.

The guy gave a shamefaced grin. 'No point carrying on being butt hurt. Besides, she's one of my best mates, so I've got to be happy for her, right?'

'Right,' Gabrielle said approvingly. 'Pierce, this is Justin, who is not only my husband's best mate, but clearly a good guy, and the most talented woodworker you'll ever meet. He can whip up anything from a built-in robe big enough to hold *all* of my clothes—' she rolled her eyes dramatically '—to a bespoke piece of art.' She lifted her chin toward the trough under the wedding arch. 'He even managed to rescue that for us. It's almost a hundred and fifty years old, and I just about cried when I moved here and discovered it had disintegrated. But Justin made it better than new.'

'Better than old, you mean,' Justin said, thrusting out a hand to shake Pierce's. 'You on the bride's side or the bride's side?'

'Neither,' Pierce said, politely ignoring the mistake. 'I guess I'm on the host's side: I know Gabrielle from back in the city. She used to handle my marketing, though she's getting pretty hard to pin down these days.'

'Easy to market a restaurant that makes the best pasta ever,' Gabrielle said. 'You'll have to check out Pierce's place when you're in the city, Justin. His wild mushroom gnocchi is to die for. I've never found better, not even in Italy.'

Pierce's gut clenched. *His* place only served brunch.

Instead of dwelling on what he'd lost, he watched Gabrielle chatting and laughing with other guests as she made her way toward her inn. The Gabrielle he'd known in the city was competent and efficient; friendly, but perhaps a little guarded. Now, although there were dozens of people to manage, she seemed relaxed. Happy. In her element, as though she was truly with friends.

A vague pang of envy wormed through his stomach. He suspected that friends would be very different to regular customers.

By the time he and Justin had herded the guests to where Gabrielle wanted them, Pierce had broken a light sweat. Without the faint haze of smog he rarely noticed in the city, the sun out here seemed to have more bite. Last time he'd visited Gabrielle he'd needed to get back to the trattoria for the evening service and hadn't had time to fully appreciate the property. The grounds were even more extensive than he'd realised. Standing near the dock, he was probably two hundred metres from the inn.

He scanned the cliffs, imagining the passage of time that had seen the water carve so deeply into the land. Birds flew in and out of small caves in the rock face, piping and calling. The broad, pewter-coloured expanse of the river appeared motionless, though he knew it flowed toward the Murray Mouth at Goolwa, over one hundred kilometres south. He inhaled deeply, the air warm and rich, a lush smell of earth and river. Despite the sun that beat down upon his back, it seemed easier to breathe, as though his lungs expanded more readily, greedily embracing the fresh air.

It was, as Gabrielle said, different out here.

Like his life now, he supposed. Different. With only the cafe to keep him busy, what was he supposed to do with the rest of his time? Financially, it wouldn't be a problem. He'd only drawn a token wage from the trattoria, relying on the cafe and twenty-five years of smart investments for the bulk of his income. He gave a snort: Dante was in for a shock if he thought he'd be pulling a decent wage from his *managerial* position.

For a second, he wondered how his parents would cope with the increased workload, but then he drove the thought from his mind. They were both healthy, and the restaurant made enough money that they could employ someone to cover Dante's shortfall. As long as they kept Dante's fingers out of the till, that was. Still, that wasn't his problem anymore. His parents had made their choice; now they'd have to deal with the consequence.

He nodded at the river, as though he had enjoyed a discussion with a wise old friend, then spun on his heel and headed back up to the inn.

As he approached, a pair of guys seated on stools near the arch started strumming a riff from Faith Hill's 'Breathe', harmonising the chorus after a couple of bars. A gasp went up from the guests as a tall brunette in a floor-length, fitted lilac dress appeared in one of the inn's twin doorways.

Pierce couldn't make out why Gabrielle had remarked he should wait to see what Sharna was wearing. She had given the impression he would feel less out of place, but the bride's elegance made him more obviously underdressed.

The guitarists fluidly switched to Shania Twain's 'Man! I Feel Like A Woman!' and a woman seated alongside them picked up the lyrics. A rustle passed over the crowd as guests bent toward one another, murmuring. Justin gave a loud whoop. 'Go, Sharn!' People chuckled, an older, hard-looking woman gave a very audible *tssk*.

Then another woman appeared in the second doorway. Pierce knew instantly that *this* was Sharna.

Her floor-length dress of soft rainbow stripes was cut in a swoop above her knees in the front, long in the back. She struck a pose: one hand pressed to the doorframe above her head, the other on her hip. Right leg in front of left, she bent her knee, the toes of her tooled leather cowgirl-boot in an incongruously dainty ballerina's *pointe*. Head bowed, her face was hidden beneath an Akubra.

The crowd burst into applause, and now Justin wasn't the only person hollering.

As the soloist kicked up a notch, hitting the chorus, Sharna lifted her head, then sashayed forward, swaying her hips to the music, the stripes of the dress billowing around her as the back trailed on the ground. She offered her hand to the first woman, and together they walked the aisle, timing it perfectly to arrive at the arch at the conclusion of the song.

The celebrant tried to settle the crowd, who seemed intent now on going straight to the party. Sharna flung reddish-gold ringlets back over her shoulder, stuck her thumb and middle finger in her mouth, and let out an ear-splitting whistle. 'I've waited long enough for this,' she called, dropping her hands to her hips. 'Shut up, you lot, before Taryn changes her mind. I'm still trying to persuade her that Gabrielle's not the only civilised person out here.'

Another wave of laughter, then the crowd settled for the short ceremony—though, by the time the guitarists and singer launched into 'This Kiss', there was no holding them back.

Though he'd witnessed both proposals and receptions in the tratt, none had ever had the pure, infectious joy of this event. Pierce edged through the celebrating guests and wandered down a side passage toward the paved courtyard at the back of the inn. Despite Sharna's quirky dress sense, he still stuck out like a sore thumb. It didn't particularly bother him: he was neither shy nor self-conscious, but he'd already caught a lot of interested glances his way, and he didn't need to draw attention away from the brides.

The air was already summer-heavy, filled with motes dancing in the last of the light, and it seemed he could reach out and collect a handful of gold dust from the air. The roses in the borders drooped, their heads exhausted but their perfume still overpowering the rich, fresh-mown scent of the lush lawn. In the gums around the lagoon behind the inn, the galahs' strident arguments mellowed as the day ended and a pair of kookaburras called in the evening.

Without conscious intent, he headed toward the barn-like side wing that joined the two-storey inn, forming an L to shelter the courtyard. Gabrielle had shown him around the more modern extension last time he was here, and now it drew him.

A kitchen was the only place he felt truly at home.

12

Samantha

'Anything I can do to help?'

Sam froze at the male voice that accompanied the bang of the kitchen door. Her reaction was ridiculous: for starters, she knew her husband's slightly nasal tone well enough to realise that this wasn't him. Plus, despite their long marriage, he wasn't considered a local—no one from Murray Bridge ever was—so the open invitation didn't extend to him. Besides, even if he had been here, there was no way Grant would swan in offering to help when there were free drinks circulating outside.

Carefully placing the palette knife on the bench, she took a steadying breath before turning to face whoever had intruded on her hiding space. Not that Sam needed to hide: she'd known most of the guests her entire life, even her brother and grandparents were out there. But she also knew small towns, knew how they loved to gossip. If she hid in the kitchen, they could talk *about* her, speculate on what had gone wrong in her marriage. Yet if she ventured out to the party, they would talk *to* her. And, with a bit of booze in them, far too many would ask for details. She wasn't an accomplished enough liar to deal with their questions, and couldn't rely on Christine to screen them all.

For the last few months, she'd waved off the questions in the cafe with 'We're just taking a break' or 'Can't chat, I'm flat out, got a phone order to fill' excuses. Nobody believed her, but with Christine in the shop every open hour—she just *happened* to like quilting in the sunshine-filled window seat—they didn't dare press any further.

But now Christine was busy circulating through the guests so she could share her purse-lipped disapproval about the ceremony—as though she hadn't spent hours embroidering *Sharna* and *Taryn* on the mulberry silk pillowcases she had wrapped and then placed, without a card, on the gift table. Christine hid her caring behind the persona she had created. And Sam totally got that.

She dredged up her own unfailingly cheery persona. 'Sorry, what did you want?' The afternoon sun bathing the courtyard created a halo around the guy in the doorway, making it impossible to see his features.

'Gabrielle suggested I could take refuge in here with you.'

Refuge? Sam stiffened: what the hell? Gabrielle had carefully not asked about her situation and, with her air of culture and calm, was the last person Sam would have suspected of flapping loose lips around the place. She crossed her arms over her chest, her facade dropping as her scowl rose. 'What's that supposed to mean?' Her words should have been a challenge, but instead came out quavery. She used to be confident—everywhere except her own home—but the past couple of years had eroded her self-assurance.

'Oh. Hi,' the guy said, his tone lifting in apparent surprise as he moved further into the room.

As her eyes adjusted to the backlighting, Sam assessed him. Black hair, flecked with grey on the sides, was neatly faded into more length on top. His dark eyes and skin hinted at genetics rather than a tan. His nose, clearly broken at some time in the past, saved him from being 'too pretty', as Ma would say.

Her gaze darted beyond him. Sounds of the party out on the front lawn billowed toward them, a cloud of laughter, music and happiness that eased the tension between her shoulder blades. She was safe, everything felt right.

The guy tapped his chest, and she choked back an urge to laugh at his collared shirt, the deep V-neck laced so that it stretched open across his upper chest. He belonged on the Gold Coast, not anywhere near Settlers Bridge. 'Pierce,' he said as though it should mean something to her.

She raised an eyebrow and a shoulder.

'We met about six months ago,' he persisted.

Six months was a lifetime, as far as she was concerned. 'Sorry, I don't recall. A lot of people come through the shop.'

'It wasn't . . . Doesn't matter,' he said, seeming to change his mind mid-sentence. 'Pierce di Angelis.' He introduced himself more formally. The name tweaked something in her memory, but she couldn't place it.

Pierce gestured toward the oven. 'Gabrielle took pity on me and suggested maybe I could help out here. To save me from further embarrassing myself.' He jerked a thumb over his shoulder, toward the empty courtyard.

She couldn't help but grin. A guy who didn't take himself too seriously made for a refreshing change. She indicated the laden bench that stood between them. 'The kids have the savouries doing the rounds, and desserts are ready to go a bit later.' It was lucky Gabrielle's kitchen was solid, otherwise the benches would be groaning under the weight of sweet dishes. Some, like Christine's pavlova stacks, would replace the vases of pastel peonies and roses as the centrepiece on the larger tables. The finger food, including jelly cakes, cream horns and tiny almond and cherry cheesecakes—which contained no cheese of any kind, but Christine refused to concede they were actually frangipane tarts, and insisted they go by the name in her 1930s CWA recipe calendar—would be distributed the same way as the savoury dishes.

Sam had deliberately kept busy in the kitchen, tidying and choosing to handwash the dishes. Having run out of distractions, she had been threatening her current nemesis with a palette knife when Pierce appeared.

'Is that the wedding cake?' he said, approaching the five-tiered structure on the bench.

'Lucky guess,' she said dryly. She had carefully ombre-blended the delicate apricot, peach and yellow tones of the first two fondant-covered cakes so the join was imperceptible.

'It's amazing,' Pierce said, walking around the island bench, as though assessing the cake from every angle. 'The colours are perfect. To go with the pastel theme on the tables, right? Fruit cake?'

She nodded. 'The bottom layer is fruit cake, to support the weight. The next is chocolate mud cake. Sharna and Taryn agreed on those two, but Sharna had me add the top three as a surprise.' Shaded from deep mauve, through lilac to amethyst, they were the ones she was really sweating on: she was worried the heat would either dry out or melt the painstakingly smoothed fondant, or that the dowels holding the cakes together would slowly sag to one side. Using a lavender watercolour palette, she had hand-painted a delicate pattern of tendrils climbing the sides of the cakes, linking the five tiers.

'Those three are to match the bride's—well, bride number two's—dress, right?' Pierce asked.

She nodded, flattered that he'd seen the connection.

'And you made this?' He sounded impressed.

'God, no, I wouldn't even attempt it.' An actual chill ran through her at the thought of being responsible for producing the enormous cake. 'The fruitcake is Christine's, Tracey did the mudcake. Then they and Roni did one of the top cakes each.' Christine had been adamant they should have only traditional sponge, while Tracey wanted to add popping candy, knowing Sharna would get a kick out of it. Roni had smartly sat back and waited for the dust to settle before quietly insisting she would do orange chiffon with thick Chantilly cream for her layer. 'Because Sharna's the biggest kid around, each cake is a different flavour. Some of them a little . . . surprising.'

'But the decorating?' Pierce dropped to his haunches to get a closer view of the lowest cake, before standing slowly, inspecting each level.

'Ah. Yeah. That was me.' She was surprised by his interest. Wedding cakes weren't a guy thing, at least not among the men she knew.

'Including these?' He pointed at the spill of lavender and blush pink flowers that formed a crescent on the top cake, before tumbling in a widening cascade down one side of the tower.

Nerves prickled the inside of Sam's mouth and she swallowed hard. She'd spent so long carefully assessing, removing and remaking flowers that didn't look perfect, but there would be something wrong. Her dad had always found fault, and she'd known Grant would, too, if she gave him a chance. 'Yep,' she said shortly. Who needed some city guy to come in here criticising? Sharna would be thrilled with the cake, and that was all that mattered.

Pierce gave a low whistle. 'These are piped buttercream, right? You've even got the stamen in there. But how did you get the colour so natural? It's like they're . . .' He clicked his fingers, searching for the word. She noticed that he was careful to move his hand away from the table. 'It's like the actual colour of the petals, not just the physical flower, is three-dimensional. If that makes sense.'

'Because the flowers are so pale, the trick is to put equal amounts of two different shades of pink in your piping bag at the same time. If you look at a real rose—Gabrielle has plenty in the garden—the pale ones often have more than one tone.'

Pierce nodded slowly, as though filing away the information, but his gaze still devoured the cake. 'Is that hand-painted fondant? Or airbrushed? And . . . no, wait.'

Her fingers tightened on the palette knife as he leaned closer. It was nice he was admiring her work—her friends had also done so, but they kind of had to. This guy? Not so much. But no amount of admiration would make up for him accidentally bumping the construction.

'The three large flowers, are they sugar roses? You know how to make them?'

'I wouldn't say "know". I watched how to do it on YouTube, and gave it a go.'

'Yeah, right,' he said, though he sounded disbelieving.

'You can find just about anything on YouTube.'

He shook his head. 'This is sensational.'

'Oh.' Sam willed herself not to press a palm against her hot cheek. She couldn't remember the last time she had blushed. 'Not really, just trial and error. You should see how much of the evidence I had to eat.'

'Ha. Best and worst part of the job, right?'

'The violas and violets are real. Crystallised. Also YouTube.' She groaned inwardly. Seriously, one compliment, and she went into information overload.

'Amazing,' he murmured. 'I can't imagine the hours of work that went into this.'

That he would even consider what it had taken was incomprehensible to Sam, and she frowned, trying to work out his angle.

'You're pulling my leg about YouTube, though, right?' he said. 'You're a professional.'

She wrestled down the instinctive urge to agree, to keep the peace at all costs. Disagreeing meant arguing. And arguing meant . . . *no*, she had to get that out of her head. 'Not at all,' she said with a dismissive wave of the palette knife. 'This is my first go at a wedding cake, and you can see I shouldn't have tried so many different-sized roses. An extra shade of purple in the spill would probably look better.'

'It's bloody amazing,' Pierce said. 'If I had half your talent, I'd be running a cake shop, not a—'

'Oh, now I've got it!' she exclaimed, relieved as her brain finally pinpointed his familiarity. 'You catered a function for Gabrielle, right?'

'Just delivered sample cakes, actually. Or tried to, but got lost in the process.'

'So you didn't make those cakes?'

'The ones you didn't try?'

He spoke teasingly, but she couldn't remember the details of their interaction. There was a lot of her life over the past few years that she preferred to blank out.

'Yeah, I made them. They were nothing like this, though. This is . . . *una grande passione*.' He spoke with one hand, pinching his fingertips and thumb together. 'There is love in this creation.'

His words were as certain as his manner, and she was surprised to realise that he was right: she had loved both the creation of the cake, and she loved Sharna, who she had known all her life.

'This isn't just a job, is it?' Pierce pointed at the cake. 'I recognise the hunger, the drive to get it right. It's how I feel about creating the perfect dish, the right balance of sauce, the silkiest pasta. You're fired by desire, but there's also a sense of dread, yeah? A fear that, even though you've put everything into it, your creation won't be perfect.'

Sam blew out a long, steadying breath. 'Exactly. I'm terrified the buttercream will be gritty—though I ate enough of it, testing each batch, to be sure that it isn't. Or that I've overworked the fondant and it's dry and will crack—even though no one ever eats fondant, anyway. Or that nothing is set hard enough, and it will melt when we get it outside. Or, you know, that a flying unicorn will land on it and take a dump,' she added with a grin, knowing that she had to sound nuts. The other women in the CWA were quietly—or not-so-quietly, in Christine's case—confident in their work, churning out scones and biscuits and cakes by the dozen to feed shearers, labourers, family and fundraising stalls.

'Interesting.' The corners of Pierce's eyes crinkled, and she realised his irises were almost as dark as his pupils. 'You don't generally come across much insecurity in this business. Most creatives are too busy posting their latest triumph on their socials to have time to doubt their ability.'

Sam nodded. 'Then all the likes show up on their page, and you wonder if anyone's actually tasted the food, or they're all just buying into the hype.' She had jealously drooled over enough posts to know what Pierce meant.

'Exactly. And it seems to become a self-fulfilling prophecy.' Pierce made a grand gesture with the sweep of an arm. '"I say I am amazing, therefore I am."'

'My ma would say it's an emperor's new clothes kind of thing. No risk of that happening here, though.' She tapped her chest. 'I don't have social media.' She didn't have the confidence to post either her baking or her plating, and couldn't imagine ever doing so. It was taking everything she had just to allow her friends to see she was branching out, to let them judge her work.

'No socials? Well, we have to immortalise this somewhere,' Pierce said, pulling his phone out of his jeans pocket. He gestured at the cake. 'Do you mind? I'll put it on my restaurant page. Well, *the* restaurant page.' His correction was accompanied by a fleeting scowl.

'Sure. Whatever.'

He waggled his fingers, trying to get her to move closer to the cake. 'Hop in the frame, you deserve the recognition. Do you want to be tagged as Sam or Samantha?'

She stiffened. She didn't need anything that would remind Grant of her existence, cause him to wonder where she was when the cafe was closed.

'No. That's fine,' she said woodenly. 'Don't mention me.'

13

Pierce

The unfamiliarity of the room woke him early. Gabrielle had done a great job at the inn, each of the opulent guest apartments decorated with a different retro vibe, paying homage to the elegance of the 1920s, thirties, forties and fifties. His room, on the upper floor, faced the river and was decorated in rich colours and metallics, in what Gabrielle informed him was a Gatsby-inspired nod to the twenties.

He hadn't bothered to draw the long curtains that rested in soft cream scallops on the plush carpet. Though the other guests had made a bit of late-night noise in the corridor, his thickly walled room seemed embracingly private, and curtains over windows that looked out to the secluded landscape unnecessary.

Now the sun streamed in through the multiple small window panes, and he vaguely wondered what sort of birds keened above the cliffs, their calls echoing mournfully through the river valley.

He was barely thinking about them, though. Instead, his mind was on Sam. He'd been surprised by the buzz he got from seeing her yesterday, and tried to tell himself that it was relief at recognising a familiar face. That wasn't the truth, though. As Mum said, he had pasta-pots full of confidence: he didn't need to know anyone to be at ease in a crowd. The kick had been because he got a better look at her than last time, when her eyes had been the standout feature in a dripping, rather bedraggled visage.

And he hadn't imagined how striking those eyes were.

Over the last few months he'd entertained the occasional late-night fantasy where Sam had been grateful for his knight-in-shining armour rescue from a storm-swept back road. Being a fantasy, he could ignore that not only was he the one who had been in need of rescue, but that Sam hadn't shown anything the least bit like gratitude for his manly presence.

Yesterday, fantasy and reality collided. Maybe because it was the first time in decades he wasn't focused on rushing between the cafe and restaurant, getting the next dessert baking or the sauce for pasta simmering. Whatever the reason, he'd been caught entirely off guard by the unfamiliar lurch of interest that tightened his chest.

Sam was pretty, in a soft, unstructured way: her toffee-streaked blonde hair pulled up into a ponytail, devoid of makeup, she looked . . . fresh. He couldn't recall what she wore, because his entire focus had been on those blue eyes, one splashed through with an avocado stripe. Her attitude, which continued to swing between cautiously friendly and downright prickly as he tried to make himself useful for the remainder of the evening, had him slightly out of balance and totally intrigued. She seemed the polar opposite to the women he usually encountered, who were either done up for a night out or, like Amanda at the trattoria, had all her assets out on display in the hope he'd notice. Which he sure as hell did, but he had more self-control than to allow himself to be seduced by a vast display of creamy cleavage.

It seemed that tiger-striped eyes, though, were a different story.

He deserted the tempting softness of the luxurious bed to stand in front of the window as he processed his thoughts. Below him, the front door of the inn closed with a solid thunk. Seconds later, a woman appeared, striking out across the lawns toward the river.

Sam? He craned forward in surprise. When she disappeared from the kitchen last night, he made a few rounds of the partygoers before concluding she must have headed home. It hadn't occurred to him that she might also be staying at the inn.

Pierce grabbed a pair of bone-coloured cargo pants from the top of his kit bag, then threw on a long-sleeved black tee, the first thing that came to hand. Though he took the stairs two at a time, by the time he reached the gardens there was no sign of anyone.

He grunted with quick irritation, and made his way down to the wooden dock that jutted out over the calm water. With the sun barely cresting the cliffs and flooding the river valley with an almost silver light, the last of the spring mornings clung to a sharp freshness.

Two ducks came in to land, their feathery butts hanging low, webbed feet out in front, as though they anticipated a need to brake hard despite the long stretch of water. To Pierce's right, several stone cottages clung to the waters' edge, the dirt road running behind them. Trusting his gut, he headed left.

It didn't take more than a few hundred metres for Pierce to realise that the route he had taken wasn't so much a path as a strip of bare earth where the swaying fronds of the willow trees bordering the river brushed the ground clean. He threaded beneath the branches of lacy leaves, breaking into a cleared space. It was cool and earthy and tranquil beneath the trees. A cave curtained in shimmering golden-green privacy.

Struck by the silence, he held his breath to listen.

It wasn't truly quiet. Trees whispered secrets to one another in the breeze, and tiny birds called as they flitted through the branches. He caught glimpses of the river, but that seemed sworn to silence, neither rippling nor splashing.

As he moved from one cathedral-like space to the next, Pierce realised that the growing labyrinth was the perfect place to hide. He would never find Sam.

He kind of understood what Gabrielle meant: it was different out here. Away from the concrete hustle of the city streets, it was hard to imagine a life that revolved around work and stress.

Or perhaps it was simply the unfamiliarity of having a couple of days off that threw him? If that was it, he fully intended to kick back and get into this sensation of relaxation.

As though his new acceptance cleared his vision, Pierce spied Sam through the swathes of delicate, feather-veined leaves.

A great root sat a couple of feet above the river, coiled like a dragon's tail, a bridge to nowhere. Knees drawn up under her chin, Sam was at the very end, where the tree plunged into the water. Watching a pair of pelicans sail by in stately fashion, she seemed oblivious to his presence.

He should back away, leave the woman to her solitude and reflection. But he'd already struck it lucky twice: if he left now, he might never run into her again.

He cleared his throat.

'Shit!' Sam whipped around, her hand slamming down to clutch at the moss-covered root.

Pierce winced. Fat chance of a positive reception now.

'You scared the crap out of me,' Sam gasped. She patted her chest, as though calming her heart. But then she grinned. 'I was miles away.'

'Figured. That's why I didn't call out.' Her hair was loose today, soft, burnt caramel waves shot through with blonde resting on her collarbones. 'I thought a cough might blend in a bit better.'

'Yeah, because the carp keep popping up out of the water and coughing at me,' she said.

Encouraged by her joke, he moved closer, flinching as a branch grazed his head. 'This place is crazy. I'm used to the banks of the Torrens: you know, bitumen walking paths, mowed lawns and trees in cages. I didn't realise that once you get outside of Murray Bridge, the river is basically wild. You can see how the escaped convicts could hide out.'

'Convicts?'

'Yeah, prisoners,' he said absently as his foot sank into the marshy ground. He would have been better off with a pair of RMs, not his Italian leather loafers.

'I do know what convicts are.' Sam's amusement was obvious. 'But South Australia wasn't a penal settlement. You know, bragging rights, we have to tell everyone that.' She clambered up, her bare feet curving to hug the slippery branch. 'Or did you go to school interstate? I don't think anywhere else likes to acknowledge our convict-free heritage.'

He shook his head. 'Nope, I'm from Adelaide. But, as my teachers would be happy to tell you, I wasn't exactly a star student.' With the hours he put in at the trattoria, it had been hard to see any use for the education school provided, other than maths and English.

'Fair enough.' Sam nodded. 'School wasn't really my thing, either. I prefer to pick stuff up, rather than have it drummed into me.'

'Life experience.'

'Or osmosis.' She chuckled. She gestured at the trees. 'Here's one for you. I know from the captain of the *Mayflower*, which is docked upriver at Mannum, that the willows were planted in the 1860s as a navigation aid. So too late for your non-existent convicts, anyway.'

'Navigation? How do the willows help with that?' He tugged the slender branch closer. Perhaps the almost imperceptibly different coloured undersides of the leaves all faced south or something.

'They don't *do* anything.' Sam was laughing at him, but he didn't mind. In contrast to the marked wariness she occasionally displayed, the laughter relaxed her face. Her blue eyes sparkled in the sunlight filtering through the wispy leaves. He wasn't close enough to make out the green stripe, but damn, he wanted to be. 'They were planted to mark the main channel so paddle-steamers didn't get lost in the tributaries. Box willows on one side, weeping willows on the other. And, for good measure, there are some basket willows, too.'

'These trees are over one hundred and fifty years old, then? Guess that explains their impressive roots.'

'Uh-uh.' She wrinkled her nose, seeming unsure about correcting him. She paused for a moment, eyeing him. 'Willows only live about fifty years. But new ones grow so fast from fallen branches and cuts in the roots, that they're now considered an invasive weed. They've been cleared out in large stretches along the Murray, there are only a few stands left on this lower part.'

'Shame.' He didn't really give a damn about the trees, just wanted her to continue talking. The hours in the kitchen last night had been bizarre: he couldn't recall when he'd last talked for so long about nothing . . . and everything.

'It is.' She looked sad, and he felt guilty for not paying attention to her words. 'These trees give . . . shelter, you know? Not just to the animals and birds, but to anyone who needs it. I can sit under here for hours, and be safe. Well, until some city-slicker wanders in on my meditation.' Her grin made it clear that she was teasing.

'*Mi dispiace*.' He held his hands open, palm up, in apology. But what he wanted was to ask her what she needed to be safe from. This rural backwater, with the river softly lapping at the base of old trees, the birds—made brave by their quiet conversation—flitting closer, was the epitome of tranquillity.

She cocked her head slightly to one side. 'Are you actually Italian?'

He didn't miss the inferred 'or just a tosser who quotes in Italian?' '*Si*. Though I've been here since I was a toddler. Why?'

'Pierce doesn't seem a particularly Italian name.'

In forty-plus years, no one had ever asked him about his name. He tapped his chest. 'Pietro,' he said, rolling the *r*. 'I guess my parents were eager to assimilate but didn't think *Peter* was fancy enough. They changed it when I started school, back in the days of *Remington Steele*. You know, Pierce Brosnan?' He waited a moment to be certain Sam made the association with the actor his mum had been—still was, thanks to the movie *Mamma Mia*—madly in love with. 'Mind, that desire to conform didn't stop them from sending me to school with salami and provolone.'

Sam snorted, the naturalness of her reaction bringing a smile to his face. 'You don't get to complain. My mum's go-to was fritz and sauce.'

'Bums and lips, according to Mum. Which is ironic, given that my parents will find a way to cook up and eat just about any organ or muscle you put in front of them.'

'Sounds like my brother, Jack. He's into this . . . nose-to-tail eating stuff.' Sam used the phrase uncertainly, lifting an eyebrow. 'Sustainable living.'

'But you're not?' He jerked around as something splashed in a puddle between the twisted roots.

'Yabby.' Her arms outstretched for balance as she walked toward him along the slippery root. Sam pointed to the small, bubbling whirlpool. 'He was creeping up out of the mud, checking you out.'

'Great. Nice place, shame about the stalkers.'

Sam froze, staring at him with deer-in-the-headlights intensity.

14

Samantha

Sam cursed her instinctive over-reaction to Pierce's words. It wasn't like he'd claimed to be a stalker—although he had followed her into the trees along the riverbank. But she wasn't the nervous kind, had never been afraid of anyone in her life. Until Grant changed, that was. The distance between her and Grant now made her increasingly aware of the myriad small ways her husband had controlled and dominated her, until she was terrified to cross him.

She shook off the mood and took Pierce's outstretched hand so she could jump from the log to the soggy ground. She ignored his questioning look, though. She didn't have to explain a damn thing to him, or anyone else.

He held her hand for longer than seemed necessary.

Her heart lurched like the side of a mattress dipping, and she felt the exact moment the devil got in bed with her. That was what Ma had always called it, those rebellious teenage moments when she bucked against some rule or expectation, or acted wild just for the sheer hell of it.

She was aware how isolated she and Pierce were. Just as she was aware of a certain magnetism about him. Despite a few hiccups—which weren't his fault—he had been good company in the kitchen yesterday. He was assured, enthusiastic and inexplicably interested in her creations, her process, her thoughts. He had mucked in to help with the dishes as the empty savoury trays returned to the kitchen. And he hadn't tried to take over direction of the distribution of the sweets. Instead, he offered help if needed, and then stood back.

The fact that she noticed those things about him were why she had chosen to disappear last night. Her life didn't need complication.

The fact that she noticed those things meant she hadn't slept well. Yet, for the first time in a long while, it wasn't fear that had kept her awake.

The fact that she noticed those things made her wonder if perhaps Grant had not succeeded in crushing her.

And that was why she had been sitting in silence, hoping the river would somehow answer her churning questions.

Now, with the devil beside her, she felt wild and free. Why shouldn't she seize the moment, live a little for once? The thought made her feel giddy and silly, and for a second she automatically closed herself down, shut off her emotions. But then she tightened her grip on Pierce's hand, using him to steady herself as she pulled one bare foot out of the mud. 'I didn't judge that landing too well.'

'You're doing well in comparison to me,' Pierce said dryly, displaying what appeared to be a canvas boat shoe, well covered in ooze.

'At least yours are on your feet.' She reluctantly withdrew her hand from his. 'I'm going to have to fight back into my shoes.' She dipped her foot in the puddle, trying to rinse off some of the mud. Normally, she balanced carefully on the root all the way back to the trunk of the tree, where her shoes waited.

The water was chilly but did nothing to shock her back to her senses. Or to cool her racing blood. What would it be like to give in to her curiosity, to flirt with another man? To feel wanted and desired for the first time in so many years? She gave an exaggerated shiver and scrunched her toes together.

'Maybe leave the shoes off?' Pierce suggested. 'I'll give you a hand back to the inn.'

Sam grinned. 'Going to lay your jacket across the puddles?' she teased.

He hooked his fingers into the neck of his tee, and for a terrified second she thought he was going to follow through. 'I would, but I don't think this shirt will cut it,' he said, with a mock remorseful shake of his head. 'I could go ask Gabrielle if she has some gumboots?'

When he'd lifted his shirt, her gaze had glued to the narrow strip of flat, tanned midriff his movement exposed. Her visceral reaction was more than mere curiosity. She lurched toward the hanging curtain of greenery, stumbling in her haste to draw it aside, to disperse the illusion of privacy the soft leaves created.

Since she was sixteen, she'd never looked at any man other than Grant. She had all she wanted in him—or so she had believed. Perving at guys would have been as logical as a vegetarian window-shopping at a butcher's display. She even found excuses not to go on the girls' night at the end of netball season, knowing they would inevitably end up at an all-male review in Hindley Street. Though last time, Grant had provided her with the excuse, saying he felt ill and demanding she stay close. There was a history of heart trouble in his family. He never knew when it could flare up.

She shoved her way out between the branches and charged across the dirt track, making diagonally for the safety of the inn's gardens. Her mind raced even faster than her feet, flashing up the events—the *opportunities*—from her past. Did the fact that she had *actively* avoided anything that might be a temptation mean that perhaps she hadn't done it willingly?

Her pace sped up, as though she could outrun the thoughts.

No, she assured herself, she had always been a homebody. Never the type to throw her knickers at *The Thunder from Down Under* when they toured.

Grant would have slapped it out of her.

Yet here she was, blatantly objectifying Pierce.

'Here, you forgot these.'

Sam didn't realise that she was charging barefoot across the clover-studded grass toward the inn, until Pierce spoke. Her sneakers appeared, dangling from his fingertips, in her peripheral vision.

'Ah, I was going back for them. Just trying to wipe some mud off on the grass,' she said, making a meal out of doing exactly that. She needed time to think, time to justify. Time to work out whether she still needed to make excuses for her feelings, because old habits sure died hard. Almost subconsciously, she feared the result of making a decision, taking an action that might displease someone else.

No, that wasn't true: she was scared of angering Grant. No one else.

But was he even still her husband? Surely not by anything but an antiquated government requirement, an imaginary bond that would be dissolved in a few more months' time.

'Did I—?' The sneakers disappeared as Pierce spoke, and she figured he was making some kind of questioning gesture. She'd noticed that he used his hands to speak. In fact, she had been mesmerised by the flow of them as he conducted his words like music. 'Did I say something wrong back there? Again.'

She winced. A reminder that her interactions weren't exactly *normal* wouldn't help her to act any more normally. 'No. It's not you. Just . . . shit.' She took the shoes and glanced at her naked wrist, as though she wore a watch. 'Wow, it's getting on.' Even though it was undoubtedly still early, and Gabrielle was generous with late checkouts, it was time Pierce left.

'I didn't realise you were staying here last night.'

She let her eyes graze his. Did he sound as though he regretted missing some kind of opportunity? She wanted to hope so. But she was also terrified by that possibility. 'Is there a reason you should have?'

He grimaced. 'Knew that was dumb even as I said it. What I meant was, when I couldn't find you around after the cake cutting, I assumed you had headed back into Settlers Bridge.'

Conversations banged and raced in her head, and she tried to choose one. A safe one. Flirting with the stranger passing through town was one thing. Imagining their brief rapport into something more was bloody ridiculous, though. She didn't need Grant to knock any sense into her on that one.

'I don't live in Settlers.' And she probably didn't need to share that with him. 'But I do need to head that way now, and open up.'

'Open up?'

'Ploughs and Pies. I've got coaches coming through today.'

'That's yours? I noticed it on the way here.' He fell into step beside her, and she hurried, the air aromatic as the still-damp grass crushed underfoot. 'But you said you don't cook professionally?'

She gave a snort of derisive laughter. 'Couldn't have put that better myself. It's just a cafe. I do the barista stuff—also untrained—and plate up premade food. That's about the extent of it.' Despite his feedback on her cake-decorating skills yesterday, Pierce didn't need to know about her experiments. Baking for the cafe could never amount to anything; the paying regulars were too stuck in their pie-and-a-vanilla slice, or savoury-slice-and-a-lamington rut, to want to try anything she made. Already, the test runs she gave away to the schoolkids were beginning to affect the cafe's profit margins, so she had decided she could only risk stocking the cake cabinet with new treats when the buses for the zoo were coming through.

The thought of the day ahead tingled excitement through her. There would be two coaches, thirty-six people apiece. After Pierce had finally vacated Gabrielle's kitchen last night and headed out to the party, Sam had snuck back. Now she had cream horns, apple teacake, apricot crumble and giant coffee-iced crème patisserie profiteroles boxed up in the industrial fridge. Although she rarely got any feedback—the coaches bearing away the still-eating customers—she liked to think that her home-baked goods were well received, and the almost-empty cabinets seemed to prove it.

'I'll have to come by and hit you up for a coffee, then,' Pierce said. 'Can't believe I've made it through an hour without one.'

Sam scowled as she reached for the inn door. Why did some unreasonable part of her insist on making his words into something they weren't? 'I'll shout you one for the road,' she said firmly, pushing open the door and striding inside.

~

She had made it *too* clear to Pierce that she wasn't interested, Sam decided as she wiped the last of the cafe tables and upended a chair onto it. He hadn't shown for his coffee, and that was just as well. She didn't need to see him again.

'There're still crumbs on that one,' Christine reprimanded as she packed her needlework away. Her decision to stitch pillowcases for Sharna and Taryn seemed to have her enthused about embroidery, although she maintained it was only because it was getting too hot to work with quilts.

'I'm sure there aren't,' Sam replied. She shifted the serviette holder and the condiments, and wiped it again anyway. Honestly, Christine acted like her mother. Well, like *a* mother. Her own mum was career-focused. When she'd split from Sam's dad, she'd started flitting around the country, chasing something more fulfilling than reporting on the sheep and wheat prices, or the local footy team's latest win. Sam had only a few years of high school left—although Jack was several years younger—so they moved in with Ma and Pops. And then Sam got married. There had been no gap year, no adventuring, no seeing the world. Grant had asked, and she had wanted nothing more than to be his wife.

She gave a mirthless chuckle: now there was nothing she wanted more than to be his ex-wife.

'What are you snorting about?' Christine asked.

'More like a sob. Having to wait twelve months to divorce is ridiculous. I didn't have to wait twelve months to make sure I wanted to marry, even though I was a kid. But I have to wait for government approval to end the marriage. It's not like they make anything out of me being married, so I don't see why they should stick their oar in now.'

Christine pinched closed the Velcro on the voluminous appliqued bag she used for her sewing. 'You're away from *that man* now. Just put him out of your mind. I mean, what's the rush?'

'I'm not rushing. It's not as though I *can* rush,' Sam said bitterly. She moved behind the cake counter, pulling out plates. 'It's just that I'm sick of worrying about what is mine, where to live, whether I'll have a business left. I owe Gabby a small fortune in rent, yet Grant gets to live in our house scot-free, as though he's never done a damn thing wrong.'

'As far as the world is concerned, he hasn't,' Christine said acidly.

'That's the truth.' She knew Christine wasn't judging her, yet the woman shared little of her own story. It was like they were in some sort of dirty-secret club, where they knew the other had paid their membership dues, but not how much they'd been charged. 'Our joint friends have unanimously declared for Team Grant.' It had been a blow to her self-esteem. Yet, on reflection, she realised that those supposed friends were actually Grant's mates and their partners. How had she not realised that she had gradually lost contact with her own friends, that Grant had slyly driven them away? He had isolated her, leaving her with only acquaintances. And Christine. Who was . . . something else. 'They feel sorry for the deserted husband. The one who hasn't paid the rates, and isn't even making the mortgage payments anymore. I had to contact the bank to ask if they could take the overdue payments out of our redraw.'

'And?' Christine crossed the cafe to stand in front of the cake counter, her attention on the contents.

Sam clenched her teeth as memory of the humiliation surged. 'I'm not the mortgagee so I can't organise it.' She screwed up the paper towel, squeezing it so hard her knuckles ached. 'Maybe it's better that way. If the bank forecloses on the house, I won't have to push Grant to sell so that I can get a share of the money. If I'm even entitled to any.'

'Of course you're entitled,' Christine said firmly. 'Even if we have to get a lawyer involved, you'll be entitled.'

Sam shook her head. 'I can't afford a lawyer. And, because there's commercial real estate involved, I'm not entitled to Legal Aid.'

'But the shop and house are in Grant's name, remember?' Christine said triumphantly. 'So he's the one who would have to pay the legal fees, not you.'

'I wish,' Sam said. 'But if Grant has to spend anything on legal rep it will come out of the redraw. Or he'll refinance the cafe. I know he sure as hell won't pay *that* mortgage, so even if I get the shop in a settlement, it looks like I end up funding both his lawyer and mine.' What more could he take from her?

She pulled a tray from the chilled cabinet. There were only two out of the two-and-a-half-dozen giant profiteroles left, and satisfaction briefly dissipated her misery. 'It's just messy, any way I look at it. But I've got months before we can work it all out.'

'I'll take those two.' Christine tapped the glass countertop. 'And two of anything else. No, no, not those,' she reprimanded as Sam reached for the tray of commercial buns. 'Two of something you've baked. Young Eric likes them much better.'

'Young Eric?' Sam's eyebrows shot up.

'Is there a reason he shouldn't have any?' Christine demanded coldly.

Sam held both hands up. 'I didn't say he shouldn't. I just didn't realise that you knew him that well.' Young Eric was the local *old bloke*, the one who had been around the town forever. Everyone accepted his presence, yet no one seemed to know his history.

'How big is this town, Samantha? Of course I know him. And every man has to eat. I don't suppose you've ever seen him in here buying himself something?'

'If I'd thought about it, I guess I'd figure he doesn't have a sweet tooth,' Sam said defensively.

'Yes. Well.' Though not known for her altruism, Christine managed to make Sam feel small and selfish. 'Pack up two of your apple crumbles. And I can't believe Gabrielle, of all people, is chasing you for rent. It's not like she needs the money now, is it?' Christine had a knack for hiding her kindness in acid and judgement.

'Oh, she isn't!' Sam said quickly. Christine was keen to believe the worst of anyone new to the district, and more than two years of good behaviour and generous donations to the town apparently weren't enough to make up for the fact that Gabrielle had moved in with a seemingly endless supply of cash. 'The only time she's said anything was to tell me that, as Sharna had been living there the last couple of years, she was accustomed to the suite not earning anything. Of course, Sharna was working for her, so it's kind of different.'

'All right,' Christine said. Her immediately pursed lips made it seem anything but. 'As I've already told you, I have a little money put away. I can help you.'

'Thank you, love—Christine,' Sam quickly corrected, knowing the older woman didn't care for the glib endearment. The word didn't trip as easily off Sam's tongue as it once had, when she'd been using overt cheerfulness to hide . . . not misery. Dissatisfaction. 'But I'm whingeing about nothing. It's just that I'm so over all of this. Like, why can't we be adults about it? Grant made it very clear that he doesn't love me, and I sure as heck don't love him anymore.' Oddly, admitting it out loud still hurt. But was the regret over the lost relationship, or the wasted years? 'Why do we have to have this drawn-out soapie death? We could both move on and have a better life.'

'In my experience, often one partner needs to find someone else before they feel secure enough to give up everything they've known.'

Sam gasped, her face heating. 'I'm not insecure!' Christine had hardly been in the inn kitchen during the wedding, and Sam had barely flirted with Pierce. The other woman couldn't possibly know of her . . . God, not even *interest*.

Her willingness to be side-tracked from the miserable cycle of her life, that's all it was.

Christine drew herself up, energised. 'I didn't mean you. But the fact you're responding so defensively makes me wonder . . .'

Sam whirled around on the pretext of cleaning the already pristine prep bench. Pierce had been a lovely diversion. It had been nice to imagine, for those few minutes, that someone was interested in her. 'Not for me, thanks. I peaked in my twenties, it's all downhill from here,' she said, deliberately cheerful.

No house, no job, no kids, no dreams.

No future.

15
Pierce

'I didn't realise you were staying over.'

Pierce halted in his tracks. Then he noticed the tiny smile playing around Sam's lips and realised she was teasing him by repeating his observation from the previous day. 'Is there any reason you should have?' he said.

She grinned, a slight dip of her head acknowledging that he'd picked up the thread and was playing the game. 'Knew it was dumb as soon as I said it.'

He shouldn't read anything into the fact that she had their conversation from twenty-four hours ago word perfect.

Pierce only remembered it himself because she was intriguing. That was the best word he could think of to describe her. Sam was demonstrably skilled, yet insecure in her ability. One moment open and friendly, the next introverted and almost . . . scared. And either she had perfect recall, or she had also rerun their conversation in her head.

He gestured across the grass, still starred with overnight dew, toward the river. 'I thought I might run into you heading down for a walk.' In marked contrast to yesterday, the rising sun was hidden by the soft purple blanket of clouds piled on top of the far cliffs, and he'd darn near frozen, lurking around, hoping Sam would make an appearance.

He would blame Gabrielle for that: she and Hayden had invited him for lunch yesterday, which they shared on the verandah of the waterfront cottage nearest the inn. He had slyly tried to get some background on Sam, but Gabrielle laughingly fended off his questions and Hayden was, as usual, a man of few words. All Pierce learned was that Sam lived at the inn, and headed out for an early walk along the riverfront each morning regardless of the weather.

Now Sam gave him a glance, one that should be annoying in its brevity, yet simply made him glad to have even a fraction of her attention on him. 'You didn't turn up for your coffee yesterday?'

He rubbed his nose for a moment, wondering how to answer. Then he caught himself: since when did he *choose* an answer? Stick with the truth, and to hell with the effects. 'That's partly because I had to duck back to Adelaide.' Or he'd chosen to, once Gabrielle shared that Sam lived at the inn. 'And also because your offer sounded like a "push off, Pierce" kind of deal.'

'Did it?' Sam quirked an eyebrow, but didn't deny that she'd been trying to blow him off. She gestured with an open hand toward the river. 'It's my day off, so I like to go a bit further.'

'After this weekend, I need the exercise.' He patted his stomach. 'Too much partying sure shows fast when you're not thirty anymore.' Or forty. He didn't want to pigeonhole himself as he tried to work out Sam's oddly unguessable age. At times she was poised, self-assured and quick-witted. But then she seemed to back off, uncertain and defensive, like a teenager still trying to find her place in the world.

'Happy fat?' She shot him a sideways glance as they crossed the purple carpet beneath the central tree in the lawn. 'You're clearly a miserable bugger, then.'

He snorted at her quick retort, surprised at the pleasure her teasing brought.

She picked up her pace across the grass, almost as though challenging him, and he easily lengthened his stride. 'So your restaurant is shut on Mondays, too?' she asked. Her question came in short, breathless bursts, which made him grin: she was definitely challenging him.

'No. I have a brunch cafe in the city centre, so I can't afford to lose the business crowd on weekdays. I close weekends, instead.'

She interrupted with a light laugh. 'How much wine was involved in your partying? You do realise it's Monday?'

'I decided to give myself a bit of time off.' A full week. He hadn't done that since he was twenty. But he wasn't about to scare her by making it sound like he'd gone back to the city to organise staff to cover him just so he could hang around here. 'And the tratt is closed Mondays, in any case.'

'Tratt?' The sun perched on top of the cloud blanket now, and she squinted up at him, impatiently shoving a wisp of blonde hair from her face, then poking it back into her ponytail.

'Trattoria. *That's* the restaurant.'

'It's a separate location? Or you run a restaurant after your brunch service has finished?' She took a step sideways, almost bumping into him, and he realised she was avoiding treading on a cloud of tiny, azure butterflies that fluttered up from the grass.

'It's separate. A family business.' He shouldn't have mentioned it. The thought, the memory, the stress, didn't belong here, out in the fresh air and sunshine. He had done well putting it aside, other than the minutes he'd been forced to pretend he had tunnel vision, focused on getting up to his apartment without acknowledging the proximity of his parents next door. Or bloody Dante.

'Not taking your shoes off?' As they reached Gabrielle's dock, he tried to divert Sam from asking the questions he could feel brewing in her.

'Told you, it's all about the exercise today.' She turned left, taking the track he'd followed the previous day. It was only wide enough for one, but he decided to walk on the slightly marshy edge closer to the trees, rather than the long grass on the left.

'So, this . . . trattoria?' She said the word carefully, yet her pronunciation was uniquely Australian, a sounding of each letter, rather than the tongue-curling roll on the double tee.

'Yep, that,' he said.

'It's an Italian restaurant? And that's why you had the Italian desserts for Gabrielle? Earlier in the year, I mean. Oh!' Sam pulled up short as a small black hen, so glossy its feathers shone metallic blue, bustled across the path directly in front of them. Behind the bird trailed two tiny chicks, headed for the river. Sam frowned. 'Where are your other chickies, swampy?' Nibbling on her lip, she scanned the immediate area. 'Jack mentioned the foxes are really bad this year. He's not far downriver from here.'

Pierce realised he had tensed at the guy's name, and it took a second to recall she'd already mentioned Jack. 'Your brother. Nose-to-tail eater?'

She lifted an eyebrow, and he was glad she didn't wear sunglasses as the expression gave him a second to admire her eyes. 'You remember.'

'It was only yesterday.'

'Not exactly important, though.' She returned to searching the vegetation, but her concern was quickly replaced by a relieved smile as another purple-chested bird with a bright red comb and beak scrambled through the long grass, chasing three more chicks down toward the water. 'Ah, daddy day care is on duty.'

With the swamp hens sorted, Sam flicked back to their previous conversation. 'So food is clearly your thing, but I can't work out if you're a pastry chef with those desserts, or a cook, based on what you were saying about creating pasta dishes?'

'Neither. Not professionally, anyway. My brunch cafe is open until a little after lunch, and the family restaurant is literally next door. I do the cooking there. Did the cooking,' he corrected.

Sam slowed, eyeing him curiously. Evidently, his tone hadn't been as throwaway as he wanted. 'You don't work there anymore?'

'I quit on Friday,' he said shortly. Yet . . . he didn't feel as cut up about it as he should.

'Wow. What are you going to do now? Just the brunch cafe?'

'I'm not sure.' He stared intently at the faint path in front of them for a long moment. 'I think maybe it's time to look for something else. Something different.'

'Out of the hospo game?' Sam stopped, her hands on her hips as she gazed across the river.

They had left the stands of willows behind, the path now leading between river red gums that would predate white settlement. Curls of shedding bark hung like dreadlocks against the mottled trunks. Branches laden with squawking ruffles of white cockatoos stretched across the waking river. Sam blew out an unsteady breath and he suspected, with the early morning air still fresh enough to burn through his nose like menthol, she was taking a break on the pretext of looking at the view. But then she pointed at a bird spiralling far above. 'There. Whistling kite. His nest is in that tree.' She touched Pierce's arm to adjust his position so he'd see the untidy tumble of branches at the top of one of the tallest gums. 'They mate for life and use the same nest every year, just keep adding to it. Renovating, I guess.'

The bird let out a plaintive, ululating cry, and he grunted in surprise. 'That call would be fairly terrifying at night. It has a kind of . . . ghostly quality.'

Sam lifted one shoulder. 'I don't think it's scary. More sad, as though he's lost something he knows he'll never get back.'

'Haunting.'

'Exactly.' He felt ridiculously pleased as she nodded approval of his word choice. 'I know he still has a mate, so that's not what he's calling for. Maybe he's sad that the world is changing around him.'

Pierce jerked back, shocked at her insight: how did she get that out of his one brief comment about his current uncertainty? 'How do you mean?' he said warily.

Sam gestured at the towering trees, the red blossoms catching the morning sun and lighting up the canopy like tiny jewels. 'Imagine, years ago this entire valley would have been full of gums like this. Now the birds fly above and can see how little of their safety remains, how what is familiar has been stolen from them. That has to make them sad.'

'Ah.' He let his arm brush hers as his shoulders loosened. When she avoided stepping on the butterflies, he should have twigged that she had an environmental focus.

'So, what were you saying about changing career?' she said.

Damn, he'd relaxed too early. He wasn't accustomed to speaking his thoughts aloud. Of course, his life might be different now—on so many levels—if it was something he'd recognised the importance of, years back. 'I wasn't really saying that I want to change career, just that I want *more*, if that makes sense. I'm forty—forty-seven,' he corrected, feeling that honesty was important. 'And it's like I'm only just getting around to working out what to do with my life. Cooking is all I know. And I do love it. But I want to focus on the parts that speak to my heart.' He tapped his chest.

Sam gestured at the track and started walking again, but more slowly this time. 'Which are?'

This, he knew. 'Working a pasta dough until it becomes silkier than the skin of a beautiful woman. Marrying it with the perfectly seasoned sauce. Creating soup that is rich and full bodied by simmering the cheapest, tastiest cuts of meat, then adding vegetables fresh from the markets at just the right moment, so they have that perfect mouth feel, but they've given life to the dish.' He dropped his hands, realising he'd been speaking with them.

'And creating those desserts you brought for Gabrielle last time?'

He shook his head. 'That's exactly what I don't want to do. There's no passion in making them, I simply follow the same recipe every time. Guaranteed results.'

'Oh.' He couldn't see her face, but she sounded crestfallen.

'It's not like what you do,' he hurried to add, realising he had sounded dismissive. 'That wedding cake, that was amazing. There was so much work and passion and love in that. That was a *creation*. Desserts in the tratt are formulaic. Plus, I don't have your flair for presentation. I saw the desserts you sent out at the wedding: everything was tweaked to perfection, immaculately presented whether you garnished with leaves or flowers or a reduction.'

Sam didn't look at him. 'That was a team effort.'

'The baking was a team effort,' he corrected. 'You were the one standing there, checking every dish before it left the kitchen. I know. I watched you.' He held his breath, waiting for her reaction.

'Working in this trattoria would be exactly that, though, wouldn't it? A team effort. Specially if it's with your family?'

'To an extent. But it's Mum and Dad's place, the final say comes down to them. Which has always been fine until . . .' He hesitated. Yet what harm was there in telling Sam? 'Until Voldemort returned.'

Her eyebrows shot up.

What would it be like to have her attention for long enough that he could lose himself in the depths of those unusual eyes?

Pierce dragged his gaze back to the path, rubbing hard at the scar tissue that ridged his nose. What the hell was he thinking? Apparently, having time on his hands might not be so healthy.

'Voldemort?'

He chuckled reluctantly, embarrassed to admit the depth of his animosity towards his brother—yet more embarrassed to claim his kinship. 'He who should not be named, or something like that, isn't it? In this case, my brother.'

'Brosnan, by any chance?'

He was confused for a second, then caught her grin. 'Mum should have gone with that. But far more aptly, Dante.'

'Ah. I didn't pick you for a Harry Potter reader.'

'You'll have to get to know me better,' he shot back. Hell, if that wasn't an invitation, he didn't know how else to phrase it.

'I definitely need to know more about Dante.'

'Great, even when he's not here, he gets the girls,' Pierce joked. It wasn't true: he'd never actually *lost* a girl to his brother. 'Dante's . . . how can I put this nicely? He's a lot younger than me, enough that Mum considers him a miracle. And, apparently, miracles can do no wrong, even if they dabble in illegal chemistry.'

Sam winced sympathetically. 'Every family has one, right?'

'Brother off the rails?'

'A member they'd rather not own up to. For me, it was my dad. He was a right bastard. Used to lay into Jack. And my mum.'

The muscle in Pierce's jaw twitched. He had decided to gloss over that particular shortcoming in Dante's repertoire. He could turn a blind eye to the rest of Dante's shit, but that one was the clincher, the fault that made him recoil from his brother's presence.

'Past tense?' He grabbed Sam's elbow to steady her as she skated over a slick mud patch.

'Yeah. He's dead.'

'I know I'm supposed to say I'm sorry, but—'

Sam held up one hand. 'Unnecessary. I hated him. And yet I—' She broke off with an exasperated grunt. 'Doesn't matter. Anyway, what has Voldemort done to get you offside? Surely not just his lifestyle choices?'

'No, I'm—' He stopped and chuckled. 'Ironically, I was going to say I'm not that shallow, that I wouldn't write someone off for their choices. But fact is, I would and I have. Dan's just . . . scum. Your typical steroid-pumped meathead with no redeeming features.' *With a DV record.* 'But I guess the real reason I'm pissed with him is pretty juvenile: my parents welcomed him back into the family business like they were waiting for him to sign up. In my family, it's always been a case of "Dante needs help". So Dante never bothers to help himself. Or, rather, Dante helps himself to what isn't his.'

'So, you quit?' A frown creased between Sam's eyes as she tried to follow the sequence of events.

He wasn't sure whether to be flattered or intimidated by her interest. Thanks to his work at the tratt, Pierce was practised in making the appropriate interested noises when people spoke without truly engaging, so Sam's apparently genuine curiosity was disconcerting. 'Yep. Chucked a wobbly and walked out.'

Sam gripped his forearm, pulling him to a halt. 'Does it hurt?' She sounded oddly invested in his reply. 'To leave everything you've worked for?'

'It should, shouldn't it?' He rubbed a hand across his jaw, her question forcing him to assess his feelings. 'The truth is, I wasn't really happy there, I was marking time. Yet I knew I couldn't up and leave my parents in the lurch. I was trapped and I would never have had the balls to quit.' He gave a humourless laugh. 'But now they've chosen Dante, so I guess him coming home freed me. And, no, oddly it doesn't hurt. I just need to work out what to do with that freedom.'

'Freedom,' Sam said, a note of wonder in her tone, as though she'd never heard the word before.

'Yeah. It's weird. I feel a bit . . . I don't know, lost, because the tratt is all I've ever known. And maybe a little guilty that my folks are going to have to deal with Dante's shit.'

'They must know what he's like?'

He snorted. 'He's never been any different, so you'd think so.'

'People can change. Not always for the best. Anyway,' Sam shrugged, seeming to dismiss her own words, 'enough with the deep and meaningful. I don't know about you, but my heart rate is definitely not getting up.' She tilted her head, indicating they should hit the path again.

He nodded slowly. 'Mine is surprisingly elevated.'

'Thought you'd be more fit,' Sam threw back over her shoulder as she set off at a jog.

But Sam had hesitated. She got his implication. And even though she was running from him right now, he didn't think it had anything to do with his words.

As though proving him right, Sam pulled up after only a couple of hundred metres, her hands on her thighs as she bent over, puffing. 'I am so out of shape.'

'If I had views like this, I'd never bother going to the gym,' he said, resting his hands on his waist and blowing out, as though he was winded, too. He pulled off his jacket. 'Want me to carry yours?'

She looked startled, but then nodded, pulling off her grey fleece and passing it to him. He refused to notice how her tee stretched over nicely rounded curves.

Sam pointed across the river. 'See those lines on the cliff?'

'Sure.' At least, he would have if he hadn't been perving. He dutifully refocused. The river was divided by a long spit of land studded with gum trees and tussocky grass. Beyond it, the cliff looked like a layered cake, each section a slightly different shade. Where the water lapped, the stone was burnt orange, then shaded up through yellows to almost cream at the top of the rock face.

Sam spaced her finger and thumb a few centimetres apart, holding her hand in front of her face so the frame she created lined up with a section of the cliff. 'Each of those wedges is a strata line. There's a thousand years between them. The sandstone is full of marine fossils.' She shot a glance up at him, almost shy. 'I've some back at the inn, if you're interested? Shark's teeth and shells.'

'Love to see them.' Though he'd never had any interest in fossils, Pierce now had a sudden desire to know more. 'Shark's teeth, though? Isn't the river fresh water?'

'Yeah. But before the barrages were put in to block the entry to the sea at the Murray Mouth, the sharks used to swim upriver. The fresh water kills the parasites on their bodies, but sharks can tolerate it.'

'You're really into all this river stuff, aren't you?'

Sam pulled her ponytail out, ran her fingers through her hair, and then retied it. On another woman he might suspect it to be a seductive move, but Sam seemed indifferent to him, and the action appeared natural. 'I can't understand how anyone can live near the river and not want to see it every day. It's like—' she blew out a long breath as she searched for the word '—grounding. Does that make sense? There's an aura of peace and timelessness.' She gave a derisive chuckle. 'Don't listen to me. It's just . . . it's just that no matter what's going on in my life—the world, I mean—the river's still here, still flowing. It puts things in perspective: it doesn't have a purpose, yet still it exists.'

'You don't have a purpose?'

She screwed up her nose, then heaved a sigh. 'It's complicated. I'm kind of between things, too. Trying to find myself. Bit late in the day for that, right?'

It was a relief to know Sam got him, rather than saw him as some guy hitting a midlife crisis. 'I know exactly where you're coming from.'

'I figured by now I'd know where my life is headed. That it would all be easy, I'd have done the tough years, the years of insecurity, when it's hard to make ends meet, but . . .' She let the sentence trail off, then gave a wry grin. 'Like Pops says, "Just embrace the shit and move forward. Because what the hell else are you going to do?"'

Pierce nodded slowly. 'Your Pops is absolutely right.' It wasn't his job to warn his parents about Dante; they had to do whatever they thought best. 'And maybe having no direction means we're free to follow our dreams.'

Sam gave a dismissive snort. 'If you happen to have one.'

'I reckon mine has been buried for so long, it's kind of dusty.' Yet the realisation that he could now pursue a dream, that he could give form to thought, raced through him. Nearly fifty, finally he could do what he wanted. 'You don't have any secret desires hidden away?' It was a leading question but he'd be happy whether she took it as a come-on, or answered rationally.

Sam pressed her lips together for a moment, her brows drawn. Then she sucked in a slightly wobbly breath. 'I'll show you something.'

16

Samantha

What was she thinking?

Sam strode along the river path as though she could outpace Pierce, despite his longer legs—and the fact that she'd invited him along. She couldn't believe she'd dribbled on for so long, told him so much. God, even that her life was complicated. But it was simply because she wasn't accustomed to having someone listen to her. She was so used to being the one asking the questions—*How's your day been? What are you up to this weekend? Is the weather too hot for you? Do you want sauce, love?*—that being put on the spot herself was a novelty. So she'd let her mouth run away with her brain, as Ma would say.

Also, Pierce's proximity did odd things to her. She felt flustered, as though making a good impression was somehow important.

Which it wasn't. His opinion was irrelevant.

Flirting. That was all she was down for. Flirting with the stranger passing through town. It was all Tara's fault, for putting it in her head. Last Thursday, she'd peered at Sam's face, then started in. 'We've got to fix you up and get you on Tinder.'

'Fix me up?' Sam had run a self-conscious hand over her ponytail. 'First of all, I'm not some old farmhouse. And second, it's only been a hot minute since I split with my husband. I'm not after any kind of relationship.' Maybe not ever.

'Relationship?' Tara snorted. 'Who wants that? I'm talking about a hook-up. A girl has needs, you know.'

'Needs? Jeez, Tars, you're all of eighteen.'

'And how old were you when you and Grant hooked up?' Tara said, the smell of chocolate sweetening her obvious triumph as she refilled the steel shaker they used to dust the cappuccino.

'Well, now I'm old enough to know better,' Sam said firmly. Yet was she old enough, or simply scared enough? She had no idea what it was like to be with any other man. 'In any case, I'm sure I'm entitled to a mourning period. You know, divorce is one of the five most stressful life events.'

'And sex is a great stress reliever,' Tara said. 'There're plenty of guys around here who'd love a look-in. How about Justin? I reckon he's always been into you.'

'Gross, Tars. I've known Juz since he was a kid!'

Tara pouted her well-glossed lips. 'Well, that's everyone in this place, isn't it? There's no one here we don't already know. It's no wonder Sharna was so desperate to leave.'

'Agreed. So there's no point in the makeover.'

'Tinder, I told you. We'll fix you up and do a photo shoot.'

'No, we won't,' Sam said firmly. 'What we will do is send you over to Lynn's to get an extra soy milk.'

'Lynn won't have that kind of thing,' Tara scoffed.

'She's been stocking it since Lucie and Keeley moved here.' Though her brother provided goat milk for his partner and stepdaughter, Lucie sometimes preferred to use soy in her organic dishes. 'Go on, quick, before it gets busy.'

Now, Sam kind of wished she had let Tara give her a makeover, perhaps snip the flyaways from the ends of her hair. Because it seemed Pierce wasn't passing through town as quickly as she had assumed.

And she wasn't at all sad about that.

But that didn't mean she had to share her dreams with him, did it? It had been an impulsive invitation, and now she needed to find something else to distract him.

As they walked upriver, the cliffs on the far side had gradually dwindled until they became only a rocky, willow-lined bank. The branches of the trees drooped in elegant festoons, the lowest lying horizontal on the placid surface of the water. About a half kilometre behind the trees, soft hills formed a protective bowl, the river valley nestled in the embrace. The remnants of a jetty jutted into the water. She pointed toward the six upright pylons, the tree trunks uneven diameters, but the same height. 'I'm sure pelicans have no spatial awareness.' A bird was perched on one of the posts, his great, feathered body overhanging the wood in every direction, huge beak and crop seeming in danger of overbalancing him. 'I don't know why they always choose such uncomfortable-looking roosts. It's as though once they've committed they're determined not to admit their mistake,' she said.

Dead centre of the river, another pelican came into view, flying so low she was sure its wingtips must touch the calm surface. The bird gave a few effortless flaps of his vast black-and-white wings, and soared higher. He circled above them, then dove toward the pier. When it seemed that, impelled by his size and weight, there was no chance of him landing, he put down his paddlelike feet and came to a perfect pinpoint halt atop the tiny wooden circle. He ruffled his feathers, then settled, an overstuffed beanbag.

Sam chuckled fondly. 'They're my favourite bird. I mean, they're just so unlikely. Can you imagine even trying to get that bulk off the ground? But they're completely oblivious to how improbable they are.'

Pierce watched the birds. 'You know, I've never seen a baby pelican. Not that we get many of any size in the city, just the occasional couple sailing along the Torrens.'

'That one's quite young,' she indicated the first bird. 'See how his markings are more brown than black? And the second one isn't a breeder. You can tell because the circles around her eyes are yellow, not pink. But you won't ever see babies, as they're hatched inland or out on the Coorong, well away from civilisation.' Sometimes, the extent of her unschooled knowledge surprised her. It was intriguing how much information could be gleaned from passing conversations. And how useless and irrelevant much of that information was—until right at this moment, when Pierce fastened his dark, intent gaze on her.

'Whereabouts inland? Further upriver?'

She shook her head. 'No. When there's inland flooding—like at Lake Eyre last year—thousands of pelicans from all over Australia fly in to breed. No one understands how they communicate the news that it's flooding, or that they're heading there for the summer break, yet off they all go.' As though to reinforce her tale, the first pelican stood, unfolding mighty wings and giving them a shake. He took a step from the perch, like it was a trust fall into the river only a metre below, then soared up into the dawn-tinged sky without creating so much as a ripple on the water.

Sam watched appreciatively, almost feeling the surge of power, the sense of freedom as the bird became airborne. 'They're the elephants of the sky, right?'

Pierce pinched the bridge of his nose, his fingers massaging the diagonal ridge that disfigured it. He pulled a comically apologetic expression. 'I think Dumbo has that covered.'

She couldn't hold back her laugh. Why was she so thrilled that he would unashamedly use a kid's cartoon as an analogy? Was it because it seemed to make him real and approachable and . . . *No.* Not desirable. That wasn't something she was willing to countenance. Not beyond the mild flirtation they'd been having. Her life didn't need more entanglement.

But she did want to prolong their interaction, to enjoy the novel sensation of having someone interested in her thoughts and experiences.

With typical spring uncertainty, a cloud drifted across the newly risen sun, reminding her that she wanted to try Julia Childs' 'Floating Islands' recipe. Goosebumps peppered her arms, but she wasn't about to ask for her windcheater back. Pierce had it slung over one shoulder, and she didn't entirely trust herself not to bury her face in it and take a good deep breath. She was going to have to book a check-up with Taylor Hartmann at the clinic, she decided as a flush chased the chill. Her hormones were definitely out of whack.

As she pushed between the trailing fronds of a stand of willows, Pierce reached above her to sweep aside the green curtain. She didn't know how to respond, so she pretended not to notice. 'I've never worked out which bank of the river each variety of willow was planted on. I guess when the river floods they spread.'

'Does it flood often?' Pierce asked, following closely as she clambered over moss-covered roots.

'Not so much anymore. Global warming, I guess. And the locks help control the water levels.'

'Locks?'

She waved her hands around. 'Kind of a cement weir across the river, with passage along one side for boats. The boat enters the passage, or lock, which is then closed at both ends, and water is pumped either in or out to match the water level on the side they're travelling to. Then the gate is opened, and the boat goes through. The biggest flood was in 1956. If you check out Gabby's cellar, you'll see the highwater line on the wall from that one.'

'But that paddock in front of her house is huge,' Pierce said. 'It's a couple of hundred metres from the river. Are you sure it's not rising damp creeping up the walls?'

'That's not a paddock.' Sam did her best Croc Dundee impersonation, hoping the humour would prevent Pierce from getting angry at her correction. 'Best not let Gabby hear you call her precious garden that.' It was cute how city guys thought any decent expanse of land in the country was a paddock. She should take him out to Ma and Pops', show him what a real paddock looked like. A hundred acres, stretching from fence to fence. 'And no, it's a full-on tidemark, two metres up the wall. The floods reached halfway up the main street of Settlers Bridge. That's why they put in those crazy high gutters along the road. Just about need a stepladder to get up the kerb if you miss the ramps.'

'You had me at cellar. It must be cool to have that kind of history in a building.'

She liked that he didn't need to insist that he was right. 'I'm sure Gabby will be happy to give you a tour.'

'She seems pretty busy. Maybe you can show me around.' Pierce's voice lowered, and it seemed the birds chittering in the trees also hushed. The willy wagtail who had been dancing along with them, his white-tipped tail switching from side to side like the swish of a Victorian lady's fan, wrapped tiny claws around a thin branch, stilling to catch Pierce's words. 'I mean, if you have time. I know it's your day off, so you've probably got better things to do.'

No, she didn't. 'I'm heading out to my grandparents' farm a bit later, but we might have time for a quickie. Quick look,' she hastily corrected, spinning on her heel and plunging through the trees so he wouldn't catch her flaming face. She was happy to flirt with the guy, but damn, why was she so bad at it?

Oh, yeah. Lack of practice.

Although there was no path through the trees, a small wharf thrust out into the river, seeming to grow from the roots of the willows.

At the edge of the dock floated her dream.

Sam blew out a long breath, full of yearning. 'Speaking of baby pelicans, isn't she beautiful?'

For a tense moment, she thought Pierce wouldn't see what she did, that he would only notice rotting planks and cracked paint, the slight list to the port side. The fallen verandah, half of it hanging over the front window like a lazy wink.

Alongside her, Pierce let out a low whistle. 'It's a . . . paddle-steamer?'

'Not a steamer anymore, but yeah, *Pelicanet* is a paddle-wheeler.' She pointed at the exposed radial network of paddles on the near side, although Pierce had obviously already noticed the historic artifact. It was hard to miss: a giant wheel with flat wooden blades mounted around a central hub, the device covered more than a third of the three-storey structure and disappeared into the water below the lowest deck.

'*Pelicanet?*'

'Yep. Baby pelican,' she said. 'Told you I love them.'

'I've never seen anything like this.' Pierce glanced down to check his footing as he walked out onto the wharf. Probably a wise move, given that the dock was in about the same state of repair as the boat, the planks woven together by the trailing roots of the willows threading under, over and through them. 'It's as high as it is long.'

'Not quite, though *she* looks like it. I guess if you add in the engine room, below decks, she'd be pretty close.' Sam pointed at the tiered structure, which always reminded her of a wedding cake, each level reducing in size. 'The top level is the wheelhouse and captain's quarters. Next is a rabbit warren of cabins. And the level at the waterline is a galley and some other stuff.'

'A galley?' The word caught Pierce's attention.

'Do you want to see?' She'd explored the boat plenty of times over the months she had lived at the Wattle Seed Inn, but always felt a little nervous, as though she was trespassing among ghosts. She would enjoy it more with Pierce.

'Absolutely.'

From the moment Sam first laid eyes on her, the abandoned-looking boat seemed to represent a fairy-tale escape. As though she could board it and float away from her problems. But she couldn't imagine what fired up

Pierce's interest so much that he was already ahead of her on the wharf.

'Is this the gangplank?' he asked, pointing at a narrow strip of warped timber lying on the wharf, parallel to the boat.

'That's what I use.'

Pierce bent to pick up the plank, manoeuvring it to span the gap between the vessel and the landing. 'After you.' He offered his hand as though she hadn't navigated the breach herself a dozen times.

And she took it.

He waited until she had crossed, then followed her onto the square front deck of the mid-level.

She slid her hand beneath the fallen verandah, feeling along the top of a window ledge, hoping there were no huntsmen spiders. One had scared the crap out of her a couple of weeks back. And, judging by the way it had scuttled straight up to the top deck, she had startled it just as much.

'Ah, I thought maybe we were going to jimmy the lock,' Pierce said, sounding relieved as she produced the key.

'We can if that's going to give you a buzz. But seeing as Anthony told me where to find the key, it'd be overkill.'

'Anthony? The pub guy from Settlers?'

'You know Ant?' She had assumed Gabby was the only person he knew in the district.

'Not at all. Just ran into him at the supermarket on Saturday. He's got a thing going with the cashier, Lynn, right?'

'Wow, mad gossip skills. You could be a local.' She smiled. 'Yes, they have a thing. But no one's sure if they realise themselves. It's been very slow burn.'

The soft lap of waves against the hull of the craft counted the silence before Pierce responded, 'I guess some of the best dishes are slow cooked.'

'Sure. But like you said, passion is better, right?' Sam cringed; she really needed to get advice on flirting. Tara would have to be good for some tips as she was on Tinder every break they had in the cafe. Not that Sam had any intention of giving in to Tara and swiping left, right or any other damn direction. But it would be comforting to have the social skills.

It was a weird reversal: she had spent years feeling superior to her friends, being the first to have a boyfriend, the first engaged, the first living with a guy, the first married.

Not the first to have kids, though.

There was a chance she wouldn't be the first divorced, either, which was good. Lachlan MacKenzie's mother had died a few months earlier, but instead of stepping up and supporting him, his wife had decided that was the moment to end their marriage. However, Emma MacKenzie had the luxury of disappearing to Adelaide with her lover, leaving her parents and ex to field the questions and community outrage.

Dirty, mismatched curtains screened the windows spanning the front of the vessel on either side of the door. Sam made a point of concentrating on getting the key into the lock as she tried to step back into the conversation. 'I mean, we're talking *years* that they've been making cow eyes at one another, yet they've only just started to show up together at events like Sharna's wedding.'

'I still reckon there's a lot to be said for taking it slow,' Pierce said. 'That way you make sure you have the recipe perfect.'

Sam frowned; though he was continuing the joke, relating relationships to food, it felt like a veiled shot at her. How much gossip had he heard?

17
Pierce

'Watch your head. And your step,' Sam cautioned as Pierce tripped over a ledge, following her inside the boat. 'That's a weather seal. To keep the water out when the river gets wild.'

'Wild?' Standing beyond him, in the gloom, Sam's features were hard to make out, but he was sure she was teasing. And he liked it. There was nothing pretentious, nothing affected, nothing *deliberate* about the way she acted. 'Can the river do that?'

'It gets choppy, but not much more than that. But this boat was built in 1890, before the locks I told you about. So the river was more natural—unpredictably flooded, then dried up. And I guess it got wild at times.'

'That'd be something to see.' He moved beyond her, the threadbare, gold-patterned burgundy carpet suspiciously spongy underfoot.

'This was the small salon, for paying passengers.' Sam pulled back a couple of curtains that fell to hip-height, knotting them in a ball to let light in.

The area smelled of must and leather, dank and mouldy. He inhaled deeply, and Sam grimaced. 'I should have been Indiana Jones,' he said wryly.

Sam looked at him questioningly.

'This place—' he gestured at the room '—it smells like adventure. Don't you reckon?'

At Sam's delighted laugh, a stupid grin spread across his own face. Sam charmed him. That was the only word he could come up with. She was unlike any woman he knew, she . . . he couldn't put his finger on what the difference was. Could it be that she was *country*? Unselfconscious, natural, real. Her face showed life experience, rather than makeup, artifice and drama.

Was that what Gabrielle had discovered here? A different kind of people, with different values, different lifestyles, different ways of interacting?

'Certainly smells of something,' Sam chuckled. 'But, yes, adventure. I'll pay that one.'

He ran a hand over the dark, ornately carved panels beneath the window. 'This is real timber.' The room—although crowded with a cracked burgundy leather chesterfield, a green table with a ratty jade tablecloth, and a couple of tub chairs—held an old-world charm. 'And those are brass light fittings?'

Sam's gaze followed his pointing finger to the green-tarnished wall sconces. 'Yeah. Apparently *Pelicanet* used to carry passengers and trade goods. That's why the decks are almost the same size as the interior. The cargo would be piled on there, covered with tarpaulins and ferried from the Murray Mouth to Echuca. Then wool would be carried back, because it was so much quicker than taking it overland on bullock drays. There were two to three hundred steamers working the Murray at the peak of the trade. Without any roads, the river was the main highway so there are cabins for passengers, too.'

'This is awesome,' he said. 'It's like stepping back in time. I can imagine punters smoking cigars, drinking whiskey and dealing out poker hands across that old table, while the boat steadily churns along the river.'

'Imagine? Or did you just relocate Kenny Rogers from a train to a boat?'

'Ha!' He rubbed the bridge of his nose and gave a rueful grin. 'You caught me: "The Gambler". You can see it, right? It just needs a couple of revolvers on the table, a spittoon in the corner—'

'And a burlesque dancer in her corset and feathers leaning over the back of the chair?' she suggested.

He held up both hands. 'Your words, not mine. I was going to artistically leave the visual with a couple of old oil paintings and cigar smoke wreathing the ceiling. Speaking of—' he pointed at the timber plank ceiling, just above his head '—that's the captain's quarters, you said?'

'Yeah, and the wheelhouse. There's a bench for charts, the gauges for the engine that drives the paddle wheels, and a huge steering wheel. That's about it.'

Pierce almost didn't know where to start looking, there was so much to explore. He nodded at a doorway further in the depths of the boat. 'Can we?'

'Sure,' Sam said. 'That passageway is where you'll find your old oil paintings. Actually, they're sepia photos, but close enough. The cabins are through there, too. You'll need your torch, though.'

The beam of his phone danced around the space, providing snapshots of the past. Though each of the tiny cabins had a window, it was covered with thick folds of velvety material in a shade between dark burgundy and black. A pair of narrow bunks with thin grey mattresses lined one wall, an old-fashioned washstand and small oak wardrobe the other. 'How is something like this just sitting here? I mean, it's living history. It should be a museum.'

Sam stayed out in the passageway, and he guessed she already knew what each room contained. 'When the trade dried up—no pun intended—because of the roads and rail, the owners scuttled their boats in the deepest part of the river. There are about ten of them sunk in this stretch, and thirty between Murray Bridge and Renmark. But a handful, like this lovely old lady, survived. Off the top of my head, there's the *Marion* and the *Mayflower* just upriver at Mannum, and a few over the border.'

He shook his head incredulously. 'I've never seen anything like this. Does she still run, or is she wedged up on the mud so she doesn't sink?'

'It seems that every few decades someone takes an interest in this old girl, so she's not entirely original anymore. She's had a bottom lift—' she grinned, acknowledging the double entendre '—and some kind of engine stuff done decades back, along with various bits of plumbing work. Apparently Hamish MacKenzie—he runs the garage in Settlers—has his commercial captain's ticket, so Ant gets him to run her every six months or so. Just up to Gabby's dock and back. But Ant's been a bit slack since the verandah came down.'

'Or since he started escorting Lynn around the town?'

Sam snorted. 'Yeah, that could have something to do with it.'

They had moved through the broad body of the lower level, past half-a-dozen of the tiny cabins, and now emerged onto the rear deck. He pointed at the stairs. 'The wheelhouse?'

Sam nodded but glanced at her wristwatch.

'Ah, sorry.' Pierce grimaced. 'Forgot you said you had to be somewhere.'

She looked startled for a moment. 'Oh, that. No, that's not until later. But I promised Sharn and Taryn that I'd be back for breakfast before they head off on their honeymoon. Then I've got to help Gabby turn out the vacated rooms. I think she's fully booked again next weekend.'

'No worries,' he said, trying not to let his glance linger on the stairs. 'Let's head back.'

His reluctance wasn't only at leaving the boat unexplored, though. He wanted to talk with Sam more, chase down the undeniable vibe between them.

Pierce needed to know more about her, how it was she could seem so open and forthright, yet still give an impression of hidden depths. She seemed to hint at secrets he was certain weren't contrived to make her seem more intriguing because, if anything, she appeared oblivious to his interest.

'I didn't mean we have to go right now,' Sam said.

He wanted to take a moment to analyse why she spoke in such a hurry, as though preventing him from walking away, but she rushed on.

'There're also those stairs.' She pointed to the opposite side of the deck, where he could easily have overlooked a small door slightly inset in the wall. 'The galley is down there. I thought you might be more interested in seeing that than the captain's set-up. You know, considering our shared interest.'

Pierce wasn't sure whether she put an inflection on the final two words, but he wanted her to. He held her gaze for a long moment. 'I'd love to go down with you.'

Sam did a double-take, and a flush mounted her cheeks. She chewed on her bottom lip for a moment then shot him a grin. 'Hope they're not your best clothes.' She brushed past him. 'It can get pretty dirty down here.'

He followed her down the steep, narrow staircase, his blood pounding in his ears. He was sure that was a come-on. Wasn't it? Why the hell didn't he just straight up ask her? He never usually had a problem speaking his mind.

Before he could make a decision, Sam thrust open a door opening off the tight corridor. 'The galley.'

Holding his phone above her head, his gaze ranged the space hungrily. It was compact, utilitarian and unloved.

Under the beam of his torch, Sam crossed the room in three paces, and balanced on tiptoes, trying to pull aside the curtain above the bench.

He came up behind her, reaching for the fabric. Really, there was no alternative: the space was too tight for them not to touch.

Sam froze, but she didn't try to slide away from the press of his body.

He tugged the curtain aside, then stepped back a few inches, until his back hit a wooden counter. He would never try to persuade a woman, much less force her. Seduction, however, he was willing to give a go. It just depended on Sam's signals, and he was determined to read them right.

Sam gestured to one side. 'Massive range for the space. I can imagine it getting very hot in here.'

Torn between testing the thread of what he wanted to believe was innuendo, and a longing to check out the kitchen, he let his gaze follow Sam's direction. Set between wooden benches, so scrubbed they glowed white even beneath the veneer of dust and velvet murkiness, the six-burner hob was huge. 'Surely that's not vintage? It looks like gas.'

'That was a previous owner's upgrade. Along with new toilets. But that's about it.'

The cupboards lining each wall were dark wood, set with heavy iron handles. Above them ranged shallow timber shelves, each with a metal rod running across the front to stop goods from falling—in that rough weather that Sam had mentioned, he guessed.

'Pretty beaten up, huh?' Sam sounded apologetic.

He shook his head. 'The lounge—saloon—and the cabins were like a trip back in time, but this . . . this is amazing. It's impossible to look at the galley without imagining the cooks, sweating to feed the crew. Think how many hundreds of meals have been prepared here.'

'Think how many hundreds more could be, if Ant ever got it up and running.'

'Running?'

Sam stroked the dusty bench, then swiped her hand on the back of her khaki shorts.

He wouldn't check to see if there was a handprint.

Nope.

Definitely not.

At least, not yet.

She waved toward the stairs. 'Years back, he had some idea of creating a floating Saturday night pub. But then, when he bought his partner out of the Settlers, I guess he figured he'd end up cutting into his own profit. So nothing more ever happened.'

'Booze and boats. Sounds fatal.'

'I'm kind of glad it didn't work out. *Pelicanet* deserves much more than to be a pub for bucks' nights and footy finals parties.'

Opening cupboards and peering inside, Pierce slid up a large hatch opposite the oven, then gave a low whistle. 'Dumb waiter. I was wondering how they navigated the stairs with trays of food, or whether there's room to eat on this level. This must go up to—' he pointed overhead

'—somewhere in the saloon, I guess?' He stuck his head into the cavity, twisting to look up at the configuration of ropes above.

Sam nodded. 'Right on both counts. The pulley is in the passageway to the cabins, but the platform is missing. I figure the service was for paying guests only, because there's a more practical dining room down here, just behind the paddle wheels.'

His phone beeped, and he shook it impatiently. 'Nearly flat.'

'Use a proper torch next time,' Sam suggested.

'You'll bring me again?'

'I'm sure you can find the way back by yourself.' She pushed off the bench and made for the door, but her tone held a tease.

'I'm sure I don't want to,' he said, quietly enough that she could pretend not to hear, if she chose.

Instead, she turned back, letting her glance graze his before dropping it to the planked floor. 'I really have to go now,' she said softly.

What the hell was that supposed to mean? So much for reading her signals.

By the time he'd processed the thought, Sam had already turned and disappeared up the narrow stairs. He followed quickly.

Although they'd been in the mostly windowless lower deck for only a short time, the weather had turned yet again, with large clouds pushing away the sunshine that had broken through during their walk.

Sam crossed the gangplank, threaded beneath the willows, then strode briskly along the path.

Pierce got the feeling that she wasn't blowing him off but was genuinely running late. So he was more than happy to stretch his legs alongside her, enjoying the freshening breeze that curled around his neck and cleared his head. As they neared the inn, he realised he was still carrying her sweater. He started to offer it to her but ducked instinctively as a twittering swirl of tiny birds made for the shelter of the willows.

'Here comes the rain. Quick, follow the finches.' Sam dashed into the trees as the lowering cloud burst, heavy drops spattering down.

Beneath the protection of the canopy, she pulled her ponytail free again, laughing as she ran her hands through her damp hair. Her cheeks pinkened by the burst of cold, she leaned against the trunk of the willow, looking up through the branches. 'Spring showers,' she said with a dismissive roll of her eyes. 'Just like that, it stops. Wasn't worth the mad dash.' She started to push away from the rough grey bark, but paused. 'Oh, wait. Yes, it was.' Her eyes grew huge. 'Look at that.'

He dragged his gaze from her to look up through the green fronds. The rain had stopped but, driven by the erratic breeze, tiny droplets drifted in haphazard patterns—spiralling diamonds, floating directionless like a snow flurry.

Sam's hair fell in silky waves to her shoulders as she craned back. The sun peeked from behind the clouds to thread through the willows, turning her unusual eyes into opals, shot through with colour. 'I've never seen anything so beautiful,' she murmured.

He liked her. The knowledge settled in his gut, heavy, but in a reassuring way. He nodded acceptance. 'Neither have I.'

And then he kissed her.

18
Samantha

Sam was one hundred per cent certain the world was combusting, the sun imploding. Or exploding. The blood rushed to the surface of her skin, her entire body tingling. She felt alive, eager to be touched.

Pierce's lips on hers were firm and experienced, not demanding but . . . certain. He didn't try to push the kiss any further, just brought a hand up to cradle her cheek as his lips moved across hers in an utterly tantalising dance, a promise of what would come if she permitted it.

When she permitted it.

But then he pulled back.

And the world rushed into humiliating focus as she wondered whether he noticed that their noses had touched, whether her toothpaste was still fresh, whether she kissed weirdly, and whether Pierce was as horribly aware of her gulp for air as she was.

She hadn't kissed anyone for so long. Grant hadn't been demonstrative since they were teens, and she had eventually persuaded herself that she didn't care for overt touching and displays of affection.

Yet now, it was as if, during the entire morning, the air had been charging with electricity, the invisible current running through them, the energy steadily building. Waiting to explode in that moment. A combustion simultaneously startling and yet, in hindsight, completely predictable.

Pierce's hands dropped to her upper arms, then fell away altogether. His dark eyes unfathomable, shock settled into the creases and crags of his face. 'God, I'm sorry. I didn't mean to—'

Sam instinctively recoiled, her armour hardening.

When Grant wasn't accusing her of playing around or begging her not to leave him for someone else, he had made it clear that she could do neither because no one else would want her. Although she knew that was his manner of exerting control, the subversive conditioning was hard to set aside. 'Of course,' she said, her words clipped, her lips burning like acid.

Pierce screwed up his face in distaste. 'I'll, ah, I'll leave now.' He gestured toward the inn, across the endless paddock of short grass that bristled like tiny spears.

'Fine.' Her tone was as cold as the gust that now blew chill off the river, all hint of summer swallowed by the grey clouds.

~

Sam adjusted the egg-collecting apron around her waist. She caressed the warm, slightly textured, speckled brown egg for a moment, then carefully popped it into one of the thirty brightly coloured pockets stitched in tiers across the fabric. Tracey had made the floral gift for Ma's eighty-fifth, last year. At least, that was what Sam had heard: Grant had fallen ill just as they were about to leave for the family party, and she'd had to stay home with him.

He had made a remarkable recovery, well enough to sit up watching Foxtel with a medicinal Beam.

'It's nice to have you back here, Samantha,' Ma said as she shooed a broody ISA Brown from a nest in the compost pile.

'I was here just last week. And the one before,' Sam protested, trying to edge around having *that* conversation.

'I know that,' Ma said. 'I mean it's nice to have you come and go again. Like the old days.'

Previously, Sam had visited her grandparents on Mondays when the cafe was closed and Grant was at work. Over the last year or so, she had told herself it wasn't worth the chance of Grant discovering what she was doing while he was at work. But now the farm had returned to a comfortable kind of familiar, like sliding her foot into a well-worn ugg boot.

'Auntie Sassa!' The blonde child erupted from the four-door HiLux ute that pulled up in the yard behind the house. Her flashing legs competed with a toffee brown blur, the tiny dachshund apparently not hindered by his short legs as he dashed across the farmyard.

Sam whipped off the apron and passed it to Ma just before Keeley barrelled into her. 'Whoa there, short stuff.'

The memory of Grant's oppression, which made her willingly miss out on time with her almost six-year-old niece, had already become muddy, like pain through a morphine haze.

The difficulty of clarifying in her own mind just how it was that Grant had gained such control over her was one of the reasons she avoided answering questions about the end of her marriage. It was far easier to tell everyone that they'd simply grown apart. The lie was less embarrassing than the truth.

'I lost a toof,' Keeley lisped, craning back to look up at Sam.

'Oh no!' Sam gasped dramatically. 'Quick, let's look for it.' She dropped to her knees, sweeping her hand across the earth.

'Lucky you're not in the duck pen,' Ma chuckled.

Sam held up a filthy palm. 'May as well be.'

'It's not here, silly,' Keeley giggled.

'Keeley. Manners,' Jack said, coming up behind his step-daughter. 'Hi, Ma. Hey, Sam, nice to see you out here.'

Sam rolled her eyes and pushed to her feet. 'What's with you guys? I've come to the farm every Monday for weeks.'

'Yep. And it's never gonna be not nice,' Jack said simply. He had a knack for straight talk.

Ma had scooped up the rest of the eggs, the apron sitting far less comfortably around her middle, even though Tracey had put extra-long straps on it. 'Let me see that missing tooth, possum,' she said to Keeley.

Keeley bared her teeth, proudly showing off the gap. 'The toofs fairy will come tonight,' she announced importantly. 'Because I put the toof under my pillow. So you can't find it, Auntie Sassa. And you have poo on your hands.'

Sam grimaced, then waved her hands close to Keeley. 'And now you have it on your face!'

Keeley squealed and dashed toward the house through a patch of yellow capeweed. Sam took off in pursuit. She avoided being alone with her family as much as possible. She loved them, no question, but she had no answers for them.

She puffed as she reached the house, and her mind flashed to several hours earlier, when she'd been equally short of breath.

For a totally different reason.

A sharp pang of loss lanced through her. She pushed away the feeling: it wasn't possible to feel loss for something she'd never even had. And it was ridiculous to imagine Pierce had felt anything, done anything other than seize the opportunity of a snog. He'd probably been carried away by the festivities, the aura of romance that Sharna's wedding had created. She'd seen more than one hook-up at the inn over the course of the weekend.

Though it was a shame: Pierce was intelligent, and she'd loved his genuine interest in the riverboat. For a while there, it had seemed that they connected on some level. And then their lips had definitely connected, and he'd bolted like a rabbit. She gave a snort.

'Something you want to tell me?' Jack had caught up with her before she reached the steps onto the shaded verandah of the old farmhouse.

'Your hair needs cutting,' she answered. She always teased Jack about his shoulder-length surfie hair.

'About the weekend, I mean. Lucie's mum tells me you weren't in the kitchen being Cinderella all alone.' Jack held the screen door open for a moment, but then apparently decided that pursuing Sam was better than waiting for Ma and the dog, and let it bang shut.

Her stomach clenched. It was typical of this town that everyone was in everyone else's business. Heck, she gossiped often enough herself. 'So? Just some city friend of Gabrielle's who wanted to hide in there.'

'Some city *male* friend. Who was later seen wandering around, asking if anyone knew where you were.'

So Pierce had told the truth about not being able to find her? Not that she cared. 'So?'

Jack caught her arm before she turned into the kitchen. He lowered his voice. 'Just be c-careful this time, Sam, okay?'

Sam winced. When Jack stammered, he was upset. 'There's no *this time* about it, Jack. I'm not interested, he's not interested. I told you, he's Gabby's mate, nothing to do with me.' She bristled at his inference. 'And, not that it's any of your business, but I'm never not careful.'

Jack put an arm across the open doorway, stopping her from going further. 'You know I always thought Grant was a dick. And we both know what Dad was l-like.' Their father was the cause of Jack's stammer. 'I reckon there was a good chance Grant could go that way, and I just don't want to see you anywhere near that type again.'

He didn't know the half of it. Their father had been a bully, but he'd never, to Sam's knowledge, been manipulative like Grant. And her mother had the brains to have her own real estate, her own career, her own money. So she hadn't been left with nothing.

'I could never understand why you hooked up with him,' Jack added, glancing into the kitchen, checking for Keeley.

'Maybe because I was sick of looking after my little brother, and wanted someone to take care of me for a change!' she flared back. The years she had spent trying to protect Jack from their father's anger had been emotionally exhausting.

Jack nodded. 'Fair enough,' he said with the equanimity that always infuriated her. 'For the record, I wasn't judging you, sis.'

'Sure as hell sounded like it,' she muttered as Ma came in the back door.

'Nope. It's just you were always an odd match. Grant is—'

'Trash,' Ma said roundly.

'—and you're good people,' Jack added, making a joke of the term to disarm her.

Sam groaned. 'You're such a freaking hippie. I don't know how Lucie puts up with you.'

'She's the one who said that you've got both green and pink in your aura,' Jack teased, ducking the light slap she aimed at him.

'Pair of stoners,' Sam grumbled. She'd rather keep the argument going with Jack than acknowledge Ma's input. She headed into the kitchen to wash her hands in the steel sink. Keeley had already bounced into there, and was on Pops' knee. 'Keeley, show Pa-pa your tooth, and tell him who's coming to visit you tonight.'

'I have fairies, Pa-pa,' Keeley said earnestly.

'Furries? You want to take the shotgun?' Pops deliberately misunderstood.

'Fair-ees,' Keeley enunciated.

'Freeze? Get a jumper on then, girl.'

'Pa-pa, you're being mean,' Sam chided. Though she adored Keeley, and loved that her brother had found family, she knew it wasn't something she ever wanted for herself.

But what exactly did she want?

~

Sam held her breath as she sieved icing sugar over the cannoli. Bent almost double so that she was at eye level with the dessert, she tried to exert mental control over exactly where the soft snow landed. She'd already done the hard bit, rolling out the pastry thinly then winding it around the stainless-steel shell before frying. She had filled some adult-rated versions with chocolate-infused mascarpone, and Nutella for the younger customers.

'You'll never sell those here,' Christine observed as Sam slid the tray of cakes into the cabinet alongside the torta di riso she had made the previous day. 'Good Aussie customers like good Aussie food. Stick with the donuts, the Kitchener buns, vanilla slices and lamingtons.'

Sam bit her tongue, sorely tempted to point out that only the last of the four was an Australian creation—and even that was disputed by the Kiwis. 'I know the locals all have their favourites. But McCues has them well covered. I wanted to do something different.' What she *didn't* want to do was analyse just why it was Italian baking that had challenged her for the last six weeks, since *that* kiss. 'Besides, these are going gangbusters in the prepacks for the coach tours.' She had bought a stack of cardboard bento-style boxes, and packed a sweet treat into each section. The boxes sold for more than double the retail value of the cakes, and she ran out of stock each time the coaches came. It seemed that most customers preferred to just buy a selection than have to debate over which delicious item to choose in the cake cabinet.

There hadn't been many children on the expensive tours throughout the year, but the driver had given Sam a heads-up that the number of coaches after Christmas were to be doubled, with the expectation they'd be booked out for the school holidays. So Sam had devised confectionery bento boxes containing skewered sour worms and jelly snakes, along with a variety of cheesecake slices, which she created in rolls and decorated to look like sushi. Keeley was given permission to take a break from her parents' focus on organic and nutritious food, and put to work taste-testing. She declared the tiramisu rolls, made with strawberry jam from the crop on her mum and dad's property, her favourite.

'Well, yes, I have to say you are doing some good business there.' Christine sounded as close to approving as she ever came. She'd taken to helping behind the counter occasionally, when it wasn't too busy, although Sam suspected that she scared away as many customers as she sold to. The kids definitely didn't hang around as much when Christine was in charge. 'These Kitcheners are yesterday's, aren't they?' Without waiting for confirmation, she popped them into a box.

'Young Eric?' Sam asked with a knowing smile.

'And what of it?' Christine demanded.

'Nothing. Just . . . what is it with you two?' She had formed her own theory, although she wasn't too sure how it made her feel about Eric's presence.

'What on earth do you mean?' Christine snapped, flicking a Chux over the counter. 'I simply feel sorry for him. Old Timers is a terrible disease. Although,' she added darkly, 'some memories are better lost.'

Sam seized on the words and took a deep breath. She and Christine were as close to being friends as was ever likely, and she had to know what the future held for her. 'So . . . Young Eric's your ex, then?'

Christine's brow lowered, her lips tightening even further than usual.

Sam's heart beat faster. If Eric was Christine's ex and she still found it necessary to look after him, even in a haphazard fashion, did that mean Sam could never break free of Grant? She had hoped that the guilt she felt over leaving him would continue to lessen, and the thought of having to confront it for eternity loomed like a life sentence.

'My ex? I have no such thing,' Christine said icily. 'I've been married to Leslie since I was nineteen.'

Sam gasped. 'But you said—I thought you'd left a relationship. You know, like me.' She thumped her own chest too hard, desperate for the camaraderie and understanding she'd come to expect from Christine.

The older woman's expression softened, yet her chin trembled, as though with regret. 'Oh, no. That wasn't me. It was—' Inexplicably, she took a deep, shuddering breath. 'It was my niece, Kimberley. I'd say my favourite niece, but she was my only one.' Her attempt at a smile wavered, deep creases of pain running from her mouth to nostrils.

Sam's insides shrank. 'Was?' she almost whispered.

Christine gave an almost imperceptible nod. Then she took another deep breath, her chest visibly rising. She set the dishcloth aside, pulled the edges of her light cardigan together, and turned to face Sam. 'Her husband killed her. And their daughter. When they tried to leave Melbourne. To leave him.'

Sam's hand flew to her mouth. 'Oh my god!'

Christine's exhalation juddered through her chest and hung on the air, crystallised fragments of pain. 'You see why I said you needed to get out before you had children? Kimberley wouldn't listen to me, she wouldn't leave, she said that she had to make it work for the baby's sake.'

A tour bus pulled up outside the cafe, expelling air like a dragon.

Christine slipped out from behind the counter, in a rush to claim her nook in the window. But she turned back to Sam. Her voice was barely perceptible over the jangle of the door-bell. 'You're about the same age that Kimberley's daughter would have been now. I couldn't watch it happen again.'

Sam could barely concentrate on serving the customers. Her heart thudded painfully in her chest, her lungs contracted. Had she ever been in the kind of danger Christine predicted, or was that all in the other woman's imagination?

As she waited for the EFTPOS machine to connect, she brushed a hand up her arm, imagining the too-familiar feel of the tender bruises that Grant's grip, whether he was admonishing her or pleading with her, often left.

She shivered, chilled despite the summer air washing through the sunlit cafe each time the door opened. Christine was right. Although she'd believed she knew her husband intimately, Sam could never have foreseen how his nature would change over the course of their marriage. And that unreliability made him dangerous.

19

Pierce

Pierce had slammed it at the gym for the last few weeks, and put in far more hours than the brunch cafe needed. Eventually, he'd had to pull back there, as he was in danger of cutting staff simply so he'd have enough to do to keep himself distracted.

In any case, no amount of activity or self-inflicted pain chased the guilt over his behaviour out of his head. What the hell had he been thinking? It wasn't like him to shove himself in a woman's face.

He jabbed the sand-filled punching bag, grunting as the impact travelled from his gloved knuckles and up into his arm.

The thing was, he hadn't been thinking. He had acted on instinct—base, primal desire. He saw her, he liked her, he wanted her.

His left fist followed the right, muscles flexing and tensing as he swung into the leather in a strong cross, then swiped a hook from his right. He followed the moves with two swift, sharp uppercuts, the smack of knuckles against the leather forcing an explosion from his mouth each time.

The air he sucked back in between his gritted teeth was laden with the bitter odour of leather and sweat. He swiped a forearm across his dripping forehead, concentrating on the punching combinations in the hope the rhythm would shut his brain down for an hour. Get it off the loop that insisted it didn't matter how often he told himself that Sam had flirted back, that she had maybe even given him the come-on a couple of times, it still didn't equate to consent.

The confusion on her face when he'd stepped back made it clear she hadn't been expecting him to kiss her. And that made him barely any better than his bloody brother.

He stalked over to the uppercut bag mounted on the wall, and slammed out a volley of punches.

'Guess you've got the look for it, bro.'

The muscles across his shoulders sheeted into a tense raft, and he clenched his teeth to hold in a snarl. *Think of the devil and he appears*, Mum liked to say. He didn't want to turn around. One of his more minor reasons for taking up boxing had been that Dante wasn't into it: no doubt the sport required too much actual hard work and didn't provide enough steroid-enhanced photo ops for his brother's liking.

'The look, get it?' Dante indicated his nose, but tilted his head toward Pierce.

'Yeah, I got it.' His mashed nose was the result of a fight they'd had when Dante lived at his place, years earlier. Typically, Dante had figured everything that had been Pierce's was now his. At the time, Pierce had other ideas. He snorted: how many times was he going to be proved wrong on that one?

'Not still sore about that, bro?' Dante chortled.

'You were both adults. Up to you how you behave.' He used his teeth to unknot the laces on his gloves, then stuck his fists under his armpits to yank the leather off.

'Not what you said way back when, though, hey?'

'Yeah, well, maybe I thought you trying to get Jem hooked on your shit wasn't the best idea.' Even though Jem should have known better.

And maybe, by then, Pierce should have known better than to care what she did.

'Don't think that's all that bothered you, though, was it, bro?' Dante's trademark cocky grin faltered. 'Look, man, I owe you an apology for that one. I was a dick. Bygones now, hey?'

Dante was full of shit, as usual. 'It's a big city, Dan. What are you doing in this gym?' Pierce stalked across to the lat pulldown and grabbed his towel, slinging it around his neck.

'Mum's getting all antsy, wanting to know why you've not been around.'

'I've been around.' Trying to scrub away the simmering anger, he rubbed his face with the sweaty towel. He really should chuck it in the wash. 'I was there for Christmas. And had dinner with them last week.'

'So I heard. When I was out.' Dante took on his familiar stance, hands on his hips to bulk himself out. Pierce wondered if his brother ever saw the bantam rooster in the mirror. 'Mum means why haven't you been around for a family dinner. Or come to the tratt to eat?'

'Mum can speak for herself.' And she had. Volubly, swapping between Italian and Australian, her hands flying.

He had seen his parents half-a-dozen times over the last month and a half. And not one visit had been without rapid-fire recriminations—loud, fast and vehement enough to make him occasionally second-guess whether he actually had done them wrong. But he only had to think of his brother, swooping in to grab everything he'd worked toward, to get over that idea.

At first, Mum tried to make it sound like they all believed Pierce was taking a break from the trattoria, a well-deserved holiday, with bloody Dante being nice enough to step in to cover him. Then she moved on to mute denial that they had shoved him aside to save Dante. Instead, she talked about next week's menu and that day's customers, as though he and Dante worked side by side at the tratt. As though he still retained a shred of interest in the restaurant.

Dad didn't say a word, just pushed his food around the plate and changed the subject as soon as possible. Every time. He'd never known Dad to have any interest in football, current affairs or climate change, but they were sure as hell covering it all now.

In a way, it was good: the guilt he'd felt at leaving his parents in Dante's hands was tempered by his anger—no, his *frustration*—at their denial of their part in it. And that made it easier to move on. He wasn't going to hold onto the past any longer.

Pierce stuffed his gloves in his bag. 'Tell them I'll be round tomorrow.'

'I'm home tomorrow,' Dante said, his tone oddly somewhere between hopeful and apologetic.

'Suit yourself. The tratt is shut, so I'll come for dinner.'

'Cool, bro!' Dante slapped him heartily on the shoulder. 'Mum will be stoked.'

Maybe not when she found out the plan that had slowly grown in his mind, like dough proving on a warm windowsill.

~

He was right. Mum threw her flour-covered hands up and acted like he had lost his mind. '*No, non uscire di casa!*' she wailed.

'I don't live at home, Mum, so I can't be leaving,' he remarked mildly. Unless he was mistaken, his father looked relieved. Dad was never confrontational, he just wanted his wife and sons happy. This was the best way to achieve it for all of them. 'In any case, I'll be back and forth for a couple of months. Maybe until Easter.' He'd had to think long and hard about whether to rip the bandaid off and only tell them when he was on his way out the door, or ease them into acceptance. Right now, he regretted not simply sending a postcard.

'And the cafe?' Dad said.

'You know the breakfast business is quiet after Christmas and well into the New Year. I've been using the downtime to train Stefan. He's keen for as many extra hours as he can get, anyway.'

'And you're okay with that? Just walking away and letting him run it like it's his own place?' Dad was a firm believer in keeping business in the family. As he said many times, he'd take his last breath in the trattoria.

It took everything in Pierce not to point out that, thanks to that philosophy, he already had experience in walking away. 'I'm not really feeling it lately. I need to change things up.'

His mind was definitely somewhere else. At first, he'd thought the old river paddle-steamer was constantly in his thoughts because he tied it to Sam. But gradually he had realised the creaking timbers and dusty windows of the vessel had an odd magic of their own. A yearning quality. The more he thought about *Pelicanet*, exploring the boat in his mind, adding the areas he hadn't seen, even researching paddle-wheelers online to get an idea of the layout, the more it seemed that a piece of history was in danger of disappearing—and, having identified the risk, he would be responsible if he chose not to do anything about it.

'But if you go, who will make the bomboloni, the tiramisu?' Mum slapped a ball of dough on the counter.

'I can't do it all the time.' She managed to sound like she'd been picking up his slack.

'Dante will step up, I'm sure.' He rubbed the bridge of his nose. Okay, so telling himself he was the big man who could move on without glancing back apparently didn't extend to not taking a shot at his brother when the opportunity presented.

Dante nodded seriously, picking up a piece of the dough Mum had rolled. 'I tried biscotti this week. Right, Mum?'

Their mother waved him away crossly. '*Si, si*. But that is not cannoli and bomboloni and crostata, now is it?' She was doing a fantastic job of ignoring the fact that Pierce hadn't worked in the tratt for well over a month. 'Do the *patroni* want a biscuit for dessert? Of course not. Biscotti is for coffee.'

Pierce noted with relief that her mood had changed from devastated to irritated. Snappy Mum was much easier to deal with. He did actually feel sorry for Dante, though. Oddly, the flash of compassion made him feel better about himself: it was exhausting holding on to such intense dislike, no matter how warranted. 'How did the biscotti end up?'

Dante shot him a glance that flickered between suspicious and grateful. The lack of trust clearly went both ways. 'Not too bad. I did triple chocolate and nut.'

'Start with hazelnut. It's simple, classic. And don't use butter or oil. Eggs only, or they go soft.'

Dante nodded too eagerly. 'Done. And I was thinking, for Easter, I'd try a white and dark chocolate and nutmeg tiramisu. You know, mix it up, get with the season.'

Pierce was a purist, didn't like bastardised Italian food himself, but at least Dante seemed to be following up his usual hot air and big plans with some actual effort.

It wouldn't last long, though. Never did.

Still, not his problem, he reminded himself.

Mum finished running the cutter across the sheets of pasta with flamboyant, angry movements, and he picked up the tray of floured tagliatelli. 'You've got the sauce under control, Dan?' he asked as he slid the ribbons into the steaming, salted pot.

'*Vino bianco e funghi.*' Dante nodded toward the copper-based frypan.

Pierce hadn't needed to ask, he could smell the mushrooms in white wine, and it had taken everything in him not to cross the room, test the sauce, adjust it with a pinch of this, a dash of that. It hurt being back in the kitchen he had made his own, and seeing Dante banging around with his pans, his cleaver, his stuff. Yet the pain wasn't as sharp as he'd anticipated. Instead, he was buoyed by a sense of reprieve, a feeling of having escaped a lengthy sentence, rather than losing a legacy. Maybe it was because he was finally allowing himself to dream bigger than running a cafe and working at a family restaurant.

No, it was the realisation that he had options, that he could pursue whatever the hell he wanted in life now.

Whoever he wanted.

He turned away from the steaming pot, banging a colander into the sink as though the cymbal clash could banish the thought.

'You've made Mum happy,' Dad said quietly as a glass of red appeared at Pierce's elbow.

'By saying I'm leaving town?' he joked. It wasn't like Dad to do the serious stuff.

'By being here now. Relationships aren't easy, Pierce. You, of all people, know that. Family is no different. Everyone has needs. It's all about balancing. Sometimes we get it right, and sometimes we don't.'

Despite the unwanted reminder of his own history, it was probably as close to an apology as Dad would get.

'I get it, Dad,' he murmured as Mum loudly oversaw Dante's sauce making. 'You've done what you think you have to. But you know the risk in having Dante in here.'

Dad stared into his own wine glass. 'A father takes risks for his son. For both sons. They might be different risks, but they are still there.'

Pierce firmed his jaw belligerently. He knew what Dad was getting at: he had trusted Pierce to run the trattoria years ago, and that had been an act of faith. But that didn't make it right to lump him in the same category as Dante.

20

Samantha

Sam pulled the front of her light sweater away from her chest. What were the chances she was menopausal in her thirties? Because this sure felt like a hot flush.

And she was certain it had nothing to do with the fact that she'd just glanced up from the busy counter to realise Pierce was sitting at a table at the back of her cafe.

And even if it did have something to do with that, the surge of heat would only be because she was still furious at the way he'd hightailed it four months earlier.

She had spent enough time reliving their interactions to decide that the flirting had been fine. The kiss had been fine. Well, more than fine. But the way he'd cut and run? The more she stewed on it, the angrier she had become.

'Oh man, he could get *it*,' Tara murmured, angling her head toward Pierce.

'Tara!' The teen's assessment did nothing to cool Sam's flushed skin.

'Seriously,' Tara said, purging the steam wand on the coffee machine. Sam prayed the noise hid their conversation. 'It's not like he's technically *handsome*, you know. But he's got that kind of . . . dangerous vibe. Don't you reckon? Edgy but confident.'

'Can't say that I've noticed.' Sam's lips were tight as she carefully arranged microgreens, fresh from Jack's organic gardens, on the side of a croissant. She sprinkled the autumn violas, their delicate whiskered faces divided by yellow and violet petals, over the golden pastry.

'I mean, it's like he's rich and accidentally hot, but doesn't care,' Tara explained earnestly. Her voice brightened. 'You should hit that, Sam. If I was ten years older, I sure as heck would.'

'Maybe if I was twenty years less married,' Sam said.

'You're not even, anymore, are you?' Tara scoffed. 'I mean, you and Grant have been over, like, forever.'

For far longer than Tara or anyone else realised, Sam thought. She had lain awake so many nights trying to put an exact date on the end of their marriage. Regardless of what she came up with, the love affair had ended years before their separation began. 'I'm sure I'm not his type,' she said, bringing the conversation back to Pierce. 'And he's definitely not mine.'

'Not yours? What's not to like in that?' Tara pursued with irritating enthusiasm. 'And you're totally his type:

you should have seen him checking you out when he came in and you were busy on coffees.'

'Speaking of coffee, can you check the alternative milks, please.' Sam needed some space. 'And put the grinds out in the passageway for Jack to pick up for the gardens,' she called as Tara pulled a pouty face and turned away.

She blew out a long breath, trying to collect herself. Pierce had liked her well enough to flirt. And he'd liked her well enough to kiss her. But then, for whatever reason, he'd run like the devil was on his tail, and completely disappeared.

Pretending to focus on preparing a roasted pumpkin, caramelised onion and feta pide, she snuck a look at Pierce. Leaning back against the wall, legs stretched in front of him, ankles neatly crossed, he was checking out the menu—the undoubtedly tiny menu, given his restaurant background. Sam rubbed her hands down the front of the gingham apron Christine had gifted her for Christmas. Well, he could bloody well sit there until he got around to reading the sign Juz had carved for her.

Years back, before she could afford Tara, she found she couldn't wait tables and work the counter—though she was always happy to deliver the carefully plated dishes, to catch the flash of pleasure that invariably rewarded the sight of good food. So Juz had carved an elegant sign requesting orders be placed at the till.

Maybe Pierce hadn't noticed it.

Maybe Pierce could sit at his little table all bloody afternoon, for all she cared.

He glanced up and caught her eye, and she automatically returned his smile.

Well, it was only polite: she did have a business to run, after all. And she wasn't going to give a single thought to how those lips had so briefly felt against hers. It was so long ago, she could barely remember, anyway.

The doorbell pinged and Young Eric battered through the fly strips, which she really needed to take down now the weather had turned.

'Christine, could you serve, please? I'll take that order at the table.' She lifted her chin toward Pierce. 'Or it'll get crowded and awkward over here.' Eric was old and doddery, prone to mumbling and indecision. Plus, if she broke her rule and went over to Pierce, it would prevent him getting a good look at her dessert cabinet, perhaps noticing her new fascination with all things Italian.

Christine tutted, wiping her hands on the apron she had taken to wearing as her help behind the counter marginally increased. Evidently, the pink-checked gingham aprons all three of them wore were now the unofficial uniform for Ploughs and Pies. 'What are you in here for, you daft old bugger?' Christine called to Young Eric, her voice barnyard loud. 'I told you I'd bring something round.' She flapped her hands toward a table. 'Go on, take a seat, then. I'll give you something hot and you can wait there till I finish. Then I'll run you home.' She shook her head as she caught Sam's expression. 'He shouldn't be allowed out alone. I might have a word with Lucie. Perhaps she can organise him some help, like she did your grandparents.'

'She's bringing Keeley by after school in a few minutes,' Sam said as she wet her hands and smoothed her ponytail. 'I suppose you can't really ask her right now, though.'

Christine directed her snort toward Young Eric. 'Silly sod is deaf as a post. I could invite him to dance a naked tango with me, and he wouldn't react.'

Sam muffled her laughter as she rounded the end of the counter, pausing to rearrange the dome-covered display of chewy Italian almond biscuits.

Christine shot a shrewdly assessing glance at Pierce. 'Planning on filling your own dance card?'

'Him? No.' Sam jerked to a halt, trying to stop her gaze darting toward Pierce, hoping he hadn't heard Christine. Although the comment was obscure enough to be meaningless to him, surely? 'He's Gabrielle's friend. From the city. He doesn't know the counter ordering rule,' she gabbled.

'Oh, I remember him right enough,' Christine said. There seemed an unusual quirk of humour to her mouth as she plated a somewhat crisped leftover pie for Young Eric. 'I recall he was mooching around Sharna's ridiculous event looking for you.'

The hot flush raced back up Sam's neck.

Christine gave a supercilious smile. 'Of course, I let everyone think he had catering questions. We don't need them prying, do we?'

Sam rather liked the way Christine took shared responsibility for the Grant drama, making it a secret between the two of them. A burden divided. 'I don't think there'd be too much risk of that.' She flicked a hand down her front.

'Don't you dare,' Christine hissed, all good humour evaporated.

Sam lurched back a step. 'Dare what?'

'Don't you dare start putting yourself down. I've watched you change over the years, Samantha. There's no denying you were a little over-the-top when you were younger.' Nothing from Christine came without some kind of criticism, veiled if you were lucky. 'But now you've gone too far the other way. You still put on this confident front, but I can see it's an act.' Christine jabbed at the counter with enough force to make Sam wince. 'I know what that man did to you, how he's made you doubt yourself.'

'Shhh,' Sam hissed desperately. She couldn't believe Christine was choosing to say her piece now. It wasn't like there weren't plenty of quiet periods in the cafe when they could speak more freely.

'He shoved you in a little box, trying to contain and control you. You've broken out of his box: don't you go building one for yourself.'

Sam checked Tara was busy wrestling the coffee machine. 'It's hard,' she muttered unwillingly. 'It's like . . . he's still in my head. I'm so used to being what I think Grant wants, who he wants, that I don't know who I am anymore.'

'Then you need to find what makes you happy,' Christine said, apparently oblivious to the irony of the permanent lines of judgement in her sour face making 'happy' the last descriptor anyone would associate with her.

A soft gasp of sad laughter burst from Sam. 'I don't even know what that is. It used to be the cafe, but now that seems . . . I don't know. Pointless? I'm always worrying about whether I'm going to be able to keep it.' She pulled a face. 'Plus, there's no point spending the next five decades experimenting with baking when folk here really only want the basics. I think serving hot pies and cakes is pretty much going to be the cornerstone of the rest of my life.'

'Not if you don't want it to be,' Christine said firmly. 'If you don't love what you do, then don't do it. Life's short. I wish my niece had understood that. Don't waste time waiting for things to get better. *Make* them better.' She stared at Pierce, looking wholly disapproving despite her encouraging words. 'And you're more than good enough for the likes of him. So if you want to go over to take his order, you do just that. No excuses, no apologies.'

Feeling that she'd just been given instructions by the boss, Sam leaned over the counter to retrieve the order pad. She took a deep breath, and headed toward Pierce. What did she say to a guy who had kissed and run? Pretend it didn't happen?

That wasn't an option, so instead she mustered her anger, knowing she would never dare unleash it. But maybe it would protect her from further hurt.

Pierce's chair scraped as he quickly stood. 'Sam. I was coming to the counter to order.' He flicked a finger at the ornately carved sign.

'No need. I've got a minute,' she said stiffly. Damn it, he even smelled good. No sheepy lanolin or tractor grease on this guy. Just soap and aftershave. But a nice smell didn't make him less of a dick. 'What'll it be?'

'An apology.'

'What?' She almost dropped her pencil.

'I mean, I owe you an apology,' Pierce said smoothly.

'For . . . ?' She so desperately wanted him to say for running away.

'For kissing you.'

'Fabulous,' she said dryly.

'I mean, it was an accident.'

'That's what every girl wants to hear.' She screwed her lips together in a fair imitation of Christine's. He should have just bloody well let this go. Why had he come back here?

Pierce reached out to still the pencil she was drumming on her notepad. 'The timing was an accident. Not the kiss itself.'

'Yeah, that's not the least bit confusing.' His touch tingled through her. How was it that Pierce was calm and confident, while she caved like a souffle in a breeze?

He flashed her the quickest smile, then rubbed the bridge of his nose.

Her agitation stilled: she'd noticed him make that move a few times. Generally when he was uncertain.

'I mean, I don't regret the kiss. I regret that I didn't make sure it was okay with you first.'

Wow. She hadn't seen that coming.

'And that you clearly weren't into it.'

'I kiss that badly?' she blurted.

'Not at all. I just got the impression that I'd taken you by surprise.'

'Well, yeah, there was that,' she muttered, aware of Tara and Christine's gazes boring into her back. If they could hear, she didn't want them thinking that she'd wanted the kiss. Not when she had only been officially separated from Grant for a couple of months, at that stage. She shifted slightly, as though the set of her shoulders would warn them off. 'Look, don't worry about it. It was nothing. History now, anyway. Bygones.'

Pierce pinched the bridge of his nose again. 'That's not exactly what I hoped to hear.'

'You *want* me to be annoyed?' she said desperately.

'Not at all. But I also don't want you to think it was nothing. I want—' He glanced over her head, finally seeming to notice the breathless interest of the rest of the cafe. He lowered his voice. 'I want you to accept my apology for the way I kissed you. But know that I'm not sorry I kissed you. If that makes any kind of sense.'

'Yeah, sure,' she said, flustered. 'Whatever.' Grant used to trick her with his riddles—and then punish her if she misunderstood. 'Just give me your order, we close soon.' She jerked her head back toward the counter, as though that proved her point.

A frown creased Pierce's brow, and she realised with a sinking feeling that he wasn't letting this go. 'Can we maybe talk some more later? Somewhere with a bit more privacy. At Gabrielle's?'

'I'm not staying there anymore. Gabby needed the room,' she gabbled, trying to hide her confusion. 'Not that she'd ever say anything, but she's always fully booked, so I figured I'd better make space.' It should have been odd, moving back to Ma and Pops' after so many years away. Instead, unpacking her bags into the chipped oak wardrobes either side of the chimney breast in her old bedroom had a sense of homecoming. The comfortable, rundown farmhouse wrapped her in the same security and familiarity it had provided through her childhood. And Ma and Pops had been good about not asking after Grant. In fact, after the first couple of weeks, her family acted as though he had never existed, the last twenty years wiped away. And as Grant seemed to be sticking to his latest declaration about never wanting to see her again, it was good all round.

'Yeah, I've been out to the inn a few times. Gabrielle said you'd moved, but didn't say where you'd gone.'

That was typical of the town, Sam thought. Everyone loved a good gossip but closed ranks when an outsider was involved. Gabby had learned that fast, and played her part well.

'And by the time I finished out there and came into town,' Pierce continued, 'you were closed up.'

He hadn't tried too hard to catch her, if schmoozing with Gabby took priority. Sam kept her features unreadable. Showing no reaction was always safer.

'How about we catch up for dinner at the pub, then?' Pierce said.

Her insides shrivelled. A stranger in either of the local pubs was enough to attract attention: a stranger dining with her on a Friday night would probably make it into the monthly newsletter that the IGA, butcher and newsagent all distributed. She shook her head. 'You're definitely not country if you think there's anywhere around here you get any kind of privacy. But I'm delivering some cakes to Gabby later, for her high teas this weekend.' She waved behind her, toward the chilled cabinet, then, remembering her new baking lines, wished she hadn't directed his attention that way. It was better than having that dark gaze fixed unswervingly on her, though.

Technically, she didn't have to deliver the goods: Gabby always picked up her order. But if she didn't think fast, Tara and Christine were about to hear a whole lot more than they needed to. Or, worse, Pierce would leave town again before she'd got her head around exactly what he was saying. 'So I guess we could meet at the inn.'

'Sure. I'm staying there, so whenever suits you,' Pierce said easily.

'Fine. I'll get you a coffee now,' she said, trying to dial the flustered interaction back to professional.

Pierce glanced at his silver wristwatch. 'I'm going to have to take another raincheck on the drink. I've got some business in town.' His eyes met hers and he moved a hand between them, the draught creating an invisible thread linking them. 'But I wanted to sort this out first.'

Sam's heart pounded as if she had downed half-a-dozen lattes herself, making it difficult to process his words. But her mind caught on one phrase: what kind of business could a restaurateur have in sleepy little Settlers Bridge on a Friday afternoon?

21
Samantha

Pierce's palm pressed her hand, which still clutched her pencil like a weapon. Then he strode across the cafe toward the counter, pulling something from his pocket. As he walked, he folded whatever it was smaller and smaller. Barely breaking stride, he dumped it through the slot on top of the old Milo can Keeley had decorated with drawings of dogs and what she insisted was a fire engine.

Sam stayed where she was until the door banged shut behind him. Then she stormed over and prised the top off the Milo can. She fished out the wadded-up package. Although it wasn't clearly labelled, all the locals knew the tin was for donations for the local Country Fire Service unit. 'It's obviously not a flipping rubbish bin,' she snapped, hoping to head off any input from Christine or Tara. 'Why would you—oh.' The distinctive yellow note trembled in her hand.

She turned at the jangle of the doorbell. Twins, a boy and girl, burst through the door, closely followed by Roni and Tracey. The older woman's armful of bangles clicked and rattled as she tried to usher the children toward the play area in the corner of the cafe.

'It's like herding cats,' Roni groaned as she headed for the counter. She gave a low whistle at the yellow note Sam held over the donation tin. 'Fifty dollars? Who's the millionaire?'

'Gabby's friend,' Sam said quickly.

'*Sam's* friend,' Tara chirruped, barely hiding her giggle.

'Who can afford that kind of donation?' Roni said as she rifled in the large bag hung with kids' toys that she carried everywhere.

Sam frowned after Pierce. 'Buggered if I know.' For someone who had chucked in his job a few months back, Pierce sure seemed to flash the cash. Well, discreetly, anyway. He could have found a new job by now, she supposed. 'Probably someone who has enough money to buy lotto tickets without making a secret deal with god about how he'll donate half of the winnings to a worthy charity.'

Roni chuckled. 'You do that, too?'

'Along with wishing on shooting stars and chasing rainbows,' Sam said dryly. Her wishes had rarely been focused on money, though. They were more likely to be a plea for a do-over. A reset point, so she could live her life the way it should be lived. So she could chase ambitions and dare to have dreams, instead of being forced to keep quiet and small, shadowed and diminished by abuse and control. But perhaps now, thanks to Christine, in some tiny measure those dreams were starting to come true.

She moved behind the counter, talking fast so Tara and Christine wouldn't have a chance to share with Roni what they must have overheard. 'Let me guess. Two cappuccinos, one extra hot. Two small strawberry milkshakes and one sprinkle donut, cut in half?'

'I'll take care of that,' Tara said. 'Or even better, Christine can do it while I help you out with your makeup.' She seemed oblivious to Christine's glare.

'Makeup?' Sam said, confused.

Tara nodded emphatically. 'You can't meet him looking like that. I swear you've no clue about contouring.'

'I'd swear you're right,' Sam snapped back, her cheeks flushing. 'And I don't need to sit with my nose against a phone watching YouTube tutorials, either.'

'TikTok,' Tara corrected cheerfully. 'And you're right, you don't. Because I'll fix it for you.'

'What am I missing?' Roni asked, looking from Tara to Sam.

'Nothing you need to know,' Christine said frostily.

'Sam's got a date with Gabby's hot Italian dude,' Tara overshared.

'No, I don't,' Sam said stiffly. She really liked Roni, but Tracey, sitting only a few feet away, was a chatterbox. Though at the moment, no one could rival Tara, who apparently had zero filter. 'It's a meeting. A *private* meeting, Tara.'

Roni winced sympathetically as she dug out her purse. 'Ah, privacy in this town . . .'

Sam rolled her eyes and blew out a long breath. 'At least you've managed to keep some of your secrets.' Roni hadn't been particularly forthcoming about her history when she'd moved from Sydney.

Roni gave a peal of laughter. 'I think it's just that my family provides enough juicy gossip—' she shot a meaningful look at Christine '—that no one gives a thought to my past.'

That wasn't quite true. There was plenty of speculation about the circumstances of Roni's life as a foster kid interstate, but she stoically refused to be drawn on it.

'Why would one feel a need for privacy anyway?' Christine huffed.

Sam shot her a surprised look. Was Christine now intending to share the stories about Grant, or did she mean that Roni should be more forthcoming?

Christine gave a curt, decisive nod, her helmet of grey hair barely shifting. 'This town is a community. A community that cares for its own.'

'It can also be a very judgemental community,' Sam warned. A few months back, she would rarely have crossed Christine, but she had come to realise that, despite her overbearing attitude, the stern woman was often actually inviting comment.

'Judgement is merely a difference of opinion,' Christine said, looking genuinely puzzled at the notion that anyone would think differently. 'It's character building. Allows you to make your point and explain it. Imagine how boring it would be if we all thought and felt the same way.' She gestured at the cafe, filled with locals. 'But, when it comes down to it, most of us have known each other all of our lives. When you marry into Settlers Bridge, you slowly earn the right to become one of us.' Christine shot a meaningful glance at Roni, who looked shocked at the inclusivity from her arch nemesis.

'Like Taylor Hartmann?' Tara said, eager not to be left out of the conversation.

'Who has been here for more than a decade,' Christine added firmly, evidently determined to keep Roni in her place. 'Besides, the only way to keep a secret is never to have one, right, Veronica? Because eventually they all come out. You do far better to let your friends protect you.'

'But sometimes it's just not the right moment to share,' Sam said desperately. It had been months since she left Grant, but she still wasn't ready to deal with the stigma of being labelled a survivor of domestic abuse.

'You're right,' Roni said, reaching across the counter to give Sam's hand a quick squeeze. 'It's important to find the right moment for you. Anyway, let's change things up a bit today. Tara, what are you like with mad milkshakes? Can you come up with something wild for the twins?'

Tara's hand flew toward the syrup pumps. 'Any allergies?' Barely waiting for Roni to shake her head, she barrelled on. 'Peanut butter and jam? Vegemite caramel? How about lamington? Or a fairy bread shake?'

'Absolutely whatever,' Roni said, drawing her card from her purse.

'Just fix up for the hot drinks,' Sam interrupted, trying to convey her gratitude for the diversion. 'Trial milkshakes are on the house. If you come up with something awesome, Tars, maybe we'll add it to the menu.'

'You know, you should look at making this into a specialty milk bar,' Tara said. 'Can you imagine the after-school crowd?'

'Worth thinking about,' Sam said absently. As Roni headed over to join her children and Tracey, she took over the coffee machine. Christine would never touch the steamy monster. Focused on tempering the milk to silky perfection, she didn't look up at the door chime. 'Be right with you, love,' she called. As she turned off the steam wand, she realised a customer was standing near the machine, rather than at the counter. 'Oh, Hayley!' She broke into a grin as she recognised one of the Murray Bridge netballers. 'Long time, no see. How have you been?'

'Not bad,' Hayley said with a tight smile.

'Still playing?' Sam dipped her chin at Hayley's fingers drumming the counter. Before every game they had to display their hands so the umpire could check their nails didn't extend beyond their fingertips.

'What? Oh.' Hayley glanced down at her short, square clipped nails. 'No, not at the moment.'

'Coffee?' Sam tapped the machine, wondering at Hayley's unusual awkwardness.

'Sure. Make it two. Flat white, and a decaf for me.' Her hand moved protectively to her stomach, and Sam recognised the small pregnant bump.

'What do you want here?' Christine's angry tone sliced through the comforting aroma of pastry and sugary treats.

Hayley's glance slewed toward Christine, and she took a step back from the counter, making room for another customer.

Sam froze, her chest tightening. After not seeing Grant for months, she had let her guard down. Now, the sight of him sent tremors of shock through her.

Grant shot her a smile that twenty years back would have turned her knees to water. 'Hey, Sammie. How have you been?'

How had she been? Stressed, scarred, frightened, powerless, lonely, angry. A gamut of emotions, and not one of them good.

For a fraction of a second, she wondered if perhaps that meant she actually missed her husband. But then the other emotions of the previous months tumbled back in: the relief at the sense of freedom, the wonder and optimism she dared feel at the prospect of a new life. Above all, the validation of being, at least in some respects, finally in charge of her own destiny. And there were those other feelings, the barely permissible ones that Pierce stirred within her: giddiness, anticipation, hope . . . along with a sense of guilt that she would even consider allowing herself to experience such things.

'Fine,' she managed.

'Good, good.' Grant wasn't listening. He had ignored Christine, but now scanned the cafe. 'Look, I was thinking, we should really get our shit sorted, right?'

Having left the house with only her clothes, almost every message she'd sent him over the last few months had suggested they do exactly that—but it was typical of Grant to claim any practical suggestion as his own. She had learned long ago not to challenge him on it. 'Sure, what do you have in mind? I've made up a running sheet of what we own, and the values. I was thinking maybe we could just divide it up? No need to get lawyers involved.'

It felt like each of her customers was holding their breath to better hear the intimate details of her failure.

Christine evidently thought so as well. 'Tara, get those shakes out to the twins. And take the coffees.'

Grant used the diversion to let his gaze dart away from Sam. 'It's not that easy, Sam. All this—' he threw an arm wide '—is mine.'

Her tongue cleaved to the roof of her mouth. Momentarily, he had seemed so rational. 'Only on paper. You know that.' Tension wormed in her gut. He couldn't cheat her of everything.

'Whatever.' He waved off her argument. 'I can't afford to pay for this and the house.'

'You haven't been,' she pointed out, her fingertips whitening as she gripped the edge of the counter. Why the hell did he pick here, now, to have this discussion? The after-school crowd would pile in at any moment. 'You haven't been making any payments at all. They're eating into the redraw, remember?'

'Well, I would be making payments if I could,' he said sulkily. 'But the meatworks canned me because I had to take so much time off after you did a runner.' He tapped his forehead, intimating that she had messed with his mind, rather than that he'd lost his job due to any fault of his own. 'I'm going to have to sell the cafe.'

'You can't do that,' she whispered furiously. 'It's my job.'

Grant poked a rigid finger at her. 'I told you, it's not my problem to fund your *hobby* anymore. And I don't have a choice. I need the money.'

'But it's not worth selling,' she insisted. 'I explained that to you.' She flinched: Grant never took it well when she tried to educate him on some point. 'Sell the house, instead. I'll use my share of that to buy out your interest in the cafe.' It meant she would walk away with nothing but the remaining mortgage for the cafe, but at least she would have a job, something to build on.

'Why the hell should I give you half of everything I've worked for?' Grant snarled.

'It's not half of what you've worked for, it's my share of what *we* worked for,' Sam said, the memory of all the years of striving and saving, when they thought they were working toward something together, now hollow and pointless.

'Divorce laws in this country are bullshit,' Grant said, his pupils mere pinpricks. 'But none of its legally yours, anyway, so there's not a damn thing you can do about it.'

'We'll see about that,' Christine snapped, not even pretending not to listen.

Grant's jaw hardened, his shoulder hunched to block the older woman from his periphery and his ears. 'Besides, I'd have nowhere to bloody live if I sold the house. It's not like I can run home to my grandparents, is it?'

Insecurity writhed within Sam at the proof he'd known all along where to find her. Though he'd done nothing with the information, it was as though she'd been violated.

'There's another way.' Hayley moved closer to the counter, lowering her voice.

Sam cocked an eyebrow. She wasn't about to thank anyone for listening in to their private business, but if Hayley had something to add that would calm Grant down and maybe make him see logic for once, she was all ears.

Hayley pressed her lips together. Released them with a resounding pop. She glanced sideways at Grant. 'Sell the house.' She gave an ingratiating smile, confirming that she was on Sam's side. 'Like you said, Sam. Then Grant can move in with me, and we'll run the cafe. That way he has a job, plus the cash from the house to cover the shop mortgage.'

'Grant live with you?' Sam gasped, the surprise almost numbing her to the fact that even her friend was proposing she be booted out of the cafe. Her cafe. 'Why would you—' She broke off as she realised that Grant didn't share her astonishment. It was as though he'd heard the suggestion before. Her gaze slid to Hayley's rounded stomach. 'No!' The denial burst from her involuntarily. She had been questioning her right to have feelings toward anyone else, yet Grant had already . . . moved on? Not only moved on, but created the family he'd always demanded? She shouldn't be jealous—couldn't be jealous, his child wasn't something she wanted for herself. Still, she registered a tiny wash of bereavement, acknowledgment of an opportunity lost. 'You two are a thing?'

Hayley slammed her arms defensively across her belly. 'Well, you walked out on him. At least I waited until then. Not like Leanne.'

Leanne? Leanne who had been one of the 'friends' she had almost considered confiding in? Leanne who had laughingly agreed that Grant was a dick when he was drunk?

Grant turned on Hayley. 'I told you, I'm not running some damn cafe.'

Sam took an instinctive step back. Grant reacted violently when he felt cornered, even when he was trapped by his own wrongdoing. Did Hayley have any idea what she was getting herself into?

She couldn't risk making things worse for the other woman, so she chose to pretend she had missed the implication of Grant's previous infidelity, although her mind instantly wanted to replay every conversation she'd had with her supposed friend to work out exactly when Leanne had started cheating with Grant. But she would process that later. Right now, her head was spinning, and Sam could see everything she had strived for at the cafe slipping away from her—all her achievements, all her hard work.

Yet could that loss be the price of her freedom?

'I'll bloody well sell the lot,' Grant continued, his tone vindictive. 'The house, the cafe. And your bloody car. I haven't forgotten that you're driving around in that, even though it's in my name. I could just report it stolen to the cops, you know.'

'I'm sure they'll be pleased to reopen their file on you,' Christine lied calmly. 'But you go ahead and sell everything. And then you can give Samantha half the money from each property.'

Sam pressed her fingertips to her throbbing temples. 'There *isn't* any money in the cafe.' Why could no one understand that? 'Its value is in it being a job, producing an income. But selling it doesn't make any sense. No one is going to pay a decent amount for the business when they can set up over the road for next to nothing.'

'Doesn't have to make sense to you,' Grant sneered. 'I can do what I like. I'll offload the bloody place for squat just to be shot of it. I've already spoken with Claire in the real estate office. It's on the market the minute she processes the paperwork.'

Sam recognised his tone. It meant that he would follow through on his plan out of spite, even if he recognised the flaws.

She was screwed. Even if she somehow eventually got half the money from the house, with the cafe sold she would have no job, and therefore no income. She would have to start over, somewhere else.

As Grant and Hayley stormed from the cafe, tears pricked the back of Sam's eyes, the telltale tingle started high up in her nose. Damn it, she never cried.

'Oh, Sam.' Tara's eyes were huge. 'I'm so sorry. What a bastard.'

'Language, young lady,' Christine reproved. 'You're right, though. I disliked him enough before, but this?'

'Cheating and beating,' Tara observed glibly and Sam flinched. She had believed at least that part of how Grant treated her was a secret; hadn't realised that closing silent, unquestioning ranks around her wasn't ignorance, but the town's way of embracing and protecting her. That was what Christine had been trying to tell her, only moments earlier.

'Tara!' Christine said sharply. 'Watch your mouth. Samantha's Ma and Pops don't need to hear anything about that.'

Sam shook her head, trying to stop their words, but the action made her tears fall.

Leaving the twins to play in the children's area, Tracey and Roni quickly crossed the black-and-white squares of the lino-tiled floor. The four women clustered around Sam like Ma's bantams flocking for crumbs.

As Tracey patted her shoulder, Sam stammered through her tears, 'I can't believe I never even suspected. I mean, not just Hayley, but Leanne. And who else? How long have I not been enough for him? Was it because I couldn't give him children?' Wouldn't give him children.

Roni put a gentle hand on her forearm. 'I was fostered when I was a kid. Multiple times. So I know what it's like to be rejected. And—' she broke off, surveying the other women as though silently swearing them to secret '—I know what it is to be abused, and to wonder if maybe somehow I'd earned that abuse. I know what it's like to feel confused and powerless and ashamed. But, honestly, Sam, it's not your fault. If someone chooses to hurt you, the rot is in him, not you.'

Sam shook her head, accepting the piece of paper towel Christine proffered. 'It's not only that,' she sniffed into it, 'it's that I feel so bloody guilty.'

'Absolutely no reason for you to,' said Christine firmly. 'Like Veronica said, none of it is your fault.'

For Christine to actually agree with Roni on any point was something of a red-letter day. Yet, though her chest ached with the effort of controlling the tears that wrenched up from her guts, Sam forced herself to explain. 'Hayley doesn't know what she's getting into. If she did, she'd run a mile.' Part of her desperately wanted to keep the humiliating extent of Grant's abuse private, but was it even her secret to keep, now? 'I know I should warn her, I should tell her what Grant's like, what he'll become. But I just can't.'

'No woman will listen to the warning of an ex-wife,' Christine said. 'It's probably best if you leave it be for a few months, until the novelty of the relationship wears off for her. Then you can try your luck.'

Sam nodded, biting at the inside of her lips. The thing was, Grant played his part so well. It was hard to recognise manipulation when it was so neatly hidden beneath a veneer of caring. But she was coward enough to seize the excuse not to tackle Hayley yet.

'Besides,' Tara said pragmatically, 'she's moving on your man, isn't she? She doesn't deserve a bailout.'

Sam squeezed her nose with the paper towel. 'No, I owe her for that. She's basically my ticket out of the relationship. Grant was never going to let me go, but now he has someone else to focus on, he'll forget about me. I've been worrying for months that maybe it was my fault he spiralled, my fault he lost his car and then his job. But thanks to Hayley—and Leanne—I realise that, really, he'd left me long before I packed up and took off. And maybe he'll be better with a baby on the way.'

'He's not worth being sad about,' Christine said, acid in her tone.

Sam shook her head. 'I'm not crying because I'm sad. These are tears of happiness. Relief.' She heaved in a ragged breath, a huge weight leaving her chest with the outflow of air. 'Because now I know I'm truly free.'

22

Pierce

Pierce ran his palms against the sides of his head, though his hair was short enough not to need tidying. He huffed out a couple of breaths, as if he was about to go for a record deadlift. It wasn't like him to feel nervous, but Sam had given him a second chance and he was determined not to balls it up this time.

Before she spotted him in the cafe, Sam had been chatty and extroverted, greeting customers with bubbly enthusiasm. It was in direct contrast to the woman he'd met months earlier, who was careful with her choice of words, listening intently as though searching for a subtext in what he said. Briefly, he had wondered whether he'd mis-recalled their interactions, had imagined the thoughtful personality. But when Sam made her way to his table, he immediately found the intriguing woman he had spent too long thinking about.

The problem was that now it was vitally important she accept his apology.

From Gabrielle's riverfront cottage, on which he'd taken an open-ended lease, he saw Sam's car head down the dirt track to the dock, before taking the sharp hook onto the pristine white crushed-gravel driveway that swept up to the inn. It was a few hundred metres walk, which should give him time to get his brain in the game. Plus make it look like he hadn't rushed over to the inn the minute Sam arrived. Even though that's exactly what he was doing.

He deliberately slowed his pace, forcing himself to take in the scenery. In a burst of autumnal fury, the sun had swept over the high roof of the inn to sink in the lagoons beyond. The willows along the river were clothed in gold, the backdrop of the sunset-lit cliffs shades of honey and copper with the river a solid thread of silver stitching together the softly mottled tapestry.

Autumn might be a time of slowing and endings, but that's not how he felt. Instead, it seemed his life was just beginning. Anticipation surged through him at the thought of seeing Sam. Although she hadn't exactly accepted his apology, she hadn't cut him off either. At least he was in with a chance of making it right. Although, did his fixation on the hurt he might have caused Sam stem, in part, from a desire to ignore any unhealed wounds of his own?

Pierce pondered the thought as he strode across the grass, but then dismissed it: Sam was fascinating, and he wanted to get to know her better. Simple as that.

He entered the inn through the door that was marked *Gentlemen's Bar* in gilt lettering above the architrave. The centrepiece of the room was a massive red-gum slab bar, behind which Gabrielle kept a modest selection of top-shelf liquor.

Her hair loosed from its customary ponytail and skimming her shoulders, Sam had her back to him.

From behind the bar, Gabrielle lifted a cocktail glass in his direction. 'Just in time, Pierce. Friday night happy hour. I picked up my RSA certification, so I'm brushing up my mixology skills. You can be a cocktail guinea pig for me.'

'I'm not sure that responsible service of alcohol and doing a Tom Cruise quite mesh.'

'She lost me at guinea pig cocktail,' Sam said, with a slightly shy smile as she turned, holding up her glass. 'Now all I can see is a small furry body with a paper umbrella in my glass.'

His heart did a bizarre flip: she wasn't going to shoot him down. 'Must be strong if you're already seeing things.' Despite his deliberately slow stroll, Sam could only have been seated at the bar moments before he came in. Yet half her creamy drink was already gone. Dutch courage? 'Hit me with your best responsible service, then,' he said to Gabrielle as he slid onto a stool alongside Sam. 'What have you got?'

Gabrielle held up her phone. 'I've got Google. What's your poison? Sam's gone for a very ladylike pina colada.'

'You like walks in the rain, huh?' he joked. Colour bloomed across Sam's cheeks, and he could have bitten his tongue. He'd replayed their kiss often enough to recall every detail, including the soft rain that filtered through the leaves, the green canopy enclosing them like a snow globe filled with glitter.

Sam stared into the depths of her glass, then her lips lifted in a tiny smile. 'I am definitely not into yoga,' she said. 'Far too unco.'

His shoulders eased, but he figured it best not to labour the joke any further. 'Can you handle an espresso martini?' he asked Gabrielle, leaning his elbows on the glossy red-gum slab.

She held up a vodka bottle. 'Not enough caffeine in your day, Pierce? I swear, I've never known anyone throw it back like you do.'

As she measured out coffee liqueur, he let his gaze range the walls. In the corner to his right was an open fireplace, flanked by shelves of books, but every other wall held pictures and paintings. 'Love what you've got happening with the artwork in here, Gabrielle.'

'A couple of the oils are my own,' she said proudly. 'I find a bit of time during the down season to spend in the studio Hayden built me, across the courtyard.' She tilted her head toward the rear of the building.

'Not the photography, though? Cheers.' He toasted her with his glass, then lifted it to indicate a set of sepia photos on the wall behind Sam.

Gabrielle flicked a glance that way, though her focus was on her phone, her hand drifting across bottles as she chose ingredients. 'Oh, they're the floods. Sam's your girl for those details.'

'For some reason they're known locally as the fifty-year floods, but those are 1917, 1936 and 1956,' Sam said quickly, as though glossing over Gabrielle's statement, even though he wanted to investigate it: *Sam's your girl*. 'So there's a bit of an issue with the math.'

'Fair enough.' He peered at one of the photos, charmed to find the setting familiar, despite the passage of time. 'Is that the main street of Settlers Bridge?' The entire lower storey of the two magnificent stone pubs at the river end of the street were hidden by a grey swirl of water.

'Yep.' Sam slid off her stool and crossed to the photo. She had to stretch to tap it. 'That's the fifty-six flood, the big one. And there's my cafe, right here. You can see that was before the council made the gutters higher to protect the shops from future floods.'

'Can you imagine how terrifying a flash flood would be? A force of nature, completely unstoppable,' Pierce said, staring at the grainy image, envisaging the loss to the businesses as a wall of water rushed through the town.

Sam raked a hand through her hair, pushing it back as she shook her head. 'It wasn't a flash flood.' She paused, eyeing him cautiously as though checking his reaction. 'The water took a couple of years to come down the Darling from the big wet in the eastern states. From Wentworth, it all funnelled into the Murray, so the water level rose by the day down here. There was sandbagging and levees, but no stopping it.'

He gave a low whistle. 'You're not worried about the inn flooding, Gabrielle? That'd be an insurance nightmare. I guess these locks you were telling me about, Sam, are enough of a control?'

Sam lifted an eyebrow, as though surprised he remembered their conversation. 'Unfortunately, the locks and weirs are designed more to keep the water interstate when the river's low, rather than prevent flooding here. We've had a few big ones since the locks went in, but the fifty-six flood was the worst.'

'To be honest, I'd be more nervous about the snakes coming down than the water,' Gabrielle said with an exaggerated shudder. 'I'd be back in the city faster than any flash flood.'

'Snakes?'

Sam gave a chuckle. 'In the big flood, one of the dairy farmers downriver at Meningie reported killing more than a thousand tiger snakes that washed up on his flats. And people were digging them out of their cellars and houses, along with the black mud, for months.'

'Ah, the cellar. You said the one here was damaged by the flood?' Pierce tossed back the rest of his martini.

Sam nodded. 'The inn's slightly more elevated, and the river broader here than at Settlers Bridge, so the water didn't reach as high. But apparently the cellar turned into an indoor pool. Isn't that right, Gabby?'

Gabrielle nodded. 'It took weeks for the water to recede, then the mud had to be hauled out by the bucketful. Luckily, it didn't get high enough to damage the floors.' She stomped her foot on the boards, and he levered up to look over the bar.

To his surprise, Gabrielle was wearing well-polished farm boots—RM Williams, or something similar. He had rarely seen her not in heels, and certainly in nothing less than a fancy leather number. Of course, being Gabrielle, she still managed to rock a high-end country look. Sam, on the other hand, wore jeans, a fuzzy peach-coloured jumper and flat sneakers. With her bouncy blonde hair and fresh-scrubbed look, she appeared . . . wholesome.

Gabrielle lifted a tray of umbrella-decorated drinks. 'We're heading more into mulled wine weather, but I'm sure my guests won't complain about free samples. Sam, why don't you take Pierce down to the cellar and show him the other photos?'

'Photos?' He hadn't mentioned his interest in Sam to Gabrielle—at least, not too obviously—but she couldn't have been a better wingman even if he had.

'Of the floods.' Sam downed the rest of her drink, as though she needed fortification. 'Gabby unearthed a stack of old pictures and had them blown up and framed to decorate the walls down there. Because everyone decorates their cellar, right?' she teased.

'That one was more Sharna's idea,' Gabrielle called back as she headed into the adjacent room where the low buzz of conversation was occasionally punctuated by laughter.

'The cellar entrance is over here.' Sam waved. 'Through the old kitchen.'

'There's more than one?' As always, the word kitchen caught his attention. Although Sam had it anyway.

She led the way. 'The kitchen in the barn wing is a newish addition. The original one is tiny. Gabby uses it as a butler's pantry.' She indicated an unusually narrow plank door.

Pierce realised he would have to turn sideways to squeeze through. Which immediately made him think of Dante's unnecessary penchant for doing the same. He grimaced. 'Seems odd to put such tight access in a place this size.'

'There's an outside hatch.' Sam's voice echoed as she led the way down the stairs ahead of him. 'The drays would pull up to unload the kegs of beer there. And Gabby used it to get out some of the large pieces of furniture that had been stored down here.'

She smelled like sunshine and sugar, he realised. 'Guess the temperature would be stable, and perfect for storing wine.' Pierce forced himself to focus on practicalities as they reached the bottom of the stairs. Sam had flipped a switch at the top, bathing the large room in a dim, golden glow. He couldn't see her remarkable eyes, but the gloom made it permissible for him to move closer, as though the lack of light somehow also made it hard for him to hear.

Sam didn't step back, but nor did she meet his gaze for more than a fraction of a second. 'Gabby's put in a decent wine cellar. Well, she tells me it's decent, I don't know a thing about wine.' She gave a cute, dismissive lift of one shoulder.

Hell, he wanted to kiss her. It seemed pointless to drag up their previous kiss yet again, but he wasn't sure how to move beyond his mistake unless Sam made it clear he hadn't overstepped the boundaries.

She ran her tongue across her lips and tilted her head. For a wild moment he thought it was an invitation, but she flicked a hand to the left. 'The wine wall is that way. The photos are over here. Gabby installed some kind of fancy light so the glare doesn't reflect off the glass.'

He followed her across to the wall filled with enlargements of old photographs. No doubt they were fascinating. At least, they would be if he could fix his attention on them.

'I like this one best,' Sam said, tapping the gleaming timber frame around a sepia print of a side-wheeled paddle-steamer. It was moored at a dock busy with people and crowded with cargo, and the river behind was overhung with white clouds chugging from the funnels of passing boats. 'It's amazing how much life is packed into this single shot.'

'It's like a moment of time, preserved in amber,' he murmured. 'Or behind glass, in this case.'

She nodded, favouring him with a small smile—the ones he'd come to like best, the ones that seemed to say she got him and she liked that he got her. 'So evocative of when the river was the highway, crowded with vessels steaming up and down. The riverside communities would have been vibrant.' Her tone became wistful. 'I like to imagine the whistle of the boats echoing from the cliffs as they steamed into town. There would have been a sense of adventure and expectation in every arrival. People would have flocked to the wharf for news and to trade.' She screwed up her nose. 'Now we all sit in isolation, staring at our phone screens for updates rather than making human connections.'

'It's odd how some things can conjure what almost feels like a memory, isn't it?' he said. 'Some photos carry their sense of place right into your soul.'

'That's exactly it!' she said, reflexively reaching for him, her hand settling on his arm. 'Taylor Hartmann—she's the local doc—has a theory that some of us have an ancestral memory kind of thing happening. She said there's research that suggests memories can be built into our DNA, so we actually inherit some of our ancestors' experiences.' She gave a light laugh, waving her hand as though dismissing her own words. 'In any case, I like to think that's what draws me to the river. My family have always lived hereabouts.'

'From what I've seen of Settlers, you all have a lot more personal connection going on than happens in the city.'

'Yeah, I guess smaller communities are definitely better than the larger ones.' A frown creased her forehead. 'Well, in some ways.'

'Is that your paddle-wheeler?' he asked, knowing it wasn't, but seizing the excuse to reintroduce the subject as he surveyed the poster-sized photo. He felt he had an obligation to discuss his plans with Sam, almost as though he risked inadvertently stealing something.

The prow of the boat was crowded with waistcoat-wearing deckhands, some raising their caps or hats to the camera, others perched upon huge square blocks.

'*My* paddle-wheeler?' Sam snorted. 'I wish. Maybe I should work on that whole "possession is nine-tenths of the law" thing, and camp out there? Then Ant would have to let me claim her.' She tucked her hair behind her ear, giving him a better view of her profile. 'I haven't even been to see *Pelicanet* for weeks. Not since I moved out of here. I'm missing the river something awful.'

'I thought you'd still be near the river?' He managed to stop short of asking her address.

'Nope. Had to head inland a bit. Beggars can't be choosers, and all that. Besides, Wurruldi is the opposite direction to my grandparents' farm.' He seized that information and stored it for later. 'So it'd be a bit odd to just turn up here to wander along Gabby's riverfront to visit an old boat I don't own, wouldn't it?'

Pierce chuckled. 'You probably should have mentioned that before. Because that's exactly what I did. And I fell in love.'

Sam frowned, her blue eyes catching the light. He was fully aware of the double entendre in his words, and, yeah, it was a bit over the top. But he had to find a way to gauge her feelings. A way that didn't involve manhandling her or stealing a kiss.

She nodded at the photo. 'Well, then you'd probably know better than me that's not the sweet little *Pelicanet*. See how it's pulling two barges loaded with wool bales, as well as fully loaded on the front decks? Regardless of whether she was running on steam or after she was converted to diesel, poor *Peli* wouldn't have had the power to haul that much. I often wonder whether she was named because she's so ungainly. You know, she kind of looks like those pelicans we saw sitting on the tree stumps, the base too narrow for their bulk.'

'Or maybe the owners were going for something of a cygnet to a swan kind of thing?' he suggested, his arm brushing Sam's side as they contemplated the photograph. 'Perhaps they had big plans for improving her?' He silently congratulated himself on the lead-in. The conversation was going exactly where he needed it to.

'I think she's perfect the way she is,' Sam said with a slight frown.

Damn. That wasn't going to help sell his idea.

'Or at least,' Sam added, flicking him a glance, 'she *was* perfect, before a load of half-arsed attempts at renovations took away a lot of her original features. Poor thing really needs a rescue mission now.'

'Have you ever considered doing that?'

She gave a soft, sad laugh. 'I've never been in a position to do anything more than dream. And, for a long time, I didn't even dare do that.'

'Why?' Pierce asked, almost holding his breath. He was usually excellent at keeping his interest at a surface level, pretending to listen without ever wanting to actually hear. Never before had he experienced such a desire—no a *need*—to know something. The sudden change from humour to sadness in Sam's tone perfectly matched her enigmatic personality: one moment bubbly and extroverted, the next wary and uncertain. She was complex, and he wanted to unwrap her layers, discover her history, explore those dreams she didn't dare allow. Why would someone living an idyllic country existence seem so introspective, almost fearful, sometimes?

'Like the Facebook relationship status, it's complicated,' she replied, though he sensed she was trying to make light and deflect his questioning.

He frowned. 'I don't know if that's actually a thing, is it? Can't say I've ever seen it on anyone's account. Have you?'

Sam shook her head. 'Told you I don't even have social media, so I'm the last person to check that with.' She turned toward the wall of bottles. 'So you got your business in Settlers sorted, then?'

He was momentarily surprised she had caught his passing reference to business. But then, it was a small town: he was kidding himself thinking she didn't know what he was up to. It was a shame, though, as he had been hoping to surprise her. 'Hands have been shaken, money has changed accounts. Deal done. But, honestly, you were my most pressing item of business today. Sam, I want to know that it's all right between us. I want to know that kissing you was okay.' It was in his nature to lay it all out on the table, but he wasn't sure how she would respond.

Sam allowed her gaze to linger on him. 'It was definitely okay.'

He tried not to exhale his relief too loudly.

'But I don't want you to do it again.'

His gut plummeted. 'No?'

She shook her head, then took a step closer, the faint, sweet smell of baking wreathing them both. 'No. I don't like kissing. It's—' She made a quick, dismissive motion with one hand, a frown between her brows. 'It's too intimate.'

His fists clenched, resisting the rejection. 'Isn't that the whole idea?' he asked carefully.

'Okay, that probably wasn't the best word. It's too possessive. Possessive and meaningless. Whatever. I don't like it.' For the first time, her gaze held his unflinchingly. 'But I do want to have sex with you.'

When he finally found his voice, he managed to say, 'I like to think that the way I do it, that's also generally pretty intimate.'

Her breath was warm on his neck. 'Take it or leave it.'

Hell, he was only a man. Of course he was going to take it.

And maybe it would be enough.

23
Samantha

Electricity ran through Sam as Pierce's hands slid to cup her shoulder blades, his chest almost touching hers. She wanted him with a physical urgency she'd never before experienced. Rationally, she knew that it was a reaction to the revelation of Grant's infidelity, that she was subconsciously trying to make up for the time she had wasted being faithful to a man who didn't love her. Yet a part of her wanted to believe that it was more than that, that Pierce appealed to her on a deeper level. Her hands pressed against his torso—he felt warm and alive, and she wanted to melt into that embrace, to lose herself in the kiss she had forbidden.

Memory of their previous kiss had kept her awake enough nights. But she had no need of a relationship, no wish for entanglement when she had only just managed to escape. She would be mad to want anything more than pure physicality.

Wouldn't she?

Pierce's hand travelled to the nape of her neck, gently kneading as though, despite her demand, he refused to rush the moment. It was so very long since she had been touched like this. There was no reason for her not to give in to the desire that surged. Grant had moved on. She owed him nothing.

But, although this would be nothing more than a physical fling, she owed Pierce honesty.

'I'm married,' she blurted. 'Well, separated, actually.' Saying the words aloud carried an odd sensation of both freedom and shame. 'Is that an issue?' In the face of his silence, she rushed on. 'For more than six months.' She could just about see him counting back, working out how long ago they'd kissed, how taboo it had or hadn't been.

Pierce's caresses stilled, and he leaned back a little, so he could study her face. 'Not for me. But then, I'm not the one with a husband.'

'Me either, in a few more months.'

Pierce's fingertips trailed enticingly down her spine. Tacit proof of his acceptance. Relief washed through her. She very much wanted to do this, but there had been enough lies and secrets in her life that she needed him to understand exactly where she was coming from.

'I've leased one of Gabrielle's cottages on the riverfront. Shall we . . . ?' He cocked his head toward the stairs.

Although she appreciated his confidence, it perturbed her, because she didn't know where the boundary lay between self-assurance and control. Grant was confident, yet it was the arrogance of a bully that carried him.

'No.' There was something safe about this dim cellar, where they were locked away from prying eyes. 'Here. Right now.'

Pierce nodded. She liked that he didn't question her decision—or worse, make her question herself. 'Your call,' he said, as though he understood her need for control.

She closed the last inch between them, her breasts crushed against his chest. He dipped his head and she tensed, leaned back in his embrace. Did he already intend to break her rule, to kiss her?

Instead, his chin nudged aside her sweater, his lips finding the naked flesh of her shoulder and tracing to the hollow of her throat, his mouth deliciously hot. He bit her neck gently, soothing the burn with his tongue, then kissed a trail to her ear.

Gooseflesh erupted across her body. Her fingers clutched desperately at his sweater, his body solid beneath the fine knit.

His hands slipped from her waist to beneath the hem of her pullover. Hot, slightly abrasive as they slid up her feverish torso.

She moaned. Her fingers crept to the firmness of his chest as she melded her body to his.

Pierce broke away with a short, mirthless laugh. Capturing her wrists, he held her so she couldn't touch him. 'I'm sorry, Sam. I can't do this.'

'You can't?' Not even when she'd basically thrown herself at him?

He shook his head. 'I'm getting the impression that this is a one-time deal. Sex, nothing else.'

She frowned, wondering what his game was. Grant always manipulated her emotions, her thoughts, to the extent that even her reactions were shaped to what he wanted.

'And if you want to call it that way, that's one hundred per cent your right.' He took a step back. 'But it's not my thing. I want a whole lot more than that. Or at least, the opportunity to see if we have something more.'

'But a fling, no strings? Isn't that exactly what every guy wants?'

Pierce released her wrists. 'Not any *adult* with half a brain. I'm not a kid, hanging out for a screw.' He shoved his hands in his jeans pockets, and she resisted the urge to follow the movement, to see if his body gave lie to his words of disinterest. 'If I'm after a workout, I can go to the gym. What I can't get there is intelligent conversation. Someone who understands where I'm coming from. Maybe even gets where I'm headed.' He looked questioningly at her for a moment, almost earnest.

When she didn't speak, he leaned back, running a hand through his hair. But his jaw was hard, and she thought perhaps his nonchalance was feigned.

'Like I said, you do you. If all you're looking for is a quick tumble, tell me straight. And I'll walk away right now.'

She bit her lips together, hard enough to taste the faint iron tang of blood. Obviously, she had to tell him to walk away.

Yet the thought of that made her breath catch, the pain in her chest sharp. He had already disappeared once when he'd said he was staying. 'Do you have to walk right now?' she ventured. 'You've got business around here, don't you?' Sam needed time to think this through, to process what he seemed to be asking.

'I don't *have* to go anywhere in a hurry. Gabrielle's cottage is on an open-ended lease. And I've been known to get totally focused on work and forget everything else.' She got the impression that the slight bitterness in his tone wasn't directed at her. 'But the ball is in your court. I'm not going to harass or chase you. In fact, I'll never mention this again, once we leave here. But let me make it clear: I'm into you, Sam. It's up to you to let me know where you want this to go.'

She nodded, although she couldn't believe that he was investing her with that power, the control. Especially as she'd given in and glanced down at the hand in his pocket. And he was obviously more than a little interested in taking the physical relationship further.

But, despite his clarity, she needed time to get her head around the fact that what he wanted was more than a quick tumble in the hay. Or in Gabrielle's cellar. 'So, this business. You're setting up as my competition?' she asked, trying to turn the conversation, though her mind whirred frantically, navigating a choice she had never anticipated. 'Tractors and Tarts has been empty for so many years, it'll be nice to see something across the road from me.'

'Tractors and Tarts?'

She was relieved he didn't seem angry at her avoidance, demanding a response or insisting she comply. 'Well, I guess you can call it whatever you want,' she said. 'But I can guarantee that no one around here will call it anything but Tractors and Tarts. We're not big on change.'

'Ah, we have our wires crossed.' Pierce rubbed the side of his nose. 'I haven't bought in there. My deal wasn't even officially on the market.'

Sam's lungs squeezed, cold shock cooling her blood.

Grant hadn't been joking. He had sold her cafe.

And she'd just tried to screw the new owner.

24

Samantha

Although Sam rose at dawn, plenty early enough for the cafe's slightly later Saturday opening, Ma already had the washing strewn across the laundry floor by the time she'd showered and wandered through. Neat little mountains, sorted by colour.

Sam sighed. 'Ma, I wish you'd let me get you an automatic machine.' Not that she had the money. 'Or, like Lucie said, access your home care package to buy one. No one uses twin tubs anymore. You can't be hauling the wet clothes out of that and into the spinner all the time.' Her grandmother was shrinking, so small now that she tottered as she reached into the bottom of the tub to lift the sopping clothes out.

'I like doing it this way,' Ma snipped back. 'There's nothing wrong with the machine, and you know what Pops says—'

'Something astoundingly intelligent, I'm sure,' Pops cut in as he banged through the back door, adjusting his braces. He'd evidently been across the garden to the outside loo—or his library, as he called it. He was happy to spend an hour there, the door wide open regardless of the weather, looking over the scruffy garden as he read his latest novel.

'In your dreams,' Ma said. 'But *if it ain't broke, don't fix it* seems to fit this case.'

'Your back will be broke if you keep hauling this lot,' Sam muttered, trying to elbow in at the tub.

'No, no.' Ma stopped her. 'I'm just doing this load then I need to put in fresh water to rinse. Go and pop the kettle on while I empty and refill the tub.'

With the laundry plumbed to rainwater, it would take fifteen minutes for sufficient water to trickle through. 'That tank is running slower than ever,' Sam said.

'Rains are starting. Just need a decent shower, and we'll be right.'

'The next downpour will probably do the tank in,' Pops said glumly. 'It's leaking like a sieve. That epoxy bonder they sold me at the hardware doesn't work. Says the surface needs to be dry before I can apply it, but as it's a leak I'm fixing, how's it ever going to be dry?'

'Is a new rainwater tank something you can get on your home care package?' Sam asked, managing to snag the wooden spoon Ma used to hook clothes from the tub. She dug deep into the grey water, dragging sopping bed sheets across to the spin basket. 'Ask Lucie, she'll most likely know off the top of her head.'

'This one will see us out,' Ma said decisively.

'Ma,' Sam groaned, 'don't talk like that.' She needed her grandparents more than she could ever express. While life was far better than it had been only a few months ago, still she felt . . . adrift. And even more so with the discovery yesterday that Pierce had bought her business. She had made an excuse about needing to get back to the farm, and left straight after he dropped that bombshell. But last night, when she should have been trying to get her head around what it would mean for her, all she had been able to think about was his insistence that the ball was in her court.

'Samantha?' Ma said sharply. 'We've lost you in La La Land. Come on, into the kitchen with you. Let's have that coffee.'

'I've already got it on,' Pops called through the open doorway.

Where Ma was a teaspoon of Nescafe in boiling water coffee-maker, Pops had a trick of making it with equal amounts of hot milk and water, and added a generous spoonful of raw honey, which Jack collected from wild hives. Sam often had Pops' coffee in the place of a meal. Today, though, she picked up an old metal Quality Street chocolates tin she had left on the yellow Formica-topped kitchen counter the previous afternoon. 'I tried something new,' she said.

'You're always trying something new,' Pops said. 'I'm chuffed to see it. Though my diabetes, maybe not so much.'

'And my waistline, not so much,' Ma agreed. 'But as we've all got to go, may as well go happy.'

'Ma!' Sam groaned again.

'Samantha Schenscher,' Ma said, dropping her married name, 'since when have you not faced up to the truth?'

'Well, took her a while to cotton on that the bastard was no good,' Pops grumbled, setting the mugs on the table in a tidal wave of spillage.

God, she'd rather discuss her grandparents' mortality than have the conversation take this turn. Sam prised the lid from the tin and clanged it onto the table, dropping into her seat in the same moment, as though the noise and movement would deflect her grandparents.

'That's not the same.' Ma didn't notice the interruption. 'Sam thought she was doing the right thing by him; it just took her a little time to see the truth of who he was. Though I hear he outed himself on that score yesterday.'

Sam scowled at the chocolate tin lid, trying to recall which of the local tattletales had been in the cafe when Grant and Hayley came through. And had they also been there when she'd talked with Pierce? How much more had her grandmother heard?

'What's this?' Pops asked, as though he and Ma didn't spend all day discussing every little nuance of their grandkids' lives.

'That bugger—' Ma never swore '—has knocked up some poor girl. Going to ruin her life now, I suppose.'

'Someone should warn her what he's like.' Pops lowered creakily onto his vinyl-covered chair.

Sam flinched. She felt guilty enough without Pops putting her thoughts into words. 'I can't say anything to her,' she said defensively. 'Because maybe Grant was only a dick with me. Perhaps there's something about me that sets him off.' Or everything. She had lived with low-grade fear for so long, it was hard to pinpoint exactly how she managed to irritate, annoy and enrage her husband.

'Nonsense,' Ma said roundly. 'He's a piece of garbage, no two ways about it. Not that I'd mention it around your brother. He's all for teaching your ex a lesson or two, and getting more worked up about it every time I see him.'

'A lesson in what?' Sam said warily. She clenched her hands beneath the table. She didn't care about protecting Grant, but her grandparents didn't need to know the depraved depths her relationship had plumbed. 'People are allowed to simply get over each other, you know. No harm, no foul. It's nothing to do with Jack.'

Ma shrugged, though her arthritic shoulder barely moved. 'I suppose he just doesn't like to see his big sister unhappy. And you shoot him down every time he tries to talk to you. Anyway—' she dabbed up toast crumbs with her index finger and crumbled them back on to the table '—tell us more about this friend of Gabrielle's.'

And there it was. Proof that Settlers Bridge kept only the secrets it chose. Her grandparents had been protected from the truth of Grant's behaviour, but the grapevine had threaded them the news about Pierce in under twenty-four hours. Impressive, considering her grandparents hadn't even been into town.

Sam folded back the greaseproof paper from the top of the chocolate tin. 'Kourabiethes. Shortbread, Pops,' she added, catching his uncertain look at the crescent-shaped biscuits dusted with powdered sugar. She placed one on each of the mismatched saucers Ma had laid on the table. Opening a ziplock bag, she garnished each biscuit with a slice of dried orange and candied lemon. Her grandparents wouldn't appreciate the plating, but she couldn't help herself.

'Lemon flavoured?' Pops mumbled, spraying crumbs.

'This lot are, which is traditional. But I've experimented with orange, too, which I think is just as nice.'

'Traditional where?' Ma asked.

'Greece,' Sam replied, before realising she'd walked straight into the trap. She cast an imploring glance at her grandmother.

'Ah.' Ma inspected the biscuit far more closely than it needed, apparently oblivious to Sam's mute appeal. 'So Gabrielle's friend gave you the recipe?'

'He's Italian.'

'Hmm,' Pops grumbled, starting to put the remainder of his biscuit down. He changed his mind, stuffing it into his mouth, instead. Obviously, that was exile enough to make his disapproval clear. 'They're all the same, aren't they? Italian or Greek, same thing.'

'Hush.' Ma shot him *the look* that had worked on Sam and Jack for decades. 'Let Samantha speak.'

'Samantha wasn't planning to,' Sam said miserably.

'Of course you were,' Ma said, as though there was no option.

Really, Sam thought, much as she loved being back at the farm and making up for lost time with her grandparents, as soon as she got her finances sorted, she needed to look at renting somewhere.

Except, now the cafe had been sold, her finances were never going to be sorted.

The thoughts chased around in her head, a guinea pig on a wheel. And that mental image took her straight back to standing at Gabrielle's bar, sipping cocktails, the silver streaks in Pierce's hair glinting beneath the lights as his dark eyes fastened intently on hers.

Flustered, she waved her hands over the table, as though she could ward off the memories of what had come afterward. 'The recipe is from the internet. Like all my recipes.'

'I'm a big fan of the cobweb.' Ma nodded comfortably. 'I'd told Jack he could find a wife on there. Or on TV.'

'That wasn't where Lucie came from, though, was it?' her grandfather said, his brow furrowed.

His confusion gave Sam more cause for concern than Ma's scattiness, which she suspected was often deliberate. 'No, Pops. Lucie and Jack met because of his property, remember? Nothing to do with the internet or TV.'

'And that's not how you met this friend of Gabrielle's either, is it, Samantha?' Ma neatly brought the conversation back.

'That's exactly my point,' Sam said. 'He's a friend of *Gabby's*. He also happens to be a chef, so we simply have some shared interests to discuss.' Her cheeks flamed at the memory of yesterday's shared interest. She stirred her coffee, letting the teaspoon clank loudly. 'This honey is candied. Did Jack say where he got it? Lucie mentioned that if the bees are collecting from canola, the honey candies straight away.'

'We're not interested in discussing bees' bums,' Ma said. 'Tell us more about this chef.'

She said it almost as though they had a right to vet her interests. Which, Sam realised, might not be such a bad idea. She sighed, keeping her gaze on her coffee. 'He's just . . . different. I was going to say educated, but he reckons he dropped out of high school, too.'

'Hmm, the less we say about that, the better,' Ma cut in. Apparently that decision was still going to come back to bite Sam even decades after the event.

'But he's got . . . street smarts. You know what I mean?'

'Of course,' Ma said. 'That's exactly what you have. Natural ability. You could be anything you want to be.'

'No, I couldn't.' Sam sighed. Ma tended to wear rose-coloured glasses. 'My grades were never much chop, and it's not like there was much around here in the way of career options anyway.' Besides, at sixteen, all she'd *wanted* was Grant. She hadn't thought beyond the moment, to what it would take to create happiness for the future.

'I wasn't talking about the past.' Ma seemed to read her thoughts. 'You're free now. You can do whatever you want. Anyway, what is it that makes this fellow so smart?'

Ma's mention of freedom thrilled through Sam. Though the world wasn't quite as open to her as Ma seemed to think, she felt much less restricted than she had for years. 'He's really passionate about cooking. And into history. And he, well, he listens.'

'What's that?' Pops joked, cupping a hand behind his hearing aid.

Sam rolled her eyes, and Ma flapped at him to hush.

'Listens because you're saying what he wants to hear?' Ma said. 'They'll all do that.'

Sam shook her head. 'No. Just listens. Whatever I'm dribbling about. And, more surprisingly, he remembers what I've said. As though he's actually interested.' She took a swallow of coffee. She had to shut up, stop listing Pierce's virtues.

Especially when she wasn't interested in them.

Well, hadn't entirely decided if she was interested. 'Anyway,' she finished up hurriedly. 'Like I said, he's Gabby's friend, and we just have interests in common.'

'And he's nice?' Ma said, helping herself to another kourabiethes.

Sam snorted. 'You're asking *me*?'

'That *so-and-so* was just a hiccup,' Ma said, powdered sugar floating in the air. 'Forget about him.'

'A twenty-year hiccup,' Sam muttered.

'Well—' Ma licked her fingers '—drink a glass of water and hold your breath, then get back out there.'

Sam's stomach tensed. Like a pelican, was she too large for the nest, and her grandparents were trying to push her out? 'But I like it fine here.'

'I know you do, love. But you're only in your thirties, and Pops and I won't be here forever. You'll be lucky to get another fifteen years out of us.'

God, she hoped her grandparents had that long. She would be lost without them.

'And you're not going to stay on the farm. You need something more in your life.' Ma patted a sugar-dusted hand on Sam's. 'It's understandable that you're nervous about getting back out there.'

Sam closed her eyes and blew out an unsteady breath. If her grandmother, without knowing the extent of the mess of her relationship, was confident Sam could start over, who was she to argue? 'But the thing is, what if I find someone else exactly like Grant?'

'Lightning never strikes twice,' Pops put in.

'Hush, you,' Ma said irritably. 'Eat another biscuit. You go on, Sam.'

'Shouldn't I be playing it safe? Swearing off men so I don't make the same mistakes?' She knew what she was asking: she wanted Ma to tell her to go ahead, to give Pierce a chance even though she was barely out of a relationship and hardly knew him.

Ma lifted an open hand in question. 'They weren't your mistakes though, were they? You're not responsible for someone else's personality, their character faults. Grant simply wasn't destined to be your forever. Why shouldn't you put that behind you and move right on?'

'Because it's not normal?' she said, though her words held a hopeful, questioning inflection.

'Who says it's not normal? Trash gossip magazines? Dr Phil?' Ma demanded.

'Life is short, Samantha,' Pops said, unusually solemn. 'I don't want to see you get hurt again. But I don't want to see you hurt yourself, either. Marriage is important, but sometimes it doesn't work out. Stop beating yourself up over it.'

Sam winced at his unfortunate choice of words, again grateful that they didn't know the full story.

'Besides,' Pops continued, 'if you lock yourself away like a nun, you're letting that bas—' he broke off with a look at Ma. 'You're letting that *bugger* win. Why should he be the only one having any fun?'

She might as well lay all her cards on the table, Ma and Pops would hear the news soon enough. 'It's not that simple. Pierce seems nice—'

'Pierce? What sort of name is that?' Pops grumbled, having apparently moved on from his wisdom-giving.

'Paul,' Ma said warningly.

'But apparently he's bought Ploughs and Pies. So that makes him my boss. Or . . . I don't know what it makes him. He said he's got time off from his business in Adelaide, so maybe he intends to run the cafe himself.'

'Ah. Well, now, that is a pickle,' Ma said, with far too much glee. 'I read a story like that once. You know, a fling with the boss. An Annie Seaton, I think it was. I must get that book from the library again. But anyway, why would you sell Ploughs and Pies?'

'Not me. Grant. And this is real life, Ma.' Sam had never had time for stories. 'Even if I thought I liked him, how would that work?'

'Seems to me you're more worried about figuring out whether you like him than you are about losing the cafe,' Ma said.

'Yeah, well, no point focusing on stuff I have no control over, is there?' she snapped, stung by Ma's accuracy.

'Depends how much you like this Pierce,' Pops chimed in. 'Could be that you don't have any control over either of those things.'

'Pops!' she groaned. 'I barely know him.' Not that she'd had any such reservations the previous day. 'We've met a handful of times.' And kissed. And it wasn't her fault they hadn't taken it any further than that.

'Then time is a-wasting, girl. None of us are getting any younger. Nor are these biscuits getting any fresher.' Pops tapped one on his plate, as though dusting off the excess powdered sugar would help his diabetes. 'Might just have to eat them all now,' he said with a wink. 'Young Keeley's coming over tomorrow, so perhaps you'd better get another lot on for her after work.'

Sam pushed up from the table, glad for both the excuse and the warning. She wasn't about to let her brother corner her anywhere he could press for more information on Grant.

Her almost ex was history now, and there was no reason for Jack to get involved. 'I'll do the chickens on my way out.'

She let the fowl out of the coop and scattered grain on the sheet of corrugated iron Ma used to keep the feed out of the dirt. Then she sloshed over to the layer boxes, the mud that caked her cracked Redbacks announcing that the rains had arrived overnight. Despite the fresh sawdust in the boxes, the eggs were filthy. She grimaced. Just occasionally, suburban life—and clean eggs in cartons—trumped country living. But she knew her cakes tasted better for the home produce. And Roni was bringing her duck eggs today, because the cafe menu was going American this week. She had brownies on the list, and duck eggs guaranteed a fudgier texture.

After this week, she'd switch to recipes that were light on eggs, because the birds were stopping laying for the winter.

Or she wouldn't switch, because she wouldn't have a job, she realised, shaking her head at the utter inconceivability of such a momentous shift in her life. Although, maybe Lucie was right, perhaps life was affected by full moons or planets aligning or some such voodoo, considering how everything seemed to be in such a state of flux. Her husband, her house, her job.

And Pierce.

The thought of having to change career now, of even trying to imagine what else she might do, should put her right off seeing Pierce, considering he was the cause of that particular chaos. Yet the turmoil she felt when she thought of him wasn't related only to the business; instead of anger, her emotions were a wild rainbow mix of excitement, anticipation, nervousness and thrill at the idea of potential and challenge.

She fumbled in her pocket for a scrap of paper Lucie had given her a while back. She tended to ignore her sister-in-law's hippie ramblings, but for some reason she'd hung onto this one: a mantra Lucie swore was the most powerful in the universe.

Sam read the words aloud, trying to invest them with a degree of certainty, rather than imploring. '*I do not chase. I attract. What is meant for me will simply find me*.'

25

Pierce

He missed the smells of the commercial kitchen. Pierce inhaled the rich, familiar aroma of the trattoria: herbs, salami and the pungent overlay of garlic.

What he didn't miss was the monotony of seeing nothing but the same walls, day in and day out.

He had headed back to the city on Saturday afternoon to chase down some supplies, and took the opportunity to grab some more clothes from his apartment. There was plenty of storage in Gabrielle's cottage, and no point in him continually wearing the same paint- or varnish-splattered clothes when he had a cupboard full of wearable stuff here. Plus, his promise not to chase Sam didn't let him off the hook when it came to presentation: there was always a chance he'd run into her.

Hell, he hoped he'd run into her. Giving her space was going to be damn hard, even with the project keeping his mind busy from dawn till dusk.

He'd been surprised when he transited through the brunch cafe to access the stairs to his apartment. There was no pull, no desire to be back there. But then, the cafe had always been a means to an end. Though he had regulars, the customers were mostly business folk, in for a great coffee, or a quick breakfast bowl, and then on their way. There wasn't one whose surname he knew.

His apartment had been the same: he realised he'd not missed the austere, organised space. It had no heart, no soul. Didn't call to him the way that . . . the way that the river called to Sam.

And maybe now, to him.

Pierce wanted nothing more than to grab his gear, and head back out to Settlers Bridge. But it would be churlish not to go next door, check in with his folks. It had been almost a month since he'd seen them. Not long, really, but long enough, when the three of them had been accustomed to spending almost every day together.

As he stood in the trattoria kitchen—which seemed far larger than he recalled, after his recent work in confined spaces—Mum appeared from the storeroom. 'Pierce!' she shrieked, throwing her hands into the air. Fortunately, they were empty: Pierce suspected she would have flung aside anything she was carrying. 'Roberto! Pierce is home.'

'Mum.' He laughed, enfolding her in a bearhug. 'You do realise I'm only a bit more than an hour away, right? Settlers Bridge isn't exactly the ends of the earth.'

She reached up to slap his shoulder lightly. 'I'm not stupid. In fact, I am so not stupid that I know you're not in Settlers Bridge, and that this Wurruldi place is even further away.'

'Wow, barely. And I just figured Settlers is much easier for you to locate. You know, so you can head that way and maybe visit.' He needed to ease Mum into the idea that he had no plans to return to Adelaide.

'And when would we find time to do that?' Mum flashed back. 'Your father, he is so busy here now—'

'You realise you can't have it both ways, Rosa,' his father said dryly, coming into the kitchen from front of house. 'You can't complain that business is quiet, and also complain that we have no time. Pierce. Good to see you, son.' He shook Pierce's hand, but pulled him in for a one-armed hug.

This he had missed, Pierce realised. The closeness of his family. Querulous and garrulous, life was smaller without them.

'I'll complain about whatever I wish to,' Mum said.

'Which is it then, Dad?' Pierce asked. 'Run off your feet or quiet? You shouldn't have hit the winter lull yet.' He was shocked by how grey his father seemed. Obviously it hadn't happened in the few weeks he'd been gone, but it was more noticeable after an absence. Pierce took after his maternal grandfather, and was at peace with the streaks of silver that had appeared at thirty-five. But seeing it on his dad was . . . confronting. And it wasn't only Dad's hair: his skin was sallow, his face lined.

Mum, on the other hand, seemed to have a whole lot more pep. 'Sit,' she urged, flapping her hands at a stool pushed beneath the long counter. 'Have you been eating?' Not waiting for an answer, she started crossly banging at pots and pans, ladling out food already on the hob. 'No, of course you have not. You boys, neither of you has the sense you were born with. How much trouble is it to put food in your mouths? You're not infants, now, are you?'

He sat, knowing he'd never escape otherwise. For all Mum's concern, the intensely physical nature of his new project meant he worked up a hunger, and he, Gabrielle and Hayden ate together most nights, taking turns to cook: Italian on his night, French on Gabrielle's. Hayden laughingly limited his input to keeping the drinks topped up, after his offer to toss a couple of chops onto the barbecue had been shouted down.

'It's too quiet,' Dad said, pulling out a stool to sit knee-to-knee with Pierce. 'We're not even getting a full service on Friday or Saturday nights.'

'Well, the food's still good, so that's not your problem,' Pierce said, spooning thick soup into his mouth. 'You always made the best minestrone, Mum. I could pick yours blindfolded.'

'The secret is the broth,' she said proudly. 'But, of course, you know this.'

'Gabrielle makes something similar. A lot of her dishes are slow cooked.'

'Gabrielle, is it?' Mum said, her spoon raised as though poised to top up his bowl every mouthful he took.

He shook his head. 'Gabrielle is well and truly spoken for.'

Mum's shoulders slumped. 'I said to Dad, if you're staying away this long, it must be for a woman.'

'Or because you don't need me here anymore,' he couldn't resist muttering. Sure, he might not want to be here now, but that didn't take away the sting of being usurped. 'Speaking of, where's Dante?' His gut clenched: more than anything, he didn't want them to say that Dante had done his usual, got bored and disappeared. Because if his brother had left them in the lurch, Pierce knew it would fall back on him to rescue them.

And, for the first time, he had his own plans.

Dad pointed over his shoulder. 'Front of house. He is training a new girl.'

'You need more staff when you're not doing so well?' Pierce said in surprise.

'Not *more*. We lost two,' Mum said with a dark look at his father, as though it could somehow, by some wild stretch of the imagination, be Dad's fault. Pierce knew his father was a pushover to work with; he was the one everyone hit up for raises or time off. Pierce was the one who'd had to deal with staff discipline, although over recent years it hadn't been an issue, as he had amassed a dedicated team both at the tratt and the cafe. With a pang, he wondered who had gone: it was like losing a family member.

Well, like losing a *wanted* family member, he corrected himself, as Dante strode in. The sight of his brother shouldn't instantly get his hackles up: it wasn't like he hadn't expected to run into Dante. Nor like they hadn't managed to have the occasional civil meal together since Christmas. But there was always going to be that juvenile part of him that insisted Dante was his parents' favourite, despite Pierce devoting his life to his parents' dream.

'You're back, bro.' Dante grinned with his customary good humour.

'Nothing like stating the obvious,' he said dryly.

'Pierce,' Mum warned.

And just like that, it was as if he'd never left. Mum was plying him with food, Dad pounding the bench while discussing finances, and Dante proudly trying to tell him about his new hire, as though it was a good thing they needed to train someone up. Everyone seemed oblivious to the fact that he no longer cared.

No, that wasn't quite true: it wasn't that he didn't care, he still wanted the best for his parents. It was that the trattoria and cafe were no longer his sole focus. Those businesses had been set aside by a new passion.

Or two.

His family worked on rotation, one or two of them occasionally dashing out the front to deal with an early customer, as the other plied him with questions and facts.

Finally, he grabbed the opportunity when both of his parents were out of the kitchen. 'Dante, what the hell's the deal with this new hire?'

'She's great. No experience, but—'

'Not what I meant,' he cut in. 'I mean why is there a new hire? Bex and Paulo have been with us for years.'

Dante shrugged, his expression sullen. It always seemed to Pierce that his brother was only seconds away from shoving out his lower lip in a full sulk. 'It was probably time for them to move on then, wasn't it? They were both getting way too cocky.'

Alarm bells went off in Pierce's head. If he was smart, he'd ignore them: it wasn't his fight anymore. 'Cocky?'

'Didn't want to take direction. Figured they knew everything.'

'They do,' he ground out. 'Whose direction didn't they want to take? Let me guess, yours?'

'Right.' Dante thumped his own chest with a closed fist. 'Mine. The manager's.'

'Jesus, Dante, Mum and Dad can't afford to lose trained staff. You screw them over, and they're the ones who have to pick up the slack. They're supposed to be semi-retiring, not covering for your sorry arse. No wonder Dad's looking shafted.'

Dante fronted up to him, thrusting his pigeon chest out belligerently. 'You need to stand down, bro. You had your turn. I've got this under control. We're going to open an extra day, that'll make up the shortfall.'

Pierce stood his ground, his anger surging in response to Dante's aggression. 'That won't bloody work. You're up for extra wages and higher running expenses. That's exactly why we close on the slow days. Save unnecessary costs. Dad and I worked it out, we've got the takings and customer numbers noted for years. I can give you the hours of the day, the days of the week, the weeks of the year, that are not worth opening. I'm telling you, you don't need to reinvent the damn wheel, Dante, you've just got to stop screwing up every damn thing you stick your oar in.'

'And I'm telling you to fucking well back off!' Dante snarled. 'You've had your chance. You've been pissing in Mum and Dad's ears forever. Getting things done your way. Setting yourself up a nice little family business, all done with their money.'

'Bullshit,' Pierce bit out. 'We were getting things done the best way for the business.' Even though he deliberately stood over Dante, a small core within him acknowledged the truth of his brother's accusations. Mum and Dad had been easy to mould. They didn't have much vision, just knew they wanted to produce good food. They'd been happy to let him take the lead.

'Shame you just couldn't hang on to the happy family bit, isn't it?'

For the briefest second, Pierce thought Dante was gloating about having ousted him from the trattoria. Then he shook his head. 'Seriously? You're still on about Jem? Man, how many times do I have to tell you, I don't give a shit about that anymore.' He dropped his hand quickly, as he realised he'd been reflexively rubbing his broken nose.

'Yeah, well, maybe that was always your problem,' Dante goaded. 'You never cared as much about anything as you did about the business. Screwed yourself over there, didn't you?'

Pierce forced an easy shrug. 'Or did myself an enormous favour. It's a matter of perspective.'

'She was the best thing you ever had in your life,' Dante said angrily, jabbing a finger into Pierce's chest. 'And she walked out on you. You don't get to take a second shot. Not with her, and not here, either.'

'Man, you are so cooked. That's ancient history.' For him, at least. But the more he thought on it, the more he realised that Dante had been fixated on Jem since their fling, well over a decade ago. Maybe Jem had been his little brother's first true love. 'Whatever,' he said, suddenly weary of the whole conversation. 'You know what, Dan? You're right. It's your turn now. Winner takes all, do what you want.'

Dante did one of his unpredictable flips, his aggression dropping, his good humour restored. He blew out a long breath, as though he was relieved. 'So we're all good, bro?' he said eagerly.

Pierce shook his head. For god's sake, Dante was like a scolded labrador puppy, fluctuating between snarling and looking for a pat. He seemed unable to accept that their relationship was irretrievably broken, that blood didn't mean they had to get along. Pierce held up both hands in surrender. 'It is what it is. Just do right by Mum and Dad, and we're good enough.'

26
Samantha

Sam could tell from the fogged windows and rear tail-lights of Christine's SUV, parked in front of Ploughs and Pies as usual, that the older woman was waiting in the car with the heater on, rather than on the shop doorstep, which she generally did to highlight Sam's tardiness.

Uneasiness churned Sam's stomach: Christine didn't actually have a job in the cafe, but it had certainly become a large part of her life over the last few months. Whether she was sitting in her window seat doing craft or, as was more lately the case, commanding Tara behind the counter, Christine was there every day the cafe was open. Sam had to wonder what Christine had done with her time before they struck up their unlikely friendship. She was going to miss Christine when they no longer had opportunity to cross swords in the cafe, that was for sure. Perhaps they would team up for some of the CWA baking contests. Christine certainly had faith in her ability now.

Sam wound a fluffy scarf around her neck—for the weather, not because she needed it, like last year—and dashed through the drizzle to unlock the front door. A chilly gust greeted her, and she was yet again glad she'd not had to spend time camped out on the floor of the storeroom this autumn.

'Don't suppose the rain will last long enough for the seeding,' Christine said, close behind her and infallibly pessimistic.

'Probably not. But I love the way the pies smell as soon as it gets chilly, don't you? I was thinking we might do some hot desserts this year, like rhubarb crumble. Oh!' Old habits died hard; it didn't matter how many times she told herself there possibly wasn't going to be a *this year.* No time like the present to break the news to Christine, though.

Sam slung her bag on the counter, reaching up to take down the Saturday aprons for each of them. 'So Grant already got his wish.'

'As in?' Christine said, doubling the tie around her stick-figure waist.

'He's sold the cafe.'

'No, he hasn't.'

She had to grin at Christine's peremptory assertiveness. If Christine did not want something to be so, then it would not dare to be so. 'He has. Gabby's friend told me that he's bought it.'

'Then *your* new friend is a liar. Which is unfortunate, as it means we'd better write him off your list of possibilities.'

'He wasn't on any list and he's not a liar.' But she already doubted her assessment: historically, she hadn't done so well. 'I mean, why would he lie?'

'I'm sure I have no idea. But I spoke with Claire from the real estate down at the Overland yesterday evening, and she hasn't even listed it yet. Which isn't surprising as she's never terribly organised. The only surprise is that your good-for-nothing ex actually got around to putting the property on the market. I thought he was all hot air, trying to impress his new girlfriend.'

'Turn on the pie-warmers, please, Christine.' Sam busied herself prepping the coffee machine, trying to wrap her head around what Christine was telling her. 'Pierce said the papers were signed and money changed hands, or something to that effect.'

'Well, that proves it's a lie,' Christine said triumphantly. 'Why on earth would money change hands the moment he makes an offer? You know that's not how it works.'

Sam didn't know. Grant had never involved her in that side of their finances. 'That's definitely what he said.' Right before she had made a gabbled excuse about needing to get back to her grandparents, and practically bolted up the inn's stairs in a flustered display of athleticism her PE teachers would have believed her incapable of. 'I guess we'll find out the details today.'

Suddenly, she wasn't in such a rush for Pierce to come in.

No, she was. Because she knew that, in his self-assured style, he'd have an explanation.

'You want to be wary of anyone with too pat a story,' Christine cautioned.

Sam banged through into the storeroom, where McCues Bakery made their morning delivery through the side door with the key she had supplied. She hefted the plastic rack of baked goods and slammed it onto the counter. 'Just yesterday you were encouraging me to seize life,' she said, though her anger was based on her own confusion. Why had Pierce lied?

'Precisely. Life.' Christine said brusquely as she loaded the warmer. 'Enjoy having the freedom to make choices, but this time make sure that they allow you exactly that: life.'

Considering what had happened to Christine's niece, Sam knew Christine chose the word carefully. She retrieved another tray from the storeroom. This one was loaded with McCues dough creations: cream-filled donut stix, passionfruit logs, bee-stings and Kitchener buns. 'I'll walk down and see Claire before lunch,' she said. 'She's open half days on Saturday, isn't she?' But why would she bother? The fact that her almost ex had put the cafe on the market without her signature made it embarrassingly obvious that she had no control over their financial affairs. She'd be better off waiting for Pierce.

Except, wasn't that waiting for a man to direct her life?

She shook off the thoughts with a sense of relief as the doorbell tinged, even though they wouldn't turn the open sign around for fifteen minutes yet.

Young Eric shuffled in, his filthy old army surplus store greatcoat swinging around his gaunt frame. His hungry gaze locked on the cake cabinet Christine had begun to fill. He twisted an old, felted cap in his gnarled hands, his farm boots even more worn than Sam's. She felt a pang of guilt: she'd never truly paid attention to him before, or noticed how he was deteriorating. Lucky Christine was more aware than she was.

'I've told you I'll bring the food to you,' Christine said loudly. She dropped her voice only slightly to add to Sam, 'Honestly, we don't need his smell in here. I daresay he only washes once a year. I must chase Lucie down again.'

'It's all right,' Sam soothed. 'No one else will be in for a while.' She looked over the counter, trying to catch the old man's gaze. 'Sit down. I'll microwave you a pie so you can get something warm in your belly.'

Young Eric looked confused for a moment, then sank in an untidy heap on the nearest chair.

Sam heated a can of beans to go with the pie. 'It's not really a vegetable,' she said to Christine. 'But at least it's warm.'

'It'll do him just fine,' Christine said. 'Heat him a cup of milk, too. Coffee in the morning gives him indigestion. Not too hot, and make sure the sugar is off the table. He can have honey.'

Sam didn't point out the sugar loading in the desserts Christine took to Young Eric every few days.

As she took out the food and a container of utensils, she winced. Christine was right about Eric's aroma. She'd have a chat with Lucie tomorrow, when they dropped in at Ma and Pops'. See what services could be located to help the elderly guy.

She set the food down, noticing that Young Eric had a row of medals pinned to the incongruous suit jacket he customarily wore through winter. 'What are these for?' Sam asked brightly.

Young Eric didn't answer, so she repeated the question more loudly, although he'd been able to hear her offer of food well enough.

Eric fixed her with jaundiced eyes that made her wonder about his alcohol intake. Grant's eyes had been turning more yellow by the year, and she'd researched liver disease, although she had been too afraid to bring it up with him.

'Murder,' Eric mumbled. 'Murder medals.'

'Don't mind him.' Christine appeared by her side with the milk. 'He's a sorry old bugger.' She placed the mug on the table. 'Here you go, love,' her tone softened. 'Get that in you to warm up. It's going to get a whole lot colder before it gets warmer. I might get the girls at CWA to patchwork some extra rugs together for him,' she added to Sam. 'There's no point giving him anything fancy, it will all have to be burned.'

Sam cringed a little and moved back toward the counter, but Young Eric didn't seem to have heard.

Christine followed her. 'No matter how hard done by you feel, there's always someone to give you perspective, isn't there?' she murmured.

~

By the end of the week, Young Eric had become a fixture, often waiting beneath the hooded verandah for them to open up. Sam's self-confidence, however, was far less constant. Day by day, her assurance was slipping. Christine insisted she'd spoken to Claire multiple times, and there was no sale in the offing. Which, rather than reassuring her, left Sam in an odd kind of limbo. She had half persuaded herself she was done with the cafe, ready for something new. Though what that was, she had no idea—especially as the thrill of accomplishment when pulling some new dish out of the oven hadn't yet grown old. But worse than the unsettled way she felt was that Pierce had disappeared.

Well, not so much disappeared, as failed to appear. She supposed he was still out at Wurruldi, staying in Gabby's cottage. Maybe he had no reason to come into Settlers.

'Hey, Samantha.' The gravelly voice intruded on her meanderings, and Sam fumbled the microgreens she was dividing from the large bag Jack had dropped by. She'd found that, in winter when people weren't so keen on having salad alongside their pastry, a handful of the organically grown herbs made a great alternative.

'Pierce. Hi,' she stammered, automatically checking how much of an audience they had. Which was ridiculous: it wasn't like she was about to throw herself at him and demand to be ravished. Not again. 'I thought you must have gone back to the city.'

Pierce placed one hand on the counter, and she noted absently that it was paint speckled. 'Only briefly. Told you, I'm not clearing out in a hurry.'

She nodded, letting her gaze dance across him. Yep, he still looked good. 'I got that, but I thought you would have been keen to get started on your new project.' She waved a hand at the cafe.

Pierce looked confused. 'I am. I have.' He displayed the paint-covered hand as though it was proof of something. 'I was hoping you'd have come by Gabrielle's sometime so you could see.'

His tone made it seem that there was more to why he wanted her to head out to Wurruldi, but she was too confused to follow that thought. 'You're helping Gabrielle with something at the inn?'

His eyes crinkled in amusement, and she realised that he was enjoying her confusion. She scowled. Grant also did that, finding a cruel amusement in the game.

'I did consider asking Gabrielle for your number after you took off,' Pierce said. 'But decided that's not in the spirit of our . . . agreement.'

Her annoyance dropped like a shield, and she stared, lost for words. When he said it was up to her to make the next move, he really meant it.

'But I figured coming into a public place for my first decent coffee in a week isn't being pushy.' Although he sounded confident, he did cock his eyebrow in question.

'Of course not.' Her hand moved automatically to the coffee machine. 'But it's hardly a public place when you own it, is it?'

He frowned. 'Own it?'

She nodded. 'That's what you said last week.'

He spread his hands open, and she saw they were callused, as though Gabby had been working him hard. 'I didn't even realise that you had this place up for sale.'

'Yeah, so you said. That it wasn't officially on the market.' She was trying not to sound aggressive, but the exchange was doing her head in. Plus, she wanted to prove that Christine was wrong, that Pierce hadn't lied. Yet he seemed to be digging himself deeper into the hole with every word.

'My deal wasn't on the market,' Pierce said carefully. 'But it wasn't Ploughs and Pies. You're not selling up and leaving, are you?' He sounded concerned, leaning over the counter, his forehead furrowed.

'I'm not . . . In fact, if you've not bought the cafe, I have literally no idea what I'm doing,' she managed. It was hard to talk to him and at the same time replay their previous conversation, the one she'd run out on. Yet, now she thought about it, had she leapt to the conclusion that he'd bought Ploughs and Pies simply because Grant's threat was fresh in her mind? Pierce had never actually said anything about the cafe, had he? 'So,' she said slowly, 'what did you buy? I didn't think much else was up for sale around here.'

'Like I said, I was hoping you might have come out to Wurruldi during the week.'

She blinked at his quick change of subject. 'I was kind of waiting for you to come here.' The blush rose up her neck. 'You know, Gabrielle mentioned you have a coffee addiction. She does a nice French press, but it's not the same, is it?' She waved toward her machine, hoping to take the heat off herself. 'How do you take it? I don't think you've ever actually hung around long enough to have one.'

'Long black, thanks. And what do you recommend to eat?'

'Depends on your taste.'

He gave her a considering look. 'Something down to earth, not overly complicated. Maybe a touch sweet.'

They were back to playing with words, and she was so out of her depth. She just didn't have the experience.

'You'll want a croissant, then,' Christine interrupted the mild panic that fluttered in Sam's chest. 'Unless you're after something a little different. In which case, I would recommend Samantha,' she continued.

Sam almost choked on her inhale, spinning toward Christine. The older woman pinned her with as close to a benevolent smile as she ever managed. 'She's adept at slipping in somewhat unexpected elements.' She let the words hang far too long, then continued. 'I would suggest you try her orange polenta cake.'

'Yes, that one's nice,' Sam babbled. 'It's served with cinnamon honey and rosewater syrup. I was doing a bit of Moroccan kitchen-chair travelling this week. You know, to spice things up . . .' Her words trailed off as she recognised the unintended innuendo.

'Sugar *and* spice, huh?' Pierce said, his words lazy and amused. 'I'm up for almost anything you suggest.'

Yeah, *almost*. 'Take a seat.' She lifted her chin toward the table he'd occupied last time, though she was the one who needed to sit.

As Pierce moved away, she gripped the edge of the counter, pinching until her fingers turned white. Pierce said he wasn't in any rush to leave, but she couldn't risk trusting his mysterious business to keep him around forever.

The problem wasn't that she didn't want him, but that she didn't know how to allow herself to want him.

27

Pierce

Leaning against the stone wall of the riverside cottage, Pierce didn't even bother pretending not to be watching for Sam.

Gabrielle came out of her cottage a few metres along the grass-covered bank, winding a caramel shawl around her shoulders. He lifted a hand in greeting, and she hesitated, glancing across the grounds toward the inn as though she needed to be there. Then she strode toward him.

'Knocked off work already?' Her breath steamed as she spoke.

'Yep, early finish.' Gabrielle was one of few people who knew of his project. 'Sam's coming by after she closes up.'

'Ah, that'd explain your distant-but-intense expression,' she teased. 'I knew there was something going on between you two.'

'Nothing going on.'

Gabrielle stuck out her bottom lip.

'Which isn't to say that I don't want there to be,' he admitted.

'Is that so? Do tell,' Gabrielle urged with a lift of her arched brow. 'What does Sam say about this?'

'Not a whole lot,' he admitted. 'I've laid my cards on the table, straight up told her how I feel. She's thinking about it. At least, I *think* she's thinking about it,' he amended.

Gabrielle twisted her lips to one side, surveying him with something that looked disturbingly like sympathy. 'You know she's been burned, Pierce? It may take her some time to come around.'

'Burned how?'

Gabrielle simply shook her head. She could be infuriating like that.

'Well, I've let her know I'm in no hurry.' He gave a disparaging snort. 'Which isn't entirely true. It's killing me, but I suppose I should be glad she didn't just shoot me down out of hand.'

Gabrielle screwed up her face, watching him for a moment as though deciding what to share. 'Just take it easy with her, okay? Hayden's known them all his life, and he's concerned she's a lot more fragile than she lets on.'

He tensed. He had assumed Gabrielle's mention of Sam being burned was a reference to her having an ex, a situation which, in his experience, always came with baggage. But this sounded like something more. 'I'm not out for a quick tumble in the country hay, if that's what you mean.'

'I don't think there's any other kind of hay, is there?' Gabrielle smiled. 'And you're totally giving away that you're as city as they come: hay is horribly prickly to do any kind of tumbling in.'

He chuckled. 'Not even going to ask how you know.' It was fortunate she didn't ask exactly what he was looking for, though. Because he had no idea what the future looked like. But he figured that was something to work out with Sam, if she was interested. All he could do was be honest with her. But what kind of baggage was she carrying? 'What do you mean, she's fragile? Because of the ex? She told me she's been separated a few months.'

Gabrielle shook her head. 'Not my business to tell, Pierce. Sorry.'

'I thought small towns are supposed to be hotbeds of gossip?'

Gabrielle pulled her wrap tighter as a chill breeze rippled across the river. 'You thought right. But there's also something of a covenant: you have to be a local to be in the know. It's taken me a couple of years to earn my position just on the fringes.' She grinned. 'I'm not about to risk that. Not even for you. But Sam's . . .' She squinted across the gardens as she searched for the word. 'She's a really good person, you know? And she's straight up. She'll tell you if she thinks you have a right to know.' She nodded at the approaching car. 'This'll be for you, then.' Gabrielle started to walk toward the inn, but turned back. 'And Pierce? Good luck.'

His friends's farewell didn't do anything for his unusual insecurity, and—too late—he wished he'd pumped Hayden for more intel on the woman the stonemason had apparently known since forever. He pushed off the cottage wall as Sam pulled up in her car.

The moment she stepped from the vehicle, laughing as her hair whipped across her face, his doubts vanished. She'd come. That was proof enough that she was prepared to give him a chance.

He had to remember not to kiss her, though. Instead, he strode forward, wrapping her in a hug. Maybe took the opportunity to close his eyes and breathe in her scent of sugar and spice. Since the old biddy in the cafe had taken over their conversation, that's what would come to mind every time he thought of Sam: sugar and spice. She was sweet, but had hidden depths, nuances and surprises.

She returned his hug unstintingly, melding into him. Pierce hoped Gabrielle was right, that Sam would speak her mind, let him know exactly where he stood. Because this hug sure felt like it was leading somewhere.

She stayed in his embrace for longer than a close friend would, then stepped back. Her eyes watered in the breeze, her nose a little reddened. 'It's bloody freezing out here.' She took a deep breath, her gaze ranging over the lacy whitecaps decorating the river. 'So nice to be back, though. I mean . . .' She twisted her lips, seeming embarrassed. 'I know I was only here a week ago, but the river always feels like coming home.'

'There's that ancestral belonging you mentioned.'

Sam rested her gaze on him.

He had noticed she did that more frequently now, unlike when they'd first met a few months back.

And if she was looking at him, Pierce was sure as hell going to look back. 'I know it's cliched, and you'll have heard it from every guy you've ever met, but you have amazing eyes.'

She snorted. 'Every guy? I grew up here, you know, so I've known most of those guys since I was born. And I can tell you, amazing was not the word they were using back when we were playing four-square in the school yard.'

'Sucks for them they missed a good in, then,' he responded. 'And you can take the compliment like I'm the only guy to ever think of it.'

'If it makes you feel special.' She said the words lightly, with a laughing inflection, but the slight pause before Sam spoke suggested she chose them carefully. Arms crossed over her chest, she hunched deeper into the fluffy, rust-coloured jumper. 'All your flattery isn't going to keep me warm, though. What was it you wanted to show me?'

Gabrielle was right: Sam was direct. He liked that. It invited reciprocity. But this was too big to rush. 'Let's take a walk?' Pierce suggested, nodding toward the golden border of naked willow trees fringing the river. Kissed by the rain, each drooping, whip-like branch seemed to have been touched by Midas.

'Absolutely,' Sam said eagerly.

In unspoken accord, they followed the riverbank upstream, taking the same path they had months earlier.

'It looks different with the trees all bare, doesn't it?' Sam said after they had wandered some way in companionable silence. 'I just love it out here. It's like . . . like my heart beats slower. I can breathe deeper, my head is clearer.'

He walked closer than was necessary, their arms touching. She didn't move away. 'Different,' he agreed. 'Yet I'm not sure that it isn't more beautiful like this. It's as though all the fancy bits have been stripped away, what you see is what you get. Sculptural trees, stark cliffs. The eucalypts impossibly white and the river almost pewter. It's raw and striking.'

'You're right,' she said, a note of wonder in her tone. 'I didn't think anyone else would see it. You know, everyone's all about water sports and suntanning on the banks and fishing. But like this, it's . . . timeless. There's not a single thing in sight that gives any indication of *when* we are.' Sam shot him a slightly embarrassed look. 'If that makes any kind of sense. Just . . . sometimes, it would be nice to be able to rewind time, to choose where to start.'

'Perfect sense,' he agreed easily, although he felt she was talking about more than the pristine, unspoiled state of the river. Pierce gestured ahead. 'I guess *Pelicanet* is the only giveaway.'

'Ah, poor *Pelicanet*,' she said wistfully. 'She's so rundown. I suppose it's like carbon dating: easy enough to work out we are well past her era.'

'If she looked like she used to, we'd be lost in time.'

'That wouldn't necessarily be a bad thing. Imagine a life where you're not constantly striving, wondering whether you're at the point that you should be, judging everything by your perceived achievements, whether they make you happy or not.'

'Gabrielle has the right idea. She came here looking for her passion. And she sure found it.' He gestured back behind them, the inn far out of view.

'In more ways than one.' Sam grinned. 'I can't even imagine what her life must have been like in the city, she fits in so well here. And my brother's partner, Lucie: she's the same, she's found herself here.'

Everything Sam said seemed to prove he was on the right path, yet nerves still pounded in his chest. If he'd crossed a line, if she felt he'd interfered, trespassing where he wasn't wanted, she would shoot him down. Pierce could take the financial loss, walk away from the project and go back to his cafe. But he didn't want to walk away from Sam. Why was her business for sale? She'd not answered his question about whether she intended to leave the area. Was she seeking escape, as he was? Yet she loved the river, why would she go? And where? 'So what's the deal with your cafe?'

'I'm the last person you should ask. Apparently, my ex has it up for sale.'

That wasn't bad news—for him, at least. It meant their separation must be final. 'He wants to recoup his share?'

'Not really,' Sam said. 'More a case of him being a pain in the arse any way he can.' A frown flitted across her face, and she seemed to check herself. 'Plus, he'll have a baby to provide for in a few months.' Her voice hitched.

'Sorry. That must be shit.'

'Probably the worst of it is knowing what everyone will be thinking. They talk sympathetic, but really they're relieved, because if thirty per cent of marriages end in divorce, they now only have a twenty per cent risk, thanks to me.'

'That's a lot of math,' he remarked mildly.

'Mm. May have missed my calling. Though statistically, I think I've copped more than one for the team.'

He wasn't certain what she meant, and his instinct was to gloss over the obvious issues, to assure himself—and her—that she could move on from her ex. Who had clearly moved on. But harsh experience told him that life wasn't that simple. 'I guess the first step to forgiveness is realising the guy is a tosser who doesn't deserve your time.'

She grinned at his choice of words. 'I'm not sure that leads to forgiveness.'

'No. Maybe more like acceptance.'

She screwed up her face dubiously. 'I don't know if I'll ever get there.' Something in his expression must have given away the lurch in his gut her announcement caused because she rushed on. 'I mean, I can totally accept that we're over. After all, I was the one who bailed on him. What I don't know if I can accept is the way he . . . behaved.' Her face had clouded, memories darkening her eyes. 'Or that I wasted twenty years hoping for things to turn around.'

'Behaved?' he said softly. 'This other woman, you mean?'

Sam gave a derisive snort. 'Hayley? She's the least of my worries. Well, no, that's not true. I am worried about her. But for her own sake. Anyway, Grant's over and done with,' she said decisively, slicing a hand through the crisp air. 'Short answer is, I've got history.'

Sam sounded as though she was challenging him, testing whether he was going to be able to deal with that fact. He wasn't entirely sure where she had been going with the story about her ex, but he'd have to rewind that later, see if he could untangle it. 'The way I see it, you've got perspective.'

She chuckled. 'Yeah. Maybe that's how I'll refer to him from now on. Anyway, it's too nice out here to discuss that *perspective*. Are you ready for some more of my useless facts?'

'I'll take anything you give me.'

She measured him for a beat. A tiny smile lifted the corner of her lips. He thought she was going to say something, make it clear that she was interested. Instead, she pointed to three pelicans, sailing in stately style down the river. 'Flotilla.'

'Pardon?'

'On the river, a group of pelicans is a flotilla. In the air, they are a squadron, and on the ground, a battalion.'

'All very regimental. I wonder who on earth comes up with these collective names?'

'Someone smarter than me. But how cool is that?'

Her enthusiasm for small details, things that would have passed anyone else by, was infectious. 'Definitely way cool.' A kite spiralled lazily above the river. An arch of beige splashed through the chocolate of the underside of each wing, the fingertipped edges fluttered minutely as he maintained his place in the thermal. Suddenly the wings folded back and the bird dived, snatching a fish from the river. Dripping scales glinted in the watery sun. 'Reckon that's the same bird we saw last time?'

'Watch and see if he returns to the nest I showed you,' she said, almost as though testing him, seeing if he remembered. He had noticed her peculiar investment in that, as though she was unaccustomed to people paying attention to her words and thoughts.

The whistling kite let out a ululating call, the noise echoing from the cliffs. 'He's headed the wrong way.'

'Or the right way for him. He's small, so he's probably one of the previous year's fledges, setting up his own nest over there somewhere.'

'The kids don't move far from home? Must be nice for the parents. Or maybe not if fledges are like human teens.'

Samantha flinched, her face closing, and he cursed silently: he'd hit a nerve. Probably to do with the ex's new baby.

She jerked to a halt. 'No,' she gasped.

Following her line of vision, he recognised his oversight. Focused on what he wanted to achieve, he'd not noticed the impact his efforts of the last few weeks had on the area. Deep ruts scarred the track, the mud gouged where heavy items had been unloaded.

'*Pelicanet!*' Samantha surged ahead, plunging through the branches of the willows as though she could reach the boat more quickly than if she stuck to the track.

'Sam, wait. It's fine,' he called. He should have prepared her, instead of trying to surprise her. He had sworn Ant to secrecy and used contractors from Adelaide to rush the work through, hoping that Samantha wouldn't venture this way until he was ready.

Sam wasn't listening. She ducked and wove, heading for the derelict pier.

He didn't have to chase fast, though. She slammed to a halt on the edge of the wharf. '*Pelicanet*.' She whispered the name this time, and his gut coiled in apprehension.

He should have discussed it with her first. *Pelicanet* was her find. Her dream. Not his. At least, not his to start with. But then the boat, the history, the vision, had taken over his mind. The project had come to represent escape, new beginnings and unfettered opportunity.

Sam turned to him, her eyes glistening. 'Someone's bought her,' she said, her tone distraught. 'I wish Ant had let me know.' She gave a defeated shrug. 'Not that I could have done anything. But they'll take her away.'

He seized her upper arms, glad of the excuse for contact, even in the face of her distress. 'Sam, it's okay. I've leased her from Ant. She's not going anywhere. Well, not anywhere she shouldn't.'

She stared at him uncomprehendingly. 'Leased her? For what?'

He gently turned her back to face *Pelicanet*, realising she'd not taken in the details. 'I have an idea that I wanted to run by you, get your thoughts on.' Though, with the news of the impending sale of her cafe, maybe he needed to fine-tune those plans? 'But first, I needed to turn Ant's planned makeover into more of a restoration—he's cool with it, as long as he's getting rent. And he'd already sorted the heritage regulations permissions. A friend in the South Australian History Trust dug out photos of paddle-wheelers of a similar vintage and helped me source the correct shades of paint. *Pelicanet* is as close to an accurate restoration as I could manage, while still having her be functional.'

'Functional?' Sam repeated in a tone of wonder. 'Functional for what?' She took a few uncertain steps toward the boat, but then stopped. 'May I?'

He spread his hands wide in invitation. 'Key is in the same place as always.' Though the glass throughout the vessel was new, as were the locks, he'd put the key on the restored wooden lintel, just in case Sam ever came by while he wasn't there.

As she approached the gangplank—a broad sheet of reinforced marine ply, wide enough to allow disabled access and lacquered to match the rich burgundy tones of the deck, she paused again. She let go of the white rope threaded through upright posts either side of the gangplank, covering her mouth with her hand.

He realised she was trembling.

'She's so beautiful,' Sam whispered. 'She looks . . . she looks just like she did in my imagination. I never saw her as broken or battered, I just saw her potential. But you . . . you've brought her to life. You've rescued her, Pierce.'

She couldn't have chosen better words to make him happier. Not unless she wanted to say something positive about their relationship.

'I've made a start. Fortunately, Ant has kept all the marine compliance up to date, so basically what I've done is cosmetic. Come see.' He offered his hand on the pretext of urging her onboard.

'Wait, I want to drink all this in, first. She looks like new, but better.' Her gaze ranged across the upper level, where the windows around the captain's quarters were shaded by rich oak internal shutters. Samantha wouldn't have been able to see into that third storey from the dock, but he wanted to make certain it was his final surprise.

'I suspect she cost more than she did in her first incarnation, but it was worth it.' Not only because the vessel was now undeniably magnificent, but because Sam looked so happy. A slight flush, which Pierce didn't think came from the chill wind, brushed her cheeks, and her eyes sparkled, the avocado streak through the grey-blue echoing the river and sky. 'I was kind of worried, after I'd started, that I'd messed up.'

'How so?'

'I realised I could be treading on your toes. You know, messing with your dream, when I had no right.'

She gazed at him for a long moment. Then her fingers laced through his. 'It's nice that you'd even think about that. But my dream, if I'd dared have it, would always have been to see *Pelicanet* restored.'

'Ah, that's just it,' he said, crossing everything he had and sending up a swift prayer that his gamble would pay off. 'She's not exactly *restored*. Well, she is, but not original, I guess would be a better way of putting it.'

'I'm . . . intrigued?' Sam said cautiously.

Pierce kept firm hold of her hand, using the other to gesture. 'As you can see, the exterior is much the same, just tarted up. The structure was sound, so it was more a polish and paint, new windows, that kind of thing. But inside . . . that's where the magic is.'

'The magic is in how you kept this from me. No one keeps secrets in this town.' She winced, as though something had occurred to her. 'Actually, that's not true. Maybe it's more that everyone's secrets get discovered eventually.'

'Ant said it would've been harder to keep it quiet a couple of years back, that he used to see more of you round the place, but that you pretty much keep to yourself now.' He was probing again, trying to discover her secrets. He got that she was separated, and evidently the ex was something of a dick, as exes tended to be. But no one would give him any actual information. 'I reckon Ant is actually a little embarrassed by his impulse purchase, and doesn't really talk about *Pelicanet* around town.'

'Oh, you've definitely nailed that,' she laughed. 'I only found out *Pelicanet* is Ant's because he pays mooring fees to Gabby. Took me forever to get it out of her, though. When I bailed him up to ask if I could have a look around, I thought he was going to turn purple. Couldn't shush me up quick enough. I'm pretty sure only Gabby and Hamish, the guy who takes *Pelicanet* out every six months, know about her.'

'Worked in my favour, though. Ant used out-of-town tradies to keep her . . . seaworthy? Is that the right term for a riverboat? Anyway, she was sound. She *is* sound. Gabrielle is a bit dark on me, though. She wanted me to use local tradies to do the fit-out, particularly a cabinetmaker she introduced me to a while back.'

Sam nodded. 'Justin. He's more than just a cabinetmaker. He has mad skills with a chainsaw.'

'But I figured if I used anyone local there'd be too much risk of the secret getting out.' Pierce had guided her up the gangplank onto the side deck and around to the main door. He reached up to the lintel, and handed her the key.

She pushed it back toward him. 'I can't. She's yours now.'

'Not exactly,' he replied, apprehension coursing through him. This was where the whole thing could go irreparably wrong. 'That's what I need to speak with you about.'

28
Samantha

Biting her lip, Sam looked up at the tall man beside her. Pierce didn't understand what he'd done. He couldn't. It wasn't just that he'd rescued *Pelicanet*—that fact was too much for her to deal with right now—but that he'd listened to her dreams.

Heck, it wasn't only that, either. He had listened, followed through with something he thought would make her happy, and now he was actually worried about her feelings. He had no way of knowing how huge each of those things were, how much they meant.

And how much they terrified her, because it would be safer to persuade herself that all she felt toward him was gratitude.

Yet she knew that was a lie.

So she held his hand. Even though she wanted so much more than that.

Sam put the hand he had pressed the key into against her chest. 'You wouldn't believe how my heart is pounding right now.'

Pierce's gaze lingered on her hand, and she felt the flush mount her cheeks. Thank goodness for the chill breeze that skittered the odd autumnal gum leaf across the toes of her sneakers.

'Pounding in a good way?' Pierce sounded charmingly uncertain.

The hell with it. What was it Pops said? *Time is a-wasting.* 'In all kinds of good ways,' she said, nerves making the words more forceful than she had intended. She waved at the beautiful boat. 'This colour makes her look so much larger, don't you think?' Larger, smaller: it didn't matter what the heck she said, as long as she kept talking fast enough to cover the awkward moment.

It was difficult to see beyond the reflected river and trees in *Pelicanet*'s gleaming windows, but she could make out burgundy curtains drawn back to the edges of the frame. The colour matched the new stencil that ran along the upper edge of each level, a Roman wreath of leaves encircling a five-pointed, burgundy-edged star. She tapped the same symbol, rendered on the centre of the timber door. 'I can see the paddle wheel on the grey backdrop, but the star is . . . ?'

Pierce chuckled. 'It's actually a cogwheel. But, like you, I figured it kind of looks like a paddle wheel. And the whole thing seemed fitting because it's the emblem of Italy.' He pointed at the green leaf circlet. 'It's an olive branch on the left—for peace, of course—and oak on the right, for strength and dignity. And that's the *stella d'Italia* in the middle. The Star of Italy. The border is always deep red, same as the ribbon binding the branches, so it fit the heritage scheme perfectly.'

'*Repubblica Italiana*,' she read laboriously, grimacing at what she was certain would be her mispronunciation. She had noticed from the dock that the elegant burgundy fresco formed a picture frame for the three pale yellow levels of the boat. The paintwork was clean and fresh, the red-gum rails rubbed back and lacquered until they shone with a lustre to match the burgundy window trims. The wheel housing on the near side had been pared back to individual red-gum slats, exposing the giant paddles.

'*Repubblica Italiana*,' Pierce corrected, using a short vowel sound on the 'e'.

'It sounds much better when you say it,' she laughed, trying to slide the key into the shiny brass lock on the timber door.

Pierce reached across, closing his hand around her trembling fist.

Now, ridiculously, he had both of her hands in his grasp. And yet it seemed neither of them was in a hurry to let go.

Pierce tipped his head toward the doorway. 'After you. This has been the hardest secret I've ever kept. I don't know if I'm excited or terrified.'

That made two of them. Sam took a breath, and stepped over the weather seal.

'Oh my god,' she murmured. She gazed around, drinking in the sights greedily. 'Oh my god, she's beautiful.'

'Go in,' Pierce urged.

Sam shook her head, unwilling to step on the plush burgundy carpet that perfectly matched the exterior trim. The lower wall panels had been stripped back and oiled until the timber emitted a deep, golden glow, the grain and whorls dark highlights. Everywhere she looked, opulent fittings gleamed: burnished wall sconces and light switches, a brass rail where chairs would hit the wall.

Covered in velour to match the trim and carpet, a pair of ornately carved oak chairs sat at each of the fifteen tables, which were hidden beneath snowy linen. The setting closest to the port window sparkled with crystal glasses and the gleam of silver cutlery. Her heart beat faster at the suggested intimacy.

The dining room—for that was what the old saloon had unmistakably become—stretched all the way to the back of the boat. The poky cabins gone, an elegant bar with glasses hung above the polished bench; a range of spirits glowing on a high shelf took up half of the rear wall. Alongside, a glass door opened onto the rear deck. Without the partitioning of the cabins, the boat was more spacious than she had ever realised.

'Gabrielle chose the artwork for me,' Pierce said.

'You two must be close?' She tried to ignore the unexpected surge of jealousy that wasn't only because Gabrielle had evidently seen *Pelicanet*'s transformation first.

'More so now than we were in the city, I guess. She seems more . . . chill out here. In any case, I know nothing about art, but I knew what kind of feel I wanted *Pelicanet* to have. Something to evoke that bygone era you love to talk about. Gabrielle pulled a heap of stuff up on the internet that she thought might be what I was going for, then helped me source the right pieces. At least, I think she did, but if you'd prefer something else . . . ?'

Sam let her gaze linger on the paintings hung on the few walls that weren't windows overlooking the majesty of the river. It didn't matter that Gabrielle had suggested them, because Pierce had chosen them to fit what he believed she wanted. He had invested money, time and thought into rescuing *Pelicanet*. For her. Her heart suddenly full, she had no idea how to respond, short of bursting into tears. 'It's perfect . . . wow.' She shook her head. 'Folks around here will tell you I'm never lost for words. But you've managed it.'

'I take it that's a good wow, then?' Pierce's relief was obvious.

And then she did know how to respond. 'I can only think of one way I'd rather be shut up,' she said, turning so they stood close. She tipped her face up to his.

Pierce gazed down at her for a long moment. His fingers moved to tilt her chin a little higher. 'Yes?' he murmured.

'Yes,' she said, stretching up onto her toes to bring their lips closer.

He kissed her gently this time, nothing like that first kiss. This was more questioning. Tender and tempting.

'Okay?' he said as they finally broke apart, though his arms were still around her waist.

Sam understood that he was asking more than whether the kiss was okay. But she still couldn't bring herself to commit to anything in words. She had to somehow find approval in her own mind before she could wholeheartedly give it to him.

'More than okay.' She grinned, choosing to turn the question into a joke. 'But you've not told me exactly what you plan—wait. What's that smell?' The rich aroma of garlic and tomato had been initially hidden by the smell of fresh paint, lacquer and furnishings. Now it was enough to make her stomach rumble.

'I thought I'd take the kitchen renos for a spin, see if I could get the food up here quick enough on the dumb waiter for it to stay warm.' He drew her toward the table set for two, overlooking the river.

The rain had drifted in, hazing the view beyond the window. Grey sky, grey rain, grey river. The bleakness threw a curtain of privacy around them, secluding their cosy little world which, she realised, Pierce had found some way of heating. The increasingly cold, stark beauty outside enhanced the inside warmth; the opulent furnishings and fittings gleaming against the wintry chill, the aroma of good food and promise of better company all contributing to the growing glow deep inside her.

Determined not to focus on the stretch of the thin fabric of Pierce's jersey as he lifted a carved chair to clear the plush carpet, Sam chuckled. 'You went for the heavy ones in case of stormy seas?'

'Wanted to be prepared for anything. I don't expect this to be all smooth sailing.'

She knew he was talking about more than just the *Pelicanet*. 'Ma reckons the bumps are what makes life interesting.'

'Good way of looking at it. I'd like to meet her.'

'You will,' she said, suddenly certain. 'You wanted to see my fossil collection, remember?'

Pierce placed a hand in the small of her back, urging her to the seat. Although his touch sent a warm thrill through her, Sam shook her head. 'Beautiful as this looks, I want to see what you've done with the galley.' She grinned. 'Also, I'm figuring I might get to the food more quickly that way. It smells unbelievable.'

'I reckon you're probably the only woman in the world who'd rather stand in a poky kitchen than sit at a five-star dining set-up.'

'You're probably the only guy who has ever made a paddle-wheeler smell like this,' she countered, following him toward the narrow stairs to the lower deck, now stripped back to polished wood rather than the dank grey marine carpet. 'Anyway, tell me more about this five-star dining.'

'It was your idea,' Pierce called back over his shoulder.

She paused, halfway down the stairs. 'I don't think so.'

'You said that *Pelicanet d*eserved to be more than a floating bar. I got to talking with Gabrielle about her set-up at the inn, and she mentioned she was looking for "experiences", as she puts it, for her bed and breakfast guests. Anyway, I couldn't get you—' Pierce stopped outside the kitchen and sent her a slow smile '—and *Pelicanet* out of my head. You said it made no sense to be near the river but not *on* the river. And that Ant had intended to make *Pelicanet* into a floating pub. Those things kept going around in my brain, and eventually I figured a fine dining option for Gabrielle's customers would take the experience she offers that one step further.'

'So you're working with Gabby?' she asked.

'Sort of. But even though I've kept the dining exclusive, her guests won't fill the seats. So she's going to look into whether we can get interest from one of the coachlines to make this a destination. You know, something like the winery tours of the Barossa Valley: a day trip along the Murray with a fine dining event and cruise at the end.'

Pierce's plan immediately fired her imagination 'Why don't you try the operators of the Monarto Safari Park coaches?' she suggested. 'An evening cruise would be the perfect way to round out a day trip there.'

'Working in with an existing tour is a great idea.' Yet, standing in the narrow corridor, Pierce looked dubious. 'But I'm not so hot on kids. Shit—' He ran a hand through his hair. 'I don't mean I dislike them, you know, as a race. Just that they don't work in this kind of restaurant.'

A smile tweaked her lips at his fluster. 'It's okay. I don't have any.'

He nodded. 'Come into the galley, let me find something other than my foot to put into my mouth.'

'We seem to have a thing for inviting each other into confined spaces.' She brushed past him to enter between the swing doors, an unprecedented sense of control thrilling through her as Pierce impulsively reached for her.

'I had the kitchen stripped out, but reused the original benchtops.'

'You really IKEA'd it,' she said approvingly as she admired the streamlined fit-out.

'I've what, now?'

'Managed to squeeze everything into a small space.'

Pierce nodded. 'I'm sure you'd know how much more efficient a compact kitchen is, especially with limited staff. Which leads me nicely into what I wanted to talk with you about.' He turned on the gas burner, shifting a pot of rich, red sauce onto it. 'Pasta okay with you?'

'Perfect. That's what you wanted to talk about?'

'Nope.' He concentrated on shaving a block of parmigiano-reggiano onto a board, but his inexplicable apprehension charged the air like electricity. 'I don't want to be working in a confined space with just anyone, so I'm hoping you'll help me out. I've seen your plating skills and your desserts, and both are areas that I either don't like, or don't shine in. I think we would work well together.'

Sam stared at him. If he'd asked her to jump into bed with him, she would have been better prepared. 'You . . .

want me to work for you?' It was odd, when she'd spent days wondering whether he'd keep her on at the cafe—only to find that she had entirely the wrong end of that particular stick—to now have him offer her a different job.

'I want you to work *with* me.'

The rich aromas now sat heavy and nauseating in her gut. She shook her head reluctantly. 'That won't work.'

'Any particular reason why not?'

She wanted to believe it was disappointment that hardened Pierce's features. Not anger. 'Well, first, I've got my cafe. For the time being, anyway.'

'You'd rather stay there?'

'No,' she said, brutally honest with herself for the first time. 'That's over. Ended, and not in a way that's left the best taste in my mouth.' Anticipating his anger, she tried to make a joke, gesturing at the garlicy sauce. 'But it made me realise there's no point pretending to be any kind of team.'

Setting aside the peeler he'd used to shave the cheese, Pierce leaned against the counter, hands braced either side of his narrow hips. 'I'm not following you.'

His tone didn't hold the annoyance she expected, yet still her stomach knotted with dread. 'I don't . . .' She rubbed her throat nervously. 'I don't deal well with conflict.'

He lifted one shoulder. 'Conflict?'

She gestured at the galley. 'There'll be a "too many cooks spoil the broth" thing. We each have our own way of running a kitchen. Our own ideas about what to put on the menu, what to plate.'

'That's part of the challenge of getting a new venture off the ground. It'll be trial and error, but that just adds spice, right? We try stuff, see if it works. Discuss the outcome and find the balance.'

'*Discussions* have a nasty way of going south,' she said bitterly. Pierce's bemused expression made it clear that he didn't understand, and she blew out a tense breath, searching for the courage to risk his annoyance. 'I don't want to ruin things between us by creating an environment where we disagree.'

'You're afraid we'll argue?' he said, a frown creasing his forehead.

Sam stared at the floor as she tried to hide the tremble of her lips. She'd told Ma and Pops that she wouldn't be carrying her scars forward into a new relationship. Yet she'd been fooling herself: the memory of what Grant had done made the prospect of history repeating more terrifying than when she'd lived it.

'Sam,' Pierce said quietly, though his tone didn't hold the ominous quality of Grant's silences, when he'd sulk before unleashing on her. 'I'm Italian. Passionate by nature. I'm also ridiculously driven when it comes to work, to the extent that I can get unreasonable. So I guarantee that we won't always agree. But I expect you to fight for what you believe.'

'I won't fight.' Her breath hitched on the word as her survival instinct surged. She should back down, agree with whatever Pierce wanted. Then escape. Never return, either to Pierce or to *Pelicanet*. That would be safest.

But it would also break her.

Pierce was silent for so long, she eventually had to drag her gaze from the floor, her fists clenched in anticipation of his fury.

His gaze was steady on hers. 'I can't promise I won't argue. But it comes from passion, not from anger. And I want you to feel safe to do the same, because I swear, on my nonna's grave, that I will *never* hurt you.'

Sam shook her head. Was he honestly that naïve? Had he never been provoked enough to discover the truth? 'No one can control their temper one hundred per cent of the time. And then . . . things happen.'

'No,' he said flatly. 'We're intelligent beings who make choices. So things don't just *happen*. Not if you're with a man who knows his limits and when to walk away. A man who recognises the boundaries and holds himself accountable. A man who lives with morals and principles, and makes the choice to control his temper.'

Anger at Pierce's logic, which seemed to discredit her experience, flared. 'Doesn't every guy claim—and probably believe—those are his values, at least to start with? Until things get tough, and he wants to make his point and it's easier to do that with a smack than waste time talking?' She welcomed the surge of emotion: it had been too long since she'd dared allow herself to verbalise her thoughts.

'Sam, we're disagreeing right now.' Pierce said, still not making a move toward her. His posture was relaxed, his tone gentle. 'And that's fine. It's safe. But I'm not going to try to persuade you to work with me, or to convince you that you'll never be in danger from me. I'll wait for you to find your way. Right now, though,' he lightened his tone deliberately and flicked a finger toward the ceiling, 'I need you to see if this food arrives hot in the service lift. I don't like our chances of getting wait staff if they have to run laden plates up those stairs.'

29
Pierce

Sam's revelation had shocked him to the point where he couldn't think, couldn't speak.

He'd had to send her up to the dining room to give himself breathing space, swallow down the rank anger that crowded his throat. How the hell could a man lift a hand to a woman? Because he was pretty damn sure that's what she was telling him had happened.

By the time he followed her up to the dining room—a bottle of Aglianico and a plate of garlic bread in hand—Sam had unloaded the food lift of the two tureens of pasta and the white bowls he favoured for serving.

'Yum, this all looks amazing and smells even better,' she said.

Apparently, their discussion was closed. He'd noticed she seemed to compartmentalise, switching from wary and introspective to cheerful and open. Was that how she'd dealt with her husband's abuse?

Pierce shook the thought away, not trusting himself to speak calmly if he allowed it in his head. 'I wasn't sure what you like, or if you have allergies or anything. So this dish,' he tapped the bowl of multicoloured pasta in a creamy sauce, 'has a light walnut sauce. The other is a traditional amatriciana with black pepper and chilli.'

'You were sure I'd stay for dinner,' she teased, indicating the table.

'I was sure I hoped you would.'

'This garlic bread makes that a no-brainer. How is it both soft and crispy?'

'Chef's secret, but I'll share it with you. Butter, garlic and herbs on the bread. When the slice hits the griddle pan, invert a saucer over it. Only fry one side.'

'So effectively it's steamed? Brilliant. Do you butter both sides? And do you mince fresh garlic, or use the jar? Don't worry—' she waved her crust at him '—I'm not going to pinch your secrets. I'm never going to win Settlers Bridge over to anything more exotic than a pizza slice once a week. I just like to *know*, you know?'

It took an effort to stop himself from pointing out how easily she could indulge all of her cooking dreams. It seemed that wooing Sam meant he was going to have to learn patience.

He frowned. If Sam wanted to keep the cafe, maybe he should have a word with his accountant, see if he could swing it.

Yet, wouldn't that be an attempt to coerce her? He had to be careful not to forge ahead, *un toro in un negozio di porcellane*, as Mum said, evidently believing Italian gave the old adage about bulls and china shops more emphasis.

Pierce stood to ladle pasta from the serving bowl while Sam busied herself pouring the wine. When he sat, he raised a glass in toast.

She held up one hand to stop him from speaking. 'May I?' At his nod, she took a deep breath. 'To the man who possibly should have a suit of armour, given his apparent love of rescuing damsels in distress.' She waved airily at the room around them, but maybe *Pelicanet* wasn't all she was talking about.

He allowed himself a smile, a glimmer of hope easing the acid of his anger toward her husband. Sam had evidently taken the time to process what he'd said. Now she would decide whether his offer was worth taking a chance on. They seemed to have a pattern: he charged at things, whether it was kissing her, taking over *Pelicanet*, or rushing her into a new business venture. But Sam sat back, assessing the situation before committing.

Hopefully that made them a complimentary pair. 'To life.' He returned the toast. 'Which is all about conflict. And resolution. And maybe forgiveness.'

Sam's face shuttered. 'Some things shouldn't be forgiven.'

'Totally agree with you,' he said, cursing himself silently. 'But I meant that I'm still angling for forgiveness myself.' Despite their brief kiss, the hand-holding and banter, he still wasn't entirely sure where he stood on that score. He needed to remind her that she was driving her destiny. And his.

'Ah, yes, that,' Sam said, circling a damp finger around the edge of the crystal wine glass, so that it sang. 'Well, I don't give much for your chances of walking away, now that you've set this up—'

'I meant it.' Pierce reached across the table, laying his hand on hers. 'If I'm in your space, if I'm making you uncomfortable, I'll totally walk away. *Pelicanet* is only leased, there's nothing keeping me here. Nothing but hope, anyway.'

'I'd like—' She broke off to run her tongue over her lips, her gaze flicking to his, then away again. 'I'd like there to be more than hope keeping you here. But you understand, it's hard for me right now? I'm afraid to want anything, in case it turns out that I was wrong. Again. And I discover I've wished myself into another nightmare.'

'I'm sorry,' he said softly. 'I'd give anything to find a way to prove that you can trust me.'

She shook her head. 'I need to be able to trust *myself*. But I cocked it up so royally with Grant, I don't know how to get back to a place where I can rely on my own judgement.'

He had no advice to offer. His instinct was to take her in his arms, to promise that he could and would protect her. But Pierce knew that life didn't work that way—and also that it wasn't his right. Sam had to find herself, to be comfortable in her own skin before she could risk letting someone get close to her.

'Anyway,' she said, her tone lightening in what he'd come to recognise was a deliberate manoeuvre: instead of indulging her fears and anxiety, Sam overtalked them by adopting a bright, bubbly persona. 'You still have to explain to me what exactly is going on with sweet little *Pelicanet*. Though, I must say, she doesn't look so little anymore, with this area all opened up. Are you going to put in more tables?'

'Could, but I figure we will probably go for more of an exclusive experience.' He used the word 'we' very deliberately. Until Sam definitively told him otherwise, he was going to include her in this. 'Catering for thirty allows privacy for each table, plenty of room for the wait staff to move around without being intrusive. And it makes it easy on us in the galley. We can concentrate on having dishes that each look and taste amazing, instead of rushing to deep-fry three dozen schnitzels and two dozen butterfish, and serving them with a dollop of coleslaw.'

'True,' she said, gazing around the room. 'So a destination dining experience to go with Gabrielle's destination accommodation?'

'Exactly.'

'We don't want to cut into Gabby's trade though. Particularly as we're using her dock.'

'You're right,' he said, setting his fork down so he could use his hands to talk. As Sam was willing to at least discuss the project, he'd allow his natural enthusiasm free rein and see where they ended up. 'But, although she whips up the odd bouillabaisse or coq au vin for special guests, Gabrielle said she'd prefer to keep her events themed. You know, lawn parties, cocktails, something around the fire pit in the courtyard. So she's dead keen for this, said it will take the pressure off her a couple of nights a week.'

'A couple of nights? You're not making this full time?'

He shook his head. 'I don't think there will be the demand. If we were to do a standard river cruise, fish and chips, sure, we could probably fill the dining room three times over. But I want to create something special. Plus, you're busy in the cafe during the day.' According to the sign on the door, she closed at three, but he'd been past enough times over the weeks to realise she stayed open till four, handing out paper bags full of baked goods to a horde of school kids. It had taken all his control not to head into the cafe each time he was in Settlers, at least to say hello to her. But he'd promised he wouldn't crowd her.

'And you'll work in your cafe in the city the rest of the time?'

He liked that she was evidently trying to place his movements in her mind. 'No. I've had that fully staffed while I've been working on *Pelicanet*.' Pierce held up his callused, paint-splattered hands, hoping she'd recognise the proof that, willing to invest both money and time, he loved the boat—the dream of a new beginning—as much as she did. 'But Gabrielle's asked me to run the inn kitchen part time.'

A gust of wind spattered raindrops against the windows, and as the sky darkened, the solar-powered fairy lights strung across the front and rear deck came to life. He'd chosen tiny ones that gave off a soft butter-coloured twinkle, enhancing the romance of the river setting.

'Oh, so pretty!' Sam exclaimed.

'Thanks. But as I'm about out of ideas now, I could really use your input.'

'Seems to me you're managing just fine. But I will tell you a secret.'

He should be happy she was confiding, but given her previous revelation, his guts knotted.

Sam tapped her fork against her bowl. 'I've never had handmade pasta before. That's what this is, right? I can't believe how different it tastes to the shop-bought stuff. The sauces are amazing—I love the fresh basil on the amatriciana. But it never occurred to me that the pasta itself could taste different, or be anything other than a vehicle to carry the sauce.' She wrinkled her nose. 'That's pretty bad for someone who says they like to cook, isn't it? I guess I didn't expect it to have a taste at all, but it's silky and buttery. And I can actually pick the different flavours.' She barely paused for breath, every bit as enthused to discuss food as he was.

Using a tine of the fork, she lifted a strand of richly coloured pappardelle. 'Beetroot, right? And this is spinach. This one, though?' She picked up a deep yellow thread, wrinkling her forehead. 'Egg?'

'Saffron. And the black one is squid ink.' He paused a beat, but instead of recoiling, Sam unthreaded a strand of the almost-purple pasta from her plate, and sampled it.

They ate in appreciative near-silence for a few minutes. Then he leaned across the table to select a piece of pale pasta from the other serving dish between them. Winding it around his fork and waiting a moment for the walnut sauce to drip off, he held it toward her. 'Can you pick this one?'

His heart rate ratcheted up, his gaze on her lips. But Samantha jerked back with a gasp. 'Wait! There's something in that.' With the curiosity of a born cook, she pulled the strip of pasta from the fork, splitting it open with her nails. He loved that her eagerness banished all propriety, that she acted instinctively and enthusiastically. 'It's . . . a flower?' She looked from the tiny blue bloom to him.

'A forget-me-not. When I saw your floral work on Sharna's wedding cake, it got me thinking. I looked into what edible flowers would work in pasta. Forget-me-nots taste kind of like cucumber, so I figured they wouldn't overpower the walnut sauce. Plus, Gabrielle had a ton of them in her gardens, so I picked and dried some.'

'How do you get the flowers into the dough?'

'Laminate them in there when I roll out the pasta sheets, before I cut it into ribbons.'

'And they don't go soggy when you cook the pasta? Well, obviously, they don't.'

'Fresh pasta only needs cooking for about three minutes, so the flowers stay intact.'

'Wait.' She waved her fork at him, frowning. 'The texture of this pasta is different, too.'

He cleared his throat, smacked a fist against his chest a couple of times, like he could quell the ridiculous excitement that tickled within—he'd found someone whose passion and enthusiasm matched his own. 'The amatriciana is a heartier sauce, so I use a fifty-fifty ratio of polenta to flour in that pasta. It gives a bit more of a chew factor, helps the sauce to stick. But this one is silkier.'

'I'm in heaven. I bet they go nuts for this in the trattoria.' Sam wound a length of the flower-studded pasta around her fork and popped it into her mouth.

'I haven't offered it to the tratt. I made it for you.' The choice of flowers hadn't been an accident.

She looked at him, then clapped a hand over her mouth, her eyes dancing. 'I was trying to give you a deep and meaningful look of appreciation,' she said, her words muffled. 'But with my gob full of spaghetti, I know I wasn't hitting the mark.'

It was her sense of humour that attracted him more than anything, he decided as his laughter rang across the room. That, and those eyes. And her passion for cooking. If anyone could understand how completely he lost himself in creating food, it would be her. 'A gob full of spaghetti looks very appealing on you,' Pierce managed.

'There is an issue with this pasta, though,' she said, wiping her thumb across her mouth.

He lifted his eyebrows.

'Well, more with the sauce. They both have garlic.'

It took him a second to cotton on to where she was going with that. Then his heart leapt. 'And the garlic bread, too. But don't you know the IDGR?'

'IDGR?'

'Intimate Dining Garlic Rule. As long as we eat equal amounts, we'll be fine. So you'd better get a move on. I've eaten three times as much as you.'

'I doubt that. I should have taken before and after photos: Ma would be thrilled to see how much I've shovelled down.' She rolled her eyes. 'Which goes to prove I can't get back into this dating stuff. I've obviously no idea how to act appropriately.'

'You know that whole not-eating thing is a load of magazine promulgated rubbish, right? Men like women who have a good appetite.'

Sam looked terribly serious for a moment. When she spoke, her voice was low. 'I assure you, I used to have a lusty appetite. I'm just beginning to find it again.'

'Sam,' he said carefully, once he could find his voice, 'I don't want to screw this up again. So I really need to know—'

'Straight up, whether I'm interested in you,' she said in her no-nonsense manner. She sat back, tossing her hair over her shoulders. 'And straight up, yes, I am. But, like I said, I need to feel my way around a bit. I mean, I like you, I really do. But I keep getting these flashes of . . . panic?' She fanned her chest, her lower lip caught between her teeth as her eyes implored him to understand.

'There's no need for you to panic. I'm not rushing this anywhere. I simply don't want to put pressure on you by flirting, if that's the last thing you want.'

'Flirting is fine. I just suck at it . . . as you've seen.' She pushed aside the glass of Amaretto he'd selected for them to finish with. 'In any case, I'd better head home so I get to work on time tomorrow. Otherwise, Christine will skin me.'

'I've got some wet weather gear upstairs,' he said. 'Just give me a sec to grab it.' He deliberately made it clear that he wasn't inviting her up to the bedroom. 'I would have brought the car, but I've been on at the tradies to minimise their access tracks as much as possible so the wharf isn't completely ruined. Not that we'll use it for passengers; we'll bring *Pelicanet* down to Gabrielle's main dock. But I wanted to keep it the way you like it.'

'I need to stretch my legs, anyway. A stroll by the river, even in the rain, will be perfect after all this. And—' Samantha paused, making sure she had his attention '—just putting it out there to make it absolutely clear: I do expect a goodnight kiss.'

30

Samantha

She liked him. She really bloody liked him in the most excruciating, exciting, terrifying way possible. Sam lay staring up at the peeling paint of the ornate ceiling rose in her bedroom, barely visible in the pre-dawn light. And it wasn't a 'maybe I do, maybe I don't' kind of crush. It was a totally debilitating longing to see Pierce again, even though they'd only parted hours earlier. An hour less than it should have been, by the time they'd stopped kissing beneath the verandah of the cottage he'd rented. Half of her—more than half—had hoped he would invite her in. But she knew it was too early.

And so did he, reluctantly breaking away to escort her to her car. He'd offered to tail her out to the farm to make sure she got there safely, but they'd compromised on swapping numbers, so she could text and let him know. Sam chuckled.

Only city folk would think a fifteen-minute drive needed a safety check-in.

'Man, you are looking like the cat that got all the cream,' Jack said as she bounced into the kitchen, still wearing her flannelette pyjamas.

'Get kicked out of bed?' she responded. 'It's early even for you.' Working their grandparents' farm as well as his own acreage, Jack often popped in for extra breakfast.

'Lucie's not feeling all that well this morning, so I'm making a round of deliveries for her before I start.' Despite his words, Jack gave off an air of suppressed excitement.

'What kind of not well?' Sam asked eagerly. She'd been anticipating his announcement for over a year. Not wanting children of her own in no way transferred to not wishing them for her brother. She knew—and he'd demonstrated with Keeley—what an amazing father he would be.

'I'll tell you my s-secret if you tell me yours,' Jack said, his stammer giving away the intensity of his emotion.

'I don't have any secrets. What I do have is a . . . friend who'd like to buy some of your organic produce.'

'A *friend*?' Jack dramatically dropped his piece of toast. 'Is that what we're calling them now?'

She didn't know what else to call Pierce. But friend was far too casual, she wanted a label that staked her claim to him. 'Sucks to be you,' she said, nodding at Jack's toast, which had landed Vegemite side down on his plate. 'Maybe a little more than a friend,' she admitted, then quickly hushed him as Ma bustled back into the kitchen with fresh eggs.

'I'm coming by later,' Jack warned. 'You can fill me in then.'

'Swap you,' she returned smartly, though she still wasn't sure whether—or what—she would tell him.

❧

'Morning, love,' Sam chirruped to Young Eric, slumped as usual in the doorway of the cafe. She'd have to dial it back a bit, or Christine would be suspicious.

Eric dragged himself to his feet, taking longer than usual to focus on her. 'He was here,' he announced with sudden clarity. His hand moved to protect the brown paper bag wrapped around something in the deep pocket of his army-surplus coat.

Sam paused with her key in the door. 'Who was?'

'Never mind him,' Christine said, coming up behind them. 'He's rambling. Fancy a hot Milo this morning, Eric? It's come in a bit brisk.' She toed his cocoon of blankets. 'What are you bringing these here for? You've a perfectly good house.' She added in a not-so-quiet aside to Sam, 'Not that you'd want to be caught dead in it. Smells like something already was. Doesn't matter how often I clean it, can't get rid of the stink.'

'Got to stay on patrol.' Eric nodded sagely. 'Keep a look out for them bastards. They'll do for you, you know. No sleeping in the foxhole. I set up a bivouac here.' He pointed at the shop doorway, then gestured at the empty street. 'And I'll do recon through the day. Keep it clear.'

Sam winced. Eric evidently had a history of looking after his country, yet now he was relegated to tatters and loneliness. And the care of Christine, possibly the world's most unlikely guardian angel. 'Let's get some bacon and eggs into you, Eric,' she said as the three of them bustled into the cafe.

'Yesterday's leftovers are fine for him,' Christine said sharply, flipping the sign to open as Sam hit the light switches and turned on the various machines and pieces of equipment.

Sam shook her head. 'We need to defrost the cafe, and nothing warms your insides like the smell of bacon and eggs. Besides, I only had time to pinch a piece of Jack's toast this morning, so I'm doing some for myself.'

Young Eric shuffled over to a table, looking beseechingly at Christine from beneath hooded eyes. 'Go on, then,' she sighed. 'While Samantha's still the boss, you can get away with it.'

Eric folded untidily into the chair as Sam carried out the cake and pastry deliveries from McCues Bakery, and started loading the cabinets. 'Won't be a minute, Eric.'

'I'll make us a coffee,' Christine said. 'We could probably open an hour later on these chilly mornings, no one comes in this early.'

Sam turned on the radio, catching the weather before the local station cut into their familiar eighties-heavy mix. She raised her voice over the music and splatter of frying bacon. 'I'd thought about that the other week. I was going to extend the hours so the cafe looks like harder work than it is, you know, make it an unattractive proposition for buyers. As though there's likely to be any around here. But . . .' she trailed off. Frying bread for her sandwich, she decided to leave Eric's uncooked: she'd noticed he had few teeth remaining.

'But what?' Christine said her face tight with grim determination as she faced off with the coffee machine. Sam had been surprised when Christine asked recently how to operate the monster.

'But . . . I'm not sure I really care what happens with the cafe anymore. I mean, I still love it. Just I'm not as passionate about it as I am about . . . other things.'

'Careful now, it's hot,' Christine cautioned Eric as she landed a mug of Milo on his table. 'It's lukewarm,' she added to Sam, as though Eric couldn't be trusted with it. 'And what are these "other things"?'

Sam slid eggs onto the bread with far more attention than the task required. 'I was offered a new job last night. Like, an extra. It wouldn't take me away from here. And I'm really tempted.'

'A job? You're not going back to Murray Bridge. You don't want to be nearer *him* than you need be.' Christine knew that jobs in Settlers were rare as hen's teeth, so anything coming up was more likely to be in the larger town.

'No, it's out at Wurruldi.'

'Gabrielle's taking on inn staff?'

'No. Well, yes, but it's not that. It's . . . I'm not sure I'm supposed to tell you.'

'But you will anyway,' Christine said.

Sam halved the sandwiches, decorating the plates with a swirl of Tracey's homemade barbecue sauce. 'It has to stay secret.'

'I think you know I can be trusted,' Christine said acidly.

'Of course.' Sam cringed at her own instinctive lack of trust, which was so much less than her friend deserved. 'Pierce is setting up a destination restaurant on the river. He's focusing on fine Italian dining, and he wants me to handle the plating and team up on the desserts.' Her voice trembled only a little on his name, and it was more to do with the excitement that flooded her at mentioning the plan out loud. Well, almost more to do with that.

'Pierce again, is it?' Christine said. 'It's about time you got something sorted out there.'

About to deny that there was anything to sort out, Sam paused. Perhaps one of the first steps to allowing herself to accept that Pierce was becoming a part of her life—whatever that entailed—was to acknowledge the fact aloud, rather than endlessly argue it in her head. But it was hard. There would be judgement, whispers that perhaps it hadn't been Grant's fault they'd split up, that maybe Sam had been on the prowl. She knew how quickly the grapevine could tangle the truth.

She wiped the edge of the plate with a paper towel, feigning nonchalance. 'A bunch of new rumours are probably a good diversion.'

Christine leaned an angular hip against the counter as she sipped her coffee. 'Stop everyone talking about what *that man* did, you mean?' she demanded in her usual no-punches-pulled fashion. 'You said you wanted to warn his new woman what he's like, yet now you're creating gossip to protect him. Is Pierce aware he's nothing but a disguise for *that man*?'

'He's not!'

'So you *do* like him?'

'How the heck do I know?' Yet she knew, all right. 'It's messy. I should just forget the whole thing, right?'

Christine laid a hand on her arm, her tone unusually sympathetic. 'If you try to protect yourself by pretending you don't care, there's a risk you'll end up not caring. Trust yourself to make the right choice.'

Sam took a quavery breath as the weight of the secret lifted from her chest.

'Besides, I'm here if he dares take a step out of line.' Christine smiled in wolfish fashion as she picked up Eric's plate. 'You should have had me in your corner years back.'

'I should have,' Sam agreed, glancing up in surprise as the doorbell pinged. They usually had a good half-hour of set-up time before they had customers. 'Morning, Heath,' she said to the new arrival. 'You're in town early. Heading to the clearing sale?'

The man, buried beneath a heavy oilskin, merely nodded in reply. He rarely said anything, and Sam, having picked up his name from his credit card months earlier, had made it a personal challenge to get a smile out of him. So far, he was winning.

She filled his takeaway coffee order, then gazed at his departing back as he strode back out into the rain. 'Know anything about him?' she asked Christine.

'Keeps to himself, that one,' Christine answered, clearly irked. 'Moved onto one of Marian Nelson's husband's old properties a while back. Must do all his running around in Murray Bridge, though. Rarely see him here.'

Despite the weather, the day was unprecedentedly busy. Or maybe it was because the chill was driving everyone in town to search out hot food. With Tara not starting until a little before lunchtime, both Sam and Christine were run off their feet all morning.

When Pierce came in at one, Sam barely had time to nod at him. Being busy didn't prevent the quiver that rippled through her at the memory of his lips the previous evening.

'Best make up your mind whether he's a secret,' Christine said as she steamed milk and Sam plated a quiche, adding homemade pickles on the side. 'Anyone with one eye can't miss that daft smile.'

Sam made a concerted effort to focus on her work, but Christine snorted. 'Course, there's not much point you trying to hide it, when he's gazing at you like a lovesick cow. Let me guess, he gets table service again?'

'If I have time,' she said, trying to make it sound like she wasn't desperate to rush over there, to simply stand near Pierce, maybe allow their hands to briefly touch.

She finished the round of orders and changed to a clean apron—tomorrow's, much to Christine's unvoiced disgust—and headed toward Pierce.

He stood, his face darkening. But his gaze was fixed on the door, not her. A stocky man entered, glanced around, then strutted toward Pierce. Sam bit back a chuckle as his odd gait put her in mind of a sumo wrestler, his arms bent at the elbows, fists held at waist level. He looked threatening, but a glance at Pierce reassured her. He had taken his seat again, looking oddly resigned as he waved the other man into the chair opposite. He shot her a regretful look, though, and her heart wobbled. Just a little.

Christine raised an eyebrow made heavy by judgement as she moved back behind the counter.

'Business meeting, I guess,' Sam said lightly. 'I'll take him a coffee. Better make it two.'

She made the second drink a standard flat white and delivered them to Pierce's table. She was a little disappointed when he didn't introduce her to his companion, who had opened a laptop and turned the screen toward Pierce. But he did let his gaze linger on hers, and a secret smile crossed his lips.

An hour later, the rest of the cafe's occupants having changed a couple of times over, the two men were still at the table.

Sam ran the back of her hand across her brow. 'Wow, that was a wild one today, wasn't it? Never seemed to be any let-up. You really should have taken a break, Christine. Tara's legs are younger, she can cover more ground.'

'My legs are plenty young enough, thank you very much,' Christine replied frostily. 'But with business increasing like this, we should look at putting on an extra set of hands. Especially when the zoo coaches pick up in spring.'

Perhaps the extent to which Christine had taken over running the cafe should offend her. Instead, Sam felt relieved. It was like she had found a good home for a cute but unwanted kitten.

'I am finishing up early today,' Christine said, fiddling with the apron strings she had knotted at the front of her waist.

'Here, let me.' Sam stepped in to help, noticing Christine's knuckles were thickened with arthritis or rheumatism.

'I'm going to pop over to Young Eric's. Lucie has organised some woman to come out and make an assessment of his place tomorrow, but if she sees it in the usual state, she'll turn tail for the city.' Christine managed to make it sound as though the scheduling was deliberately engineered to cause her the maximum inconvenience.

'Don't you overdo it,' Sam cautioned. It was funny, all these years she'd considered Christine an interfering busybody. Not once had she taken the time to recognise the good the woman did for the community.

Which wasn't to say that Christine wasn't interfering, but everyone had their faults.

Business had hit the usual two pm lull so, after delivering another round of coffee to Pierce's table, Sam finally made a drink for herself. 'Tars, can you grab the mail from the post office, love?' she called as the teenager scuttled toward the door for a late lunch break.

'Sure.' Tara swiftly drew the door shut to keep the frigid blast of air outside. A swirl of dried leaves managed to sneak in, though, and Sam fetched the dustpan and broom from the storeroom.

She startled as the door slammed open again, the bell tinkling in wild distress.

Habitual fear rippled through her as Grant strode in. But Hayley was with him so, with an effort, Sam pulled herself together: he was happy now, and she was happy. There was no reason for resentment on either side.

'What the hell is this?' He shook a fistful of papers in her face.

She took an instinctive step back, bringing the dustpan up between them. Her throat ached in learned response to his aggression. 'I've no idea,' she managed.

'I fucking signed to sell the shop, but I wouldn't have agreed to the bullshit price if I'd known it was your offer.'

'What are you talking about?' Sam said. Yet a premonition clutched her chest with a fist of ice. Had Pierce made an offer on the cafe for her? God, she hoped not. Because she had finally realised that the cafe was permanently tainted by its association with Grant, and she was ready to move on.

But even more importantly, she wasn't ready to be bought. Not by anyone. She had been owned once—and it wasn't going to happen again.

31

Pierce

Pierce surged out of his chair as the guy in the cafe doorway yelled at Sam, standing over her.

But Sam shot a furious glance toward him at the same moment Dante put a restraining hand on his arm. 'Don't get involved, bro.'

He shook Dante off impatiently. Stayed standing, assessing the situation.

The guy struggled to tear a wad of papers in half, the frustration obviously not improving his temper. 'You get that bloody crone to pull out now. She's got three days cooling off; you tell her she needs to cancel the contract, or I'll damn well do her.'

'Grant,' the woman who'd entered the cafe with him interceded. She pulled on his arm. 'Calm down. You got what you wanted for the place, let's just be shot of it.'

Grant. Sam's ex. Blood pounded in Pierce's temples, urging him into the fray.

'Shut the hell up, Hayley!' Grant rounded on the woman. 'I told you before, it's none of your damn business.'

Sam's shoulders relaxed, as though she was relieved Grant's focus was elsewhere. But as Hayley's hand moved to protect the pregnant rounding of her stomach, Sam stepped closer, snatching the papers from Grant.

Pierce tensed. What the hell? She was deliberately redirecting her ex's anger toward herself.

Sam's tone was low and furious, yet oddly calm. 'I have no idea what you're raving about.'

Grant smacked the papers from her hand, but she didn't glance down as they fell to the floor. Pierce's fists clenched: she hadn't looked away because she'd known it would be dangerous to drop her guard.

'Like hell you don't know!' her ex yelled. 'You've had that old bitch in your pocket for months. Now she's acting for you.'

'Christine? Christine bought the cafe?' Sam's tone was incredulous. Either she was a brilliant actor, or she'd had no idea what was going on.

'You set me up,' Grant roared, looming over her.

Pierce took a step forward, but Sam risked a glance toward him and gave a sharp shake of her head. She turned back to Grant. 'I didn't. But while you're here, Hayley—' her shoulders shifted to include the woman in the conversation '—I owe you an apology, because I should have had the guts to warn you before. The way you see Grant behaving right now is the way he's always going to be. If you stay with him, the best you can hope for is that he keeps it behind closed doors.' She gave a bitter laugh. 'Or maybe that's the worst of it, isn't it, Grant? Because you're a big man behind closed doors, where no one can see you.'

Pierce's guts twisted. Adrenaline urged him to get over there, to get between them, to protect Sam. Both from the current danger and from past hurt. But instinct told him that she wouldn't appreciate it.

'Don't you start with that shit, Sam,' Grant said belligerently.

'Or what? What will you do now? My guess is nothing, because there are witnesses,' Sam spat defiantly. 'And don't even think of lifting a finger against Christine, because half-a-dozen people just heard you threaten her.'

'I wasn't threatening, you know that.' His tone suddenly turned appeasing; the guy's switch in mood was worthy of a double-take. 'You just rile me up. You know you do.'

'I've heard you blame me often enough, that's for sure. But it's no good turning the puppy dog eyes on me now.' Sam sneered. 'That trick used to make my heart flip. Now it just makes my stomach turn. Because I know you. I know what you are. You're a coward and a bully.'

'Why do you have to try and hurt me, Sammie?' Grant wheedled. 'After all these years, everything we had?'

'Everything we had that you so slyly put in your name, you mean? And you want to talk about hurting? You really want to go there?' Sam unobtrusively put space between her and the other woman, drawing her ex away as she goaded him. 'You want to discuss exactly how you hurt me? The ways that I had to hide from everyone? Or, even worse, the ways that don't show?'

'Jesus,' Pierce grunted through his clenched teeth.

'Keep out of it,' Dante warned.

He shot Dante a look of loathing. The last thing he needed was relationship advice from his brother.

'You know what?' Sam snarled at Grant. 'The hell with keeping your secrets. You don't deserve my loyalty.'

Realising he was losing the fight, Grant was backing from the shop. 'You haven't heard the last of this,' he muttered. He yanked the door open, but made a point of holding it wide so Hayley could precede him.

Pierce wasn't sure whether he was exerting his authority, or trying to disarm his girlfriend with courtesy.

'He's regrouping,' Dante noted as Grant stalked past the window, Hayley fussing after him. 'He'll be back for revenge. No guy wants to be taken down by a woman like that.'

'You'd know, wouldn't you?'

'What do you mean, bro?' Dante spread his hands wide in question.

Pierce shot a desperate glance toward the counter. He wanted to check on Sam, but she had disappeared into the back room. He was torn between rushing after her or affording her some privacy. 'You just got out of jail, remember?' he ground out, reluctantly resuming his seat. He didn't bother to look at Dante, his entire focus on the closed door, waiting for Sam to reappear.

'So?' He felt rather than saw Dante's shrug. 'What of it?'

The nonchalance dragged his gaze back to his brother. 'So you're every bit as bad as that piece of crap.'

Dante's hand fisted, slamming on the table. A cup skated over the edge, smashing on the floor. 'The chick said that dude was hitting her? Don't you *ever* put me in his category.'

Pierce shook his head incredulously. 'You're cooked, man. You just did time for DV.'

'I did the time, but I didn't do the crime.' As usual, Dante's anger passed as quickly as it arrived, and he was jovial again.

'Bullshit.'

'No, bro. Look.' Dante leaned in close, as though they'd share a brotherly secret. 'Karls was beating on me, okay? She got pissed-as and fell down the stairs at the club. Sure, I cracked the shits at her, I admit that. But she laid into me. Then she called the cops.' He sat back, his innocence proven. 'She had bruises, I didn't: what were they going to think?'

'I'd say they were probably going to come to the right conclusion,' Pierce muttered, unwillingly fascinated by the story his brother was weaving. He shouldn't be. That was Dante's talent, spinning bullshit into gold thread. Yet his brother's apparent embarrassment gave the tale a degree of credibility.

Dante shook his head, thrust out a blubbery underlip. 'I didn't even bother to argue it. I mean, how would it look? Saying a sheila whaled into me when she's the one who's black and blue, with a chipped tooth?'

'But you went to prison, man.'

Dante snorted. 'Yeah, because it got written up as DV with bodily harm.' Unbelievably, he flashed a grin. 'Plenty of other times I should have gone down—though not for shit like this—so it was only fair to take the rap. Plus—' his countenance changed, suddenly serious '—I figured lock-up was going to be the best place for me to get clean.'

Pierce snorted. 'Well, that's a new one. Junkie goes to jail instead of rehab.'

'I'd have taken rehab as a challenge, found a way to get the gear in to beat the system.'

'Same in jail, surely?' He couldn't help but be riveted by the convoluted workings of his brother's mind.

'Not so much. I knew if I went in on a DV I set myself up to be on the outer with some of the cellies. Not to mention the lobsters.'

'Lobsters?'

'Meat in the arse, shit in the head. Screws.' Dante drained the last of the second coffee Sam had brought them earlier. 'Anyway, there'd be no one in lock-up looking to do me any favours, you know what I mean? Made it easier to stay clean. And made me focus on this.' He tapped his bicep. 'It pays to bridge up in the gym there.' He moved his arms into his familiar wide-elbowed stance, so Pierce would understand. 'You gotta look intimidating, and you can't afford to be drug fucked when you're in or you're just asking to get jazzed.' He dropped his arms, puzzlement sweeping his face. 'Anyway, I told you I've kicked the shit.'

'You've told me plenty of things over the years.' Pierce stood. 'I've got to go check on Sam.'

'Sam? Ah, she's the chick—I mean girl—you mentioned over Christmas, yeah?'

He didn't think he had, and his jaw tightened in annoyance. Not much got past Dante.

His brother gave a low whistle. 'So that piece of work is her old man?' He seemed to think for a moment, then gave a decisive nod. He cracked his fingers by pressing his hand to the table and levering up his palm. 'I'll sort him, bro.'

'Just stay the hell out of it, Dante. If anyone is going to sort him, it'll be me,' Pierce growled. Damn, he wanted to thump the crap out of Grant.

'Trust me, you don't want to risk getting in shit for that,' Dante observed.

'And you do?'

'Haven't you noticed, trouble finds me regardless?' Dante sounded resigned. 'Reckon no matter what I do, I'll end up back inside one day. You're the golden child, mate. That's why Dad said to see you about this,' he tapped the computer screen.

'Why didn't Dad ask me himself?'

Dante eyed him levelly. 'Guess he feels bad asking you to help sort out money problems when he gave me the job against your advice.'

If Dante had levelled a backstabbing accusation at him, Pierce would have taken a shot back. But his brother's quiet acceptance left him replaying the conversations with Dad in his head, guiltily checking if he had been as arrogant as Dante's statement made him seem. 'Look, it's not that I didn't think you should get a second chance—'

'Just not a fifth or sixth, right?' Dante said, though his grin seemed forced. 'Trust me, I get it, bro. But I don't know how I'm supposed to convince you that I'm straight now.'

Pierce stared hard at his brother, then shook his head. 'Me, either, Dan. And I'm bloody sorry about that.'

'Fair call.' Dante nodded. 'It is what it is.'

Pierce cast another glance toward the door Sam had disappeared through. The teenager who worked for her blew in off the street, and headed in the door's direction, so he reluctantly sat and pointed at Dante's laptop. 'All right, listen up. Dad's getting shafted by the milk prices. Why have you changed suppliers?'

'Toby cut me a deal. He's got a cash and carry, handles all our dairy now. The cream, ricotta, yogurt, mascarpone and milk. It's all above board.'

'Looks like the only cream is going into his own pockets.' Pierce punched up numbers. It had taken them the best part of an hour to hone in on the anomaly, not helped by Dante's unwillingness to be open about anything he'd done to change the status quo in the trattoria. 'Didn't you notice the accounts are higher?'

'No, they're lower, bro, look at this.' Dante leaned across him, poking a stubby finger at the screen.

Pierce brought up another spreadsheet, lay it alongside the one Dante was using. 'How do you figure?'

'Look at the invoice total,' Dante said smugly. 'It's two thirds of what you were paying.'

'Check how many invoices you've received since I left.' Pierce pulled the information up on screen. 'Old mate is billing you almost weekly, ten days, though he's not putting a date on the accounts.' He flicked back a screen to prove his point. 'Plus, he's sending the accounts at random times so you're less likely to notice, and changing the credit period. Five days to pay, ten, seven. Look, these two invoices came in only a day apart. He's figuring the accounts will get swallowed in the paperwork, and someone will pay them without noticing. Which you have been doing. The regular supplier sends the account at the end of every month.' He tapped the bottom of one of the historic accounts. 'So this is the total for the full month. Which means your account for two thirds the amount is actually about twice as high as the original. It's not even a sophisticated set-up.'

Dante looked crestfallen. 'Jesus. So the cun—cunning bastard set me up.'

'Saw you coming,' Pierce agreed. 'Let me guess, a friend from lock-up?'

His neck turtling into his shoulders even more than usual, Dante shook his head. 'Wasn't a birthday party in there, bro. Made no friends.' He scowled at the screen. 'The bloody mother freakin' stoner. What now? Guess I'll go sort him out.'

Pierce sighed. 'Just stop with the "sorting people out" business. It's not the way the real world runs, Dante.'

'It's the way mine does,' his brother muttered sullenly.

Pierce winced, wondering if that was true. He and Dante certainly did live different lives. And, whether that was by choice or not, it went some way to explaining why his brother was who he was. 'Clear all his accounts, pay them up in full but cancel orders going forward. I'll ring the old supplier in the morning, reinstate the regular order.'

Dante rubbed an eye with the heel of his hand, for once no smartarse comeback at his disposal. 'Jesus. I fucked it, didn't I?'

'It's no biggie.' Pierce closed down the screens. 'If that's the worst of what happens, the tratt can weather it.' He took a deep breath, surprised by the sense of clarity, of *lightness*, that accompanied the dwindling of his long-held hostility. 'Look, Dan, I know you want to make your mark, but pick your battles, okay? You don't have to change everything all at once to prove you can do it better than me.'

Dante snorted. 'Really? You've no bloody idea what it's like there, Pierce. Mum and Dad don't say anything, but I know they're judging me all the time. I know they're comparing me to you. And I know I'm coming up short. They're just waiting for me to take off and you to come back.'

'Are you planning to?' Pierce said quietly.

'Planning to what?'

'Take off.'

Dante's chin dimpled as he twisted his lips together. 'Not this time, bro. I'm settled. Look, I don't know how to tell you this, so I'm just going to say it straight: me and Jem hooked up again. I know you won't like it, but we always had something, you can't deny it.'

The news didn't surprise him as much as it should. 'Not going to deny it. Also, I don't care. Good luck to you both.'

Dante nodded slowly, his countenance clearing as though he'd got a weight off his mind. 'Don't reckon Mum will be too keen on having her in the tratt, but she's a good waitress.'

Pierce stood, holding his hands up to stop Dante in his tracks. 'Don't get me involved in that one. I'll help you sort the books, but you take on Mum on your own.'

Dante looked pathetically hopeful. 'You will help sort out the books, though?'

'Sure,' Pierce said, distracted as Sam reappeared behind the counter.

'Thanks, bro. And I'll see you right, too,' Dante said.

'Cheers man, whatever.' Pierce was already crossing the floor toward Sam. He'd give her all the space she wanted—once he was sure she was okay.

32
Samantha

There was no doubt that Pierce definitely knew all her business now, Sam thought as he strode across the cafe. There was anger in his walk, yet she knew intuitively that it would never be directed at her.

For half a second, she tried to force herself to caution, to remind herself she wasn't a good judge of character. But then she caught his eye. And remembered that this man listened to her, respected her. And shared her passion. Her interest in him wasn't some deluded teenager's hunger for affection, nor a desperate wife's attempt to convince herself her marriage was worth saving, that she hadn't made the same mistakes as her own mother.

'Are you okay?' Pierce pitched his question low to prevent the handful of other patrons from hearing. As though they hadn't just sat through a whole dinner-and-show presentation.

'I'm fine.' She gave a wry smile. 'Maybe *too* fine. It's like I simply don't care anymore. That chapter is closed. I'm ready to move on.' She gave Pierce a long, direct look, loaded with meaning.

He wanted to know where he stood? Well, she was telling him. Seeing Grant again, noticing the way he treated Hayley, the way he flipped from aggression to wheedling, had totally killed any last tiny flicker of care she felt toward the man. 'I've come to realise that my most painful experiences are my most defining moments. I mean, I so desperately wanted to be wrong about Grant, to believe that I was being over-dramatic, that he wasn't really as bad as I thought. But he just proved me right in front of everyone.' She swept her hand to include the townsfolk in the cafe, who weren't even pretending not to be hanging on her every word. 'And I think now I'm supposed to act distraught and fearful, be unable to trust. But instead, I'm just—' she dusted her hands together '—done.'

Pierce's smile was slow to come as he processed her words. But when it arrived, it was uninhibited, the brilliance of the summer sun topping the river cliffs. 'And the cafe?'

'Sounds like Christine has bought it. I guess if she wants me here, I'll work for her. But still, I'm . . . free.' The word tickled up through her chest, full of joy.

'Free to take on a new challenge?' Pierce's voice resonated through her as, both hands on the low counter, he leaned closer.

'Mind of a businessman, heart of a dreamer,' she murmured. 'That's a very sexy combination.' Who even was she? The altercation she had been dreading, the irreversible outing of her secrets in front of the town, was supposed to shatter her. Instead, she felt larger than life. Invincible. She had faced her demon. And she had bloody well won.

Pierce's gaze locked on her lips. 'You're doing me in, Sam,' he cautioned. 'We need a safe word.'

'Safe word?' Her heart hammered. She kept her eyes on him, knowing everyone in the cafe was watching them. She should keep a TV turned on in the corner.

He nodded. 'For if you ever feel confined, or if where we're headed is too much for you. I want you to know that if you need to, you can get out any time you like. I get that you don't like disagreeing with me, that it's hard for you. So we need ground rules, a way you can bail without feeling in danger.'

'Compassion,' she blurted.

He lifted a dark eyebrow.

'That's my safe word.'

'Okay. You want out, just tell me I need to find my compassion. I swear I'll back right off.'

Watching him for a long moment, she processed his offer.

She didn't think she was going to need a safe word.

Pierce reached across the counter and took her hand, his thumb caressing her palm. 'I have to head back to the city for a day or two with my brother.' He tilted his head toward the back of the cafe and she realised with a jolt of surprise that he meant the stocky guy with neck and knuckle tatts, who sat watching them intently. 'But we'll have dinner when I'm back. Work out our next move—' his lips curved deliciously slowly '—in a whole lot of areas.'

Unfamiliar anticipation coiled in her stomach. She was eager for everything Pierce was offering.

~

'Guess I should be handing these over to you?' Samantha said to Christine as she unlocked the cafe.

'Up you get.' Christine ignored her, using one hand against the window to maintain her balance as she nudged Young Eric, who was slumped in the shop doorway, with her toe. 'Honestly, I don't know why you've taken to getting here so early. You've a perfectly good house.' She glanced at Sam and lifted an eyebrow. 'Using the term very loosely, obviously.'

'Keep telling you, I gotta watch. He was here,' Eric mumbled as he creaked to his feet, the newspaper he always carried in his coat pocket falling to the stoop. 'They try to infiltrate, see.'

Sam retrieved the newspaper, glancing at the cover as she passed it to him. She did a double-take. The yellowed and tattered *Murray Valley Standard* was from the sixties, although she didn't suppose Eric had been carting it around for that long. The grainy photo on the front page sat beneath a headline about the Vietnam War.

'Plotting an ambush, he is.' The old digger nodded wisely, shoving the paper back into his pocket alongside the bottle wrapped with brown paper. He tapped the side of his nose. 'But I've got him under surveillance.'

Christine sighed, bundling Eric through the door. 'Is it just me, or is he getting worse?'

'Well, he'll be your problem soon enough,' Sam said, trying again to introduce the subject of the cafe sale.

'Mine? Hardly,' Christine trumpeted. 'You can still deal with him. Oh, I see what you mean: I heard that man was here yesterday shooting off his mouth. Honestly, it irks to have to pay him a single cent. But Claire at the real estate gave me a heads-up that she had a couple from the city booked in to look at the cafe next week. Can't have that happening now, can we? So I got that contract signed so he wouldn't have a chance to gazoop me.'

'I think you mean gazump,' Sam corrected with a secret smile. 'Though if Claire is your friend, surely she wouldn't have taken your offer to the other buyer to give them a chance to beat it?'

'There are friends and there are friends,' Christine said dourly. 'And Claire is on commission, remember. Seems to me if she was willing to sell the property for *that man*, she'd be willing to deal with the devil himself. Also, if I tarried any longer Lynn at the IGA would snap it up. I swear she has plans to own the entire town. Anyway, Ploughs and Pies will be ours soon enough.'

'Ours?' Sam said.

'You don't expect me to run this ridiculous place by myself, do you? Although, I must warn you, there are going to be changes. For starters, the décor. I have in mind a nice little fifties-style milk bar look. Pop in some booths—'

'Will I still have a job?' Tara piped up, joining them and taking her day's apron from the hook.

'If you can stay off your phone long enough to make milkshakes, you will,' Christine shot back.

Sam knelt to load a tray of cream horns into the refrigerated cabinet. 'Christine, you know how I mentioned Pierce's business?'

'Ooh, Pierce. Seriously, how hot is that guy?' Tara gushed. 'Though did you notice the dude he met here yesterday? That one looked hardcore. I wouldn't mind knowing a bit more about him.'

'I wouldn't mind you getting on with your work,' Christine reproved, apparently already invested in her upcoming role as owner.

Sam pushed to her feet, continuing her line of thought. 'I'm not sure how much time I'll be putting in there. Pierce wants me to handle desserts and the plating, but we'll only start off with a couple of nights a week. Of course, there's the baking to be done, both for here and the restaurant.'

'And certain other distractions to be taken care of, I daresay,' Christine said, tightening her mouth. But her eyes twinkled as she glanced Sam's way. 'Perhaps, if she shows a little more initiative, Tara might find herself with extra hours.'

'On it, boss.' Tara finished tying her apron and rushed to prep the coffee machine. Jobs were hard to come by in Settlers Bridge.

The morning passed quickly in the familiar, sweetly scented rush. Sam suspected she should be feeling nostalgic, sad this was one of the last weeks she would own the business. Instead, all she could think of was *Pelicanet*. And Pierce. And tomorrow night.

Plus, Pierce had promised that next week Hamish was taking *Pelicanet* out on the river, and she was already planning what she could cram into a picnic basket—other than champagne—for the maiden voyage. Could it even be considered a maiden voyage for a boat that was one hundred and fifty years old? No matter. It was most definitely the maiden voyage for the fully refurbished, newly loved *Pelicanet*. Sam couldn't believe the turns that her life had taken, to see her sailing upon the river in the boat she'd fallen in love with.

With the man that perhaps she could fall in love with.

A ripple of excitement ran through her at the thought of how much she still had to explore in the boat. Although they had investigated the galley and dining room levels, she had been trying to take in the 'big picture' type stuff, her mind in too much of a whirl to grasp all the changes and improvements Pierce had funded. And she'd not yet seen what he had done with the captain's quarters and wheelhouse.

'Samantha, are you going to serve?' Christine called from the back room, asserting her not-yet-there authority. Though really, Christine hadn't needed to sign a contract to do that: for the last six months, she'd been as likely to boss Sam around as she was Tara.

Sam gave the inside of the pie-warmer one last wipe, tossed the cloth into the basket she kept under the counter, and smiled at the attractive woman who approached the counter. 'Morning, love, what can I get you?' she said cheerfully as her gaze flicked to the window. It was always surprising to see an unfamiliar face in the cafe when she wasn't expecting a zoo coach. A shiny new Mazda hatchback filled the view, just beyond the dripping overhang of the bullnosed verandah.

The woman, perhaps a handful of years younger than her, tilted her head back to read the menu on the wall behind the counter. Chalked in fancy scroll lettering, it had taken Tara a full day to perfect, and Sam had joked that the menu could now never be changed.

'I think . . .' The woman tweaked the collar of the open fawn trench she wore over skinny jeans. Sam knew that even if she had a million lazy dollars at her disposal, she would never manage such apparently effortless elegance and confidence. 'There are about a dozen things I'd love to try.' Her wistful sigh was clearly meant to convey that she wouldn't destroy the temple of her body with such fare. 'But I'll settle for an almond latte.' Her perfectly glossed lips curved to display equally perfect teeth, and her dark gaze met Sam's unflinchingly. 'Pierce tells me the coffee is awesome here. And if anyone would know, it'd be him.'

'Oh. That's great,' Sam said, slightly on the back foot. She smoothed her apron, futilely hoping today's deep maroon wasn't speckled with chocolate powder or icing sugar. Her hair was no doubt curling wildly from the damp pause in the shop doorway that morning, and, though she had promised Tara that tomorrow she could do her worst with her makeup, today she wasn't wearing a speck.

The woman tucked her dark hair behind one ear, still not breaking the long, assessing gaze. 'He said he wanted to get back to Settlers Bridge sooner than he originally planned, so suggested we meet here. And I'm going to hazard a guess that means you're the one trying to steal him from me?'

Though the words were delivered in a light, bantering style, Sam froze. Tara fumbled the steel milkshake container nearby, but Sam didn't turn. Her heart pounded too hard, slamming her ribs. 'Pardon?' she said to the woman at the counter.

The woman tapped her fingers on the counter, one after the other, as though she played the piano. Acrylic nails created a staccato drumroll. 'Oh, he hasn't mentioned me, has he? Typical.' She thrust out her hand. 'I'm Jemma. Jemma di Angelis.'

33

Pierce

Pierce made the mad dash from his car to the verandah overhanging the row of shops in the Settlers Bridge main street. It hadn't taken a great deal of time to sort Dante's problem at the tratt, but Mum had wanted him to hang around. Mostly so she could feed him up, as though he didn't know how to cook for himself. He'd originally intended to stay in the city another night, but when Jemma said she was happy to make a day trip and meet him near the river, he'd seized the opportunity to get back earlier.

Jemma's car was parked in front of the cafe, and he glanced at his watch. As usual, she was early. Her hardcore type-A personality was part of what made her difficult to live with: while she was driven and professionally focused, she was also impatient and demanding. And she lacked tolerance for anything she considered artistic. Which included his passion for food. Jemma ate only to live, and he'd never been able to break that habit.

He ran his hand across his hair, sheeting off the rain before he pushed open the cafe door. A blast of warmth and the familiar rich aroma welcomed him, and he strode to the counter. 'I should have got here a half-hour early, just to pip you at the post.'

Jemma turned, flung both arms around his neck and kissed his cheek. In affection, at least, she was his match. 'You'd think that, by now, you'd realise you don't have a chance of beating me.'

Sam stood behind the counter, and his heart surged. But then he realised she looked inexplicably bleak. He cast a quick glance around the cosy cafe: if that bastard of an ex was here again—'Sam? Are you okay?' He leaned across the counter, reaching for her hands.

She jerked back, shaking her head.

'Ah, I called it right,' Jemma crowed. 'I knew this had to be Samantha.'

Christine appeared at Sam's elbow, her hard, dark eyes punishing him even before her mouth opened. 'Your wife just introduced herself.' Her mouth snapped closed, her glare daring him to argue.

He didn't need to look around the cafe again, there were only four people in there. 'You brought Mum?' he asked Jemma in surprise.

She wasn't particularly close with her mother, their personalities far too different to make for an easy relationship. And, though she tended to focus on her career far too much—a trait she got from himself—his daughter wasn't so oblivious that she'd bring his ex along to meet the woman he'd fallen in love with.

'Of course not,' Jemma scoffed. Then her face cleared. 'It's the flipping names, Pierce.' She turned to Sam and Christine. 'My parents are wholly uncreative and saddled me with Mum's name. Jem and Jemma.' She gave him a mocking glare.

'Wasn't my call,' he laughingly defended himself. Then he realised Sam's face was pale, two high spots of colour in her cheeks burning feverishly bright. 'Sam?'

'It's not the names . . .' She shook her head distractedly. 'You never said that you're married.'

'Was,' he corrected immediately.

Sam nodded, her rigid stance relaxing a little, and he winced. He rarely thought of his long-distant marriage so it hadn't occurred to him to bring it up, yet he realised now that she might see the omission as a deliberate attempt to hide the truth. Given her history, Sam would be sensitive to any perceived manipulation.

'Or that you have a *daughter*?' Sam continued, the last word pitched with a questioning inflection.

'One and only, because he stopped once he realised he couldn't top this.' Jemma grinned, waving a hand at her own front.

'Because I was sixteen when I got her mum pregnant, seventeen when we were married by special licence and Jemma was born,' he said tightly. 'And twenty-six when we divorced.'

'And I'm almost thirty-one, if you're trying to do the math,' Jemma chipped in, oblivious to his tension. She always got a kick from the attention their small age gap brought.

Sam nodded slowly, trying to digest the facts, and his chest cramped. If she thought he'd lied, he knew Sam would have no reservations about walking away from him. 'So only child, or only one from that marriage?' she said quietly.

'Only child.'

'And only marriage,' Jemma butted in, shooting him an admonishing look. 'Honestly, Pierce, you're worse than the guys I date. You have to put stuff out there, not assume we're going to figure it out. You know, *use your words*, Dad.'

He could barely even form the words, yet Pierce couldn't help a flash of wry amusement as Jemma grabbed the opportunity to quote what he'd said so often when she'd been a tantrum-throwing kid, and then a sullen teen. She'd come good, though, when she found her career passion and focused her formidable intelligence in that direction. He sucked in a ragged breath, knowing that what he said now were probably the most important words he'd ever utter. 'I've been married once, have one child who, as you see, is an adult, and have been divorced for more than twice as long as I was married. I should have told you earlier, it's just that it all happened so long ago, I never give it any thought.'

'Thanks very much,' Jemma muttered sarcastically.

'Which is why it never occurred to me to mention any of it to you, Sam,' he finished doggedly.

'Humph,' Christine snorted, though he couldn't tell whether it was disbelief or judgement of his past.

Sam bit her lips together, her gaze on him, and he knew his words were being weighed and assessed, his trustworthiness judged. And he also knew that if she didn't say anything, that would be the absolute worst outcome: it wouldn't be because she accepted what he said, but because she was too afraid to make waves.

'I've not been seriously involved with anyone since Jem because I've always been more invested in work than relationships. I haven't met anyone who could understand my ambition, or share my passion. Not until now.' Pierce didn't care if it sounded like he was pleading. He refused to accept that this could be the last time he got to stare into those amazing eyes, the last time his hands touched her, the last time he breathed her sweet, spun-sugar fragrance. But if Sam decided she didn't trust him, that he'd been deceitful rather than thoughtless, she would never give him a second chance.

'Christine,' Sam said softly, her gaze never leaving him, as though determined to read his reaction, 'I was saying, before Jemma came in—'

Surely the fact that she'd use his daughter's name had to be a good sign?

'—that I might not have as much time for the cafe in future. This is probably as good an opportunity as any to ask Pierce exactly what sort of commitment he expects from me, so we can work out if you can offer Tara those extra hours.'

Hell, he was glad he was close enough to the counter to be able to surreptitiously lean against it. He was in a cold sweat, but numb with relief. That honesty, the directness he'd admired in Sam from the outset, meant that she wasn't about to play mind games with him. She'd assessed the situation, made her decision and was prepared to move on.

The teenager behind the counter must be Tara, because she gave a little squeal of excitement and clapped her hands together once. He wasn't sure if she was applauding the chance of extra hours, or applauding for him. But, man, he felt like cheering himself.

34
Samantha

If she had retained even a lingering doubt about his sincerity, the sight of Pierce was enough to dispel it. Backlit by warm yellow light, he opened the door to the riverfront cottage before she knocked. As though he'd been waiting for her to pull up. The silver flecks in his hair caught the light, and his muscular arms, only slightly softened by the fine knit jersey he wore over blue jeans, wrapped her with an easy confidence.

His calm assurance was contagious, immediately settling and reassuring her. This was where she was meant to be. Not only in his arms, but setting out on this new adventure. By his side.

'I forgot to ask whether you wanted to eat here, or on *Pelicanet*.' Pierce's feet were bare, and he gestured toward the cosy interior of the cottage.

Sam hesitated. 'I know it's crazy in this weather, particularly when it looks so inviting in there. But, *Pelicanet* . . .' How could she explain to him that the vessel silently called to her?

'Special events need a special place,' Pierce said, understanding her unspoken thoughts. 'I packed a picnic basket. And blankets and a torch.'

Any other guy would think she was crazy for wanting to tramp the muddy riverbank on a wintry evening, when the last of the light had already slipped beneath the dark surface of the river.

'Come inside for two minutes, while I grab my shoes.'

'Or I could come inside for two minutes and we could make out, and then you could grab your shoes?' she suggested.

'Or that,' he said, drawing her in and pushing the door firmly closed.

It was longer than two minutes, and she wasn't feeling the least chilly by the time, massive cane picnic hamper in hand, Pierce wrapped an arm around her and guided her toward the river path. 'Fortunately for you, Samantha Schenscher—'

She liked that he'd gone to the trouble of discovering and using her maiden name.

'—my mum's minestrone travels well in a thermos. And pastizzi are probably better eaten at room temperature.' He shivered as a squall danced across them to find the water. 'Not that this is room temperature.'

Pierce dropped his arm from her shoulders so they could walk more quickly in the bouncing light from the torch she held. Catching her free hand, he guided it into the pocket of his jacket.

'Are you keeping my hand warm for my sake, or your own?' she laughed up at him, blinking the ice tears from her eyes.

He snorted with sudden amusement. 'I love how you say whatever comes to mind.'

Sam threaded her fingers through his. She didn't need to pretend it was too fast, too soon or any other damn thing. They were well and truly adults, they had no one to please but themselves and could make and remake their destiny as they chose.

The crisp air frosted their breath into tiny crystals in the torchlight and their conversation faltered as, unanimously intent on reaching *Pelicanet,* they covered the kilometre of night-shaded path in silence punctuated only by panting as the cold air hit their straining lungs.

As the dark shadow of *Pelicanet* loomed before them, Sam found her breath. 'It seems a shame to start the generator and ruin the not-silence.'

'Not-silence?'

She paused, hands on her waist as she tried to get oxygen back into her lungs. 'Listen. It's quiet but not. There are possums moving through the trees over there. Or, you know, possibly river rats. But *possums* sounds cuter. And something scared the pigeons out of their roost on the cliffs.' She tilted her head toward the river. She loved closing her eyes, putting a picture to each individual sound: the splash as a fish leapt, chased by a nocturnal predator. The wind swaying branches with the soft music of a rain stick. Fluffing and stirring in bird nests, the occasional squawk of annoyance.

She felt Pierce nod alongside her. 'I like your not-silence. It's soothing. And fortunately,' he drew her onto the dock, 'yesterday we had large capacity batteries installed. So we have all the mod-cons, without the noise of the generator.'

She needed to correct his 'we' usage.

But not right now.

Because there was *Pelicanet*, welcoming them home.

Pierce unlocked and dropped the laden basket in the dining room, before flicking the brass switch near the door. He exhaled noisily as the room glowed golden. 'There's always that moment, with batteries, when you're afraid it's not going to work.'

'There's always that moment with *everything*,' she corrected. 'Pops says the best way to get something running right is to shut it all down, and then restart.'

Pierce nodded. 'Pops is a wise man, I think.'

'You'll be so in with him if you go with that attitude.'

Somehow, she was in his arms again. He gazed down at her. 'I'll take all the coaching I can get.'

Sam felt safe in his embrace, yet a tiny part of her wanted to insist that she didn't allow herself that luxury. She fought it down. She refused to drag the broken parts of herself into her future. She returned his kiss unstintingly, but when they separated, she surveyed him seriously. 'You do understand that I've nothing to offer, don't you? I mean, the business was in Grant's name, as is our house and every other darn thing. I'm probably going to walk out of this marriage with less than I had going in.'

Pierce shrugged with a monumental lack of concern. 'Then we build something new. Something better. Though—' he gazed out of the darkened window for a moment, and all she could hear was the soft lapping of the river against the old timbers '—I know someone who might be able to help you with that. No promises, though.'

'I don't like my chances,' she said. 'Grant knew what he was doing. And if I am entitled to anything, I know he's going to fight me for every cent. The point is, I want you to know I've nothing I can offer you other than labour. And, you know, company.' She had slid her hands beneath his jersey, his flesh firm and hot. But then she withdrew them in a rush, realising it could seem that she was trying to coerce him. The thought made her smile: it was a novelty to be in the position where any portion of the power in the relationship was hers.

'Company. And clearly, honesty,' Pierce said. 'And friendship, and shared passion. And, maybe one day, something more.'

She was taken aback by his forthrightness.

'Remember your safe word, Sam,' he murmured, then paused, waiting for her nod of acknowledgement. Or perhaps to see if she would use the word.

She didn't. There was no need, because she knew she could talk with him. 'Is there any point hoping for more? I mean, it's not practical.' She took a steadying breath. They weren't kids, didn't need to hide behind euphemisms, testing each other to see who would dare use the word first. 'And anyway, *love* disappears.'

Pierce shook his head. 'We both know that love *can* disappear,' he corrected. 'That doesn't mean it has to. And as for practicality—is there an iota of sense in rescuing a hundred-plus-year-old boat to run an occasional and limited dining service? Nope. Neither financial nor business. But we love her. So we'll make it work.'

Never had Sam imagined someone would share her attachment to *Pelicanet*, to the sense of timelessness the riverboat evoked, the connection to stories of lives long gone that hid in her creaking timbers. She nodded slowly, breathing deep the smells of the history they had saved. The new history they would create. Together.

'One thing, though . . .' She hesitated. God, it wasn't a conversation she ever wanted to have, but if she expected honesty, Pierce had a right to the same. 'You mentioned that you're not keen on kids. Does that mean you don't want any more?'

Pierce winced. His jaw worked for a second. 'Is this going to be a deal-breaker, Sam? Because, honestly, I don't. I'm nearly fifty, I've done the kid thing once, and I wasn't that great at it.'

His reply should have made it easy, but there was still a chance Pierce would consider her *less* once he understood the depths of her selfishness. But she wasn't about to lie; not to him, and not to herself. 'I often wonder whether we're destined to repeat our parents' mistakes. Mine, in case you're wondering, were pretty ordinary. Both as human beings and as parents.' She took a steadying breath. 'So I've decided I will never have children.'

Pierce slid his hands up her arms. 'If that's something that would have been important to you, I'm really sorry you've been forced into that position.'

She needed a moment to process the emotions that swept through her. Relief that he didn't try to persuade her that she'd be fine as a mother, and that she both should and could want children. Gratitude at his honesty and easy compassion. Perhaps a tiny touch of sorrow at the knowledge she would never carry his babies.

And yet there was something already growing inside her: joy. Excitement. Anticipation for what life might now hold.

'Thanks. But I think . . . I think I may have found something else to attach my affection to.' Her gaze travelled the room, lingering on the details. 'You know, you still haven't showed me what you've done with the wheelhouse. If you're getting Hamish to do your captaining—is that the term? Ship driving? Boat handling?—are you turning the upper deck over to him?'

Pierce bent to kiss her. His lips were assured, the caress both tender and demanding. 'Not a chance. He gets a tiny wheelhouse, now, but the rest of the renovations up there are only for us. I wanted to show them to you last time but thought perhaps it wasn't the moment.'

She could barely breathe, yet she managed to force out, 'I think now might be the right time.'

His hands were in the small of her back, and drifted deliciously up her spine to cup her shoulder blades. 'I have to warn you, I'm nervous.'

'Performance anxiety?' she teased. If anyone should be nervous, it was her. Yet what she lacked in experience, she would make up for in eagerness. Her heart beat faster at the thought of being closer to Pierce, touching him, exploring him. He stirred feelings that she'd never suspected she could harbour. Yes, she wanted him to make love to her. She wasn't a stranger to lust. But the difference was, if Pierce said that they were going to cook together instead of having sex, she'd be just as happy to focus on that shared passion.

Well, almost as happy.

'More that I'm anxious about what you'll think of my improvements.' Pierce bent to pick up the basket. 'I'll duck down and put this in the fridge.'

'I'll come with. I need to have another good look at what you've done there, too—make sure I wasn't imagining it. I couldn't take it all in before.'

Pierce led the way down the narrow stairs to the small galley. 'Proof of how easy it is to build on a good foundation, I reckon.'

She smiled, appreciating the way he made his point in a manner she could ignore if she chose. There was honesty in his pursuit. And she knew she owed him the same. She took a moment, searching for the right words. 'I wasn't enough for Grant,' she said quietly, as they stood surrounded by the trappings of their joint passion. 'And I'm worried I won't be enough for you. You have this crazy idea about my ability and experience . . .' She let the words drift off, but really she wanted to say, *And me. You have this crazy idea that I'm good enough for you.*

Pierce drew her into his arms. 'You've got that totally the wrong way around. Grant wasn't enough for you. Maybe, when you were kids, when you met, then he was enough. But you grew and he didn't. At least, not in healthy ways. Samantha, you are enough. More than enough. For me, you are just perfect.'

35

Pierce

The bed was on the small side, but he didn't mind in the least. Any excuse to press himself closer to Sam was welcome.

During the night, she must have snuck from the covers and opened the timber blinds that surrounded the cabin on three sides. Now the grey winter dawn, dappled with the rosiness of a hard-won sun, lit the small room.

'It's perfect,' Sam murmured from where she nestled into the crook of his shoulder.

He leaned down to kiss her forehead. 'I didn't realise you were awake. What's perfect, the dawn?'

She snuggled closer, her fingers idly playing with the hair on his chest. 'Just . . . everything,' she purred. 'I've dreamed of what it would be like to wake on the river, to feel *Pelicanet*'s heartbeat as the water pulses beneath her creaking timbers. To hear the birds' dawn chorus in the willows on the riverbanks. Do you think animals have worries? Or is that only a human thing? Maybe they don't think about the future.' Her voice had dropped to a drowsy mumble and he thought she had fallen back to sleep. But then she pressed her lips against his torso. 'Anyway, even in my dreams, I never dared imagine being here with you.'

'I'm afraid I'll have to puncture that dream.'

She stiffened, he could feel her hold her breath.

'Because I'm going to the galley to make us a coffee.'

Sam groaned. 'I promise I'll make you the best cup you've ever had, if you'll stay in bed with me for just five minutes more,' she cajoled, throwing one silky thigh across his legs, as though she had a hope of pinning him down.

'I think I'll die without coffee. Besides, I need to refuel.' Sam had surprised him. She'd started out shy, but had quickly turned wanton and wild, as though she couldn't get enough of him, couldn't get close enough. And that suited him perfectly.

But right now, he needed to rehydrate.

He sat on the edge of the bed, leaning down to pick up his jersey from where Sam had tossed it on the floor. She snatched it from him. 'I'm claiming this. You get the pants.' She pulled the shirt on, her head popping out, hair adorably mussed.

'I'll freeze in only jeans,' he protested.

Sam knelt on the bed, shuffling closer to him across the quilt. 'I'll warm you up.'

He slid his hands beneath the jersey, adoring her soft flesh. 'I'm already feeling warmer. But I still require coffee.'

Pierce stood, able to see out of the window without crossing the tiny cabin. 'Hey, you need to look at this.'

Sam clambered off the bed, coming to lean against him. He draped an arm around her shoulders. Beyond the glass, mist covered the river, making it seem they floated upon a cloud.

'Oh!' Sam gasped. She twisted so she could wind both arms around his waist, but still see out of the window.

Through the mist, a lumbering shadow gradually took shape. A pelican, his great wings beating in a slow, steady rhythm, appeared. He drew level with the boat. Behind him, slightly to the left and the right, another pair of pelicans appeared, and then another, the five flying in a V formation along the river.

'A squadron,' Pierce said.

'You listened,' Sam replied softly. She shifted beneath his arm to look up at him. 'I think maybe that's what I love most about you: you listen.'

His heart kicked, but he kept his gaze on the river. He had to respond carefully, not give her any excuse to retract the statement. He'd suspected his own feelings for a long time now, but had avoided admitting the full magnitude, even to himself, in case she shot him down.

'My mum and dad have always been pretty tight, but I never believed in soulmates,' Pierce said, keeping his gaze on the river. 'Actually, I guess I didn't really give it any thought. Too busy, you know? But now, it seems it's all I can think about.' He was aware of the breathless tension in the woman beside him. 'From the first time I met you, Sam, I've not been able to get you out of my head.'

'The *first* time?' Sam said, with a lilting giggle.

He exhaled in relief. Of all the things she could have said, all the roadblocks she could have thrown up, the escape routes she could have devised, the safe word she could have employed, Sam chose to tease him.

'Okay, the second time,' he corrected with a grin. 'You *were* pretty soggy and a little crazed that first time.' Maybe it was too early to lay all his feelings out on the table, although they'd been intimate in more than one way the previous evening. They had made love, both fast and frantic, and long and languorously, exploring each other's body. But they had also talked. Talked like he'd never talked with a woman—no, had never talked with any person—ever before.

Prior to last night, he'd had intense feelings for Sam, had cared about her and had most definitely desired her. Had suspected it could become much more.

This morning, he knew he was all in. Completely and irrevocably in love with her.

'I guess there could be something in it,' she said, snuggling into him as though she, too, couldn't get close enough. 'The soulmates thing. I mean, maybe you can read my mind. After all, you did restore *Pelicanet* perfectly. And then there's this room . . .'

He grinned, recalling her astonished reaction the previous night, when he'd thrown open the door to what had once been a poky, dark cabin. He'd had it rebuilt so that only the wall partitioning off the wheelhouse was wood. The others were tempered glass, carefully inset in timber frames so that, from the outside, *Pelicanet* retained her original look. The double bed was custom made: elevated, to maximise the view from the windows, but also to allow pull-out storage beneath. The panelled wall disguised shallow cupboards, configured as wardrobes, drawers and a bookshelf, each hidden door operated by pushing on the timber.

'So it meets with your approval?' he said, turning to increase the contact of their bodies. Sam fit his embrace so perfectly. Solid enough that he wasn't worried he would crush her, yet diminutive against his frame. Somehow she managed to feel . . . real. That was the thing about Sam, he'd decided: she was real. The way she talked. Her forthright honesty. The exuberant impulsiveness tempered by learned caution. And the way she felt in his arms.

'You definitely weren't in my head when you came up with this,' she said. 'I'd never have thought of it. The only way you're going to lose points on this one is if you tell me you had Gabrielle in here designing it for you.'

He liked that she openly admitted to her jealousy, instead of sniping and hinting, using her suspicions as an excuse to pick an argument. 'No, this one I managed myself.' He pushed the panel to open a small door. 'With you in mind.' As the door swung outward, it revealed a crammed bookshelf. 'I know you said you like to teach yourself new skills, so I thought maybe we could look at doing some hands-on learning of this stuff together.'

Sam ran a finger over the spines of the DVDs and books he'd selected, reading the titles. '*Edible Art*, *Italian Street*

Food, Heritage Recipes, Sushi and Sashimi.' She stopped a third of the way across the shelf. 'Sounds time-consuming. Not to mention challenging. You really think we could make a go of this?'

'I know we can have fun trying. If it works, it works. If it doesn't . . .' He tilted her chin up so she met his gaze. 'If this doesn't work, *we* try something else.'

Though she pressed her hand to the side of his face, Sam looked worried. His heart clenched, his gaze on her lips as he willed her not to say the word. *Compassion.*

'Pierce, I've only just begun to find myself.' Sam's whisper was broken, as though the words tore from her. 'And I'm terrified that if I become invested in someone else's dream, I could lose myself. Lose everything. Again.'

Catching her hand, he held it against his jaw, her palm warm and soft. 'Sam, I only want you onboard if this is your dream as well.' He reached behind her into the recessed bookshelf. 'I was hoping you'd go through all the titles and find this, but . . .' He held the paperwork toward her, willing his hand not to shake. 'Jemma's a lawyer. Proves apples can fall a long way from the tree, right?' He hoped to see a spark of amusement chase the worry from Sam's face. 'She came to Settlers yesterday to drop this off. Obviously, it's only a draft contract. To be legal it needs your signature, too.' He took a deep breath. It was now or never. 'When I realised you were into the idea of turning *Pelicanet* into a restaurant, I made Ant an offer. I've got three days to withdraw.'

Sam frowned. 'I love the idea of you owning her, but why would your contract need my signature?'

'Because I listed us as joint owners.'

She gasped, stumbling back a half-step and almost falling as the bed brought her up short. 'I thought I made it clear? Working for you is one thing, but when I get a divorce settlement—*if* I get anything—I'll need to put money into somewhere to live. There's no way there'll be enough for me to buy into *Pelicanet*. I'm so sorry.' She looked . . . devastated.

And the expression gave him hope.

'Sam, I stole your dream.' He waved a hand at their surroundings. '*Pelicanet*. She was truly yours, the home of your heart. You shared her with me.' He rubbed his nose, searching for the right words. 'I get if you're not ready to talk about any kind of happily-ever-after. Also, I accept that you may never be. So this is purely a business partnership. There's no reason the financial input has to be equal. I'm capitalising on your knowledge of the area and the local tourist trade, and tapping into your network and the goodwill you've earned through Ploughs and Pies. That expertise will be your share of the initial investment. I don't have those insider advantages, so instead, I'll put in the cash. Check the contract. I had Jemma write in that if we ever decide to sell *Pelicanet*, it's a fifty-fifty split at current market value.' He gave a grin, trying to tone down his desperation. But this dream wouldn't work without her. 'Kind of the prenup you have when you're not having a prenup.'

36
Samantha

Sam giggled as she raced back up the stairs ahead of Pierce. She couldn't believe this new side to herself, how light, how *happy* she felt. Her hard-learned caution had demanded she reject Pierce's contract a few hours earlier. But she'd rebelled. Pops was right, life was for living. And this would give her everything she could ever want: Pierce and *Pelicanet*.

'Hey, not fair,' Pierce called. 'How come I'm carrying both coffees?'

'You need to brush up on your basic service skills,' she teased. 'We're going to have to operate with a small staff, because there's little room to move around one another.'

'If you can guarantee this view, I won't be complaining,' he chuckled, close behind but slightly below her now.

The knowledge that he wouldn't suddenly flip, his mood turning dark, thrilled through Sam. She didn't have to cultivate what she said, how she acted, to please him. She knew he was a man of contrasts: when they talked work he was dedicated, serious. When they discussed food, his hands flew to express his passionate emotions. And when he loved he was tender, playful, charming. And sexy as all hell. But never was he dangerously unpredictable.

As she ducked through the low doorway into the captain's quarters, her phone vibrated noisily on the timber boards. She scooped up her clothes and the tumbled linen from the floor, laughing as Pierce set down the mugs, his exploring hands hampering rather than helping her. She finally found the phone and pressed to answer before her brain registered the caller.

'Sam?' Tara's voice was high-pitched, as though she'd been trying to get in touch for ages. Which she possibly had, Sam thought guiltily. But it was Monday, so the shop wasn't open.

'Yeah, Tars, what's up?'

'You've got to come, quick.'

Tara's tone paralysed Sam's lungs with fear. 'What's wrong?' She could barely get the words out. She swivelled so she could communicate her concern to Pierce, switching the phone to speaker.

Fists clenched, a frown creased his face as he watched her. Over the other side of the room his phone started to vibrate too, the timing ominous. He glanced toward it, obviously torn about whether to answer.

Premonition rippled through Sam. 'Tara, what the hell's wrong?' she yelled.

As Pierce surged across the bed to snatch up his phone, Tara took a great sobbing breath, her words unintelligible for long seconds. 'It's the cafe. You've got to come. Now.'

Pierce's hand closed over her shoulder. 'Gabrielle's on my phone. Ploughs and Pies is on fire.'

'No!' Her phone fell from her nerveless fingers. As she scrabbled into the clothes Pierce handed her, Sam ran through lock-up in her head. Had she, in her hurry to finish up at the cafe and meet Pierce, left something turned on?

No. She'd followed the same routine for years, could do it in her sleep. Besides, leaving an oven or warmer on wouldn't cause a fire. Would it?

Pierce had dressed in seconds. 'Gabrielle's driving down to the wharf to pick us up.' He took her by the shoulders as she tried to force her suddenly rubbery legs into her jeans. 'Sam, it's okay. Breathe. It's just a *thing*, all right? A building, a place. We can fix it.'

His words made her pause, oxygen flooding her lungs. 'Of course. You're right.' Christine was more vested in the cafe than she was now—'Christine!' she gasped, snatching up her phone. She had to check that the older woman knew what was going on. The cafe had been Sam's for so long, it was feasible no one would think to alert Christine. 'Tara, are you still there?'

The teenager was sobbing.

'Tara?'

'I'm here.'

'Is Christine there yet?'

Pierce led the way back down the stairs and they pounded across the wharf, his hand firmly gripping hers as they navigated the damp, twisted willow roots.

'Tara?' she yelled.

'I can't find her!' Tara finally managed.

Pierce bundled her into Gabrielle's car and Sam managed a smile. 'Don't worry, Tara, Christine will get there as soon as she hears. Stop crying, okay? It's not that big a deal.' She winced: considering what had happened to Tara's brother a couple of years back, even a building fire was probably a very big deal to the younger woman.

'Sam,' Tara's hysteria dropped to a whimper, 'they've found something in the cafe.'

'Something?'

'Someone.'

'A trespasser?' She snapped upright, the pieces falling into place. Grant had gone looking for the cash he often accused her of stashing at the cafe. She had never believed him when he claimed he'd lost his set of keys. Hot fury chased away her shock. 'That bastard! I'll—'

'You don't understand!' Tara wailed as Gabrielle's car flew along the dirt road out of Wurruldi. 'Christine said she was going in today because she wanted to do some planning for her new set-up. She was so excited about it.'

'She won't be there yet. It's far too early.' As she spoke, Sam realised that, although it had been dawn when they woke, she had persuaded Pierce to go back to bed before they headed down to the galley to make coffee. And then they'd made love there, too.

It wasn't that early anymore.

Still, Grant wouldn't touch Christine, even if she had turned up while he was torching the place. There had been far too many witnesses when he'd made those threats about her for him to risk following through.

Gabrielle changed down the gears, driving in white-knuckled silence, her concentration on the switchbacks leading up the cliff.

'It's a body,' Tara gasped, her voice breaking as the connection cut in and out. 'They found a body.'

Sam's jaw locked as bile filled her mouth. She couldn't move, couldn't even turn to look at Pierce.

He reached across the seat and took her hand. He didn't speak. What could he say?

'Tara, you don't know it's her,' Sam managed to squeeze the words past the tightness of her throat. 'I'll call her.'

'I've been calling her. Her phone's not even ringing.'

'I'll get her,' Sam insisted, her voice thick with tears. She had to be able to reach Christine. The older woman had become her best friend. Her protector.

Her mother.

They drove in silence as Sam repeatedly dialled the number, staring unseeingly out of the window as they hit the bitumen road. This couldn't be happening, not when she was finally free of Grant. Not when everything was going right. Not when Christine had found happiness in the cafe.

'Yes?'

The abrupt voice startled her so much she couldn't respond.

Pierce snatched her phone, though it was on speaker. 'Christine?' he barked.

'Who is this?' Christine's terse, unmistakable voice snapped.

'Oh my god, oh my god,' Sam grabbed for the phone. 'Christine? Are you all right?'

'Of course I'm all right. Really, how dare *that man* come past my place, drunkenly yelling abuse at that hour of the morning. Or any hour. But how did you hear about it already? I've literally just walked out of the police station. And they insist they don't have a patrol to spare to bring him in at the moment. How ridiculous.'

Sam could barely hear Christine for the blood pounding in her ears. 'Wait, you mean you're at the cop shop?' she said.

'I believe I made that clear,' Christine said. 'I'm not about to let that kind of behaviour pass without reporting it. We both know how *that man* likes to push the boundaries.'

'You're safe? In Murray Bridge?' Sam sobbed, relief making her weak.

'Well, that's relative, isn't it? I'm reasonably sure this part of Murray Bridge is safe,' Christine said. 'Samantha, what on earth has got into you?'

Sam took a tremulous breath, trying to sound calm. 'There's been a fire at the cafe, I'm heading there now. Could you meet me there?'

'Of course.' Christine's practical tone barely changed, 'I'm on my way.'

As the call disconnected, Sam let her head fall back against the seat. The large, solid stone houses that sat opposite the dairy flats on the outskirts of Settlers Bridge flashed past the windows. Her eyes ached and her temples throbbed. But it didn't matter. Christine was okay. Tara was okay.

But then, who—?

Pierce's phone pinged and he glanced down at it. His hand tightened around hers. 'Fuck.'

'What's wrong?'

'My brother. Oh, Jesus.' He let go of her, dragging a hand down his suddenly bleak face.

37
Pierce

Pierce stared at the message, willing it away.

Saw you right, bro. That little problem of yours? Sorted.

'What's wrong?' Sam repeated, leaning toward him, shaking his thigh, as though she could loosen a response.

'Dante. He's done . . . oh, fuck, he's done something bad.' And it was his fault. Dante had said he'd sort Grant out, and Pierce had ignored him. Like he had all of his little brother's life.

And now there was a body and a burned-out building.

'Jesus. Dan said he knew he'd end up back in jail, no matter how hard he tried,' he groaned.

They turned into the main street, crowded with CFS vehicles and flashing lights. Sam was out of Gabrielle's car before it'd stopped rolling.

Pierce took off after her. He needed to call Dante back. Hell, he needed to get on to Jemma, see if she could organise a lawyer for her uncle. But, more than anything, he needed to support Sam.

Because, even though her friend was safe, she was about to discover that her almost ex-husband wasn't. And no matter what Grant had done to her, he doubted that Sam wished him dead.

Especially not this way.

Tara spotted them before they reached the paved centre divider of the windswept street. 'Sam!' She darted across the road, weaving between emergency services vehicles.

'I found her, Tara. It's okay.' Sam grabbed the younger girl, holding her still so the words could penetrate. 'Christine is fine.'

Tara sagged against her. 'You're sure? Oh god, I was so worried! I mean, she's a bit of an old cow, but still, she's Christine, right? I was sure it—' She stiffened and jerked back to face the shop. 'Wait! But then who . . . ?'

'I've no idea.' Sam shook her head. Arms around each other's waists, the two women started across the road.

Pierce hesitated. Should he tell them? Warn Sam it was her ex in there?

He didn't have to make up his mind straight away: a police officer stopped them. Nothing as organised as a crowd barrier, just a hand barring their way, a stern look keeping them in check.

He took the chance to dial Dante, pressing the phone close to his ear to keep the call private.

'Bro,' Dante crowed. 'All good?'

'Good?' He struggled to keep his voice low. 'Jesus, Dan, you have to call Jemma. Tell her I said you need her help. I can't make the call right now, I'm at the cafe. But don't say a damn word to anyone until you've spoken to Jemma, you hear me?'

'What's wrong?' The concern in his brother's voice was electric. 'Are you okay? Talk to me, bro. What's going down?'

He'd failed his little brother one too many times. He had to at least guide him. Except . . . he couldn't protect Dante. Not from this. 'Grant,' he hissed.

'Who?'

'The ex.' Jesus, did Dante do this so often he couldn't keep track of who he'd topped?

'You mean he's come back to give you grief?' Dante sounded astonished. 'Jeez, the guy's got balls, didn't credit him with that. I was sure he got the message. Damn, I'm sorry, bro.' Now he sounded despondent. 'I wanted to fix him for you.'

'Don't say that.' Pierce cupped his hand around the phone. 'You're going to make it worse for yourself. Hell, I don't think you can make it worse, can you?'

Guided by Sam, they had edged along the street, slowly gaining ground on the cafe. From this vantage point, Pierce couldn't make out any damage. But the blue plastic tarp rigged across the recessed porch beneath the bullnosed verandah blocked his view.

'He's not the kind to go to the cops,' Dante scoffed. 'Besides, he admitted he's been hanging around your woman's cafe, planning to do it over. So I set him straight. Trust me, bro.' Dante clicked his tongue, a sound of irritation. 'I mean, yeah, I said that with the tratt, too, but this is my territory. I know what I'm doing. I told him to steer clear of both his ex and you. He's a Murray Bridge lad, recognised a couple of the names I dropped. Though I gotta say, it's blowing my mind that he'd come back at you already.'

'What do you mean, come back at me?' Pierce ground out. He needed to get off the phone, make sure he was a hundred per cent there for Sam. But his brother was about to go to jail because he'd been desperate to gain Pierce's approval. 'How the hell is he supposed to come back at me from this?' He lifted his chin toward the cafe, though Dante couldn't see.

'Look, I'm on my way. I'll go straight to his. I'll mess him up a bit this time.'

Pierce jerked back. 'Wait. I thought you said you sorted him?'

'Well, I chatted to him.' Dante sounded shamefaced. 'I didn't want to go in too hard. But he got his warning shot, so I'll do it right this time. Okay, bro?'

'Jesus, no, Dan, no!' He was shouting now, and Sam turned to him wide-eyed. He tried to give her a reassuring smile. 'Dan, you mean you didn't . . . hurt him?'

'Not yet.'

He sagged against the window of the shop they'd stopped in front of. 'Dante, listen to me. Don't do a thing, okay?

Not a damn thing. Don't come here, don't go to Grant's place, don't call Jemma. You got it?'

'Grant?' Sam mouthed.

'He's okay,' Pierce reassured her. Realistically, though, he was the one who needed that reassurance.

His brother wasn't going to jail. Not this time, anyway.

But there was still a body in the cafe.

38
Samantha

From what Sam could see, craning her neck from the verandah outside the IGA, it didn't seem the cafe was damaged at all. In fact, if it wasn't for the CFS trucks and utes, and the three police vehicles parked at odd angles to block off the main street, nothing would seem amiss.

'What is all this nonsense? What a lot of vehicles for a small fire,' Christine snapped, her acid tone so sweetly familiar that tears sprang to Sam's eyes.

She turned and flung her arms around the older woman.

'My goodness, what's that for?' Christine said, though she patted Sam's back for a moment before retreating.

'I thought . . .' Sam gestured toward the cafe, but realised that, with nothing to see, the movement made no sense.

'You still have insurance I presume, and I took out cover when I signed the contract, so it'll be fine,' Christine said prosaically. 'But what on earth are you all doing, huddled out here?' She signalled the police officer to come closer. 'We're the owners, so you can escort us in now.'

The officer was brave—or foolish—enough to shake his head at Christine. 'No one can go any closer until we establish whether it's a crime scene or an accident. There appears to be a butane cylinder involved, but we have to rule out natural causes. In any case, nobody's going anywhere until forensics have finished, and the body is on the way to the morgue.'

Pierce's arm slipped around Sam's waist, drawing her comfortingly close.

'Body?' Christine froze, her hand still in the air. She closed her eyes for a long moment.

Was she flashing back to her dead niece? Sam reached out and patted Christine's arm, recognising the futility of the action, but not knowing what else to do. Pierce's physical presence comforted her, and she wanted to do the same for Christine.

'Eric,' Christine murmured, her tone heavy with sorrow. 'Eric and that ridiculous campfire contraption he used.'

'Oh my god!' Sam clapped a hand across her mouth. 'Of course.'

'Eric?' Pierce repeated.

'An old guy, an army vet. He comes by for hot food, but he's been turning up earlier and earlier. A few weeks back, he set up camp in the doorway with a portable stove thing, and a couple of blankets Christine gave him.'

'He doesn't have a place?' Pierce asked.

'He does.' She drew a ragged breath. 'But he's got it in his head that he has to protect my place.' The sadness of Eric's life tightened her throat. Caught in the tragedy of his memories, he had believed he was doing her a favour. And his confusion had led to his death.

'He was right,' Pierce said bleakly. He glanced at the police officer, apparently making sure he was too busy taking information—or, more likely, directions—from Christine to overhear them. He drew Sam further aside. 'Dante just told me that Grant has been hanging around. Admitted he was planning to break in.'

'Oh my god,' Sam groaned. 'Like he hasn't taken enough from me.' Then the full import of Pierce's words hit and she staggered back: Grant had always been fascinated by fire. Whether deliberately or accidentally, blinded by his need for malicious revenge, her husband must have killed Young Eric while robbing her cafe. She'd never be able to move beyond this moment, the recognition that it was her greedy desire for freedom that had caused the old man's death.

Pierce rubbed the bridge of his nose, frowning. 'But I'm not sure that's what happened. In fact, depending on the timing, Dante might be Grant's alibi. Seems Dan was at your ex's place, putting the hard word on him to steer clear of you.'

'He what?' she blurted, though a part of her mind was grasping at the life raft, the possibility that her husband might not be a murderer, that she might not be to blame for Young Eric's death. 'Why would your brother say anything to Grant? I don't even know him. And my business is none of his.' She was stung to anger by the ingrained need to keep her secrets close, even though she knew with an unshakable certainty that Pierce was one of three men in her life that she could trust without reserve: Pops, Jack and Pierce.

Pierce grimaced. 'Dante was in the cafe when Grant came by, remember?' But it's more complicated than that. I'll explain later, but the short version is, it's my fault. He figured he was doing me a favour by taking care of Grant.'

'Your fault *that man* finally learned what it's like to be bullied?' Christine interrupted tartly as she returned. 'Seems to me that you're due commendation rather than condemnation, then.' Though her tone was sour, Sam caught the glint of approval in her eye. Then Christine turned back to the shop and sighed heavily. 'That poor, silly old bugger.'

'We don't know it's him,' Sam tried to console her. But she knew all right.

Whatever the cause, Young Eric had died on duty. Protecting her.

Epilogue

'Close your eyes,' Christine directed.

Sam did as she was ordered—even playful, her friend sounded stern.

Taking her by the elbow, Christine led her from the side passage of the cafe to the front of the building. With her eyes closed, still Sam recognised the familiar sounds and smells of her childhood, her life. The occasional car dawdled past, the noise smooth and distant on the wide road. A wolflike howl came from the end of the street, near Ant's pub, and she knew Tracey was in town with her keeshond, Bear. Tracey always joked that the dog couldn't stand to let her out of its sight, and Bear seemed determined to prove her right.

The air was spicy with the scent of nasturtiums spilling from the pots alongside the verandah poles, and bees made music among the flowers.

'Step,' Christine said, as though Sam didn't know the way into her own cafe. Well, what had been her cafe, until four months ago.

She didn't need warning about the step, anyway, because Pierce had one arm around her waist, and lifted her before they reached it.

Eyes closed, she allowed a thought for Young Eric. The coroner had ruled his death an accident, and she chose to think of it as peaceful: he had fallen into a permanent sleep at his sentry post, and the gas burner tipped over. The naked flame caught his greatcoat, which had apparently slowly smouldered for some time before the newspaper he always carried in his pocket ignited. As it flared, the fire had spread to the interior of the cafe. Fortunately, that damage had been cosmetic, not structural.

'For goodness' sake,' Christine muttered testily to Pierce, 'Sam can manage the step herself.' But the suppressed excitement in her tone was impossible to mask. An air-conditioned breeze wafted over Sam as Christine pushed open the front door. Instead of the familiar tinkle of the bell, a wave of fifties Elvis rockabilly flooded out.

'She's here, she's here.' Sam caught Tara's excited whisper, almost hidden by an unfamiliar rustle she couldn't identify. Pierce chuckled, deep and reassuring, and she let herself melt against him. She would never have enough of this man. Though he'd told the truth about his passionate nature, and got fired up when they knocked heads over their business, he was dependable. She was learning that they didn't have to agree on everything, she was entitled to an opinion and could safely share it, knowing Pierce would never exact some petty revenge as punishment.

'Come on, Christine. Let me open my eyes now,' she pleaded. 'I can't take all this secrecy.'

'One moment.'

She felt Christine move away. More rustling, like heavy fabric shifting. A giggle from Tara.

'All right, you may look now.'

For half a heartbeat, she didn't want to, knowing her Ploughs and Pies was forever gone.

But then her heart gave a giddy leap. Because what did it matter? Life was so much better now than she'd ever dreamed possible. Gabrielle had given them a permanent lease on the riverside cottage, though they spent many nights 'camping out' in the snug captain's cabin aboard *Pelicanet.* To their surprise, demand for the exclusive dining venture had outstripped their ability to provide, and they were fully booked months ahead. Pierce had wisely suggested they increase the price and limit the customers, so they maintained their passion for the adventure, rather than burn out.

'Wow,' she breathed as she opened her eyes. Gone were the serviceable tables and chairs. In their place, bright red vinyl banquettes lined the walls and centre of the room. A jukebox stood in one corner, a life-sized model of Elvis in another. On each shiny black table was a small tin caddy. Designed for carrying old-fashioned pop bottles, now the red enamelled containers held sauce and mustard bottles, napkins and cutlery.

Sam gazed about, barely able to take in all the changes. Shelves of fifties memorabilia surrounded the blackboard behind the counter, which now offered a variety of hamburgers, hotdogs and loaded fries. Literally, the last kind of food she would have expected Christine, the CWA matriarch, to champion. It seemed her friend was a woman of many surprises. As she turned to remark on that revelation, Sam took a surprised step back, pointing at Tara and her younger sister, Chloe, who stood alongside Christine. 'Oh my god, look how cute you are,' she exclaimed.

Dressed in black swing skirts, nipped in at their waists and then flared wide with layers of stiff red tulle, the three sneaker-clad women's pristine white blouses were partially hidden behind frilled aprons. The ribbons on their ponytails and their lipstick matched the red aprons, although the bright slash on Christine's tight mouth was worth a sneaky second glance.

'Go on, off you go. I'm not paying you to preen and dawdle.' Christine shooed away the two girls. Giggling and deliberately swinging their ponytails, they darted behind the counter.

Sam was almost relieved to see there was still a small array of traditional baked goods in the retro diner's glass-fronted, chrome-edged cabinet, but prominent place was given to trays of brownies, cream-covered strawberry shortcakes, fluffy slices of angel food cake and marbled chocolate fudge cake. 'This is incredible, Christine. I'd never have had the imagination to come up with something so . . . quirky.'

'That's because you're practical.' True to form, Christine managed to make the label sound somewhat disparaging. 'Leslie and I went to Graceland for our anniversary. Three times. Deep down, I guess I've always had this dream—so I suppose I should thank Young Eric for lighting a fire under me, so to speak.' The sudden flash of black humour startled Sam, and Christine shook her head. 'Death comes to us all, Samantha. No point being miserable about it. Come on, sit down. I assume I'll have to let the rest of this rabble in.' She gestured toward the doorway, shadowed with eager locals.

~

'Christine's cooking was every bit as good as I'd expect,' Sam said, leaning closer to Pierce in the seclusion of his car. 'But it's going to be a very long time before I can see any logical connection between her and burgers.'

'I guess people are rarely what we see on the surface,' Pierce responded, his attention on the road winding between the centuries-old gums on the river flats near Wurruldi.

'Ooh, deep,' she teased.

He chuckled. 'Judging by the crowds, she's got a winner on her hands.'

Sam put her hand on the centre console, palm up. Pierce took his left hand from the wheel, threading his fingers through hers, then lifting her hand to kiss her knuckles. 'Half of the customers were from Murray Bridge,' she said. 'So I'd say she'll be looking for even more staff very soon. There's nothing like that diner anywhere around here.'

'And you're okay with what she's done?' Pierce was the only person who could ever understand how much of herself had been invested in Ploughs and Pies over the years.

'Absolutely. I divorced Ploughs and Pies months ago. It was time for me to move on to . . . *better* things.'

Pierce smiled, knowing she wasn't talking only about swapping jobs. That was one of the many things she so liked about him: while they could discuss anything and everything, they also shared a deep, unspoken level of understanding.

At the riverfront, Pierce took a left, heading along the widened track toward the private willow tree wharf where *Pelicanet* was moored.

'Camping tonight?' she asked. There was nothing more wonderful than waking on the boat, and she never slept better than in the small bed, wrapped in Pierce's arms, cocooned by *Pelicanet*, soothed by the river.

'We can. But I have something to show you.'

He turned the car off and, hand in hand, they ducked beneath the drooping, heavy-foliaged willows and clambered across the roots which had become part of the dock. *Pelicanet* bobbed at her mooring, like she was happy to see them.

'Wait here,' Pierce directed.

Sam leaned against the bow rail, tipping her face up to the sunshine. After a moment, she turned to gaze out across the river, the willow trees drinking from its milk-coffee serenity. A pair of pelicans sailed in stately fashion near the far bank. Parrots darted through the trees, multi-coloured jewels studding the foliage. The kite called for his mate, a clear whistle, descending down the scale.

'Samantha.'

'Oh!' Absorbed in the scenery, she hadn't noticed Pierce's approach. Tara was right about him being totally jumpable. His signature mix of debonair ruggedness never failed to thrill anticipation through her—garnished, as always, with a sense of disbelief. Could this man really want to spend their forever together?

Pierce held a book-sized box tied with a burgundy velvet ribbon.

She raised one eyebrow in question.

'Easiest way to find out is to open it.'

She carefully undid the ribbon, then lifted the lid from the box. A pair of industrial-sized, glass salt and pepper mills nestled in a bed of tissue paper.

'Local pink pepper from the peppertrees, and Murray River salt crystals,' Pierce explained. 'I had them custom made. Because that sea salt you finished your dark chocolate ganache with last month—' he kissed his fingertips '—the ideal touch on an exquisite dessert.'

'And who doesn't like pepper on their pasta?' she said. 'They're perfect.' She held up a bottle to admire the translucent pink salt against the deeper cerise of the jar of pepperberries. In ornate scrollwork, the letters *S&P* glinted in the centre of a silver plaque hung from a fine chain around the bottle.

'Multi-purpose grinders?' she said, turning over an identical plaque on the second mill. 'I'd have thought steel for the pepper and ceramic for the salt, so it doesn't corrode.'

'They're definitely individual.' Pierce moved closer and she breathed in the heady smell of *him*. 'Like us. For a while there, I thought we might be like oil and water, totally different, never able to mix. Though I'd still have made this thing work, you know? But then I realised that we're actually the perfect pairing. You're the salt of the earth, Sam. You're practical, honest, genuine.' His hand traced softly down the side of her face. 'And, like salt, I can't live without you.'

She tore her eyes from his gaze to examine the engraved disk again. 'And you're fiery and wild and peppery.'

'You can add hot in there, too, if you like,' he suggested.

She chuckled. 'Don't want to give you a big head, no matter how well deserved. Would you settle for "I appreciate the spice you add to my life"?'

'Fair,' Pierce said, resting his hands on her hips. 'And you know that salt and pepper should always be together, right?'

'Because they complement each other perfectly,' she murmured.

Pierce's dark eyes drew her deeper. 'Because they're soulmates.'

Sam's heart actually hurt and the breath she drew in was ragged with emotion. Pierce was always open about his feelings, but the salt and pepper analogy was so perfect for them, it seemed to say more than all his declarations. 'They keep each other in balance,' she suggested, still trying to cling to the prosaic, rather than allow herself to plunge down the slippery slope of passion and love.

Yet with Pierce there to catch her, she knew she risked nothing more than the most joy-filled ride.

He chuckled. 'There's my girl. Trust you to be practical when I'm trying to be all new age and sensitive and stuff.'

She wrinkled her nose in pretended apology. 'Sorry. You know me.'

'I do. And I adore you. But I am trying to impress you with all my non-school learning. Here's another one for you: a few centuries back, a man was considered rich if he had salt at his table. I want that wealth, Sam. I want you at my table. Always.'

There was silence for a moment as his lips touched hers, firm but tender, a promise of love rather than passion. Yet she knew the passion was also there, spicy, peppery, waiting to be fanned into flame.

The breeze caressed the water, wrapping them in gentle spring warmth, rich with renewal and potential. And Sam realised she was ready to embrace all of that. The hell with being careful: it was time to take a chance on life again.

Pierce swept aside the hair that drifted across her face. 'What do you think of changing things up and using Salt and Pepper as a name for the restaurant? That way, we keep *Pelicanet* for ourselves. And S&P,' he tapped the mill, 'could be our logo.'

'I think, Mr di Angelis, that you are brilliant.' She and Pierce didn't always agree, and that was fine. But it was exceptional when their minds, motivations and desires meshed so seamlessly. 'Look, it's our initials, too. Sam and Pierce.'

Pierce's shadow of a smile meant he had already made the connection and waited for her to catch up. That was the thing about him, Sam realised: he neither led nor pushed her. Instead, he waited, so they could move forward together when she was ready.

And she wanted to move forward with him. The pair of them, side by side.

'S&P.' Sam wound her arms around Pierce's neck, giving herself to him completely. It wasn't surrender, but a melding. Body and mind. They belonged together.

The ancient timbers of *Pelicanet* rocked beneath them in the invisible current, bobbing in gentle approval.

Acknowledgements

Anyone who follows my social media will know that I dread finalising the acknowledgements—simply because so many people have input into or impact on the story that I'm terrified of forgetting to mention someone. This is not made any easier by the fact that, by the time I write the acks, I'm a couple of books further on, so my head's no longer in the right story. I know, I know—the problem could be fixed with a little organisation, such as writing the acknowledgements in a timely manner, not at the last minute! But, let's face it, that's never going to happen.

So, fingers crossed for me, let's dive in . . .

As always, thanks to Taylor (aka The Kid on my social media posts). We dreamed up the idea of setting a book on a paddle-wheeler while cruising the Murray on the oldest paddle-boat in South Australia, the tiny *PW Mayflower*, for my dad's eightieth birthday. Seated on a hard bench in beautiful summer sunshine tempered by a brisk breeze, we churned from the tiny, historic riverport of Mannum through timeless surrounds: drowned gum trees, soaring cliffs and wide flood plains that just begged to have a story told. Normally our book brainstorming is done on road trips—but apparently the 'inland highway', as the Murray River was known in the 1800s, works just as well!

I love including my passion for the past in stories, and the Murray is an intrinsic part of the history of South Australia, featuring prominently in the ancient Ngarrindjeri Dreaming stories. The heyday of the river trade saw the majestic stretches and winding tributaries crowded with steamers, barges and mission boats. If you are interested in the history of this era, many of the small riverside towns have monuments and plaques—and I can highly recommend the Mannum Dock Museum.

I was unsure whether a vessel as small as my imagined *Pelicanet* would be capable of producing restaurant-quality meals, so Taylor and I took several trips on the Captain Proud Paddle Boat from Murray Bridge, which does a terrific three-hour cruise and meal. Really, this research stuff is awfully hard! I baled up the captain of the craft, Josh Lehmann, at the helm (I think there was only one door into the wheelhouse: sorry, Josh, no chance of escape). Josh provided a wealth of information about the river and historical river trade and loads of tech detail about engines and paddle wheels, navigation and nautical distance. As usual, much of the research didn't make it into the book, but it was invaluable for adding detail and colour to the story, so thanks for your time and expertise, Josh.

My eldest daughter, Samantha—thank you for allowing me to steal your name, though not your story (well, not *this* time, anyway!).

My fabulous team at Allen & Unwin—I'm always hesitant to add names, as there are so many people working behind the scenes to get my books out that I know I won't cover everyone. But, as always, my wonderful publisher Annette, who indulges my frequent off-path meanderings as I pitch different projects instead of staying focused! And particular thanks to my brilliant editor, Courtney, who reads my manuscript more times than any person alive yet retains a passion for the details. I was thrilled to have Deonie Fiford's expertise added to this book: with Courtney, Christa and Deonie on board (see what I did there?) the book is probably about five thousand waffling words shorter than my original version. And my special appreciation to Nada Backovic, who designs the perfect, most evocative covers for my stories.

Special thanks to Courtney's sister Georgia, who sorted out my rookie wedding cake baking mistakes.

My partner, Stephen, has proved to be a walking thesaurus: I don't know of anyone with such a talent for plucking the required synonym out of thin air—particularly when my request (demand!) for help is usually me grunting the offending word without even supplying a sentence for context. Another twenty years and you might have redeemed yourself for doubting I'd ever break into the industry!

Thanks to my mum, who is by turns vocally enthused and outraged by my tales of the challenges of this industry—and is unfailingly prepared to hear the same whingeing from me every second day. And Dad, who apparently can't make a visit to either the airfield or the doctor's surgery without touting my books to anyone daft enough to listen. My apologies to those of his fellow pilots who've not been permitted to leave the airfield without promising to purchase!

Karly Lane, Maya Linnell, Sandie Docker, Rachael Johns and Darry Fraser: you've all been fabulous sounding boards over the past year, and I appreciate the heck out of you.

To The Not-So-Solitary Scribes Scribblers' Ink writing group, many of whom helped to promote my books after I had consecutive releases plagued by Covid-lockdown dramas—Jodi, Penelope, Chrissie, Emma, Sueanne, Joanne, Jem, Leanne, Pamela and so many others (I'll keep a few names for the next book!)—your friendship and support is cherished.

Special shout-out to my followers on Facebook and Instagram who flooded me with book title suggestions—and particularly to Tanya (@read.by.the.librarian on Insta), who came up with the title 'The Willow Tree Wharf'—and it stuck!

And, finally, thanks to you—the readers and reviewers. It is your support that brings Settlers Bridge to life.

Thank you all.
Lee x